"You want to scream? Go ahead. No one will hear you out here," he said, as if daring her to.

"I would if it would help," she shot back. "Can't see how that'll make it easier to be around you, though."

"*I'm* the problem?" He almost sounded sincere, but damn—that grin! It ~~was~~ ???y, she had to give him that, but a little ~~??? a~~ lot sexy—wasn't about to mak~~???~~ he was getting whiplas~~???~~ ne minute his hand ~~???~~ the next he coul~~???~~ or a bigger wall betwe~~???~~

"Glad y~~??? ???s~~ from my point of view," she said, knowing full well his was a question, not a statement.

The smile faded from his lips and his hand flew behind his back. "Get down."

She dropped to all fours at the exact same time his gun came around and leveled at a spot where her head had been seconds before.

DELIVERING JUSTICE

BY
BARB HAN

First Published in Great Britain 2016
By Mills & Boon, an imprint of HarperCollins*Publishers*
1 London Bridge Street, London, SE1 9GF

© 2016 Barb Han

ISBN: 978-0-263-91916-5

46-0916

Our policy is to use papers that are natural, renewable and recyclable products and made from wood grown in sustainable forests. The logging and manufacturing processes conform to the legal environmental regulations of the country of origin.

Printed and bound in Spain
by CPI, Barcelona

USA TODAY bestselling author **Barb Han** lives in north Texas with her very own hero-worthy husband, three beautiful children, a spunky golden retriever/standard poodle mix and too many books in her to-read pile. In her downtime, she plays video games and spends much of her time on or around a basketball court. She loves interacting with readers and is grateful for their support. You can reach her at www.barbhan.com.

This book is dedicated to: Allison Lyons
for making every single book better.

Jill Marsal for always being there
and ready to answer every question.

The great loves of my life: Brandon,
Jacob and Tori, the best people I could ever
hope to have in my world (I feel crazy blessed!).

Patricia Allsbrook for the last-minute save
(thank you, thank you!) and always being
such a steady, calming force.
And her daughter, Paulina, for her quick wit
(what are you, a twenty-year-old?) and warm smile.

And Babe for *always* being the one
I can't wait to talk to every night.

Chapter One

For a few seconds as Tyler O'Brien scaled Diablo's Rock and pushed up onto its crest, everything in the world was peaceful. Looking out onto the land that breathed life into his soul, he couldn't imagine a better place to be.

Tyler's gaze swept down and he muttered a curse as he stared at an overturned four-wheel ATV with an unmoving body splayed out underneath.

A dead body was not part of Tyler's lunch plans.

Tyler hated accidents. He and his five brothers had inherited the cattle ranch two months ago after his parents had died in an "accident." New evidence had the sheriff opening a homicide investigation before the will was out of probate.

"You okay?" he shouted, wishing for a response but not really expecting one. Not with the way the body was pinned under the ATV. It was too far away to get a good visual on the person. Yet Tyler had seen enough scenes like this one to get a good feel for how it would turn out.

Cell phone coverage was nonexistent on this part of the ranch so he couldn't call for an ambulance or the sheriff. He'd left his walkie-talkie with Digby, his gelding. Most ranchers used ATVs and pickup trucks for convenience when checking the vast amount of fencing on a ranch the size of The Cattlemen Crime Club. But Tyler figured his horse needed the exercise and it made him feel connected to the land to do things the way his father had. His ranch hands used ATVs, and for a split second he feared one of them might be below, but the area around Diablo's Rock was Tyler's to check.

Maybe someone had their wires crossed. Or a group of thrill seekers had wandered onto the land and one got separated.

His pulse kicked into high gear as he moved into action, digging the heels of his boots into the rocky forty-foot drop one careful step at a time. He scanned the horizon looking for the rest of the ATV party. There was no sign of anyone else as far as the naked eye could see.

Diablo's Rock wasn't a good area for people new to ATVs and only an idiot would come out here alone. There were black bears and copperhead snakes, badgers and all manner of wildlife running around this part of Texas. The land was beautiful and its danger only enhanced Tyler's respect for it. It was a reminder that people weren't always at the top of the food chain. An unprepared person could end up at the wrong end.

The closer Tyler descended toward the body, the more his pulse spiked. He could tell that the figure was smaller than a man, and that definitely ruled out one of his employees.

As he approached, he could clearly see the creamy skin of long legs, which meant the woman either had on shorts or a dress. He assumed shorts considering the fact that she wore running shoes. Neither outfit was appropriate this time of year, which struck Tyler as odd if she'd been planning on this excursion. Wouldn't she dress for the occasion? Thanksgiving was right around the corner. The average temperature in November was in the sixties in this part of Texas and this week had been colder than usual, barely breaking fifty with a blanket of cloud coverage most days.

A good part of the reason he'd intended to eat lunch on the rock was that the sun had finally broken through and its heat would reflect on the surface, offering a warm place to eat.

Then again, maybe the visitor hadn't planned on being out there at all. When Tyler got closer, maybe he'd recognize her face. The notion she could be someone he knew pricked his throat as if he'd swallowed a cactus.

People wandered off trails and did all kinds of random things while on scheduled hunting expeditions, but there was nothing on the calendar and the safety record on their land was unblemished. Right up until now, he thought.

The ATV had flipped over and was on top of her. At first blush, she looked trapped. He shoved thoughts that she could be a young runaway or in trouble to the back of his mind while he moved around the ATV, trying to get a better look at her positioning.

Her body was positioned awkwardly and close to the handlebars, but she wasn't being pinned by them as he'd first suspected.

On closer appraisal, the ATV wasn't touching her at all. And that was the first positive sign he'd had so far. He couldn't tell how bad the damage was to her body from this angle and he didn't see any signs of her breathing.

As soon as he rounded the side of the vehicle, he noticed blood splattered on the rocks next to her head. He was no expert at analyzing an accident scene but he'd heard enough stories around the campfire from their family friend Sheriff Tommy Johnson to know the splatter most likely came from an injury to her head. An impact hard enough to create that amount of blood wasn't good.

She was facedown in the dirt with her head angled toward the side he was standing on. Not that he could see past that thick red mane of hers.

This didn't look good at all. He'd make the short hike back to Digby in order to use his walkie-talkie to call for someone to pick her up. And it was such a shame that a young woman's life had been cut short.

"We'll get you out of here soon," Tyler said softly, dropping to his knees to get a better look at her face. She wasn't wearing a backpack nor did she have a purse. A physical description might help the sheriff identify her.

Tyler brushed her hair away from her face, expecting to see her eyes fixed, and then checked her neck for a pulse. She blinked sea-green eyes instead and mouthed the words, *Help me.*

She was alive?

Shocked, Tyler nearly fell backward. His pulse pounded even faster as he located hers on her wrist, which was strong.

"You're okay. I'm going to get you out of here." Tyler had enough training and experience to know better than to move her. He needed to reposition the ATV so he could better assess her injuries.

Just as he pushed up to his feet, her arm moved and then her leg. Was she trying to climb out from under the machine?

"Hold still, there," he said. "Let me get this out of the way."

Tyler dropped his backpack and hoisted the ATV upright and away from her body. It popped up onto all four wheels. His right shoulder pinched at the movement, the old injury liked to remind him of the reason he didn't have a pro baseball career anymore, and he rubbed the sore spot trying to increase blood flow.

The mystery woman had managed to roll onto her side and was trying to climb away.

"I'm not going to hurt you so you don't have to go anywhere," he said. "I have water. Are you thirsty?"

She nodded. Based on her pallor and the freshness of the blood on the rocks, she couldn't have been out there for long. That was the second good sign so far.

He had medical supplies in his saddlebag, enough to dress a field wound. He could tend to that gash and try to stem the bleeding while they waited for help to arrive. It wouldn't take long to scale Diablo's Rock, get to his horse and then return with provisions. But he didn't like the thought of leaving her alone.

"What's your name?" He went down on a knee next to his backpack, pulled a bottle of water out of the main compartment and unscrewed the cap before offering her the bottle. He shrugged out of his denim jacket, draping it over her.

She looked like she was drawing a blank in the name department as she took the water and poured the liquid over her lips. They were pink, which was a good sign. She couldn't have been out there for long.

It didn't surprise him that she'd temporarily forgotten her name and other details about her life, given the blow she'd taken to her head. Tyler had witnessed plenty of concussions out on the baseball field. The good news here was that she could recover, a huge relief considering he'd started the afternoon thinking he would be reporting a body.

"Do you have ID?" he asked.

She looked panicked and disoriented.

"Mind if I check in your pockets?"

She shook her head, angling the bottle to get more water

into her mouth than her last attempt. Again she failed miserably.

He scooted closer to her.

At this distance, he could see the dirt on her clothes. The cotton long-sleeved shirt was a deep shade of green that highlighted her lighter-colored eyes.

"Let me help you." He cradled the base of her neck with his right hand, ignoring the spark of electricity shooting through him. He shouldn't be feeling attracted to her. A sexual current couldn't be more inappropriate under the circumstances. He didn't care how beautiful she was. And she was beautiful, with her sea-green eyes, creamy complexion and heart-shaped mouth. He'd force himself to look away from her lips if it didn't mean that he'd spill water all over her face.

But feeling a real attraction to a woman he'd found lying helpless on his land a few minutes ago?

Nice one, O'Brien.

When she signaled that she'd had enough to drink, he set the bottle within her reach and then pushed up to his feet. "Okay, I'll just check for that ID, okay?"

She nodded her agreement and winced with the movement.

"Did you come out here with anyone?" he asked, chalking his physical reaction up to his overreactive protective instincts.

Looking startled, she glanced around.

Then she shook her head. Another fact she might be fuzzy on, given that hit she'd taken to her forehead.

"A group?" he continued.

The only thing he knew for certain was that she wasn't from around Bluff. It was dangerous for tourists to get lost on a massive ranch like his. She was darn lucky he—and not a black bear or hungry coyote—had found her.

She squinted her eyes. A raging headache was one of the side effects of a concussion. Luckily, that could be dealt with by popping a few pain relievers. Tyler had those in his pack, too, but the doctor would want him to wait to give them to her.

Tyler didn't want to notice her full hips or sweet round bottom as he checked her back pockets.

If he could think of another way to search her front pockets, he'd be game. As it was, he had to slip his fingers into them and ignore the way her stomach quivered.

It was safe to say that she had no ID. For the moment, neither of them knew who she was. Maybe her handbag or backpack had gone flying when she'd crashed. He scanned the ground, taking a few steps in one direction and then another.

No cell phone or purse could be seen anywhere and that struck him as odd. Tyler couldn't think of one woman he knew who would go anywhere without her cell. And that fact put a few more questions in his mind that he didn't have answers to. Like, if she was alone why wouldn't she have supplies or ID?

The panic in her eyes didn't help matters, either. Of course, waking up to a stranger and not being able to remember who she was or where she'd been would cause a certain level of panic in any normal person. Hers bothered him and he wished there was more that he could do to put her at ease.

He pushed his feelings aside as just needing to offer comfort to a stranger. It couldn't be anything more than that. He'd only known her for ten minutes, and when it came right down to it, he still didn't know her. He didn't even know her name.

"I'm going to send for help," he said.

Her eyes pleaded, filled with more of that panic he

didn't like seeing, but she didn't argue. Then again, she hadn't said anything except "help me" since he'd found her.

"It's okay. I'm coming right back. I promise," he added to ease her concern. He whistled, hoping the family's chocolate lab, Denali, was somewhere within earshot. He could keep her company. After a few seconds of quiet and no Denali, Tyler said, "My horse is tied up on the other side of that rock and I need to get there so I can contact my men and send for medical attention."

She didn't relax but she nodded, wincing again at the movement. That was going to be one helluva headache when the dust settled.

As Tyler got to his feet, he scanned the area for any signs of wildlife. In her weakened state, he doubted she could fight off a flea. He pulled out his pocket knife anyway and her hand met his faster than he'd thought possible for hers to move.

"It's okay, I'm here to help."

She nodded as she took the knife.

"I'll be back in a few minutes." He filed her reaction away as another interesting thought. If she'd come out alone, what was she really afraid of? Him? Animals? She'd come out by herself without identification or a way to defend herself. This patch of land wasn't anywhere near a road. Clearly, he'd never met the woman before but he didn't have to know her to realize that she didn't look the type to wander off on her own on a four-wheeler. Not that she looked weak or like she couldn't handle herself in most situations. But the type of clothes and shoes she wore didn't fit with the activity and those expensive running shoes belonged out here about as much as a woman wearing a light jacket in the cold.

She didn't give the impression that she was a bandana-wearing thrill seeker. Nor did she particularly strike him as a granola-eating nature girl. Especially since the latter wouldn't be in the driver's seat of a four-wheeler.

There was another thing that bugged him as he walked away from the accident. He'd noticed another set of tire tracks when he scanned the ground for her personal belongings, which meant there could have been another person involved.

If she and a friend had ventured onto his land by mistake, what kind of jerk would leave her alone in her condition?

Then again, with no cell service the other person might've been forced to go for help.

And it wasn't like Red was talking. All she'd said so far was, "Help me." Pretty much anyone in her situation would say the same thing.

Tyler quickened his pace. If there was someone on his land searching for reception, he needed to get a search team out while there was still plenty of daylight. The accident might've already been called in. If the person wasn't familiar with the area he or she might not be able to lead rescuers to Red.

Even so, a person would have to be new at this to panic and leave an injured person alone with all the dangerous wildlife here on the ranch. A darker side of him also noted that this would be the perfect way to cover up an attempted murder.

Tyler wrote the sentiment off as the result of learning that his parents had been murdered. He would like nothing more than to solve the case that had been made to look like an accident. Thinking about it made him angry. Who would want to hurt his family?

He shelved those thoughts for now.

Another one struck him about the mystery woman. If the scene back there had an attempted murder, then the murderer could still be around. With her lying there vulnerable and alone, it wouldn't take much to finish the job.

Tyler crested Diablo's Rock and took the back side just as fast shivering in the cold breeze. He'd tied Digby to a tree in a spot where his horse could decide if he wanted to be in the shade or not.

The gelding was standing in the sun, right where Tyler had left him. He blew out a breath as he pulled his walkie-talkie out of his saddlebag and got hold of his foreman, Russ.

"What can I do for you, boss?" Russ asked.

"There's been a four-wheeler incident at the base of Diablo's Rock. A woman took a pretty bad hit to her head. She's not going anywhere without help."

"You don't know who she is?" Russ asked. It was more statement than question.

"Never seen her before. She doesn't have any ID on her and I'd put money on the fact she has a concussion."

"Sounds like a mess," Russ agreed. "Hold on for one second, boss."

Tyler would never get used to the title even though he owned just as much of the ranch as his brothers. Together, they had a ninety-five percent interest—or would as soon as the will was out of probate, which would take another ten months. The other five percent had been divided between Pop's only living brother and sister a few years ago. Uncle Ezra and Aunt Bea didn't agree on much of anything except being taken care of. The two of them were as alike as a water moccasin and a frog.

Pop had included them both in ownership of the ranch to help take care of them financially as they aged, since Bea's daughter had left for California and Ezra's only son had died before his tenth birthday. The family cattle ranch was the biggest in Texas, both in land and net profit. As if that wasn't enough, the hunting club brought in more money than they could spend, much to the benefit of the many charities their mother had loved—a tradition Tyler and his brothers had every intention of continuing in her honor.

Even though the family had money and the boys had grown up knowing that they stood to inherit the highly successful family business, none had relied on that inheritance. All six O'Brien brothers had a deep-seated need to make their own way and depend on themselves. None were like their aunt or uncle, who seemed content to ride their successful brother's coattails. Especially Uncle Ezra, who had been angling to sell his interest or be given more control over the hunting club in recent months. Tyler's older brother Dallas figured the man was getting bored in his old age and wanted more to keep him busy.

Tyler hoped that was all there was to it, especially since it was his job to keep the peace. Of all the sons, he was the best negotiator and he'd talked Ezra down for the time being. They'd already set aside one percent of theirs for Janis, their housekeeper, who would be wealthy enough not to work for the rest of her life. Although, she'd said she was way too young to retire.

"I have emergency personnel on their way to the Rock," Russ said, interrupting Tyler's heavy thoughts—thoughts he'd volunteered to ride fences to try to stem in the first place.

Ranch hands called Tyler a Renaissance man for doing things the old-fashioned way, but the truth was that it was as good for Tyler's soul as it was for Digby's health. Being out on the land on his horse made him feel connected and whole in a way he couldn't easily explain, nor did he care to examine.

"Let Tommy know about this, will you? Someone might

be sick with worry looking for her," he said. The sheriff had been Dallas O'Brien's best friend and like a brother to the rest of the O'Brien boys. He'd grown up on the land. His uncle, Chill Johnson, had worked for Pop as long as Tyler could remember. Tommy had come to live with his uncle after his parents died.

"Will do, boss. I'll see if the sheriff can meet you at the hospital to take statements. Maybe he can help figure out who she is." Russ knew Tyler well enough to realize that he wouldn't be able to walk away until he knew the mystery woman was all right.

Silence meant Russ was taking care of that phone call right now, which was good because if someone had already reported her missing, then Tyler might be able to bring back more than medical supplies. He might be able to give her an identity. And if that second set of tire tracks had someone frantically searching for help, Tyler could ease that burden, as well.

"Sheriff said no one called in an emergency or missing person's report," Russ said.

Tyler feared as much.

"Said he'll meet her at the hospital since he's tied up on another interview right now," Russ continued.

If no one was looking for her, then Tyler had to consider other possibilities for those tire tracks.

"Much appreciated," he said to Russ. "Have someone ready to take Digby from me so I can head to the hospital as soon as I get back to the barn. And send out a search team in the chopper to make sure there's no one out here lost."

Tyler thanked Russ before ending the transmission and starting the journey back toward the redheaded mystery. He couldn't completely ignore the fear that he'd return to a lifeless body. She'd been upright and responsive so he'd take those as positive signs. Being away from her while she was vulnerable had his blood pressure spiking faster than a pro volleyball player. He picked up his pace, needing to see for himself that she was still okay.

At the faster speed, he crested Diablo's Rock in half the time. Part of him wondered if she could have managed to crawl away. She'd seemed determined and half-scared out of her wits—a combination that could be dangerous—or deadly—and left him wondering what really had her so freaked out.

He found her right where he'd left her. His pulse had slowly wound back to a decent clip when he saw that she was still conscious. And yet something else he couldn't quite put his finger on was eating away at him. What was the creepy, fire-ants-crawling-on-his-spine feeling about anyway?

Danger, for one thing, in the form of poachers. Sure, there were poachers in South Central Texas. People looked for trophies and illegally hunted on the large ranches in the area, which created a dangerous situation for all involved.

The O'Briens worked diligently to keep the land free of people who trespassed to hunt or steal game, so that risk should be minimal. If it wasn't poachers, then what was it? The fact that so many things didn't add up?

A beautiful single woman alone on a four-wheeler in territory she didn't know and wasn't dressed for? Yep. That made about as much sense as a deer eating barbeque.

"Help is on the way," he said, trying to give her hope to hold on to, wishing he could do more. He knelt next to her and opened his medical supply kit.

"Thank you," she managed to get out.

"My apologies if this hurts." It was going to hurt. That gash on her forehead was deep and had him worried. He poured clean water over it and then dabbed antibiotic ointment onto an oversize gauze bandage, pressing it to her forehead to stem the bleeding. She seemed determined not to give in to the pain. Or maybe she was just too weak.

It didn't take long for the cavalry to arrive. Tyler heard the chopper moving toward them before he got a visual on it. A helicopter was the only logical choice for rescue workers to use in order to access this part of the land. Otherwise, they'd have to take her on one helluva bumpy ride to get her to a main road, and that could jeopardize her condition.

Tyler saw the chopper moments before the pilot landed.

From there, it was only twenty yards to reach him and Red. The land was flat enough to manage easily on foot.

As emergency personnel neared, the mystery woman squeezed Tyler's hand.

He glanced at her and saw that same look of fear in her eyes. What was that all about? Didn't she realize this was the help she needed?

Depending on how bad that blow to the head was, she might not recognize them as the people who would help her. That had Tyler more worried than when he'd found her. Just how badly injured was she?

The blow she'd taken to the head looked bad. He'd give anyone that. But her panic looked like she was in one of those horror flicks being chased by an ax murderer.

"It's okay. I know these men. They'll take care of you," he tried to reassure her. Tyler had known the EMTs, Andy and Shanks, for years. They were good guys. Dougherty would be piloting the chopper. Tyler didn't need to see him to know that.

So what was up with the way she kept squeezing his hand, looking like she was trying to say something?

Chapter Two

The heel of Tyler's boots clicked against the white tile floor in the hospital hallway as he neared room 367 to check on Red.

He removed his gray Stetson before crossing the threshold, pausing long enough to finger comb his hair and chew on the facts. No one had reported the mystery redhead as missing or reported the accident. That had not been the news he was expecting and it made him worry that some other outsider was on his property, hurt, lost or just a damned fool who was hunting illegally and ditched the redhead when her ATV overturned. Something he couldn't quite put his finger on had his radar on full alert and it was more than just finding her in the condition he had.

Tyler pushed open the door at Bluff General and walked inside Red's room. Her eyes were closed. The bed had been raised so that she was halfway sitting and she had an IV attached to her left arm. He'd seen enough of the inside of hospital rooms to know the IV most likely contained fluids and possibly antibiotics to stem infection. All good things that her body needed to recover.

In fact, the fluids seemed to be working magic already because there was a rosy hue in the creamy complexion on her cheeks now. Her forehead had a proper bandage on it and his makeshift head wrap had been replaced with clean, white gauze.

Since she looked to be resting peacefully and he didn't want to disturb her, he figured this would be a good time to visit with her doctor and find Tommy to see if he'd managed to get a statement or put a name to Sleeping Beauty here.

Her eyes fluttered open and he felt like a fool for staring at her.

"How are you?" he asked, for lack of anything better to say. Even through the gauze and tape she was stunning.

"Better," she managed to squeak out. Her throat sounded scratchy. It was the dry air.

He set his cowboy hat down on the chair and moved next to her bed. Now that she seemed able to speak, maybe he could find out if there were others on his land or if he should call off the search.

"What's your name?" he asked.

She made a move to speak but coughed instead. Her gaze locked onto a large white mug situated on the wheeled table next to her bed just out of reach.

"You thirsty?" he asked as he moved to the mug.

"Yes, please" came out on a croak.

At least she was talking and making sense. Those were good signs.

"Were you alone earlier?" he asked as he held the oversize mug filled with ice water toward her. She eagerly accepted but didn't answer.

After a few small sips, she leaned her head against the pillow, but her eyes never left Tyler's face. Those sea-green eyes stayed fixed on him, panic and fear still there.

"Do you know who you are?" he asked, setting the mug down on the tray and then repositioning it so that she could reach water whenever she wanted.

"Jennifer," she said, throat still scratchy but sounding much better. Her voice had a nice pitch to it. "Who are you?"

"Tyler O'Brien. My brothers and I own the land you were on earlier."

Her gaze darted toward the door and then her eyes widened in fear, so Tyler turned to follow her line of sight.

A decent-looking man in his early thirties walked in. His gaze ricocheted between Jennifer and Tyler. He was several inches shorter, so Tyler guessed he was around five foot eleven. He was on the thin side, built like a runner, and had sandy-blond hair. A fresh-looking pink sunburn dotted his tanned nose and cheeks.

Tyler didn't recognize him.

"Honey," the man said with a sigh and he seemed to pour on the drama if anyone asked Tyler. "I've been so worried about you."

Tyler glanced at Jennifer in time to see a moment of sheer panic, so he stepped in between them, blocking Tan Face's path.

"Name's Tyler." He stuck out his hand.

"What happened to you, honey? Are you all right?" Tan Face said, sidestepping Tyler and his hand.

"Hold on there, pal," Tyler said, placing his hand on Tan Face's shoulder, ensuring he couldn't get to Jennifer's bedside. "I didn't catch your name."

"James Milton," he said, puffing out his chest like a cobra, looking none too thrilled that Tyler had put a hand on him.

"Do you mind?" he asked. "My fiancée is lying in a hospital bed and she's none of your business."

Fiancée? Tyler didn't normally misjudge situations. His instincts were usually spot-on. Red seemed scared of the man. But if the two of them were engaged then he needed to take a step back. Some lines shouldn't be crossed no matter how irritated the man's presence made Tyler.

He let go of the man's shoulder. It might be better to take a wait-and-see approach to this one. Tyler told himself that he'd leave as soon as he knew she was going to be fine. Besides, he needed to make sure she had no intention of suing him for having an accident on his land. As crazy as that sounded, he'd heard of people doing that and more.

He ignored the little voice that said he was lying to himself about why he was sticking around and that it had to do with an attraction.

Milton made a dramatic scene of rushing to Red's side once he was free of Tyler's grasp. The man was fresh-from-a-shower clean and had on dress slacks and a button-down shirt. Not exactly the kind of clothes one would wear on an ATV adventure, so the logical question was why would he let Red go alone if he cared about her as much as he professed?

"I didn't know what to think when you disappeared," Milton said to her.

Tyler folded his arms and leaned against the wall. The panicked expression on Jennifer's face intensified. He'd probably regret this later, but he had to ask, "About that, James. What happened exactly?"

"I'm fine," Red interjected, her gaze darting from Tyler to Milton.

Tyler didn't have a strong reading on the guy other than general dislike and her reaction wasn't helping. Milton's concern came off as insincere. Tyler had learned long ago to trust his instincts. This guy looked like he was putting on a show.

The door opened and the sheriff walked in.

Milton turned and the look on his face when he caught sight of the sheriff was priceless. Also, it strengthened Tyler's intuition that this guy was up to no good. This was about to get interesting.

Tommy introduced himself to Jennifer and Milton, and then shook Tyler's outstretched hand.

"I've been worried sick about you, darling," Milton said, turning to Jennifer, and Tyler thought the man was over-selling.

She managed a weak smile.

Tyler noticed that she stiffened when Milton took her by the hand. Not exactly a warm reception for her fiancé, and that got Tyler's mind spinning with scenarios, none he liked.

"Do you have ID?" Tommy asked.

"Did we do something wrong, sheriff?" Milton produced two Louisiana driver's licenses. His and Jennifer's.

"Just routine under the circumstances in which—" Tommy glanced at one of the plastic-covered cards "—Ms. Davidson was found."

When Tommy took down the information and then returned the cards, Milton refocused on Jennifer.

"I can't believe I almost lost you," he said, his voice had more syrup than Granny's pancakes when she'd started losing her sight but refused to wear glasses.

If anyone asked Tyler's opinion, and Tommy would as soon as they were alone, he'd say the guy was a fake. That didn't exactly make him a criminal.

"Mr. Milton, do you and Ms. Davidson mind answering a few questions?" Tommy asked.

"Don't take this the wrong way, Sheriff, but I'd like to spend some time alone with my fiancée," Milton said.

Tyler would bet his horse Milton would. He stifled a snicker.

"But I do understand that you're just doing your job,"

Milton added and Tyler was sure it was part of the con-
cerned-fiancé act.

"Given that you seem to sympathize with my position,
I hope you won't mind if I ask Ms. Davidson a question,"
Tommy said.

"Of course," Milton responded.

"Ma'am, would you be more comfortable giving me
your statement alone?" Tommy asked. "I'd be happy to
clear the room."

Milton balked at the request. Before he could puff up
again, Tommy held out a warning hand.

"It's part of the job," he said to Milton. Then he turned
his full attention to Jennifer. "Ma'am?"

She looked to be contemplating her answer.

"Why on earth would she want that?" Milton's cheeks
turned a shade of red as he focused on Jennifer.

Her weak smile died on her lips as soon as he turned
back to the sheriff and didn't that make the hair on Tyler's neck stand at attention. Was she being manipulated?
Abused? Milton didn't seem to want her to speak up for
herself.

Tyler ground his back teeth, thinking about a man being
physical with the opposite sex.

"No, thanks," she said to Tommy.

"Were the two of you riding ATVs earlier today?"
Tommy asked Milton.

"Yes, and I lost her on the trail so I left and went back
to our motel to wait for her," Milton said.

Tyler's eyebrow shot up about the same time as Tommy's. Tyler also noted that she'd deliberately kept the truth
from him earlier about being alone on the trail. He'd seen
the tracks himself. What was she hiding?

The two of them might have gotten into a fight and it

could have gotten physical. He could've taken off and then she could've chased after him before the crash.

"You decided to leave her unprotected in unfamiliar territory?" Tommy asked.

"We'd had a fight." James turned toward Jennifer with a stern look.

"I searched everywhere for her once I lost her on the trail. I figured she was mad and needed to blow off steam."

"Do you realize there are black bears in these parts of Texas?" Tommy asked, incredulous.

"No. I didn't. I would never…" Milton let that sentence hang in the air. "I searched for her everywhere and couldn't find her so, like I said, I decided to give myself time to cool off, as well. I went back to my room, got worried, and when she didn't answer her cell I called around local hospitals."

"But not the police station?" Tommy asked.

Milton shook his head.

"Did you take off before or after she'd been in an accident?" Tyler asked, since he hadn't had a chance to brief Tommy on the situation yet.

Milton whirled on Tyler.

"What's that supposed to mean?" he asked.

"I was just wondering if you knew she'd been in an accident before you took off to 'cool down' as you said," Tyler elaborated.

"If I'd known anything had happened, I'd have stayed with her," Milton shot back, turning his attention to Jennifer with another overexaggerated look.

That rang more warning bells.

And there was another thing bugging Tyler. If these two were engaged, wouldn't she be wearing a ring?

"You said the two of you were getting married," Tyler began. "Set a date yet?"

"We're working on it," Milton said. "Why?"

"Just checking to see how far along your plans are," Tyler said coolly.

"And why would that be any of your business?" Milton asked, not bothering to hide his disdain. He'd been reasonably respectful to Tommy since he was the law, but the man must see Tyler as an inconvenience. A lot could be said about a man who treated people poorly if he saw them as beneath him.

Tyler shrugged, his casual demeanor was clearly getting to the guy. "Thought it was customary for the woman to wear a ring."

Milton's gaze shot to Jennifer. "We haven't made it that far. I just asked her."

Tyler studied Jennifer's reaction. Her expression was blank, her eyes dead as she forced a smile.

She was doing exactly what Milton said and yet she feared the man. Had Tyler read this situation wrong? Sure, none of it was adding up and she looked less than thrilled to be around Milton, but no one was forcing her to be with the guy.

Tyler couldn't figure why anyone would stay in a bad relationship. And yet it happened all the time.

"There are two sets of tracks leading up to the accident. And one left. How do you explain that, Mr. Milton?" Tyler asked.

"I can't because I wasn't there," Milton responded.

"Is that true?" Tommy asked Jennifer.

She glanced up at Milton first, and then nodded.

If she was going to corroborate Milton's story, then maybe Tyler needed to mind his own business. He'd tried to defend a few buddies who were in the middle of domestic fights and had learned just how quickly tempers could escalate. Tyler wasn't afraid of Milton; he could handle that jerk. But he couldn't make Red leave the guy.

If she wouldn't give him anything to work with, then he had to come at this from another angle.

"Have the two of you had any lifestyle changes lately?" Tommy asked Milton, picking up on Tyler's tension. "In preparation for the wedding?"

Milton's face scrunched up. "No."

"Haven't taken out any life insurance policies on each other? Named the other as the beneficiary?" Tommy pressed.

"No. Nothing like that." Milton's face looked ready to explode from anger. "Am I under arrest, Sheriff?"

Not yet, Tyler wanted to say.

"Can I see you in the hall for a minute?" Tyler asked Tommy.

"I was just about to suggest the same thing," Tommy said and then turned to Milton. "I'll be back as soon as I take a statement from the landowner."

The door had barely closed when Tyler turned around and asked, "How is it that a man could, first, leave his fiancée outside in a strange place alone and, second, not call the police when she's missing for hours?"

"Good questions," Tommy said. "He's a jerk. I just don't have anything that I can charge him with. I need something solid in order to take him in."

"Did you notice how scared she looks?" Tyler asked. "Or the fact that he was so concerned about her that he decided to take a shower before he bothered to figure out where she'd gone or what might've happened to her?"

Tommy frowned, nodded. "It's not illegal, though."

"His story doesn't add up and he'll most likely run out of town the minute our backs are turned." Frustration ate at Tyler.

"You're right on both counts, but he has every right to

go where he pleases for now. As far as I can tell no crime has been committed."

"He's hurting her." Tyler clenched his fists.

"Which is a shame, but not against the law unless someone witnesses it or she steps forward on her own to press charges."

"It should be." Tyler knew this guy was up to no good.

"I'll stay on him. If he so much as makes a wrong turn while he's in town I'll question him for it," Tommy said.

"There has to be more you can do than that," Tyler said.

"We can scare him," Tommy said after thinking about it for a minute. "We better get back inside. I don't want to leave him alone with her longer than we have to."

"I have a few more questions for him," Tyler said through clenched teeth.

Tommy paused before opening the door. "Go ahead and ask everything you want. See if you can get him to mess up and admit to something. Without her willing to go against him, we have nothing otherwise."

Milton stood, rising to his full height when they reentered the room, which was still considerably less than both of the other men.

"Earlier, you said you lost your fiancée after a fight?" Tyler took up his position leaning against the wall near the doorjamb.

"She was tired and decided to turn back but I wasn't ready to go, so I told her how to find her way to our original meet-up point." Was Milton changing his story?

"I thought you said the two of you got into a fight," Tyler said.

Milton glanced down and to the right, a sure sign he was about to lie.

"That's what we fought about," he said, quickly recovering, as pleased with himself as if he'd just won the big stuffed animal at the state fair.

Clearly the man had just made another mistake. First he said he lost her, then he said that she turned back on purpose—which was it?

"You can't have it both ways, so pick one," Tyler said point-blank.

"Well, originally she said she was going to turn back, but then I got a bad feeling about her being out there alone in a place she didn't know and so I turned back to look for her, thus find her." Another satisfied smirk crossed Milton's features.

If that wasn't a sack of dung bigger than a bull, Tyler didn't know what was. Who did Milton think he was fooling?

Tyler's right hand fisted. He flexed and then forced it to relax.

"Good that you had time to clean yourself up, you know, while you were so busy being worried about your fiancée here," Tyler pressed.

Another frustrated pause.

"When I couldn't find Jennifer I figured she got angry at me for leaving her, so I decided to be ready to smooth things over when she came back to the motel," Milton said.

"Even though you couldn't find her when you went looking for her? You still assumed she'd be able to find her way back?" Tyler asked, not letting up. "And where was this meet-up point you mentioned?"

Milton didn't answer.

In all honesty, the man could walk out at any time. But then, that would leave Jennifer alone with Tyler and the sheriff. No way did James Milton want that.

"What are you doing in town, anyway?" Tyler continued.

"We came for the…nature. We wanted to get out of the city for a long weekend and decompress before kicking our wedding plans into high gear," Milton said. "Life from here on out is going to be crazy, isn't it, honey?" Milton shot another look at Red.

"What trail were you on? Do you remember anything about it that stuck out?" Tyler asked.

"Not really." Milton shrugged.

"Was it rocky or were there trees?"

"Trees," Milton said, trying a little too hard to sound convincing.

"Which direction did you come from?" Tyler asked.

"We came from the north," Milton supplied.

Tyler didn't immediately respond.

"You sure about that?" he finally asked.

"Yeah. North, right, honey?" Milton said, glancing down at Jennifer.

She managed a weak smile and a nod.

No one got to Diablo's Rock from the north on an ATV. Tire tracks at the scene indicated the opposite. Tyler slanted a look at Tommy.

"That's impossible," Tyler said. "Tracks came from the south."

Anyone could get confused in an area they aren't familiar with, but this guy wouldn't be confused about direction because he was wearing one of those expensive compass watches.

"Guess I didn't notice." Milton shrugged. "If I'm not under arrest, then can we be finished with this conversation?" His lips flattened, indicating his patience had run out.

Well, guess what, buddy? So had Tyler's.

And they were far from done.

Chapter Three

"Where's the doctor?" Milton asked, rotating toward Jennifer and effectively turning his back on Tyler and Tommy. "How much longer do you have to stay in here?"

"In a hurry to go somewhere, Mr. Milton?" Sheriff Tommy asked, blond eyebrow arched.

"I'd like to get her home where I can take better care of her," Milton said. "It's impossible to get any rest in one of these places."

"And where is home?" Tommy asked.

"Louisiana, like on my license. You saw that earlier," Milton said. "You'd like to come home with me, wouldn't you, darling?"

There he went with that *darling* business again. Tyler wanted to vomit. Again, Milton was pouring it on a little thick.

While Tommy was finishing his interview, Tyler excused himself in order to talk to Jennifer's doctor, Dr. McConnell.

McConnell was a no-nonsense middle-aged woman who'd been working at the hospital since graduating medical school. A local, she wore jeans and boots under her white coat and she'd been a close family friend since longer than Tyler could remember.

"Is there any chance she's being abused?" he asked McConnell when he was sure they were out of earshot.

"I'm bound by oath not to respond to that question," Dr. McConnell said. "However, since you found her, I don't mind telling you that she has quite a few bruises on both of her arms."

"I'm guessing that's a yes," he said.

"She's been through a lot." McConnell frowned. "I'm not saying she's been abused, but even if she has there's no way to prove anything. And, of course, nothing can be done unless a victim is willing to talk about it or press charges."

"In theory, would you have offered that kind of help by now?" he asked.

"I would've. We're not talking about a child here, where I'd be forced to report suspected abuse and Tommy could step in," Dr. McConnell said. "I can only help patients who want it."

Tyler didn't like what he heard.

"When I see a patient with bruising like we've discussed, I'm always sure to have another conversation with her. I can promise that she'll know that there are folks who can help. I'll offer assistance, but it'll be up to her to accept," Dr. McConnell said, placing her hand on Tyler's shoulder. She had to reach up, considering she wasn't more than five foot three.

"Much obliged to you, doc," Tyler said.

"Before you go, any word on the investigation? It's been two weeks since I submitted the results from the third-party analysis of the toxicology report," she said, and he knew that she was talking about his parents. She'd been one of his mother's closest friends and he could see how much the doctor missed her in the dark circles under her eyes. The recent news that his parents had been murdered hit their friends hard, their children harder.

"Nothing so far, except that Tommy is reviewing the case file personally," he said. Tyler and his brothers benefitted the most from their parents' deaths so they'd be at the top of anyone's suspect list. There were no other leads at the time.

Dr. McConnell gave that a minute.

"Give your brothers a hug for me," she finally said.

"I will."

Walking toward Jennifer's room, Tyler's footsteps fell heavy. Even though he wanted to take James Milton out back and teach him a thing or two about why real men didn't hurt women, the reality was that there wasn't much else he could do at the hospital.

Tommy seemed to be wrapping things up by the time Tyler returned to the room. As much as it soured him to do so, Tyler shook James Milton's hand. Milton's wasn't moist or hot, indicating that he was fairly relaxed about the situation.

But should he be?

A man who hit a woman might be a practiced liar. Tyler didn't care much for people who couldn't be bothered to tell the truth. And this jerk was poised to walk right out the door and go scot-free. He hadn't violated any laws that Tommy could arrest him for. Tyler could see Tommy's frustration written all over his face.

"One last thing," Tommy said to Milton. "Did you have permission to ride on the O'Brien ranch?"

"Permission?" Milton echoed. His eyes widened when he heard the name O'Brien. Most people knew it and had a similar reaction.

"The land that you and your fiancée were riding ATVs on is owned by the O'Brien family," Tommy continued.

"It's protected by a fence and No Trespassing signs are posted everywhere. I've been out hunting on that property myself. So, my question to you is, were you aware that you were breaking the law when you took your recreational vehicles on the land?"

"Well, no, we hadn't planned on being on his property. We got lost. Is that a crime?" For the first time in the interview, Milton looked like he might break a sweat.

"Being lost? No. Trespassing on someone else's land and destroying their property? Yes." Tommy turned to Tyler. "Will you be pressing charges today, Mr. O'Brien?"

Tyler might not be able to stop Jennifer from walking out of the hospital with this jerk but he could slow them down.

"As a matter of fact, I will," Tyler said, shifting his gaze to Milton. "You say that you innocently got lost, but how do I know that you weren't out on my property, illegally hunting?"

"I don't own a gun, for one," Milton shot back.

Tyler figured that Tommy could check the gun registration database all day long and not find a gun registered to James Milton. That didn't mean he wasn't carrying one anyway. There was no shortage of illegal guns on the black market and in the hands of people who had no business with them.

"I can't know that for sure. Besides, you might've ditched it when you realized you were close to getting caught. In fact, I have another scenario worth the sheriff's consideration," Tyler said.

"Care to enlighten me?" But Milton's gaze said the opposite.

"How about this? You take your fiancée here on a hunting trip on my land. We offer excursions but you don't want to pay the price. You decide to do things on your own. But then you hear someone and you know you're about to get caught. Rather than risk it, you take off, leaving your fiancée to fend for herself. You go hide in your motel room waiting for her to come back. You clean up because you don't want to risk anyone realizing you might've been outside. But here comes the problem. Your fiancée gets herself in trouble and ends up in the hospital, so you make up this wild story about the two of you fighting to cover for the fact that you were illegally hunting on my property," Tyler said, his gaze zeroed in on Milton.

"You can't be serious." Milton's gaze darted from Tyler to Tommy as he took a step back. A few more and he'd be in the corner.

"Sure I can," Tyler shot back, watching Milton's reaction.

"Can I see your hunting license, Mr. Milton?" Tommy asked.

Milton balked. "I don't have one. I've already told you that I don't even own a gun."

"Did you realize that you'd need one?" Tommy continued.

"I didn't come here to hunt. I wasn't out looking for game on his land." Milton shot daggers toward Tyler before narrowing his gaze when he looked at Tommy again. "I'll ask again. Am I under arrest?"

"If you were, we'd be having a different conversation right now, Mr. Milton. One that would include reading your Miranda rights to you. Since I haven't done that yet, you're free to go." Tommy turned toward the door. "But I have every intention of investigating Mr. O'Brien's complaint. In which case, I'm advising you not to leave town until this dispute has been resolved."

It was weak. Tyler knew enough about the law to know that, but Tommy was betting that Milton didn't realize it.

"I have no plans to go anywhere until my Jennifer is better. And then I have every intention of driving out of this town and back to Louisiana," Milton said.

"Mind if I speak to you privately, Mr. Milton?" Tommy shot a wink toward Tyler so subtle he barely caught it.

Tyler immediately caught on. He grabbed the pen and paper off the wheeled tray table and jotted down his cell number. Then, he moved to the bed next to Jennifer.

"You sure you're okay?" he asked.

She nodded, looking resolved. If she was engaged to Milton, then wouldn't she seem more comforted by his presence? Tyler figured he could rack his brain trying to solve that and other mysteries for the rest of his life and still come up short. There wasn't much else he could do or say if he stuck around. Red... Jennifer, he corrected himself, seemed intent on staying with this jerk. Just in case she changed her mind and wanted a friend, he folded up the piece of paper into a tiny square.

"You change your mind or need anything, call me." He managed to slip it under her pillow before Milton returned.

Tyler figured it might help him sleep at night, knowing he'd done everything he could.

Heck, who was he kidding? Those sea-green eyes were going to haunt him.

TYLER'S CELL BUZZED. He glanced at the clock on his nightstand. It was hours until the sun would rise. The noise should've jolted him awake but his eyes had barely closed all night thinking about Red.

He threw off the covers and walked over to the dresser where his phone sat on its charger, thinking what he really needed to clear his head was a night on the town and a stiff drink.

The number didn't look familiar but he answered anyway.

"I don't have anyone else to call. Please help me." The frail voice on the other end of the line belonged to Red.

Was she ready to talk? To get out of the relationship with Milton? To get help?

"Are you there?" she asked. Panic raised her voice a couple of octaves.

"Yes." he said. "As long as you're ready to tell me what's really going on."

"I'm sorry about before. It's just…" She paused, sounding almost too tired or scared to finish what she started to say. "If he finds out I'm talking to you, to anyone, then I'm dead."

"Seems to me that he's going to hurt you either way, Jennifer," Tyler said.

"My name isn't Jennifer. It's Jessica," she confided.

"I saw your driver's license," he said, chalking up the mistake to her head injury.

"Please, give me a chance to explain," she begged. "I'm not who I said I was. I know who I am and my name is Jessica."

Chapter Four

"Okay." The handsome cowboy paused as if he was seriously considering what Jessica had just said. "Is the license a fake?"

"No."

"Well then, I'm the one who's confused," he said, his voice gruff from sleep.

Jessica didn't know Tyler from Adam and yet his calming voice and masculine strength had her believing she could trust him. There was something about the tall cowboy that made her believe he would protect her.

Then again, it wasn't like she had a lot of options. The game had changed somewhere along the line and she hadn't expected Milton to try to kill her. He didn't even know that Jennifer had an identical twin, let alone that Jessica was posing as her sister.

"What's really going on?" Tyler asked.

How much should she tell him? *Could* she tell him? She needed to say enough to convince him that she wasn't crazy.

"I wish I knew," she said honestly. All Jessica thought she was supposed to be doing was subbing for her party-girl sister, Jennifer, in order to give her time to fix whatever needed fixing. Since no one in Jennifer's circle knew she had an identical twin, the two figured they could pull off a switch and no one would be the wiser. "I need to contact my twin sister and I can't do that while *he's* watching my every move."

"You're a twin?" Tyler sounded surprised but not shocked.

"Yes. Sorry for lying to you earlier," she said quietly into the phone, praying she wouldn't disturb Milton, who was sleeping ten feet away from her bed. Jessica despised lies. Anyone could ask her ex-boyfriend, Brent, about that. He seemed to be an expert at manipulating the truth when they'd been together.

Jessica refocused. She'd waited all night for Milton to doze off, and this might be her only chance to reach out for help. She'd be released sometime tomorrow afternoon and if she didn't get away from Milton it would be all over. Jessica's memory was still spotty but one thing was clear. She needed to get away from that man while she was still alive and connect with her sister before he figured her out. He kept asking her where she'd hid "it." Jessica had no idea what he'd been talking about. Her sister had warned her that Milton believed she had something valuable and had said to pick a place to take him. When she'd taken him to the O'Brien ranch and told him she'd buried it nearby, he'd slammed a rock against her head.

"What are you asking me to do?" he asked in that deep raspy voice.

"Get me out of here," she whispered. She was taking a huge risk in calling the cowboy. Milton could wake at any second. She had no idea what her sister had gotten herself involved in, but it must be pretty darn bad for that man to want her dead.

"Is he there right now?" the cowboy asked.

"Yes."

Milton stirred in his sleep and Jessica panicked. She

hung up the phone before he could catch her. If hospital staff didn't show up every hour or so she figured Milton would've already found a way to finish the job. The fact that his earlier attempt to kill her had been staged to look like an accident made her believe that he didn't want to be associated with a murder investigation.

If Jessica didn't figure out what was going on and find her sister, they'd both be dead. Losing contact yesterday had settled an ominous feeling over Jessica. She wasn't sure who she could trust anymore, except the rich cowboy who seemed determined to help. He sent her pulse racing for a whole other set of reasons she didn't want to examine. But she'd called him as a last-ditch effort to try to help her escape and find her sister. Was that a mistake?

Milton rolled onto his other side in the chair next to her bed, causing her pulse to race.

Jessica had no idea how long she'd been lying there, staring at the white ceiling, when a pair of nurses walked in pushing a gurney.

Milton shot straight up and rubbed his puffy eyes. "What's going on?"

The nurse shot him a warning look before checking the chart affixed to the foot of Jessica's bed. "We're taking our patient for an X-ray."

Milton stood, blocking her path to Jessica.

"At this hour?" he asked, puffing out his chest, and Jessica noticed he'd done that earlier when he tried to intimidate Tyler. It hadn't worked with the rich cowboy.

"This is a hospital, sir. We run 24/7," the nurse shot back and she didn't appear affected, either. "Now, if you'll step out of the way on your own it'll save me the trouble of calling security and having you removed from the building. We can do this any way you want. It's your call."

Jessica grinned despite trying to hold it in. Luckily,

Milton's back was to her so he couldn't see her face. The man frightened her.

The nurse could see her, though, and she winked at Jessica as she brushed past him.

Between the two nurses, they detached Jessica from the monitors and hoisted her up onto the gurney.

Milton made a move to follow them into the hall, but the lead nurse put up a hand to stop him. "I don't think so, sir. No one but the patient and X-ray tech are allowed where we're taking her."

His agitation was written in the severe lines of his forehead, and his eyebrows looked like angry slash marks. Jessica worried that wouldn't bode well for her later. Then again, he'd made his intentions pretty clear.

Milton stood in the doorway, watching, as Jessica was wheeled down the hallway. She could almost feel his eyes on her and she'd never be able to shake the horror of turning to find him standing there, rock raised in the air, and then a sharp pain before everything went dark.

With him in the room, she hadn't been able to sleep a wink for fear he'd make sure she never woke. But that didn't make sense, did it? Would he be so bold as to kill her in the hospital where he could be discovered? Especially now that their situation had drawn so much attention. He'd gone to great pains to make his first attempt look like an accident. Jessica had every intention of figuring out why he wanted to kill her sister and what she'd gotten herself into by agreeing to help.

The nurses made a right turn at the nurse's station and then broke into a run. Before Jessica could manage to get a word out, they stopped. A blanket was tossed over her head as she was ushered off the gurney. Her claustrophobia kicked into high gear but she resisted the urge to fight against it, taking a deep breath instead of giving in to panic. She could only pray that the nurses could be trusted.

"DON'T SAY A WORD," Tyler said, turning the light on his phone toward Red as he took off the blanket.

"What are—"

"You asked me to help and that's what I'm doing," he said, hating how scared she sounded, looked. He expected her to argue or put up a fight. Instead, she wrapped her arms around him and buried her face in his neck.

"Thank you," she said, and he could feel her shaking.

Tyler would do whatever it took to help Red. The mystery woman stirred up all kinds of unfamiliar feelings. And seeing her in an abusive relationship dredged up all kinds of bad emotions from the past…feelings he couldn't set aside as easily as he'd like. He'd told himself that he'd agreed to help her solely based on the fact that she was a woman in need, but there was more. The best Tyler could do was let Red explain herself. He intended to get to the bottom of what was really going on.

"Can I use that phone?" she asked.

"As soon as you tell me why you're with that jerk."

Shock widened her sea-green eyes. "I'm not. We're not. It's just that everything's so complicated right now. I'm not sure how to explain."

"Start at the beginning."

"I need to get ahold of my sister first, so I can sort this out. Please."

Tyler figured he needed to buy some goodwill so he handed over his cell.

Red made a phone call and it ran straight into voice mail.

"That's not good. She should be picking up." Exasperation ran deep in her voice. She called another number.

A sleepy-sounding woman answered.

"Where's Jennifer?" Red asked.

Tyler now knew that she'd been posing as her sister. It was a trick his twin younger brothers had played on the family more than once when they were growing up. It had all been good-natured fun. But Red's life was on the line.

And then a thought dawned on him. Red wasn't in a bad relationship with Milton, her sister was. Maybe she was giving her sister time to get her bearings enough to leave the jerk. She might've been the one to deliver the message. A guy like Milton wouldn't have taken news like that lying down. Had he gotten angry, found the nearest rock and bashed her in the head?

"What do you mean she just disappeared?" There was outright panic in Red's voice now as she spoke quietly into the phone. "No. Don't call anyone. Don't tell anyone. Promise me you won't look for her."

Red's shoulders slumped forward and tears rolled down her cheeks as she ended the call. She closed her eyes as if trying to shut out the world.

"Tell me what's going on and we'll figure something out." Tyler's fingers itched to hold her but making that move was a slippery slope. "Does he know who you really are?"

"No. And I have no idea what I've actually gotten myself into," she said, pinching the bridge of her nose. "My head hurts."

"You can start by telling me what your sister's relationship to James Milton is," Tyler said.

The mention of Milton's name got her eyes open in a hurry.

"We can't talk here." She glanced around. "Where are we anyway?"

Tyler didn't like the idea of taking her out of the hospital without knowing exactly what kind of danger she was in and from whom, but he had no choice under the circumstances. Milton would be asking questions soon and wouldn't be satisfied without an answer. Tyler needed to get her away from the building. He pulled out a bundle of clothing. "Here. Put these on."

"Scrubs?" she asked, and when he nodded she turned to face the other way.

He took the cue to untie the back of her gown and had to force his gaze away from the silky skin of her shoulder as she slipped out of the cotton material. In addition to the surgical scrubs, Dr. McConnell had provided a bra and panties and shoes. He needed to call her in the morning to thank her for arranging everything on such short notice.

Luckily she'd believed the story about Red wanting out of the relationship. Since she'd planned to release her the next day, McConnell didn't see the harm in giving Red an out tonight. She'd joked that it was already morning somewhere and made him promise to let her stop by his place after rounds to check on her patient. Lying to McConnell sat sourly in Tyler's gut. He'd explain the situation when he could. His first order of business was getting Red away from Milton and to safety. Then, the two of them would have a conversation about delivering justice to Milton.

"What now?" Red said, turning around to face him.

"Put these on." He handed her a surgical mask and hair covering. "And then meet me downstairs near the ER. If he sees me he'll think something's up. I want to give us as good of a head start as I can."

She took a deep breath and he assumed it was to steel her nerves.

"Okay. Let's do this," she said.

"You go first. That way, if he's wandering around and happens to see you, I won't be far behind," Tyler said.

"Once you walk out the door, make a right toward the stairs. I don't want you waiting around for an elevator. The ER is on the first floor so you'll have to make it down eight flights of stairs on your own. Can you handle it?"

She nodded and all he could see were her eyes, the green stood out even more against the light-blue face mask.

"Okay, then. Once you're down, I'll meet you at the ER bay," he said. "Don't forget to take off the mask before you walk out of the stairwell."

Red stood at the door for a long moment. She pressed her flat palm against it but stopped short of opening it.

Then she stole a last look at him before walking out and to her right.

Tyler figured he needed to wait a bit before he followed. It would take all his self-control not to hightail it to Red's room and deliver his own brand of justice. Milton needed to see what it was like to fight with a man. But that would only alert the creep to the fact that Jessica was on the run. Since Tyler couldn't be in two places at once, he waited a few minutes, then pushed the door open. If Milton saw him at all, it could be game over.

Besides, there was a lot more to this situation than met the eye and Tyler needed to get to the bottom of what was going on before he let his fists fly. He'd take Jessica to the ranch for tonight. There wasn't a place around with better security than home.

Tyler made it down the hall and then to the elevator without incident. In the ER, Red was standing right where he'd told her to and a part of him sighed in relief. He couldn't be sure that she wouldn't bolt as soon as she had the chance and he had all kinds of questions that needed answers.

Then again, she was in a strange town. Running from the one person helping her didn't make a bit of sense.

So far, Red had told Tyler that she'd stepped in for a sister who was now missing. Twins. He shook his head as he walked toward her. Wouldn't his little brothers Joshua and Ryder have a field day with this? Red and her sister's trick would be right up their alley. Even though they weren't actually identical, his youngest brothers looked enough alike that they got away with a few too many pranks, switching places to confuse people.

Tyler took Red's arm and led her out to his waiting SUV.

"What has your sister gotten herself into?" he asked as soon as they were safe inside his vehicle. He turned the key in the ignition and backed out of the parking space.

As he meandered through the lot and onto the highway he expected her to speak. She didn't.

"We can turn back and I'll ask Milton, if that makes you feel better," he threatened. No way would he go through with it but she needed a little motivation to get her talking.

"I told you before, she's my twin sister. She's in trouble."

"What kind?"

"I don't know exactly what's going on," Jessica said, staring out the front window.

"Then start with what you *do* know," he said.

"I got a call from my sister three days ago asking if I could take time off work to help her out," she said. "She needed me to step into her life and go on a trip with a friend of hers for a few days while she fixed a problem. She said go along with whatever he said, so I did. This isn't the first time I've had to bail her out of a bad situation, so I agreed."

"Is your sister involved in something illegal?"

"Before yesterday I would've been ready to fight if you asked that question about her. Now, I'm not sure what she's gotten herself into," Jessica said on a heavy sigh. "She's not a bad person. I normally get called in for a relationship that has gone south and she doesn't have the heart to break it off herself. I show up and help ease her out of it. At least that's how it started five years ago. It kind of grew from there."

"So you had no prior relationship with Milton?"

"We're not engaged, if that's what you're asking, and neither was Jenn," she said with an involuntary shiver. "I'd never seen the man before two days ago. My sister sent me with him. She said I could trust him and to go with him and pretend that I knew what he was talking about. We checked into the Bluff Motel and he started demanding that I tell him where something was. Some kind of box. I can't remember clearly." She touched the bandage on her forehead.

"Is that how you ended up on my property?"

"Yes. I picked a remote place thinking that he'd give up when we couldn't find the box right away. He got angry instead. Demanded that I tell him where it is, told me to stop playing games. I said that I'd tricked him and had no idea where the box was. The next thing I know I'm being hit in the head with a rock," she said, leaning back against the headrest. "Where are we going, by the way?"

"My ranch," he said.

"Maybe you should just take me to the airport and drop me. I can grab a flight or rent a car there and drive to Louisiana. I have to find my sister."

"In case you haven't noticed, you're in no condition to drive anywhere. Milton still has your ID so renting a car or getting on a flight is out of the question," Tyler countered. "And then there's the issue of him trying to kill you. We need to update the sheriff first thing in the morning."

"No. We can't."

Was she serious? She balked pretty darn fast when he mentioned Tommy.

"This is his town and he has a right to know the truth. You should be pressing charges against that jerk who tried to kill you," Tyler said. "In case you hadn't noticed, he seems intent on finishing the job."

"I have," she retorted, motioning toward her forehead. "But I have no idea what's really going on, I can't remember everything, and I've already put my sister in danger by leaving the hospital. All I know for sure is that Milton isn't the one in charge. Until I know who's trying to hurt her, I can't bring in the police. You can drop me off at a bus station."

She wouldn't last a day without money or transportation, and she seemed to realize it about the same time Tyler started to tell her.

"This must look bad to an outsider," she said. "But I have to ask you to keep everything I've told you between us. Give me a little time to figure out what happened to my sister and help her."

"She might be hiding."

"Or hurt," she said.

"In which case, doesn't it make more sense to bring in the law?" Tyler turned in to the ranch and security waved him ahead.

"This isn't a good idea. I shouldn't have called you and gotten you involved," she said, and he could hear the fear and panic in her voice. Not a good combination.

She looked exhausted, and his first priority was to get her inside where she could rest.

"Let's not make any decisions tonight," Tyler said, pulling up to his two-story log-cabin-style house. Their parents had built each of the brothers a home on the expansive ranch in hopes they would someday take their rightful places at the helm. Tyler's was on the south side to take advantage of the sun. Most people hated the heat in Texas but it couldn't get hot enough for Tyler. His mom used to joke that he had to be cold-blooded because of how much he loved summer.

He'd spent most of his childhood outdoors, throwing a baseball, football or whatever was around with one or more of his brothers. His childhood had been happy and filled with loving memories, and his blood boiled at the thought that someone had wanted his parents dead. They were kind, respected members of the community. His mother had one of those hearts that had no bounds. Pop was honest, albeit stern.

Tyler pulled into his attached garage and parked his SUV.

"Hold on," he said as he slid out of the driver's seat and then rounded the vehicle to open her door for her.

"Are you hungry?" he asked, offering a hand.

"I'm more thirsty than anything," she said, putting her fingers in his.

A frisson of heat fired through his fingertips and he noticed how small and delicate her hand was by comparison. He pushed those thoughts aside. His mind was still reeling over how much he'd misjudged his last girlfriend, Lyndsey. The last thing he needed was another complication in his life. "We can fix that."

There was a noise at the front door, a scratching sound.

Tyler opened the front door and let the family's chocolate lab inside. He patted his old friend on the head and scratched him behind the ears.

"This is Denali," he said to Red.

"Is he yours?"

"Denali?" Tyler glanced up. "Nah. He belongs to everyone. He drifts to each of our houses now that we're home, and he's been known to stay in the barn from time to time."

"He's beautiful." She hesitated. "And big."

"This old boy won't hurt you," Tyler said.

She moved a few steps closer and bent down. Denali jumped up at about the same time and her cheek met a wet nose. Jessica let out a yelp before reaching to scratch Denali behind the ears.

"You hit his favorite spot. Don't be surprised if he follows you around now," Tyler said.

She smiled as he helped her into the kitchen and for the first time could see just how weary she looked. Even in an exhausted state, Red would be considered beautiful with those big eyes, thick lashes and creamy complexion.

"I have some homemade chicken soup in the fridge. How does that sound?"

"Impressive. You cook?" She eased onto a bar stool at the large granite island.

"Not me. I had some delivered from the main house."

"This ranch is amazing. Are you telling me there's even more to it?" she asked. She glanced around the room as he divvied up the soup into two bowls and heated them in the microwave.

Tyler couldn't help but laugh. "More" was an understatement. "Each of my brothers has a house on the ranch, and then there's the big house my parents lived in. They kept one wing open for guests of the hunting club we own."

"What kind of ranch is this?"

"We raise cattle and provide hunting expeditions."

"How many brothers did you say you had?" she asked as he set a steaming bowl in front of her.

"Five. Six if you count Tommy. He spent most of his childhood here. He and my older brother Dallas have been best friends since before I can remember." He took a seat at the island next to her. "Be careful. It's a little hot."

She blew on the spoon before taking a mouthful. "Either I'm *that* starved or this tastes even better than it smells."

Denali had gone to sleep at her feet.

"Probably a little of both but Janis Everly is an amazing cook. Her soups are a whole experience in and of themselves," he said with a smile. It was true. The woman could cook. "You should see the main house during the holidays. Everything's decorated to the nines and the whole place smells like cinnamon and nutmeg. Janis cooks every kind of cookie imaginable. She dresses up like Mrs. Claus and delivers them just about everywhere in town."

"She sounds like an amazing woman," Jessica said.

"She's a saint for putting up with us all these years," he said with a laugh, liking the smile his comment put on Jessica's face as she bit back a yawn.

He showed her to one of the guest rooms after she'd drained her bowl. A few hours of rest should clear her thoughts and let her come to her senses.

Then they could get to the bottom of whatever was going on. And even though she'd protested, he had every intention of bringing in the law.

Chapter Five

The *rap, rap, rap* against the front door shot Tyler straight up out of bed and to his jeans, which were laid out across a chair next to his bed. The machine-gun-like knocks fired again. Tyler hopped on one leg trying to get his second leg in his pants and stay upright.

He shook his head like a wet dog, trying to wake up, and glanced at the clock. Almost six thirty. What on earth?

He took the stairs several at a time and saw that Tommy was standing on the other side of the door.

"What's going on?" he asked as he opened the door and motioned for the sheriff to come in.

"I'm here on official business," Tommy said, and the tone of his voice didn't sound good.

For a split second Tyler thought his friend might be bringing news about his parents, except that he would've called all the O'Brien's together first. So this had to be about Red.

"You want a cup of coffee?" Tyler asked, moving toward the kitchen.

"No, thanks. I've already been on duty for an hour." Tommy followed. "I'm here to talk to you about a murder."

Tyler stopped in his tracks and spun around. Those words had the same effect as a good, strong cup of coffee. "Let me guess. Milton's dead?"

"No. He's missing. We haven't identified the victim yet," Tommy said.

"What does this have to do with me?"

"The body was discovered at the Bluff Motel," he said with an ominous sigh. "In Jennifer and Milton's room. I have to ask. Where were you an hour ago?"

"Here. Asleep," Tyler said, and he could see that his friend didn't like asking that question.

"Have you been here all night?" Tommy asked.

Tyler's phone records would tell the story so he decided to come clean. "No. I went to the hospital to check on Red after she called and said she was ready to leave the jerk. I brought her home with me."

Tommy's eyebrow arched severely.

"What else was I supposed to do?" Tyler asked, his shoulders and hands raised in surrender as he stood there in the kitchen in an athletic stance. "She reached out for help and I said I'd protect her. Dan Spencer was working the security gate when we came home and he can tell you that we arrived around three o'clock this morning. I fed her soup and put her up in the guest room, and that's all."

"She's here right now?"

Tyler nodded, motioning upstairs.

"Get your coffee. It's going to be a long day," Tommy said, taking a seat at the granite island.

A few minutes later Tyler joined him with a fresh mug filled with strong coffee. He took a sip. "You want me to wake her?"

"I'll need to talk to her," Tommy said.

"What happened to Milton?" Tyler asked. "He was at the hospital with her when she called asking for help."

"He must've left after you got her out of there," Tommy supplied.

Tyler took another sip, letting that information sink in.

"He must've realized pretty quickly that something was up at the hospital."

"How'd you get her out of there without him knowing?" Tommy asked.

"Dr. McConnell arranged it on the condition she could check up on her at my house. She sent in a couple of nurses saying they were taking her for X-rays. I took over once they got her safely away from him." He paused long enough to take another sip. "I tried to convince Red to press assault charges a few hours ago."

"But she refused," Tommy finished. He knew the drill all too well. Except that this was no run-of-the-mill abuse case.

Tyler nodded. He'd let his friend make his own assumptions for now. But he had every intention of filling Tommy in as soon as he could.

"What happened at the motel?" Tyler asked.

"A couple in the room next door heard two men arguing, banging noises against the wall and then a few minutes later a car sped away. They didn't think much about it at the time, figured someone had too much to drink. The noise woke their baby and the husband got sent out to the car to get extra supplies from a diaper bag. When he returned he noticed the door next to his was still open. He thought it was strange and decided to check it out, make sure everyone was okay. That's when he saw a man splayed out on the floor, bleeding out. He tried to administer CPR and yelled for his wife to call 911," Tommy said.

"But it was too late," Tyler said.

Tommy nodded.

"Sounds personal," Tyler said.

"Very personal," Tommy echoed. "He stabbed him with a hotel pen, which means he grabbed anything he could find. Then he panicked and ran without thinking about closing the door behind him, which leads me to believe that he wasn't expecting the confrontation."

"Any chance this was a random mugging?" Tyler asked. Red was in more danger than she realized. If she truly was covering for her sister, and he believed her story, then Jennifer was into something very dark and dangerous. He also believed that Red had no idea what was going on and he found himself wanting to help her even more.

The truth lay somewhere between Texas and Louisiana, and Tyler had every intention of finding it.

"Nothing appears to be missing, although we won't know what happened for sure until we talk to James Milton." Tommy leaned against the counter. "If it had been a coincidence, though, he would've reported it."

"You're expecting to get the truth out of that man?" Tyler coughed.

"About as much as I'd expect a deer to drive a car. This whole scene looks like self-defense, but then Milton took off in a hurry, leaving behind his clothes, shaving cream, pretty much everything he brought with him as far as we can tell." Tommy dragged his boot across the tile floor. "And I'm left wondering why he would do that and not go straight to my office."

"Seems strange."

"Everything about Milton is off. From his fiancée ending up in the hospital and him expecting us to believe that lame story about losing her, to a man being stabbed to death in his motel room."

"What about the dead guy? Have you identified him yet?" Tyler asked, trying to absorb just how much danger Red was in. He also hated lying to Tommy, allowing him to believe that Jessica was her sister. He had every intention of clearing up the misunderstanding as soon as he spoke to Red. Tyler despised lies and they were racking up.

"No. He had ID on him but it was fake." Tommy's boot toe raked behind his other foot.

"What about transportation?"

"We're still working on the rest of the pieces." Tommy glanced up and tilted his head to the left. "We have no leads. Unless Jennifer knows what's going on."

"I can vouch for her whereabouts last night. She's been with me the whole time."

"The neighbor heard male voices. We aren't looking for a female." Tommy said. "And yet that doesn't rule out the possibility she might be able to fit the pieces together for me. Right now I have a dead stranger at the morgue with a fake ID, and a man on the run who could be anywhere or right under my nose looking for Jennifer. Based on his actions yesterday, I'd say the man doesn't want to leave town without her."

"I didn't trust or like that guy from the minute I laid eyes on him, but I'm just as confused as you are. She hasn't told me a thing since we got here." He glanced at the star-shaped metal clock in the kitchen. It was ten minutes until seven. "I'd hoped to give her a few hours of sleep before I talked some sense into her and brought her down to the station to press charges against Milton. At the time, I thought that SOB shouldn't get away with hitting women."

"That's not all he does," Tommy said on a heavy sigh. "The problem is figuring out what else he's into before I have another dead body in my town."

And if Tyler could save Red in the process that would be even better.

"It goes without saying that I'll need to speak to his fiancée to find out if he had enemies," Tommy added.

Why did the sound of the word *fiancée* string Tyler's neck muscles tight? He nodded, feeling the tendons cord and release.

"Did the witness hear what the two were arguing about?" Tyler asked.

"He said he was half-asleep but he thinks he remembers hearing him ask something about a necklace and where the girl was," Tommy said.

"They argued about Red?" Tyler did his best to act surprised. Damn, he hated withholding information from Tommy. But the surest way to lose Red's trust would be to go behind her back by telling his friend everything he knew. Tyler feared she'd strike out on her own and end up getting herself hurt again or worse…dead. She was in so far over her head she couldn't see right from wrong anymore, and Tyler was her best bet at finding the straight and narrow again. She seemed like a good person in a crazy situation, and Tyler of all people understood her need to protect her family.

"I believe I will take you up on that cup of coffee," Tommy said.

"Help yourself," Tyler said, draining his cup and pushing to his feet. "I'll go wake her so you can talk to her."

He could take a few minutes to prep her for what was to come, he thought as he knocked on the door of the guest room. He hated the idea of waking her before she'd had solid sleep. There was no movement on the other side so he cracked the door. "Jessica."

No answer. She must be out cold. His ringtone sounded from down the hall as he pushed open the door to her room. The bed was empty and there were no clothes to be seen. The door to the adjoining bathroom was wide open but he checked inside anyway.

Jessica was gone.

Tyler darted into his own room and answered his phone before it rolled into voice mail. The call was from Dan in security and Tyler knew right away that Jessica had hit his radar.

"What happened," Tyler asked.

"Sir, a white female is being detained in the guard shack. She was seen running across the south side of the land after exiting your house," Dan said.

Tyler needed to make a decision. Bring her in and let Tommy question her, or make an excuse and talk to her first? He opted for the second. "Take her to the main house for me and wait there with her."

"Yes, sir."

Tyler ended the call, threw on a shirt and made his way downstairs where Tommy waited in the kitchen.

"I'm afraid she's gone," he said, stuffing his cell in his pocket.

"What do you mean gone? Do I have anything to worry about with her?" Tommy asked, setting his cup of coffee on the counter.

"She's afraid and she's been traumatized. There's no way she could've been involved with the stabbing because she was with me. I know you have to handle this like every other case, so I already told you that Dan at the guard shack can corroborate our story. The only reason I didn't call you before is that she didn't want me to involve law enforcement even though I told her it was the right thing to do." Tyler hedged, hoping his excuse would hold water and Tommy would chalk her disappearance up to her being abused. "I'm sure one of the guards will see her. In the meantime, she's been through a lot and I'd like to get out and search for her myself. She doesn't exactly trust men right now."

"By all means," Tommy said. "Bring her by the station for a statement when you find her. Or give me a call and

I'll come right over. Time is the enemy in a homicide investigation."

"I will," Tyler said, hoping he could convince her that Tommy was on her side. Having help from someone in law enforcement could prove beneficial.

"This mess could take a while to untangle. A man like Milton probably has a lot of enemies." Tyler grabbed his keys from the counter.

"I'd bet money on it." Tommy was already walking toward the door. "I'm heading over to the motel now. Maybe we'll know more once we process the scene."

"While I have you here, have you made any progress on your investigation into Mom and Pop?" He thought about Tommy's comment about time being the enemy of a murder investigation. Were all the leads cold on the O'Brien case?

"I'm sorry. I don't have anything new yet. You'll be the first to know when I do." Tommy excused himself and walked out the door.

Tyler grabbed a pair of socks from the downstairs laundry room and slipped into his boots. He was ready to head to the main house when someone knocked on the front door. He could see Red with Dan standing next to her.

"What happened?" he asked as soon as he opened the door.

"I'm not ready to talk to the sheriff. I decided to take a walk and this guy forced me to go with him," Jessica said, chin up in defiance. Determination filled those sea-green eyes.

"I'm sorry, sir. I tried to take her to the main house but she went ballistic," Dan said, looking exasperated. "Given her condition, I thought it was safer to bring her back to you."

"Thank you. I can take it from here," Tyler said to Dan.

"Yes, sir." Dan excused himself.

"Are you okay?" Tyler asked Jessica as soon as he closed the door behind her. He couldn't help but notice the red marks on her arms and wrists, still fresh from yesterday, as he ushered her into the kitchen. And she was shivering.

"Me, yes. At least for now. My sister is the one who is in trouble," she said, rubbing her arms to warm them.

"Pull another stunt like that and I might not be able to help you," Tyler warned, his anger raised from a place deep inside…a place that made him feel helpless and weak. He bit back a curse as he retrieved a blanket from the couch and handed it to her.

"I can't make any promises. I'll do whatever it takes to make sure my sister is safe." Jessica draped it around her shoulders before folding her arms across her chest in a defensive position.

"Come and sit down. I'll get you a cup of coffee." Tyler didn't wait for her to make a move toward the kitchen before he walked over to his counter. He poured two fresh mugs. He needed to tell her the news about what had happened back at the motel and he needed to find a way to do it without scaring the hell out of her. "You like sugar or cream?"

"Black is fine," she said, accepting the mug and taking a sip.

"You want to sit?" Tyler asked, motioning toward the bar stools at the granite island.

Red seemed to catch on to the fact that he had news. She set the cup on the counter and turned to face him, hands fisted on her hips. "What is it? What's happened?"

There was no good way to put this, so he decided to come out with it straight. "A man was found dead in your motel room."

"Milton?" Red sank to her knees. Her skin paled. Tyler

crossed the room and helped her onto the stool a few feet away from her.

"No. Not him." Anger tore through him again when he realized how badly she was shaking, this time from fear not cold.

"How?" she asked, looking utterly stunned. "Who?"

"Tommy doesn't know the answer. The guy had a fake ID so they'll start trying to identify him. As for how, he was stabbed to death after arguing with a man who we suspect was Milton," Tyler said. "A witness says the two were fighting about a woman and a necklace. I'm guessing the woman is your sister and you by proxy. Any idea what the necklace is about?"

"THAT'S THE FIRST I've heard about it but maybe that's what is in the box," Jessica said. Hold on a second. Was it? A memory pricked, like a sudden burst, and then it dawned on her as she brought her hand up to the bandage on her forehead. The bump to her head must've confused her and made her forget. "My sister wanted him out of town. She needed to get him out of the way as she investigated something... I can't remember what. But she told me to go with him and agree to help him find the box. Once we got here, my sister told me she was getting close and to drag this out as long as I could."

"And that's exactly what you did," he said, and there was anger in his eyes.

"Right before I got my head smashed with a rock after telling him I'd tricked him and had no idea what he was talking about." She pulled the blanket from her shoulders and set it down.

"Feeling like he'd been duped must've made a man like Milton angry," Tyler said.

"He'd rented the ATVs and we were on your property

by the time I fessed up. I remember that much. I'd stalled as long as I could. He got so frustrated his face turned red and he started demanding to know where the box was." She glanced at the bruises on her arms. "I expected him to be upset but I never thought he'd try to kill me."

Tyler's grip on the coffee mug intensified.

"He kept hinting at my neck when he talked about the box. I thought he was threatening me, you know, for show, because I never expected him to try to hurt my sister. Now I realize he must've been referring to a necklace."

Tyler's eyes widened. "I wonder…"

He retrieved his smartphone and pulled up a news story. She squinted at the screen to get a better look at the headline: Infinity Sapphire Stolen from Prominent Louisiana Family.

She quickly scanned the story. "This is the most famous necklace in America that isn't stored in a museum?"

"Seventy-seven-point-seven carats total weight," the handsome cowboy added. He stood so close that his scent filled her senses—a mix of woodsy aftershave and warmth, deep and musky—and it stirred up all kinds of inappropriate sensations.

"You know about this necklace?" She took a step back, needing to put a little space between them, and tried not to memorize his unique aroma.

"The couple that owns the necklace attended an art auction hosted by my family recently. I didn't get a chance to talk to them. I prefer to be outside when all that's going on." He paused, turning the phone over and over in his hands. "Forgive the question, but I have to ask. Is there any chance your sister's a jewel thief?"

"None. Zero. I'd bet my life on it," she said, and she pretty much already had. "Whatever's going on can be cleared up as soon as I speak to her. She might not even know how much danger she's in. I have to find her before Milton or anyone else does."

Jessica was already up, pacing, when the cowboy touched her shoulder. It was all she could do to ignore the frissons of heat zinging through her.

"We will." His honest dark eyes seemed like they could see right through her. He was gracious to help her as much as he had already, but this situation had detoured to a very bad place and she didn't feel right putting anyone else at risk.

"It's too dangerous for you to be involved. Someone is dead because of this necklace. I can't ask for your help anymore."

"Let me be the judge of that," he said quickly. "Besides, I'm not going anywhere until I know you're safe."

Looking into his eyes, she could see he meant it and she figured it was most likely some kind of cowboy code. But she couldn't let anything happen to him, and especially not since he was being so generous helping her.

She started to protest but he stopped her with that same look.

"This is the situation as I see it. You have no transportation, no purse, and you have no idea who's after you. To make matters worse, you won't go to the law. So forgive me when I say that you don't have a lot of options right now. I'm willing to help and I'm your best bet to keep you alive and find your sister." He folded his arms and spread his feet in an athletic stance. "If those are your goals, and I believe I'm correct in saying they are, then I don't see how you're in a position to refuse my help."

He was right about all of it. There was no denying what he said was true. "I do want to live and you're absolutely correct about how desperate my situation is. But I still think it's a bad idea for you to get involved any further.

Milton's out there, somewhere, probably looking for me. He must think that I know more than I'm saying or that I'm getting the necklace for myself."

The cowboy's slight nod said he agreed. He made a sound of disgust. "What exactly was his relationship to your sister?"

"All I know is that they dated a year or so ago. I thought he was out of the picture but I guess they stayed in touch. She dated society men and I'm sure it's a small circle."

"Did she mention anything specific about why she decided to leave him before?"

"There were a lot of things. Like, for instance, if a hostess said their table would be ready in twenty minutes and it wasn't, he would become and angry and didn't care who knew." She looked at Tyler whose dark eyes penetrated her poorly constructed armor. She wanted to lean on someone, on him, even temporarily. "I knew he was a creep, but Jenn didn't mention anything about him being physical with her."

"Violence can escalate." Tyler's boots scuffed across the floor as he paced. "I'm sure Tommy will run a background check on him as part of his investigation." Tyler stopped and held up his hand. "I know what you're going to say, so don't bother. But we will need to get Tommy more involved at some point."

She started to protest but he just shook his head. "I won't go behind your back, so don't worry. But we have to bring in the law. We'll talk more about that later. Right now, I want to hear more about Milton."

"Jenn said he was upstanding but she might not've known him as well as she thought she did. He is…let's see… I know she told me…oh, right. He's a lawyer."

"He didn't sound like one when Tommy interviewed him," Tyler said.

"Right. He's a corporate guy, mergers, I think."

"That explains the shiny shoes and his lack of knowledge about criminal law," Tyler quipped, walking past her and once again filling her senses with his scent.

"I don't know much else. I'm not even sure where he works but I'm guessing he's with a corporation in or near Baton Rouge where she lives." Jessica held up her coffee mug and breathed in the smell of dark-roasted beans.

"She said he was a jerk but she didn't give details?" He shot her a look of disbelief. "Sounds unusual for twins."

"I remember thinking she might've been too embarrassed to talk about him in detail, like he was seeing someone else while she thought they were exclusive or something along those lines." Jessica braided her fingers. "The relationship didn't last long. She didn't call me in to break up with him, so they might've remained friends or run in the same circles. That's about all I remember. I had no idea he was capable of actually hurting her. And now my memories are patchy about the past few days."

"Not surprising, after the hit you took to the head," he said.

"I think I'm awake enough for the day." She set down her empty mug. "Mind if I get cleaned up in the bathroom?"

He stopped pacing and stared at her for a minute. She knew exactly what he was thinking. "I'm not planning another escape, if that's what you're worried about."

His cheeks dimpled when he smiled. "There's a spare toothbrush in your bathroom. It's still in the wrapper. I'll have breakfast delivered."

She figured it would do no good arguing with a cowboy whose mind seemed made up, so she resigned herself to accepting his help.

"Tell me one thing, though," he said as she started to

leave the room. "How'd you sneak out this morning? I mean, you were on the second floor and I didn't hear you leave."

"I couldn't sleep, so I heard the sheriff when he pulled in. The alarm code was easy because I watched you enter it last night. You seemed like a nice person but after being with Milton I had no plans to take that chance. I slipped out the side door."

She kept to herself how relieved she was that she hadn't gotten away for exactly the reasons he'd mentioned earlier. She was broke, alone, and had no means of communication. Not to mention the fact that she had no idea where she was and there would be all manner of wildlife outside that door. Plus, she was barefoot.

She was also desperate and she had a bad feeling about her sister's current situation. "Jenn might be trying to reach me on my cell. Can we go to the motel room and check if it's still there or is there no way now that it's a crime scene?"

"We can do whatever you want. But first, we're heading into the station so you can give a statement to one of the sheriff's deputies," he said matter-of-factly. "And if you want to stay above suspicion you'd better act like an unhappy fiancée."

Chapter Six

"Do you think he believed me?" Giving her statement to the deputy had taken Jessica all of fifteen minutes, mostly because she didn't know anything. She'd played the shocked fiancée as best she could, forcing tears that came only when she let herself think about her sister.

"You didn't give him a reason not to," Tyler said.

Jessica sank into the tan leather seat of the SUV as they drove to the motel room she'd shared with Milton. An involuntary shiver rocked her body at thinking about being in that place with him.

She should've been able to see right through that fake smile of his. Milton had charm in spades when he wanted to turn it on, and she could see why her twin would've been attracted to him. He was good-looking and had a professional job with what Jennifer would see as plenty of earning potential.

Jennifer had always wanted more out of life than the meager childhood they'd had in Shreveport. Both of their parents had worked low-wage jobs to support the family. Their mother had owned a cleaning service, her father had made a living doing seasonal yard work, and all three kids had had to pitch in to help summers. Jennifer had always imagined herself living in one of the grand Southern colonials they'd cleaned while Jessica had always been the more practical sister. She'd been able to see right through the men who dated Jennifer for superficial reasons and then dumped her when it was time to find a proper wife.

Tyler steered onto the highway. All makes and models of trucks blazed past them.

"I was remembering my last conversation with my sister. She said that she was involved in something and she needed to figure a way out, to clear things up. Or at least, I think that's what she said." Jessica gingerly fingered the wrap on her forehead.

"Which could mean that she is guilty of taking the necklace," Tyler said, and she couldn't argue with his reasoning. That's exactly what this would look like to an outsider. Except that she knew her sister better than that. Jennifer could be flighty and she definitely liked a good party and hanging out with the highbrow crowd, but she was honest.

Convincing the handsome cowboy of that was a whole different story. She couldn't prove that her sister wasn't involved. All she had to go on was how well she knew Jenn. *Twins for life!* had been their mantra since they were little girls and most of the time it felt like they could read each other's thoughts. Jessica had no such magic now and the silence was terrifying because she feared her sister was in grave danger.

"Jennifer might come off as insincere, and sometimes she is, but she's also good underneath all the layers. Freshman year she went to Houston for college. I helped her move into her dorm and we went shopping to pick up a few extra supplies. We get in the car and Jenn realizes that the clerk had forgotten to charge her for a twelve-dollar pillow. It was late August in one of the hottest summers on record in Texas. Jenn's car had no air-conditioning. But Jenn was worried that the clerk would get in trouble for the mistake. Drenched in sweat, she marched back inside to let him know."

She stared out the front window. "I consider myself an honest person, but I would've returned to pay for the pillow another day or waited until the sun went down. Not Jennifer. No amount of begging could change her mind. By the time she got back I was dripping so I made her stop off at the nearest gas station so I could buy a cup of ice to rub on my sizzling skin." And that was just one of many examples that came to mind.

Jessica could tell Tyler all day that her sister would never take something that didn't belong to her, but she had nothing concrete to prove it and he had no reason to believe her. "I can see how this looks and if I was you I'd probably assume the worst and that she was a bad person—"

"Hold on there. No one said anything about jumping to the worst-case scenario. We need to think through every possibility and I'm going to have to ask hard questions along the way. If you say your sister couldn't have stolen something then I believe you," he said. "Let's work with the assumption that she had no idea what was really going on but got herself tangled in this mess. That makes more sense anyway, because you two are close and based on my intimate knowledge of twins she wouldn't knowingly put you in danger. Someone could've used her. Even made it look like she was the one who took the necklace to cover for themselves."

"That necklace is worth a fortune. I'm betting Milton isn't the only one trying to find it, aside from my sister," she said. "With millions on the line, a lot of bad people would come out of the woodwork."

"Which could explain the man at the motel and if that's true, then I doubt Tommy will be able to identify him. He could be a treasure hunter or working for organized crime."

"One of how many?" She touched a sensitive spot on her head and winced.

"There will be a lot. Some of them will be official. Insurance companies hire interesting people to help investigate and recover merchandise like that, and a necklace worth millions would be insured to the nines," Tyler said. "And then there's the black market."

Just the thought made her head hurt even more. "And my sister is tied up right in the middle of this, of all these vultures."

"It would seem that way. Tommy is going to be following the same paths and I'm going to have to bring him in at some point," Tyler said, and she thought about it for a long moment.

"Okay. But not without discussing it with me first." She figured she could hold Tyler off long enough to get her bearings and for them to make enough progress for her to walk away and make sure he wasn't in danger. Eventually she'd have to break out on her own. "I need to speak to my sister. It's the only way to be certain of what we're dealing with. I talk to her and everything will be cleared up."

"You couldn't reach her earlier."

"True." She chewed on her bottom lip. "I need my cell. She may have left a message or a clue. I bet she's been trying to reach me and I haven't been able to answer. I hid my phone because Milton was creeping me out. That's why I didn't bring it with me when we went out on ATVs. I was afraid he'd take it and then he'd know." Jessica sat straight up in her chair, remembering a little more. "I find my cell and we get answers."

THREE-INCH-WIDE crime scene tape, Big Bird yellow with bold black lettering, stretched across the door of room

121 of the Bluff Motel. The sun was out and it was finally warming up a little.

A sickening feeling sank low in the pit of Jessica's stomach as she walked across the black asphalt toward the room she'd been forced to share with Milton. It was bad enough that a man had been killed only fifteen feet away, even a man who was after her sister or James Milton didn't deserve to be stabbed to death, but she could feel the sense of despair hanging in the air. Knowing what had happened and seeing the evidence right in front of her made everything that much more surreal. A man was dead. Her sister was missing.

Jessica's stomach clenched and she tried to stave off nausea. The sheriff ducked under the tape and moved toward them. He was holding a paper bag—evidence?—which he handed to a deputy.

"I couldn't be sorrier about what happened here," the sheriff said with a genuine look of compassion. "Has your fiancé been in touch with you?"

In the moment, she'd almost forgotten about keeping up that charade.

"No, he hasn't. But thank you very much, sheriff. This is all such a shock." That much was true. Everything about the past thirty-six hours had turned everything she knew upside down and twisted up her insides. "I'm afraid I lost my cell so I don't know if he's been trying to contact me."

Tommy nodded, which she took to mean neither he nor his deputy had found it.

"See anything in there that might help you figure out what happened?" Tyler asked, diverting the sheriff's attention, and she was grateful for that.

Jessica didn't have that same ability to fudge the truth with people that came so easily to her sister. In her heart, her sister was a good person incapable of hurting a soul.

Of course, Jennifer never would have called it lying. She'd prefer to say something like *bending the truth*.

Tears leaked from Jessica's eyes. Her sister had to be all right. If she'd gotten herself involved with men worse than Milton, Jessica was even more worried.

"I ran James Milton through the system," Tommy said to her. "How well do you know your fiancé?"

"I learned a great deal more about him recently. Why?" Jessica wasn't sure where this was going and she didn't like lying to someone in law enforcement.

"What did you find?" Tyler asked, drawing the attention to him again.

Jessica shot him a grateful look.

"He has a record," Tommy said matter-of-factly.

"For what?" Tyler asked as Jessica gasped.

Tommy looked from Tyler to her. "I'm guessing by your reaction you had no idea."

"No. I would never have even guessed." Jessica didn't have to fake her reaction. She was genuinely shocked and even more worried for her sister. If the sheriff confused her reaction for feelings for Milton so be it. "You think you know someone."

"I made a call to Baton Rouge PD and he's pretty well known for having gambling issues."

"Meaning the issue is that he loses," Tyler added.

"They don't call it a problem when they're winning," the sheriff said wryly. "He's wanted for questioning in several cases the PD is trying to clear up, everything from small cons to extortion. They booked him on a small-time charge."

"I had no idea," Jessica said honestly as she tried to digest this news. She'd discovered that her so-called fiancé was a con man who'd set her up. More questions for Jenn were mounting. Jessica wondered if Milton had heard about the necklace and decided to steal it and cash in. Maybe he had debts to pay with the wrong people and one of those could've been the man that had been killed.

"Ever hear of Randall Beauchamp?" the sheriff asked.

"He's the head of one of Louisiana's wealthiest families," Jessica said. "And I've heard that he doesn't make all his money from legitimate sources."

Had Jennifer gotten herself mixed up with one of the biggest crime families in Louisiana?

"The Baton Rouge police chief seems to think that Randall Beauchamp is on the hunt for a stolen necklace worth millions of dollars on the black—"

Before Tommy could finish his sentence, Jessica sank to her knees. Nausea threatened to overwhelm her. Her world tilted on its axis as the reality of her sister's situation set in. Jennifer was as good as dead.

Was Milton working for the Beauchamps? Maybe he was greedy and wanted to sell the necklace in order to settle a gambling debt. Or maybe he needed the money to disappear.

Bile burned the back of Jessica's throat as she felt herself being lifted up by strong arms.

"You don't have to do this right now" came Tyler's masculine tone, and it sent a warm current running through her. "We can deal with all of this later."

"It's okay," she said as he led her to the passenger seat of the SUV. She turned to face him. "I need to do this."

The sheriff stayed put. A deputy had brought over something he must've wanted to show his boss and the two were engaged in conversation.

She and Tyler were just out of earshot. "I need to find my phone."

"Tommy or one of his deputy's might already have it."

Jessica shot him a look.

"No. There's no way Tommy will release evidence in a murder investigation. He can't."

Jessica looked him dead in the eyes. "I hid it in between the mattresses."

"Hold on" was all he said and then he walked away.

THE DEPUTY WHO had been talking to Tommy put an evidence bag in his cruiser as Tommy disappeared inside the cordoned-off room.

"Hey," Tyler said to Deputy Garcia. "Mind talking her off the ledge?"

Tyler motioned toward Jessica, hating that he was about to lie to his friends again. He'd known Garcia since middle school.

"What's going on?" Garcia asked.

"She's still in shock about all this. First, she decides to leave an abusive relationship and now a man turns up dead in her fiancé's motel room. I think she's blaming herself in some weird way, like if she'd stayed with him then everything would be okay," Tyler said, praying his friend bought into the lie. "And now finding out that not only was he abusive but he was a criminal seems to have put her over the edge."

"Not sure what I can say to help but I'll try." Garcia shook Tyler's outstretched hand before walking over to Jessica.

There were only two law enforcement officials on the scene that Tyler had noticed so far. Hopefully Jessica could keep Garcia occupied while Tyler worked on Tommy.

Tyler glanced at Garcia, who had his back turned to him, and then ducked under the crime scene tape.

The room had worn dark blue carpeting and two full-size beds with heavy bedspreads that looked exactly like the curtains in his Gran's old house. Beds, perfectly made, were to the right and there was a plywood desk and a dresser made of the same quality against the wall to the left. This was the sort of place that most likely bolted the furniture to the floor and nailed pictures to the walls.

Noise came from the bathroom beyond and Tyler figured Tommy was there collecting evidence and looking for clues.

He ran his hand along the box spring of the second bed, figuring that Milton wouldn't want Jessica sleeping closest to the door in case she decided to bolt.

Bingo.

He tucked the phone in his front pocket and then turned to sneak out.

"You shouldn't be in here," Tommy said, standing in front of the closet leading to the bathroom. His arms were folded and his feet braced.

"I was just looking for you." Damn. Tyler was a bad liar.

"I'll give you a hint. I'm not in one of the drawers of the nightstand." Tommy hadn't bought the line.

"This?" Tyler turned to the nightstand with the phone and alarm clock on it, stalling for a few seconds while he tried to think up an excuse. He saw a pen and notepad with the hotel logo on it. Snatching them up, he then turned toward Tommy. "I was looking for these."

Tommy's cocked eyebrow said it all. "Don't touch anything else. I don't need your fingerprints all over my crime scene."

At least he didn't seem to realize that Tyler had shoved something inside his pocket.

"What did you want with me?" Tommy asked.

"Glad you asked. I wanted to talk to you without Red in the room. Do you think there's any chance she knew what was going on?"

That seemed to ease Tommy's concerns. "Her reactions

seem genuine to me. This is catching her off guard. Why? You think there's a chance she knew?"

"Not really. I just wanted to make sure I was on the same page as you after she reached out to me," he said.

"She thinking of leaving town anytime soon?" Tommy asked.

"Good question. She hasn't mentioned having family to take care of her. We already know she's from Baton Rouge. I don't think she's in a big hurry to go home, considering Milton could be there now."

"Men who abuse women like to cut them off from the rest of their family. So, even if there is someone she might not've spoken with them in months or years," Tommy said.

Tyler clenched his back teeth. "She may have had a dust-up with her family about him."

"She'll need counseling and a lot of support. Even though Milton can't hurt her anymore she needs help dealing with her emotions." Tommy's hands had relaxed and he'd slipped them inside his pockets.

"Milton's a first-class jerk."

"My guess is that the lawyer got himself in trouble with some gambling debt and that could be responsible for the timing of their trip. He might've hoped things would cool down back home," Tommy said.

"We didn't trust him from the beginning," Tyler added.

"Nope. He's a scumbag. I'm planning to dig deeper into whether or not he had a life insurance policy on Miss Davidson. She may not have known he'd taken one out and her *accident* seems even more suspect now. An insurance payoff could clear up any debt Milton had and set him up nicely."

"Good point. I didn't like him from the get-go and I like him even less now that I know about his background. She said he was an attorney and an upstanding citizen. Guess he put on a good act," Tyler said.

"Love is blind," Tommy quipped. "I see it all the time in my line of work." He paused. "She seems like a nice person."

Tyler nodded.

"I see that you're helping her out and she needs a friend. How far do you plan to go?" Tommy asked, accusation in his tone.

"Why wouldn't I lend a hand? She needs a place to catch her breath. It's been a crazy couple of days for her. I figure I'll help her get straight, maybe get Doc McConnell in to speak to her, and then send her back to Louisiana where she belongs."

"Be careful," Tommy warned.

"Of what? Her?" Tyler blew off the comments.

"Yes. I know you, Tyler O'Brien. You're not going to be able to turn your back on someone who needs a hand up. This woman's been through a lot and I'm warning you as your friend not to get too involved."

A throat-clearing noise came from the doorway. Jessica stood there. "Are you ready to go now?"

Tyler nodded and shot Tommy a warning look. Although he wasn't thrilled that Jessica overheard the conversation, he was relieved that she'd given him an out. He used it to walk out the door and past the tape.

Once they were safely inside the SUV and he was sure no one could hear, he said, "I found it."

"My phone?" There was a mix of apprehension and excitement in her tone. And fear.

He nodded. "We'll check it out as soon as the motel is safely in the rearview."

"Thank you," she said, adding, "and he's right, you know. A man is dead. This is dangerous—"

"That's not your fault," Tyler interjected.

"No, it's not. But I'm heading toward the people who killed him and that isn't safe for you." She didn't miss a beat.

"It's not for you, either. Will knowing that stop you?" he asked.

"No. My sister's in danger and I can't walk away. I have to find her. I don't have a choice," she said impatiently.

He took his right hand off the steering wheel once he got the SUV up to speed on the highway and squeezed her left. The contact sent a jolt of electricity up his arm. "Neither do I."

Tyler managed to dig into his front pocket while keeping the wheel steady. He produced a cell and placed it in Jessica's hand.

"Now, let's see what's on this phone."

Chapter Seven

Tyler made sure no one was following them before exiting the highway. He located the closest parking lot, a Dairy Queen, pulled in and parked.

"There are three calls from my sister," Jessica said, and her face had gone bleached-sheet white.

"Put the phone on speaker," he said.

She did.

Sis, I'm so sorry that I got you involved in this mess. This is so much bigger than I imagined. I'm worried about you. Call me ASAP and get far away from James. He isn't who I thought he was. I gotta go. Call me.

Tyler shouldn't be surprised at the likeness of Jennifer's voice. After all, his twin brothers' voices were similar, too. And yet it still threw him off.

The message also confirmed what Tyler already knew, Jessica had no idea what was going on. He'd trusted her and confirmation that he hadn't made a mistake in that trust eased a little bit of the tension cording his shoulder muscles.

"She sounds good," Jessica said, wringing her hands together. Fear, anxiety and apprehension were embedded deep in her eyes.

Are you okay, sis? You're not calling me back and I'm

starting to get worried about you. If James has hurt you in any way... Click.

"What's that noise in the background?" Tyler asked. "Do you recognize any of the sounds?"

Jessica tilted her head to the left and leaned toward the speaker. "I hear zydeco music and that must mean she's with her friend. He lives in Spanish Town. That's encouraging. She'd be safe with him."

"You said there are three messages," Tyler said, holding off his warm and fuzzy feelings for now. Jennifer had already misjudged one so-called friendship but he didn't want to burst Red's bubble of hope just yet. With millions of dollars on the line, Jenn shouldn't trust anyone.

Sis, run. Jennifer sounded out of breath, like she was running, and there was the sound of splashing water in the background. There was a long pause. *Wherever you are, run. Hide until I tell you it's safe to come out. Oh, God, I hope you're okay. If James figured you out don't believe anything he says. I had no idea what was going on. Don't go to the police. Don't trust anyone and especially not... NO!*

Jessica heard her sister scream.

...I've gotta go. I'll figure a way out of this, I promise. And then I'll meet you on the bayou.

Her words came out at a frantic pace now. Another scream came through the line and then there were sounds of a struggle. More screaming and a male voice telling her to stop kicking. He yelled a profanity and then came the sound of her phone being dropped in water.

A desperate Jessica held the phone so tightly her fingers lost color and now matched the pallor of her face. Anger quickly overrode all other emotions. She banged her fist on the dashboard. "They got her. It's the only logical reason the calls stopped."

"Do you recognize the man on the recording?" Tyler asked.

"No."

"What did she mean about the bayou?" he asked. Maybe he could nudge her out of an emotional state into logical thinking. Get her wheels turning.

"It's just a saying we have between us. Doesn't really mean anything." She turned to him, those sea-green eyes wide. "But they have her and now they'll kill her."

"Can I see that for a second?" Tyler peeled her fingers off the phone and scrolled through the call log. She was worth millions to them. They wouldn't kill her. He didn't see the need to bring up the fact that they would most likely torture her to get that information. "The last call came in while you were in the hospital."

"They got her so they no longer needed Milton," Jessica said. Good, she was using her anger to switch gears and think this through, and that was the best chance they'd have of finding Jennifer.

"That's one thought. Another is that someone else, a freelancer, has gotten in on the game. This necklace is famous and, like I said before, it's worth is going to bring people out of the woodwork to find it," he said, needing her to have a realistic picture of what they were facing and hoping he'd be able to convince her to bring Tommy up to speed. Tyler never went back on his word. He wouldn't go behind her back.

"She was at The Bluebonnet Swamp Nature Center during that last call," Jessica said.

"How do you know?"

"She's my sister and that's where she'd go if she was in trouble." Jessica's matter-of-fact tone had him convinced. "Plus, I heard her sloshing through water and there were sounds of nature all around her in the background. And I heard her slap her skin from mosquitoes a couple of times. This is the first place she'd go to hide because that's where I used to find her when she had a bad breakup with one of her boyfriends. She knows the area and probably figured it would be a good place to lay low, which also means she didn't want to involve her friends by staying with them."

"We'll start there." He handed her the phone and put the gearshift in Reverse.

"That's got to be a six-hour drive from here, at least," she said, sounding defeated. "Plus the call came in yesterday. She won't still be there, not if that jerk got to her, and I know he did. That's the only reason she wouldn't call again."

"Maybe she lost her phone. I heard the sound that it made hitting the water," he offered.

"She would've borrowed someone's to call and check in with me. We never go more than a day without talking and it's been at least twenty-four hours since her last attempt."

Tyler believed her, having witnessed the same phenomenon firsthand with Ryder and Joshua. Those two spoke daily.

"Baton Rouge is only an hour away from here by plane." He redirected the conversation. Last thing he needed was her dwelling on the negative.

Tyler made a few calls using the hands-free Bluetooth feature preloaded on his SUV and had set up their flight and itinerary by the time they reached the airstrip. He just hoped like hell they got to Jennifer first.

THE FLIGHT WENT off without a hitch and a private car waited at the airport. Jessica's stomach had braided into an unbendable knot the second she'd heard her sister's voice on the third message and it hadn't let up.

"You said before that few of her friends know about

you," Tyler said, ushering her into the backseat of a stretch limousine with blacked-out windows.

"That's right."

"I'd like to keep it that way," he said. "Especially since we believe she's been taken and others may not realize that."

"I wouldn't exactly call this incognito." She waved her arm in the air.

"Sometimes, the easiest way to hide is to be in plain sight."

The limo zigged in and out of traffic terrifyingly, but then southern Louisiana drivers were notorious for fast lane changes, tailgating and high speeds. Even being from Louisiana, Jessica had a difficult time navigating traffic in and around Baton Rouge. Don't even get her started on the bridges or thoughts of the alligators that lurked beneath them.

Rain threatened and a wall of humidity hit full force as they stepped out of the limo, stealing Jessica's breath. She'd get used to it in a minute, but those first few breaths after stepping out of an air-conditioned car were always staggering.

Tyler paid their entrance fee into The Bluebonnet Swamp Nature Center.

"I promise to pay you back as soon as the sheriff releases my personal belongings," she said earnestly, thinking about everything he was doing for her and hit hard by the realization that she'd never be able to equalize this debt.

He waved her off.

"No, seriously." It was important for Jessica to feel like she could cover her own bases. That was the only thing she didn't like about her sister. It was too easy for her to flash a smile and let someone else do the work for her. And even though Jessica had that same smile, she'd always known it would get her and her sister in trouble if used improperly.

Tyler mumbled something she didn't quite catch. She'd let it go, for now. A man as good-looking and wealthy as Tyler O'Brien was most likely used to getting his way. But he hadn't seen stubborn until Jessica put her mind to something. He'd learn just how persistent she could be when this was all over and she could put her affairs back in order. For the time being, though, she had to live off his generosity if she wanted to find her sister in time.

"There must be dozens of boardwalk trails here." He stood behind the Nature Center building looking at the maze of wooden paths.

"She likes a certain place. There's a bench close to an old cypress tree. The branch is huge. They built the walkway beneath it. Follow me," Jessica pushed past him, plucking at her shirt as beads of sweat rolled down her chest even though the temperature was barely seventy.

Jenn's favorite bench was a good ten minutes' hike from the Nature Center building. At their pace, they made it in seven. "There it is."

She ducked under the cypress branch, a good three feet wide, and dashed to the bench, wanting to soak in everything from the last place she knew her sister had been.

Tyler walked to the bench and dropped to his knees to get a better look at the water.

"I hope you're not planning on going in there," she warned.

"It's not like I want to," he said. "But we might be able to locate her phone."

"We?" No way was she getting in water with snakes and alligators. Jessica involuntarily shivered. "You know what's in there, right?"

"Sure do."

"I can't help my sister if I'm in the belly of an alligator chewed up into little pieces," she said, frustrated. Because she would do anything to save her sister, including jumping into that murky green water that scared her beyond belief.

Tyler's chuckle was a deep rumble in his throat and it sent a sensual vibration skittering across her skin. She was about to be eaten by an alligator and the cowboy she'd brought with her was causing her to have inappropriate sexual thoughts.

"At least let me take my shoes off first."

"How deep do you think the water is here?" he asked.

"A few feet, four at the most."

"Look for bubbles before getting in." He was lying flat on his stomach on the boardwalk, watching the surface of the water. "I'd rather wait at least twenty minutes but we don't have that kind of time, so I want you to look hard."

Wasn't that reassuring? A serious case of the heebie-jeebies trickled down her spine as she moved to the other side of the boardwalk. Okay, she could do this. She needed to talk herself up for a minute to steel her nerves, but this was going to be no big deal. She scanned the water intently, watching for any signs of life.

"I think I should be good here," she finally said, stopping twenty feet from her original spot.

Tyler popped to his feet and moved a good ten feet from his first location. "All right, then. We're looking for her cell or anything that might indicate she was here."

He ducked through the slats in the wood and then she heard the splash that said he was in the water on the other side. Jessica took in a deep breath, held it, and then slid through the wooden slats on her side. The murky green water was cold against her stomach as she waded through waist-deep water. Moss gathered on her stomach and she nearly lost her cool. Every survival instinct inside her begged her to get out of there and run away.

Jenn needed her. The fear and desperation in her sister's voice would keep Jessica on the right path.

"Something just brushed past my leg," she said, letting out the breath she'd been holding.

"We better move quickly before someone sees us and kicks us out," Tyler said.

Jessica dropped down, trying to feel her way around in three-foot-high water. All she touched was slick rocks and she tried not to think about all the bacteria lurking around and what that would do to a cut in, say, her finger.

Every noise made her jump. Every animal sound made her heart race. Every scrape of her finger across a new surface made her pull her hand back.

After searching for what seemed like an eternity and coming up empty, she returned to the boardwalk and scrambled out of the water. She quickly checked her body for leeches or any other creepy-crawlies. "Did you find anything?"

"No." The water-sloshing sound came from the other side of the walkway.

"It's useless." And worse yet, felt hopeless. She should've known this would be a dead end.

THE ARCHITECTURE OF Spanish Town was mostly post–Civil War. Rows of early twentieth-century homes of wood construction lined the narrow streets. Houses were small but had large front porches and there was more pink in one place than Tyler had ever seen. "What's up with the flamingos on all the lawns?"

But "on the lawns" was an understatement. They hung in front windows and stood on porches. There was even one on a roof.

"People used to look down on this area as having questionable occupants, so everyone decided to give them something to stare at," Jessica said. "Mostly artists and musicians live here."

"And what do we think we'll find amongst all this plastic fowl?" he asked. Their shoes and clothes smelled like swamp. The limo driver hadn't wanted to let them back inside wet. Tyler had had to slip the guy extra money to convince him it would be a good idea. He'd also promised to pay for having the limo properly cleaned and aired out, which he figured he owed the guy.

"Jenn has a friend here. I might be able to trick him into thinking I'm her."

"The zydeco music playing in the background of the first message?" he asked.

"Yes. I'm hoping she confided in him, but she might have just wanted a place to lay low. His name is Elijah, by the way." She scanned the houses. "I'm just not sure where he lives, exactly."

"Do you think it's safe to go in like this?" he motioned toward their soaked clothing.

"Probably not, but what choice do we have?" she asked with a shrug.

"We need to play this smart. Not attract too much attention. Someone could be watching Elijah's place and we're soaked to the bone. Give me a few minutes." Tyler fished his cell from his front pocket and made a call. "Janis, can you book a room for me at the Hilton in Baton Rouge?"

"Fine but I'm putting you in the Presidential Suite," Janis said.

"Okay." Normally, he'd argue. There was no need to put him up in the best suite in any hotel. But this time, he had a lady with him and the two-bedroom suite would give her the privacy she needed. They were still practically strangers, even though it felt as if he'd known her for a lot longer than thirty-seven hours. Rather than try to get inside his head about what that meant, he requested fresh clothes in a woman's size five to six to be delivered to the hotel. And then he asked for men's. Janis already knew his sizes. "Casual stuff in a breathable fabric. Also, I'm going to need hats and maybe a few ladies' scarves. Think you can get all that to my room in the next hour?"

"Does a dog have fleas?" Janis quipped.

"Thank you, Janis. You already know I think you're the best." Tyler buzzed the driver who rolled down the partition between the cab and the backseat. "Can you take us to 201 Lafayette Street?"

"Yes, sir, Mr. O'Brien," the driver said.

"I'm going to need your services 24/7 while I'm in town," Tyler said. "Is that a problem?"

"No, sir." A smile lit the driver's face.

"Thank you. I'll double your current rate."

An even bigger smile curved the driver's lips. "You don't have to—"

Tyler put his hand up. "It would make me feel better for inconveniencing you on such short notice."

"I don't know what to say. Thank you."

"What's your name?" Tyler asked.

"Zander, sir."

"How about you call me Tyler? Every time I hear 'Mr. O'Brien' I look over my shoulder to see if my father's standing behind me."

Zander chuckled. "You're the boss, Mr.—" he glanced in the rearview with a sheepish look "—Tyler."

"Thank you, Zander." Tyler turned to Jessica. "You haven't eaten since breakfast. What sounds good?"

"Nothing, I'm okay."

"You need to keep up your strength." He placed a call

to the hotel manager and arranged for soup, sandwiches and bottles of water to be waiting when they arrived. Tyler ended the call to Jessica's wide eyes.

"Can I ask a question?"

He nodded.

"I've seen your place and where you live is beautiful. There's more security than a...a...maximum security prison. So, I hope I'm not being rude, but just how rich are you?"

Tyler couldn't help but laugh. He never really thought of himself as wealthy. Rich in land and family, maybe, but not rich in the loads-of-money-in-the-bank rich. Maybe it was the way he'd been brought up. Pop had had his feet firmly planted in the soil and all the boys had followed suit. They cared more about running their horses—speaking of which, Digby needed exercising—than running up credit cards. But by all measures, they were loaded. "Guess I never think about it."

"How can you not?" she asked, eyes wide. "When I first met you I thought you were some kind of ranch hand, which was fine by me. You seem so...normal. But now I see that you own your own plane and can fly it rather nicely, by the way. You can snap your fingers and have almost anything you want delivered or arranged...am I on the right path here?"

"Not everything," he said. "And nothing that really matters."

"Tell me one thing you can't make appear?"

"My parents." He didn't miss a beat. "No amount of money can bring them back. We're about to have the first Thanksgiving without them, without Mom's cooked goose and all the trimmings, and it feels odd. She was all the warmth in the holidays. Her meals. Her traditions that me and my brothers used to think were corny as kids. That's the stuff you miss, the little things. The way she used to make these maple cookies in the shape of leaves and the whole house smelled like pancakes and cinnamon. Now all I can think is how my own kids won't ever bake pies or cut out paper snowflakes with her."

"I'm so sorry." Jessica touched his arm, and it was as though her words reached into his chest and filled some of the emptiness in his heart. He'd heard those three words more times than he could count in recent months and yet this was the first time they'd had healing power.

"Your mother sounds like an amazing woman," she said.

Tyler nodded, fearing that if he said any more he'd get choked up. Next thing he knew, Jessica had braided their fingers together.

"There's no way to replace the people we love and no amount of money can fill that void. My sister has essentially turned her back on us trying to do just that—make a bank account somehow fulfill her life. I never understood that about her. I love her with all my heart, don't get me wrong, and money's nice. Living without it stinks. But just like that old saying goes, it can't buy love. It's refreshing to hear that your family has it right."

Tyler agreed. "Being close with my brothers helps, having their support makes losing our parents easier to get through. This first holiday will be hell for all of us, but we have each other and that makes a huge difference."

"I can imagine," she said. The empathy in her voice made it seem like things would be even better in the future. He wondered if she'd lost someone important to her.

Zander stopped in front of the Hilton and opened the door to the backseat. Tyler exited first and held out a hand to Jessica. "My lady."

She took the offering with a smile, glancing down at their swamp-filled clothes.

The hotel's manager greeted them at the door. "Mr. O'Brien, what a pleasure to have you back."

It must've taken great effort for her not to wrinkle her nose at the smell of the two of them, Tyler thought. He had to give her credit, she held strong. The manager was tall and brunette, curvy, in her late thirties. Her name tag read Annabeth Malloy.

"Thank you for having us, Miss Malloy," he said, shaking her outstretched hand. "This is my guest Miss Archer."

A bellhop arrived as Annabeth acknowledged Jessica. He'd given a fake name to make Jessica feel more comfortable. She seemed ready to climb out of her skin from the attention they were receiving.

"Devin will help you with your bags," Annabeth said.

"I'm having a few items delivered," Tyler said with a nod toward Devin.

"Of course. Devin will take you to your suite. Please let me know personally if there's anything I can do for you or Miss Archer."

Tyler thanked Annabeth and followed Devin to the elevator, taking Jessica's hand and pulling her close. It was the best way to shield her from any watchful eyes in the hotel lobby. The way she fit with his arm around her felt a little too right. And that was something else Tyler didn't want to think about too much. He had enough going on without further complicating his life. And keeping her alive long enough to find the truth was at the top of his agenda.

"You've been quiet since the car ride," Tyler said, handing Jessica a bag filled with clothes and undergarments, which she eagerly took.

"I feel bad about what I said earlier about your money." She hadn't meant to be a jerk, but she had been. She'd judged him solely based on his money and that made her exactly like the people she despised, the kind of people who only cared about superficial things. The cowboy was nothing like that. He hadn't even hinted at the kind of money he and his brothers had, and she figured he wouldn't have, either. He'd been kind to her and had done nothing but offer help. So what if his presence put her on edge.

"I don't think you're showing it off in any way. In fact, I was a little surprised you had any. No offense."

That deep rumble of a laugh broke free from his chest again and it sent sensual little tingles up and down her body. "I don't know what to say."

She'd showered and was covered head to toe in a thick cotton bathrobe provided by the hotel and yet she was keenly aware of being completely naked underneath.

"It's just that you look so…normal." His skin was olive colored and tan, and his hands were rough, as if he worked outside.

"What did you expect me to look like?" Thankfully, he seemed amused as he sat down at the expansive oak table in front of a wall of windows that she was sure would frame the best views of the city if the curtains hadn't been pulled shut.

She'd smelled the food the second she'd stepped out of the shower, and despite thinking there was no way she could eat under the circumstances her stomach growled. And he was right, earlier; she did need to keep up her strength.

"Fancy, maybe? Like J.R. Ewing or something," she said, and that solicited a full belly laugh from Tyler.

"Sorry to disappoint you," he said.

"You didn't," she said a little too quickly, and it caused her cheeks to burn. "What I mean to say is that I like that you're normal."

"I could always break out my bolo tie and Western shirts if you'd be more comfortable," he quipped.

"Great. Now you're making fun of me." She reached across the table to slap his arm but he caught her wrist and held it. She didn't immediately move to take it back.

Suddenly the air in the room was charged, and her breath caught in her throat as he drew sexy little circles with his thumb.

Chapter Eight

A tense expression crossed Tyler's features, like he was trying to figure out his next move. He let go of Jessica's wrist and picked up his sandwich instead. "I hope you like BLTs and soup. This won't be as good as Janis's but it'll keep us from starving."

"I'm just happy not to smell like swamp water anymore," she said awkwardly.

"I know you were hoping to find something there and I'm sorry we didn't," he offered.

"Anything would've been nice, some kind of direction." There was so much heat and intensity crackling between them it seemed odd to talk around it.

"Sometimes it's good to be able to rule a place out. My friend Tommy has the motto No Stone Left Unturned during an investigation. It's surprising how a small detail often means the difference between a trail going cold and cracking a case wide-open," he said.

"So, we go back and try to find Elijah's place in Spanish Town," she said.

"Does he know about you?"

"She kept me separate from the rest of her life, even her friends. I doubt she told anyone about me, so he should be quite surprised when her sister shows up on his doorstep."

"Or not."

She cocked her head sideways. "What do you mean?"

"Earlier you suggested trying to fool him into thinking you're Jenn." He paused long enough for her to nod. "She said not to trust anyone. I think we should take her advice to heart. We'll know if he's involved based on his initial reaction to you."

"I hadn't even considered the possibility that one of her friends could've gotten her into this mess, but you're right."

"Let's hope they didn't. But if she's innocent, and I believe you when you say she wouldn't steal, then she either tripped into this or someone set her up," he said. "There aren't a lot of people who would have access to the Infinity Sapphire. We'll track who might've come into contact with the owner over the past few weeks. I'd like to trace your sister's movements as well, but that is a little bit trickier since we don't want to bring you out in the open."

"Speaking of which, I need to do something different with my hair." She rolled a strand around her index finger.

"Supplies were delivered while you were in the shower," he said. "There are hats to choose from. Scarves. We should probably dye your hair and have it cut but your natural color is beautiful."

Butterflies flitted through her stomach at the compliment and she was pretty sure her cheeks flamed. But Jessica wondered if there was anything he couldn't get at the snap of a finger. This was definitely a different lifestyle than the one she knew and it made her more than a little uncomfortable. A man with this kind of money was more Jenn's type. "Thank you."

She finished her sandwich and soup, surprised she was able to clear her plate and bowl. Her body was hungrier than she realized. After changing into linen shorts and a button-down silk blouse, she tried on a couple of hats before settling for one in taupe with a wide brim and a silk scarf wrapped around it. There were tan strappy sandals with just enough of a heel to give her a little more height. She looked in the mirror and hardly recognized herself. That was most likely a good thing, because even though all of what she wore was out of character for her, she didn't want to look like herself right now.

Jessica applied light makeup, more gifts from the generous millionaire, before walking into the living room where he sat at the desk on his cell phone. Tyler was so down-to-earth that she hadn't thought of him as being wealthy—at least, not until he started flying planes, ordering limousines and generally snapping his fingers to make pretty much anything show up.

None of that should have shocked her, except that he didn't fit the *millionaire* stereotype. Based on her sister's dating stories, rich men sounded like playboys or self-obsessed jerks.

She never could understand what Jenn saw in them. Jenn was beautiful and she could easily turn heads. Even though she and Jessica were identical, Jessica normally looked quite different from her sister. Jessica's hair was pulled up in a ponytail most of the time. She wore very little makeup. And her favorite outfit was a tank top and jeans.

Tyler was different from Jenn's usual men. He was almost staggeringly handsome and definitely good-looking enough to be a playboy, but she was pretty sure he'd laugh if someone said that out loud.

He finished his call and set his cell on the desk in front of him. "The owner of the Infinity Sapphire, Emma-Kate Brasseux, will be home this afternoon."

THE IDEA THAT Tyler could be walking Jessica into the belly of the beast sat in his gut like shards of broken glass. On the other hand, he was darn certain there was no way she was going to let him talk to the owners of the necklace without her. There was far too much at stake. He'd have to be careful not to cross any boundaries with Tommy's investigation and local law enforcement would also be involved. Now that the stolen necklace was common knowledge and the motive in a murder investigation, Tommy would send someone to speak to the Brasseuxs, which was why Tyler wouldn't call ahead and make an appointment to speak with them. He wanted to check things out first.

On the ride over, Tyler wanted to know more about Jessica. "Where's your family, other than your sister?"

"Shreveport, where we grew up. It's just my parents. We had an older brother who died when we were in high school. It affected us both but Jenn hasn't been the same since."

"I'm sorry for your loss." Tyler couldn't imagine losing a sibling so young.

"My brother, Jeffrey, had just turned eighteen and graduated high school when he signed on to work the pipelines in Alaska. Dad had been out of work for a while and my parents were having a hard time keeping food on the table. Sending one of us to college was out of the question.

"Jeffrey noticed an ad in the paper and saw it as his ticket to help the family while getting out on his own. Times were tough and he couldn't find a local job. He hadn't been gone for three months when we heard the news there'd been an accident." Her voice broke, and he could tell that even now it was difficult for her to talk about it.

"Sounds like he was an honorable and brave young man, trying to do the right thing by his family," Tyler said.

Jessica nodded as a tear spilled down her cheek. Tyler thumbed it away. Contact while she was so vulnerable wasn't a good idea. And neither was taking her in his arms, but he did it anyway. He lied and told himself that his actions were purely meant to comfort her. There was so much more to it than that, though...bringing her into his arms calmed his own torn-up heart.

"We were all devastated but Jenn took the news hardest. Something inside her just broke after that. She stopped hanging out with our friends and slept all day for a solid month. When we finally convinced her to get out of bed she was different. She started wearing makeup and spending more time alone. Then she found babysitting jobs and used all the money to buy nicer clothes. In school the next year she started hanging around with rich boys. I think she associated our financial situation with losing Jeffrey. She couldn't get off to college fast enough, relying on school loans to make it happen. It lasted a year before she quit school and moved to Baton Rouge. Said she needed a fresh start. There, she kept her family, including me, under wraps and didn't want us to meet her new friends. I think she was ashamed of us."

Tyler could feel her shaking in his arms, so he hauled her tighter to his chest. The limo had stopped but he didn't care. The only thing that mattered right then was the shaking woman in his arms, the feel of her skin underneath his weathered hands and the way she looked up at him with those big eyes.

So he dipped his head and kissed her. Her body stiffened and then relaxed against him. The shaking stopped as she parted her lips for him and her breath quickened. She brought her hands up around his neck and tunneled her fingers into his hair.

Tyler knew this was charting a dangerous course. He'd cut out casual flings after his first year of college and this woman had already broken through barriers that normally took other women months to breach. He should back off, let go.

He couldn't.

So he deepened the kiss, ignoring all the warning bells trying to sound off inside his head. Jessica dropped her hands, clutching his shirt, and that quieted his internal protest.

Her hand wandered across his chest and he pulled her onto his lap.

The air inside the limo crackled with desperate need.

Desperate.

Tyler didn't like the sound of that word when it came to him and Jessica.

He pulled back and looked into her eyes, a mix of desire and desperation staring back at him.

And that last part was a mood killer.

When they made love—correction, *if* they made love— there'd be nothing desperate about it.

"The car stopped," he said, unable to move...wishing he'd seen something else in her eyes—or just good old-fashioned lust.

"I know." She brought the back of her hand up to her lips and eased off his lap.

Tyler needed a distraction, so he signaled Zander to lower the partition.

"Where would you go to find someone if you didn't know their last name or address?" he asked, focusing on why they were there. The trip to Spanish Town hadn't taken long. Other than Elijah's name, they didn't have much to go on.

"And they live here?" Zander asked.

"Yes."

"Then I'd go to the market. It's a place up ahead where all the locals gather to eat," Zander said. "I can point you in the direction but you're not going to find out where someone lives if you pull up in one of these. It's a tight-knit community."

"With lots of artists who have an affinity for pink flamingos, or so I've noticed," Tyler joked, trying to ease the tension.

Jessica smiled and that helped. He wasn't sure how he'd allowed things to get so out of hand in such a short time, but he vowed not to let it happen again.

"Here's what you want to do." Zander pointed to the street in front of them. "Go down here about two blocks. Make a right and walk halfway down the street. The market is dead center of Spanish Town. You can't miss it. If the person you're looking for lives around here, someone will know him or her."

Tyler thanked Zander and asked him to wait right there on the corner. The short walk in the thick humidity, even with cooler overall temperatures, had Tyler plucking at his shirt. Texas was dry in comparison even though his state had seen more rain last year than in any he could remember. He took Jessica's hand in his and she smiled up at him. With that second smile something happened in his chest and he chalked it up to residual feelings from what had happened in the limo. "I think we can get further if people believe we're a couple."

Damned if a hurt look didn't settle in her eyes that knocked the wind out of Tyler. He didn't want to care about Jessica beyond helping to save her and her sister. So what the hell was happening to him? He didn't do mushy feelings but he couldn't ignore the warmth in his chest every time he was near Red. He told himself that it was her situation tugging at his heart. Her brother was gone and her sister's moving away must've hurt like hell. He could never imagine Joshua and Ryder in that situation. But, hey, life was crazy sometimes. And, sometimes, strange things happened.

The market was a grocery-store-turned-eatery where locals gathered for breakfast and lunch. The building was painted fire-engine red and a retractable hunter-green awning covered the sidewalk dining space. The lunch crowd was running thin but Tyler asked for a table for two outside so he could chat up the waitress.

He ordered a shrimp po'boy and two cups of coffee, even though they'd just eaten.

"Will that be all?" the waitress asked. "Dorinda" was stamped on her gold-colored name tag in white letters.

"Yeah, I guess it will. Although, I wonder if you could help me out." Tyler hesitated and she leaned forward. "Our friend Elijah used to play around here. I got a new cell and lost all my contacts." He made an annoyed face that seemed to resonate with Dorinda. "I thought we'd reconnect while we were in town. You know where we can catch him?"

"You just missed him. He was in here a few minutes ago," she said with a small shake of her head.

"Think I can still catch him?" Tyler made a move to get up.

"Stick around long enough and he'll be back." She motioned toward a waitress inside. "He picks her up as soon as her shift's over."

That was even better news because they didn't know what he looked like. "Do you have any idea what time that will be?"

Dorinda glanced at the white plastic watch on her wrist. "I'd say another hour to an hour and a half."

"Thank you. I can't wait to see that old son of a gun," he said, a little worried he might be overacting.

"Can I get anything else for you, hon?" the waitress asked.

Jessica bent her head forward, face in her hands, as if she had the worst headache of her life. Wearing sunglasses and a wide-brimmed hat, she wouldn't be easily recognized. "Aspirin."

She lifted her head up and laughed. So did Dorinda.

"I told him to stop me after the third Ruby Slipper, but do you think he did?" Jessica said, feigning frustration. She coughed and shook her head.

"I hear you. I'll be right back with those coffees." Dorinda winked before she turned and walked away.

"I hope Elijah comes back soon," Jessica said, scanning the streets. She had to be uncomfortable out in the open like this.

"I have no intention of allowing anything to happen to you."

Chapter Nine

"We should wait on the corner for Elijah," Tyler said. "We don't know what he looks like but we know who he's coming to pick up. This way no one will get suspicious if he walks right past us."

Jessica agreed as she followed him. He stopped and turned toward her, shielding her from the street.

"Are you doing okay?" he asked, and then brushed the tips of his fingers against her cheek in a move that sent sensual shivers skittering across her skin.

Her back was against the telephone pole at N. Seventh Street and Spanish Town Road, directly across the street from where they'd eaten. Cars twined down the skinny road.

Jessica nodded as she studied the activity. "This guy walked by a few minutes ago."

"Which one?" Tyler's gaze swept the sidewalk casually.

"This guy in the white pants, white hat." She intentionally looked in the opposite direction.

"He seems to be interested in us," he said, and he couldn't ignore the possibility that the police or others—men with guns—wanted to find the same person they were looking for.

The next thing Jessica knew, Tyler's hand had cupped her neck. He mouthed the words, *Trust me.* And then he dipped his head, hesitated, slicked his tongue across his lips and kissed her.

Her body instantly reacted. She reached for him, wrapping her arms around his neck and parting her mouth enough for his tongue to slide inside.

She thought she heard a groan from deep in his throat as his arm came around her waist and his free hand splayed against her back.

Deepening the kiss, he hugged her—her body immediately molding to his. Her breasts swelled and ached for his touch. Her body reminded her just how long it had been since she'd had good sex…and it had been far too long. She instinctively sensed that sex with Tyler would shatter her in the best possible way.

His body pressed hers against the telephone pole and she imagined how he would feel on top of her, pressing her into a mattress. She could feel his rapid heartbeat through their clothes.

He pulled back first and rested his forehead on hers. From across the street someone shouted, "Get a room!"

The comment made both of them laugh, his was that low rumble from deep in his throat and it was so darn sexy. He started to say something, then stopped, and she half feared that he was about to offer an apology. That was the best kiss she'd had in…in her whole life, and a part of her wanted to celebrate it, not feel awkward that it had happened.

"Damn," he said and his voice was low.

"I was just thinking the same thing," she said with a slow smile. His hand stayed steady against her back and she was grateful because he was the only thing holding her upright at this point. Her bones felt like Jell-O. She'd heard that a kiss could make a person go weak at the knees but this was the first time she'd experienced anything close.

"I've been wanting to do that again since we stepped out of the limo," he whispered.

"Maybe you should try it one more time." She tunneled her fingers into his dark curly hair.

He didn't seem to need much encouragement because he delved his tongue inside her mouth with bruising need. His body pressed against hers, sandwiching her, and desire sprang from deep within. In that moment, she got lost.

Tyler seemed to regain his senses first, pulling back. All the warmth in the cowboy's eyes turned to something else…something that looked a lot like confusion, and it caused her heart to squeeze.

"We should be watching out for Elijah. He could be here by now."

"Did I do something wrong?" she asked.

"You? Hell, no. But I just crossed a line that I shouldn't have, and I apologize," he said.

Where had that come from? And to make matters worse, he just apologized for kissing her.

Embarrassed, she sidestepped him. "Don't be sorry. I participated just as much as you did."

"Come over here. I'll kiss you, honey" came from a few steps away with inappropriate smooching noises.

If that didn't set her cheeks on fire, then waiting wordlessly with the cowboy standing next to her did. Sure he regretted their actions after having a chance to think about it. Jessica didn't doubt she was attractive, especially when she put on nice clothes and some makeup, but this wealthy cowboy was out of her league and he had to know as much as she did that it would never work between them. It would be smart to keep her guard up with him. As soon as she found her sister and settled this mess, she'd go back to her life in Shreveport, a life that made total sense.

The waitress, Elijah's presumed girlfriend, came out the

front door, lit a smoke and leaned against the front glass of the restaurant. Someone knocked on the window from inside. She made a face and moved over to the newspaper boxes at the side of the red building.

A full twenty minutes later a vintage El Camino pulled up. It had been partially restored, looked like a work in progress and had the beginnings of a mural painted down the right hand side.

The waitress pushed off the wall of the market. Now on her second smoke, she looked at the driver of the El Camino. She hesitated, made another face and then started walking toward the curb.

Jessica pulled off her hat and glasses and rushed toward the El Camino. "Elijah."

The man driving was in his early thirties and fit the description of a Louisiana musician to a T. He wore a chestnut fedora with a white hatband and red feather. Both arms were covered in tattoos and he wore a dark tank underneath a denim shirt with rolled-up sleeves. He had a silver thumb ring on his left hand, dark hair and eyes, and a mustache and goatee.

"Jenn, where the hell have you been?" he asked, eyes bright.

A moment of panic engulfed Jessica. Could she pull off being her sister when so much was on the line? Sure, it had been easy enough when she was stepping in to ease Jenn out of a relationship. But this? This was so much more nerve racking.

Jessica smiled as she pulled Tyler over to the El Camino's passenger side so Elijah could get a good look. She came up with the best lie she could. "I met someone and we ended up at his place in New Orleans."

Elijah shook his head and smirked. "I should've known. You could at least answer my texts."

"Lost my charger." She shrugged, figuring that was exactly something that would've happened to her less responsible sister.

"Actually, she lost her phone altogether," Tyler said, sticking his hand out. "I'm George For… Ford."

Jessica, arm around his waist, pinched him. Seriously? That slip might've just cost them. It would be a miracle if Elijah bought that…

"Good to meet you," Elijah said, no hint of distrust at Tyler's hesitation.

Even so, Tyler didn't seem to be good at this undercover thing. Or maybe lying didn't come naturally to him. That was a good thing considering her ex, Brent, had seemed to wake up with lies coming out of his mouth. Lies like *you're the one I love* and *what we have is real* were right up there with *she didn't mean anything to me.* Her name had been Katherine. And Jessica had believed him the first time. Then she'd stumbled across his secret email account and had been forced to ask him if Katherine had been the one he was talking about, or was it Naomi, Judy or Blanche?

Thankfully, Elijah didn't seem to notice Tyler's mistake.

"I see you've moved on from one millionaire to another," Elijah said with a wink.

Was she supposed to know what that meant?

The waitress pushed past them and plopped into the passenger seat, looking annoyed that she hadn't been acknowledged yet.

"My friend, Susannah." He looked from the waitress to Jessica.

"Girlfriend," Susannah interjected with an annoyed slap to his right forearm.

"Nice to meet you," Jessica said, appreciating the distraction. If Elijah didn't look too closely or ask too many questions then she could keep up the charade.

"Well, George, the next time you whisk my girl out of town without telling anyone make sure she checks in with me, okay? Big Beau's been looking for you, by the way." He made a face at Jessica.

The reference drew another blank.

Then again, Jenn had been secretive lately. She'd said she was dating someone important but didn't say who.

Tyler glanced from Elijah to her. He slid his arm around her waist—she ignored the quiver that rippled through her stomach—and squeezed her so her side was flush with his. He repositioned her in front of him and wrapped his arms around her.

"Do I need to be worried about Big Beau?" he asked against her neck loud enough for Elijah to hear, his breath heating her skin.

She shook her head and her cheeks heated. Thankfully, her blush was authentic. Her body was a pinball machine of electrical impulses with Tyler this close. At least she didn't have to fake an attraction. Jessica might have the ability to sell a lie, she'd done it for her sister, but that didn't mean she enjoyed doing it.

Elijah looked at her and it seemed like he was really examining her. That wasn't good. "Are we good for Thanksgiving, then? My place?"

"Of course," she said raising her voice a few octaves like Jenn did when she was flirting. She twined a strand of hair around her finger and smiled, using all her sister's charms against him.

"You're not going to ditch me for him, right?" he asked, pain from the past still present in his eyes. She felt bad for him because she knew exactly what it was like when Jenn decided to make other plans. It was warm in the sunlight and cold in the shadows.

"Why would I do that?" she frowned. Exaggerating

the expression was exactly Jenn's style and made Jessica want to throw up in her mouth a little bit. Her sister had a flare for drama.

Elijah shot her a glare. "Now, that's a good question. Why would you stand me up when we have plans?"

Jessica loved her sister and she'd never want her hurt, but she could get easily frustrated with Jenn's personality and the way she treated people at times. Elijah stared at Jessica and she realized that she'd missed an inside reference between Elijah and Jenn. She'd missed a cue and now Elijah was suspicious. Frustration nipped at her. It was difficult to think straight with her back pressed against Tyler's pure muscle-over-steel chest.

This situation was getting sticky.

"I hate to take her away from you, but we have reservations," Tyler said, catching on.

Elijah had already looked her up and down as though suddenly realizing this was not an outfit Jenn would ever have on her body. Panic was beginning to set in. The exchange wasn't a total loss. They'd gotten the name Big Beau from him but who the heck was that?

The waitress in the passenger seat was looking a little annoyed. "Good. Maybe we can go now?"

There was a hint of jealousy in her tone. Did Elijah have real feelings for Jenn? Maybe that was the weird vibe she was picking up on from him.

"Stop by later," he said, ignoring Susannah, who looked even less thrilled now.

Tyler tugged at Jessica's hip. She almost forgot to blow a kiss to Elijah and that was something her sister always did before she walked away. Jessica turned and thanked heaven she had, because Elijah was staring expectantly. She blew the kiss and he smiled widely before pulling away.

"He almost caught me," she said to Tyler as they doubled back to walk to where the limo had parked. "My sister always blows a kiss. It's the silliest thing and I nearly forgot to do it."

Tyler squeezed her, keeping his arm around her as they walked. "You did good. He seemed suspicious at first when you missed that personal reference, but then he relaxed."

"I really thought I blew it," she said honestly. "Thank you for saving me."

"No problem. And now we have a name," he said with more than a hint of pride in his tone.

"Think we can go back to the market and ask around?" she asked.

"It's not safe for us here," he said. The weight of those words was heavy on her limbs. He was right. They'd dodged one bullet with Elijah and they needed to get out of Spanish Town.

"Big Beau. That could be anybody," she said under her breath.

"We'll have to ask around, but my guess is that someone will know who he is."

The limo was parked exactly where they'd left it. Zander stepped out as soon as he saw them and then opened the back door.

"Where to, Mister Tyler?" Zander asked.

"18008 North Mission Hills Avenue," Tyler said, conceding the *mister*.

"I'm probably just being paranoid, but do you get the feeling that someone's been following us?" Jessica asked.

"Yes, and I haven't decided if that's a good or bad thing yet."

18008 NORTH MISSION HILLS Avenue was one of those luxurious, one-of-a-kind New Orleans–style estates. Tyler had said the Brasseuxs lived there. The grounds looked like a park and it reminded Jessica of the grand homes of the old South. The place had been meticulously constructed with old brick, a slate roof and patios, and an oversize front porch with columns and one of those Southern-style front entrances. It was exactly the image that came to mind when Jessica thought of old Baton Rouge money. A golf course wound through the neighborhood and she guessed there had to be at least four or five acres of lush, flawlessly groomed grounds around this house alone.

Zander pulled up to the front gate and idled the engine. The partition slid down. "This the place where you're headed, Mister Tyler?"

"Doesn't look like we'll get past the gate without an appointment," Tyler said.

"No, it doesn't. What would you like to do?"

Tyler's hand was already on the door release. "I believe we'll get out here. Why don't you circle around the neighborhood? I'll call you as soon as we're ready to be picked up."

"Yes, sir," Zander said.

Jessica followed Tyler into the unseasonably sticky air, missing the air-conditioning as soon as she stepped out of the limo.

"I hope we make it to the main house. Security could be all over us long before we make it halfway across the yard," he said.

Surprisingly, they did make it. Majestic live oaks surrounded the house. As they neared, she saw something that made her heart jump in her chest—the partially painted El Camino parked at the side.

Jessica froze. "Elijah's here?"

Tyler shot her a look that warned her to be on guard. "We have no idea if we're here because we outsmarted security or if we're right where they want us. Either way, I'd like to get a closer look."

"He must be involved," she said quietly and mostly to herself. There must've been something she'd missed in their conversation. He hadn't missed a beat when he saw her. But then, she wasn't the best judge when it came to liars. Jessica had the sometimes unfortunate tendency to take people at face value. "Do you think this means my sister is somewhere safe?"

"It very well might." There was a note of sympathy in his voice. He was trying to give her hope and she appreciated it. She would hold on to it and not give in to the despair nipping at her heels.

The veranda stretched on for what felt like days, wrapping the entire front and left side of the mansion. There were half a dozen white rockers positioned to take advantage of the view of the front gardens. She followed Tyler to a window and peeked inside. She'd already seen the hand-painted stained-glass windows from the front yard. But what they could see through the window was the picture of opulence.

The crystal chandelier hanging over the foyer was fit for a king. Jessica moved to the next set of windows to the left and saw a receiving room that looked like something out of a Southern plantation magazine. A marble fireplace mantel was the focal point of the room. There were perfectly preserved vintage gold-leafed French furnishings. This place was the very epitome of grandeur—a world that was very foreign to Jessica. Even though it was beautiful, it was also intimidating and felt like something out of another time and place, albeit perfectly preserved.

"Whoever decorated this place must've died in the Civil War," Tyler joked, and she was once again reminded of how different he was from the picture of wealthy people that Jenn had painted.

She couldn't help but laugh and it felt good to break the tension. "I can't see Elijah anywhere."

"I don't like that one bit," Tyler admitted.

Jessica's stomach dropped when she heard the sound of a boot stepping onto the wooden porch. She whirled and there he was, fifteen feet away, the barrel of a gun pointed at her.

"Don't even think about doing anything stupid, cowboy," Elijah said as Tyler spun around.

"Funny seeing you here," Tyler quipped, holding his hands up in surrender. "I'm here to see the Brasseuxs. Emma-Kate's expecting us."

"She and Ashton aren't here right now," Elijah said with an ominous smirk.

Jessica thought when she'd first seen Elijah's El Camino that he was somehow in league with the Brasseuxs. Now she wondered if that had been a mistake. Maybe he was just a common criminal and they were innocent victims. "Where is she?"

"Who?"

"Don't play dumb. You know exactly who I'm talking about," Jessica said.

"Jenn? Let's just say she won't be in the way anymore." His voice held no emotion.

Jessica cursed and made a move toward Elijah, blinded by anger.

Tyler stopped her by grabbing her arm. "Don't. That's exactly what he wants. Don't give him any reason to shoot you."

She conceded but took another step forward, hoping she could get Tyler close enough to make a move. Elijah couldn't shoot both of them and she might be able to create a diversion long enough to give Tyler an advantage. She knew nothing about guns, though, so she had no idea if Elijah could fire multiple rounds in a few seconds or if he'd need to cock the hammer every time. Tyler squeezed her elbow and she took that as a warning.

"What do you want with me?" she asked, still trying to stall so Tyler could think of a plan. She knew he wouldn't make a move as long as that barrel was pointed at her chest. She didn't need to be an expert to know that a shot this close would do serious damage.

"Who the hell are you? Jenn never said anything about having a sister," Elijah said and his voice was a study in calm. His disposition, relaxed shoulders and steady hand said that he felt in control, and he was for the moment.

"It's none of your business who I am," she shot back, anger getting the best of her again. The gentle, reassuring squeeze to her arm came a second later. "Where is my sister?"

Elijah sighed. "That, I don't know."

"You're lying." Jessica ground her back teeth to keep from saying anything else that might provoke him. She saw a figure moving toward them using the live oaks as cover out of her peripheral vision. Zander?

"Now that you're here, I have to figure out what to do with you both," Elijah said.

She needed to distract him so Zander could get closer. "My sister trusted you. She thought you were a friend. Why would you do this to her?"

His laugh was almost a cackle. "Your sister looks out for number one. Just like I do. She, of all people, would understand me putting myself first."

"She wouldn't hurt a flea and you know it."

"Tell that to Mrs. Brasseux," he quipped. "After all, Jenn was sleeping with her husband."

Was her sister having an affair with a married man? Was that the reason she'd kept her new man's identity a secret?

"Take me to her. Please," Jessica begged, trying to process that last bit of information.

"He can't," Tyler finally spoke up. "He isn't the one calling the shots."

"That's not your concern. And that goes for both of you," Elijah shot back defensively. His lips thinned. His gaze narrowed. Tyler clearly had struck a nerve.

"Then tell me who is," Jessica said. Her sister had always spoken highly of Elijah. "If you cared about my sister at all you wouldn't do this."

"Move." Elijah motioned toward the porch steps.

Tyler urged her forward, moving his hand low on her back.

"Hands up where I can see them," Elijah said.

"Where are the Brasseuxs?" Tyler asked.

"Let's just say they're preoccupied at the moment. Now move." Elijah gestured with the barrel of his gun. He was taking them to his El Camino. There was no trunk, thankfully, because Jessica was claustrophobic and she feared she'd have a panic attack.

As they rounded the corner of the big house, she noticed there was another car parked in front of the El Camino, a white sedan. The El Camino had been blocking the second car from view. Jessica heard a click and the trunk automatically opened.

Jessica's chest squeezed and the heavy air thinned as she thought about climbing into that trunk. No way would her claustrophobia allow her to go inside there willingly. Her body began to shake. If she could keep her cool, Elijah might take her right to Jenn. Then again, he could just take them into the bayou, shoot them and dump their bodies into the swamp for the alligators to pick apart.

More than anything she wanted to glance backward to see if Zander was making progress toward them but she couldn't risk giving him away.

Elijah made Jessica and Tyler walk in front of him, and he was giving them a wide enough berth to make it impossible for Tyler to disarm him. He sure thought like a criminal for someone who'd been parading around as a musician. If what Elijah had said was true and he had no idea where Jenn was, then Jessica and Tyler were in big trouble.

A struggle sounded behind them and a bullet split the air. Jessica instinctively ducked, but before she could get her bearings someone was on top of her and she was face-down on the concrete parking pad with a masculine body shielding her. Tyler's body. And he had a calming presence.

"Stay low," was all she heard him say before another shot fired. "Get behind the house as fast as you can. Don't look back."

Panic nearly closed her throat as the pressure of his body eased and she scrambled for cover. She couldn't help but look back to see if Tyler or Zander had been shot. All she could see clearly was Tyler diving into the fray. There was blood on the concrete and her heart stuttered as she rounded the corner, looking for something she could use to help the guys. No way would she leave them alone to deal with Elijah if there was something she could do to help.

There was nothing around so she ran to the back porch and tried the door. Locked. Dammit.

Another shot was fired and she ran to the corner of the building to see what had happened. Before she could get a good visual, Tyler was helping Zander toward her as the El Camino sped off. Blood dripped from the arm dangling at Zander's side and she rushed to help him. "What happened?"

Zander winced as he moved. "Bullet grazed my shoulder. I'll be fine. I saw you two in trouble and had to help—the police wouldn't have come in time."

"We appreciate it." Tyler helped Zander to the rear porch. "Where's your cell?"

"Back pocket." Zander eased to one side as Tyler fished out the phone.

"I'm calling for an ambulance. We'll stick around until they get close and then we have to go. Her sister's in danger and we can't afford to lose any more time," Tyler said as he pulled off his undershirt and tied it around Zander's shoulder just above the wound while checking to make sure Elijah wasn't circling back. "You're going to be fine. Have the police check on the family inside the house, if anyone's there."

Zander nodded. "Don't worry about me. Nothing but a scratch."

Wasn't that pretty much the same line all men gave? If the situation weren't so dire, Jessica would laugh.

"Keys fell out of my pocket. Heard them drop over there somewhere." Zander motioned toward a pool of blood. "Take the limo and get out of here."

Tyler handed the cell to Zander, who explained that he'd had an altercation and needed help.

Jessica located the fanned-out keys. "Got 'em."

"Then go," Zander pressed after ending the call.

"Not until help arrives," Tyler said.

"I'll tell the cops that I ran into someone in town who asked me to drop him off here. I'll give them the description of the man who drew a gun on you and Jessica. That way the police will be looking for him and not either of you." Zander took his cell phone and wiped it down. "Can't have your prints on here."

"What will you tell them about your limo disappearing?" Tyler asked, thanking Zander.

"I'll figure something out. Don't worry." Zander shooed them away as sirens sounded far in the distance. "I'm fine. Now go."

"We'll check on you later," Tyler said, embracing Zander in a man-hug. "Thank you for everything you've done. We wouldn't be alive without you."

Jessica's sister, on the other hand, might not have been so lucky.

Chapter Ten

"Do you think it's possible what Elijah said is true?" Jessica asked. The Louisiana humidity made it difficult to breathe.

"That your sister was having an affair with Ashton?" Tyler navigated the limo onto the highway.

"She had a new man in her life and she refused to tell me who he was," she said, tapping on the dashboard.

"Makes for a good story. Your sister is having an affair with a wealthy man. Tries to get him to leave his wife but he won't. She steals his wife's family heirloom for revenge," he said.

"When you put it like that, it sounds like something on a TV crime show."

"Exactly. And it sums everything up nicely except the part where your sister's not a thief," he said, and then glanced over at her. "You haven't changed your mind, have you?"

She hesitated. "Not really. I know my sister. But then I wouldn't have believed that she was involved with a married man, and yet she is."

"True." There was no conviction in his voice. "She may not have known he was married when she met him."

Good point. For all her social climbing, she was still

a small-town girl at heart. A sophisticated liar could pull the wool over Jenn's eyes.

"Also, in the last message she said not to believe what Milton would say about her. Maybe the same holds true for Elijah. I think we need to talk to your sister before we jump to any conclusions," he said.

"What do you think the name Big Beau really means?" Jessica asked.

"He could've been throwing the name out to get a reaction from you," Tyler said.

"A reaction from my sister," she clarified. "Or so he thought at the time."

"My bet is that Big Beau is an actual person," Tyler said. "We'll start there. The only other clue we have is the bayou."

"I still don't know if that's significant." She couldn't help the desperation in her voice.

"Milton's still out there somewhere, most likely looking for you," he said. "It would help if we knew what your sister had been doing and where she'd been leading up to this. Does Jenn keep a diary or journal?"

"No. She's not really the type to actually write anything down. Her cell phone is a different story. If we could find that then we'd get more of the picture of what's going on. She and her cell are inseparable." Jessica pinched the bridge of her nose to stave off a headache. "Where to next?"

"We need to find a good place to hide this limo and get back to our hotel to clean up and figure out our next move." Tyler pulled a business card out of his pocket. He handed the card and his cell to Jessica, temporarily steering with his left hand.

Annabeth Malloy, the hotel manager?

"Call her number and put the phone on speaker," he instructed.

A few seconds later the familiar voice was on the line.

"This is Tyler O'Brien—"

"Of course, Mr. O'Brien, how can I help you?"

"I'd like to enter through the service door. A society reporter's been bothering my friend and I and we'd like to shake him."

"No problem at all, sir," she said. "I'll make the arrangements and have someone waiting for you."

"Excellent. Much appreciated," he said. "There's one more thing, I'd like my limo safely stored until I need it again."

"Absolutely," she said confidently.

"Much obliged, ma'am."

Jessica got lost in her thoughts for the rest of the drive, rolling over the new information about her sister.

The service entrance was dead quiet and empty, not a soul in sight. The sticky humidity made Jessica want to shower all over again. Adrenaline had faded. She was tired and hungry. At least the air-conditioning in their suite evened out her temperature.

"I need to clean up." She disappeared into the bathroom, not wanting the cowboy to see the tears brimming in her eyes. The past day and a half had been surreal and a very real fear engulfed her every time she thought about her sister. Some people believed in twin telepathy and there were moments when Jessica did, too. Instances like this one, when she was overwhelmed with fear for her sister and she was sure something bad was happening.

"If we put our heads together, we'll figure out where your sister is," Tyler reassured her as she stepped out of the bathroom in fresh clothes. This time, she'd opted for a simple T-shirt and cotton shorts with running shoes. Her hair was thrown up in a ponytail; it kept her neck cooler that way.

She nodded but didn't say anything. What could she say? Her sister had never felt farther away.

"You could get away with calling yourself a college student dressed like that," Tyler said in an obvious attempt to change the subject. He seemed to pick up on her mood. "LSU isn't far and that look should help you blend in."

"Thank you. I think."

"It was meant as a compliment. Order whatever you want from room service. Would you mind asking them to send up a burger and a beer for me?"

"Not at all." In fact, both sounded really good right now.

"Thanks. I'll just be in there taking a cold shower." He seemed to realize the implication in that last part and he cracked a dry smile. "For that reason, too, but I need to wash the blood off me."

Jessica couldn't help but smile. For a wealthy guy, he was the most down-to-earth man she'd met. The images of the type of men her sister had dated paraded around in her head. She imagined flashy suits and designer casual wear. This cowboy was pretty much the polar opposite. And he looked damn good in his jeans and boots, so much better than those superficial types.

Normally, she'd notice more about the handsome cowboy, but all she could really focus on right now was Jenn. Besides, her thoughts were only more confused about Tyler after the couple of kisses they'd shared.

Jessica absently dialed room service and ordered dinner. The sun was going down and they still had no answers. Questions swirled. All they knew for sure was that her sister was in trouble, so nothing new there.

Tyler joined her fifteen minutes later, wearing only a pair of jeans that sat low on his hips. His rippled chest was tanned and muscled. Working on a ranch sure as heck did a body good because he had a six pack below solid steel pecs.

"Food should be here soon," she said, trying to force her eyes away from his chest. "And I'm not any closer to figuring out where my sister could be than I was this morning."

The couch dipped under Tyler's weight as he sat down next to her. She'd pulled a notepad and pen from on top of the nightstand and made a few scribbles on it. Mostly, the word *bayou* sat in the middle of the page and she'd circled it over and over again until it looked like one thick mass of wires.

"We just need one break. That's all. And we'll figure this whole thing out. What else do you remember about coming here with her?" the handsome cowboy asked, and no matter how many hours she spent with him she'd never get used to the sound of his voice. Its deep timbre stirred her somewhere low in her belly, and the flutter of a thousand butterflies rippled through her every time he spoke.

"She used to order in a lot when I visited. I didn't really think about it much before but I guess she didn't want to be seen with me." She wrote down the words *Big Beau.* "Do you think Elijah was just trying to throw us off?"

Tyler shrugged as the phone rang. They both looked at the land line.

"Could be the front desk," Jessica offered.

Tyler answered. "It's Zander. He's calling from a phone at the ER."

She heard very little from Tyler's end, which meant that Zander was doing all the talking. The instant Tyler hung up, she asked, "Is he okay?"

"He's doing fine. Said one of the bullets tapped his shoulder and the other grazed the inside of his arm and his ribs, missing anything that could cause serious damage. The doctor said he's very lucky." Tyler walked over to the couch and she couldn't help but admire his athletic grace. Basic biology had her evaluating whether or not he could protect her, given that they were in such dangerous circumstances. "They're treating and releasing him."

"That's the best news I've heard all day." She sighed with relief.

A knock sounded at the door. Tyler shot her a warning look. "Get out of sight until I give you a green light."

She moved into the bedroom and stood behind the door where she could see through the crack.

Tyler pulled a handgun, she wasn't sure what kind, and held it behind his leg as he opened the door with his left hand.

"Come on in," he said to the room service attendant.

The attendant wore a white sous chef shirt and black pants. He looked legit as he wheeled in the tray. "Would you like me to set up at the table, Mr. O'Brien?"

"No, thanks. Just leave it there." Tyler pointed next to the table. "I can take it from here."

He pulled a few bills from his pocket and tipped the attendant without revealing what was in his other hand. "Smells fantastic."

"Enjoy, sir," the waiter said with a smile.

Tyler closed the door behind him. "It's safe."

Even though the waiter was gone and the coast was clear, the tension stayed in the room. Jessica hated living like this, afraid of her own shadow. But her identity had been revealed and soon everyone would know that Jenn had a twin sister.

"What are you thinking about?" Tyler placed the gun securely in the side table.

"How they're not going to stop until they find me. They know about me now. Our advantage is gone."

He motioned for her to sit at the table, so she did. He put a plate in front of her and pulled off the metal cover to reveal the best-looking hamburger she'd ever seen. Or maybe she was just that hungry.

"I also ordered a fresh pot of coffee," she said. After that adrenaline rush, the beer didn't sound as good as coffee. She didn't want anything to dull her senses and she was a lightweight when it came to alcohol.

He must've been thinking the same thing because he set the beers aside in an ice bucket. "I'll keep these cold for later."

By the time she took the last bite of her burger, Jessica had downed a bottled water. She poured a cup of coffee afterward. "Want one?"

"I can get it."

"I'm right here." She cocked her eyebrow. She hadn't noticed it with all the drama going on around them, but this cowboy seemed to prefer to do everything for himself. "I don't mind. Really."

"Don't go to any trouble."

"It's none at all." She poured a cup and handed it to him. "See how easy that was?"

He chuckled. "My parents taught us to be independent. We grew up working the ranch right alongside Pop. Mom spoiled us but pretended not to. She always said we were blessed and not spoiled. Either way she managed to bring up six independent boys. Although," he smiled, "some might call us stubborn."

"Sounds like you grew up in an ideal family."

"We did. And it ruined us. We all have a difficult time letting others in," he admitted and there was something dark in his eyes now. Regret?

"Doesn't sound like such a bad thing. The situation I'm in now reminds me to be even more careful who I trust," she said. "Even someone with the best of intentions can hurt you."

"Trust can be a good thing. When it's earned." Had he trusted Lyndsey too soon? He'd believed that she knew him and understood his priorities. And then she'd demanded that he walk away from the ranch forever if he wanted a future with her. She'd said their life was in Denver, where her family lived. Needless to say, being given an ultimatum had gone over about as well as filthy ranch clothes in church and begged the question, why would she demand something like that if she really knew him?

She'd walked out and the nagging question remained: How could he have loved someone he knew so little? Even so, when Lyndsey had left he didn't think he'd ever breathe again. Surprisingly, his body functioned even when he wasn't sure he wanted it to. Losing his parents at the same time had been a double blow.

Speaking of family, when this ordeal was over and Jessica was safe, he needed to touch base with his brothers and Tommy about the investigation back home. It was easy to set aside his pain and focus on someone else's problem for a change. Tyler had focused on his own until he'd gone numb. All he could think about was the note Lyndsey had left behind. *Enjoy your life and try to put someone else first for a change.*

For the past few weeks he'd tried to figure out if there was any truth to what she'd said. He'd dated around since Lyndsey, but it had felt like he was ticking a box, making sure he was playing the field.

Tyler could be honest enough with himself to admit that Lyndsey hadn't been completely first in his life. He chalked it up to their differences. She was outgoing and liked to hang out with friends at the bar after a long day. She was flirtatious and he'd almost convinced himself that he didn't mind. He was the complete opposite. Tyler kept more to himself, preferring to trust only those who shared the O'Brien last name.

And after a long day, he wanted a good meal and a cold beer under the stars. If there was a woman involved, then he could think of other things he wanted to do, as well... things that involved both of them naked.

There was something special about looking up at the night sky in Texas, the wide expanse of midnight blue with bright specks.

Lyndsey was most likely right. He probably needed to make more of an effort with people. He was good at nego-tiating and analyzing all sides of a business deal to come up with a fair solution and that's why he was in charge of handling contracts and disputes. He had managed a tem-porary truce between Aunt Bea and Uncle Ezra recently and that had taken some serious skills. But dealing with emotions, especially his own, wasn't his strong suit.

Enough focus on the things he didn't have the first idea how to fix.

Tyler needed to straighten out his thoughts about the current situation. "Let's go back to the beginning and think this through. Milton was one of your sister's exes, right?"

"Yes. She dated him for a short while last year but they stayed friends after, or so she thought." Jessica sat on the couch and folded her right leg underneath her bottom. She sipped her coffee and set the mug on the table.

"Is that the reason she figured he wouldn't catch on that you were subbing for her? He must not've known her very well," Tyler said.

"He didn't. Not really. But then my sister's personality has many layers. I'm not sure I know all of her. I never imagined she'd be in any kind of trouble like this and yet here we are. And then there's the affair."

"We now know that Elijah is involved," he said.

"Up to his eye teeth," she added.

"How close were the two of them?"

"I'm guessing he reminded her of home, barely scraping by," she said. "He must've felt familiar to her and helped her miss us less."

"I can't help but wonder how a musician and a corporate lawyer would know each other. It doesn't seem that they would travel in the same circles," he said. "Not to mention the fact that Milton couldn't possibly be currently practicing law with his criminal record."

"That's a good question. My sister is the only connection I can find. She never dated Elijah to my knowledge." Jessica sipped her coffee.

"But that doesn't mean he didn't have feelings for her."

"No. You're right. In fact, I'm pretty sure he did based on the way he looked at me before. There was no way she'd go out with him, though," Jessica's eyes lit up just then. Her eyes weren't the only thing he noticed. There were other things, endearing quirks about her that he liked. For example, the corner of her mouth twitched when she was nervous. The movement was so slight he almost missed it the first time. He'd also noticed that her tongue slicked across her bottom lip when she was about to lie. He'd seen that a few times when she spoke to Elijah and was grateful that she hadn't done it while talking to him.

Her laugh was almost like music and made him want to hear it more often. He vowed to himself to take her out to dinner when this was all behind them and make her laugh until her stomach hurt. Also, she blinked when she wasn't sure what to say next.

But the main thing he noticed was how sweet she tasted when he kissed her. And just how right she fit when he'd held her in his arms.

"I'm worried about the Brasseuxs." She sighed sharply. "And I feel like a hamster on a wheel. Every time I ask questions I go round again."

"I keep wondering what they and Elijah have in common. Or Milton, for that matter." Tyler stabbed his fingers through his thick hair. "I mean, the Brasseuxs could've had some interaction with Milton socially. But Elijah? I can't find a connection there."

"I know one," Jessica said.

Tyler arched a brow.

"My sister," Jessica said quietly. "What if she's not as innocent as I want to believe? What if she stole the necklace to get back at Ashton and then her so-called friend Elijah sees an opportunity to make some money off of her? Everything could've gone sour and she got herself in more trouble than she could handle."

"You don't really believe that, do you?" he asked.

"I don't want to, but that's where the evidence points," she said. "You know what? I'm tired. I need to get some rest."

Chapter Eleven

Jessica tossed and turned in her bed, unable to sleep for the nagging feeling that she was missing something important. She drifted in and out, straining to think. At three o'clock in the morning it finally dawned on her. She bolted upright and must've screamed because Tyler burst into the room a few seconds later.

"What happened?" he said, his low, sexy voice still gravelly from sleep. He rubbed his eyes and moved to the bed.

"I didn't mean to wake you," she said, forcing her eyes away from his muscled chest. This wasn't the time to think about those ripples of pure steel and how soft his skin felt to her touch. Or the warmth his body possessed.

"I'm a light sleeper." The mattress dipped under his weight. He had on boxers and nothing else.

"It came to me in a flash and I realized what I'd been missing. Do you have your smartphone?" she asked.

He jogged into the next room, returned a moment later and offered his cell to her.

She pulled up the internet and entered *The Bayou* into the search engine. Hope filled her chest for the first time. "It's an actual place. The Bayou. She said that she'd see me in the bayou, which I assumed was a general reference, except that there really is a place. She took me there the very first time I visited and never again. It was one of the only public places we went. It's really far on the outskirts of town. Actually, saying it's near any kind of civilization is being generous."

"What kind of place is it?" he asked.

"A hole-in-the-wall that only locals know about. See?" She shoved the phone toward him with an address highlighted on Google Maps. "It doesn't have a website, per se, but it's listed as a business. This is the address."

He took the phone and examined the web page. "This is a good place to start."

In her excitement at this first real lead, she launched herself toward Tyler and threw her arms around his neck. The covers pooled around her knees.

"This place looks…interesting to say the least. It's literally surrounded by a swamp." His free arm circled her waist.

Jessica realized all too quickly that her thin cotton tank top was the only thing standing between them. She started to pull back.

He dropped the phone on the bed next to her knees.

"Oh, no you don't," he said, hauling her against his chest. His other arm wrapped around her bottom.

Before she could talk herself out of it, she kissed him. With a quick maneuver, he had her on his lap, straddling him, and she could feel the warmth of his erection pulsing against the inside of her thigh. Jessica deepened the kiss. Tyler was all hotness and fire and manliness. His hands palmed her bottom. She liked the feel of him…real…and rough…and still so surprisingly gentle. She scooted closer until her heat was positioned against his straining rod. The thought of sex with Tyler sent a thunderclap of need pounding through her, making her stomach quiver.

His hands roamed her bottom as she pressed her almost-naked breasts flush against his chest.

A throaty, sexy growl tore from his throat and she could feel his muscles as they flexed. Their breath quickened as her hands searched down his back, lingering on each ripple, memorizing his strong lines.

And then five words she didn't want to acknowledge wound through her thoughts. *Is this a good idea?*

She barely knew the guy and yet she'd already trusted him with her life. And a certain intimacy had come out of that, which couldn't be denied. But did she really know him? Sure, the sexual tension between them was thicker than the Louisiana humidity. She had no doubt sex with Tyler would be amazing. And then what?

They were from two different worlds. He'd go back to his life on the ranch. She'd go back to hers in Shreveport, helping her parents and running the family business, which wasn't much but enough to keep them going financially. She couldn't imagine leaving them to fend for themselves.

Her brain cautioned her not to get ahead of herself. The future was a long way away. She had tonight. She was feeling the effects of an exciting breakthrough. And there was nothing wrong with mindless sex.

THE IDEA OF taking a breather when Jessica's skin flamed against his touch was almost unthinkable.

Except that he cared about her and they were stuck in a weird space between needing to blow off steam and needing to be with each other. The former was a no-brainer. That's where Tyler existed most of the time. The latter scared the hell out of him.

Calling on every ounce of strength he had, he forced himself to slow it down a few notches.

The other side of the coin was that he realized she'd

been through a lot and most likely needed an outlet for her stress. While that would normally be right up Tyler's alley, for reasons he couldn't explain it bothered him with Jessica.

"This is not a good idea right now." He lifted her up and set her on the bed next to him, doing his level best to squash the disappointment roaring through his chest and the little voice in the back of his mind cursing him out. That was the same piece of brain that controlled everything south and he'd learned as a teenager not to listen if he wanted to stay out of trouble.

"Oh" was all she said, and he could hear the surprise and disappointment clearly in her tone.

"You're beautiful, don't get me wrong. But anything happening between us is not going to work," he managed to say.

"It's okay. You don't have to spare my feelings." Her cheeks blushed and that ripped right through him.

Did she think he didn't want to have sex with her? How could he not? She had all the attributes he admired in a real woman. She was smart, had sexy curves and was damned near irresistible. In fact, if he didn't do something to cool his jets in the next minute or two he couldn't trust himself not to haul her into his arms again and take her right then and there on her bed. Before he went all caveman on her, he needed a cold shower. He'd explain later…when he figured it out for himself.

"We're going to talk about this, but not right now." He pointed at the phone. "First, we find your sister."

Before she could protest, he walked out of the room and straight into a cold shower.

IF THAT DIDN'T rank right up there as one of Jessica's most embarrassing moments in life, she didn't know what did.

Clearly Tyler wanted her. There was no denying the erection she'd felt against the inside of her thigh. Was there something horribly wrong with her that he couldn't follow through on that desire? Maybe he'd finally realized what he was doing and decided to put a stop to it. Everything had happened so fast that Jessica got swept up in the moment. The attraction between them was real, but there was more to a relationship than physical pull. And he was right. They needed to focus on finding her sister.

Guilt washed over Jessica for losing focus. Jenn needed her and she'd gotten momentarily wrapped up with the handsome cowboy.

Shaking it off, she dressed in jeans and a cotton shirt. Throwing her hair in a ponytail she tried not to focus too much on where they were going. There'd be mosquitoes in the swamp. Alligators. Bacteria. And all sorts of creatures eager to feed off human flesh and blood.

And if thinking about that didn't give her pause, nothing would.

Then there were the people themselves to contend with…people who preferred life off the grid with no cell service or contact with the outside world.

She took a fortifying breath and turned toward the living room. Tyler stood there, dressed and fresh from a shower, staring.

"Ready?"

"As much as I'll ever be," she said, thoroughly confused by the mixed signal.

He picked his phone up from the bed and made a call.

"Who are you calling in the middle of the night?" she asked, slipping on her running shoes. If she was going to hike through the swamps in the middle of the night, then she figured that she'd need to be comfortable.

"It's not safe to drive around in Zander's limo anymore. I'm arranging transportation," he said.

"LET'S GIVE OUR eyes a few minutes to acclimate to the darkness before we head out." Tyler adjusted the seat of the SUV that had been organized for him by the hotel manager. He didn't normally play that card, the one that had him waking up a hotel manager in the middle of the night, but this felt like a real lead and waiting until morning could be the difference between life and death for Jessica's sister.

He'd also arranged for a flashlight but he wanted some peripheral vision as they made their way through dense woods to The Bayou.

"How far is it from here?" she asked.

"About twenty minutes on foot." He'd parked off the highway near the gravel road leading to the place. Any lights on that road would give them away and he didn't want anyone to know they were coming. He had no idea if The Bayou was a safe place or not. Given its coordinates, he couldn't imagine that it was…this was a place people went to fly off the radar. He grabbed a package of bug repellent wipes out of the bag he'd arranged to have in the vehicle, opened one and held it out. "Rub this on any exposed skin, neck, arms."

She took the wipe and her fingers grazed his palm. Again he regretted not following through with sex earlier. He still couldn't figure out what was wrong with him. The tension between them was a distraction they couldn't afford and he half figured a rousing round in the sack would help with that problem. Maybe then he could fully concentrate on finding Jenn instead of thinking about the curve of Jessica's sweet bottom in his hands.

Tyler tore open a packet of bug repellant and wiped his arms and neck. The last thing he needed was a case of West

Nile to take home, and he sure as hell could use a distraction from thinking about Jessica's backside.

"We'll go in dark, meaning I'll cut off the flashlight when we get near the clearing to the building. If we're lucky, everyone on the premises will be asleep. If we're not, there'll be dogs and people with guns who will wake up when they bark. Based on the Google Earth picture, it looks like the kind of place there'd be Dobermans or pit bulls. So, not only will we go in dark but we'll go in quiet."

His eyes were adjusting to the darkness and hers were huge with fear.

"You want to wait it out here?" he asked, his voice more curt than he'd intended.

Her reaction was immediate. "No. I'd do more good with you and I'm not sitting out here alone."

He silently cursed at himself for not being able to stop thinking about their encounter in the hotel room. "You know how to handle a gun?"

"They scare me to death."

"Well," he conceded, "then we'll find something else for you to—"

"But that doesn't mean I can't get over it," she interrupted. "I'm not *that* afraid and especially if it means getting my sister to safety or keeping one of us from getting shot."

She held out her flat palm and he could see her hand tremble in the light of the full moon. He had to hand it to her. She got extra points for bravery.

"The safety is on." He molded her fingers around the SIG Sauer. "It's important to get a good feel for how it fits."

She brought her other hand up and cupped the butt. "I got this."

"You gave me the impression this was the first time you'd touched a gun."

"I said that I was scared to death of them, and that part's true, but my dad taught me how to shoot when I was twelve because he kept guns in the house."

"Was he a hunter?"

"No. We lived in a bad part of town and he wanted me to be ready in case he couldn't be around." She opened the magazine and checked the clip. "This should do but I'm hoping that I won't need to use it."

"Make sure it's aimed at someone besides me if you decide to shoot," he said, only half teasing. After his stunt back at the room she had to be angry with him. Heck, he was angry at himself. He still didn't know why a bout of conscience had come over him.

Taking a beautiful woman to bed didn't normally have him getting inside his head about not being in a relationship with her. *Damn, O'Brien.* He'd really loused that one up. If he got another chance with Jessica, and he was pretty sure that wasn't going to happen based on the wall she'd erected between them, he wouldn't waste it like he had the first time. But then second chances rarely happened in the real world. Tyler muttered a curse.

"What did you say?" she asked, looking at him oddly.

"Nothing." He hesitated. "Are you ready?"

"As much as I can be," she said softly, and her blatant honesty pierced his heart.

Yeah, he was going to live to regret his actions in the hotel. Because walking away from a woman with that much strength and beauty was going to be the end of him. But, hey, just like his short-lived baseball career and his last relationship had proved, everything had an expiration date.

Tyler tried to let this thing with Jessica roll off his back, ignoring the fact that it had more staying power than a determined bull on rodeo day.

THE SOUNDS OF a swamp in Louisiana at night were not something Jessica would ever get used to. There was a clicking sound to her right as she navigated the dense forest of live oak. Everything sounded alive, even the trees, and more awake than in daylight. Something rustled in the undergrowth a little too close for comfort and her heart skittered as she stepped over gnarled roots.

Crickets chirped, her skin crawled and the sound of footsteps slogging through muddy water sent her pulse racing. This was home of the alligator.

Owls hooted in surround sound and she could tell they were literally all around her as she stepped in the marsh. Something moved underneath her shoe. She bit back a scream and reached for Tyler.

He positioned her beside him and she kept her gaze focused on the light beam that hit a tree and then bounced to the ground and back. Step by step she held her breath, trying not to focus on the chorus of insects. Heaven only knew what other creatures were lurking in the dark. She couldn't help but check for a set of eyes as the light skimmed the deeper water right next to them and she prayed they wouldn't end up waist deep as they trudged along.

Who in their right mind would come out this far from the city and into this unknown? If her sister had been taken, and Jessica was fairly certain that was the case, then this would be the perfect place to dispose of a body.

Focusing on the worst-case scenario wouldn't help their investigation or her mood, so she did her best to shove those thoughts aside as she plucked her heel from the slick soil. It was impossible to move through the vegetation without making a sound. Every time she stepped, it was as if the ground refused to let go.

Tyler squeezed her hand and stopped. The light from the flashlight disappeared, plunging them into utter darkness.

Jessica's heart beat in her throat as she took a tentative step forward. Trust wasn't her strong suit but desperation had her willing to do pretty much anything to find her sister. The total blackness ignited her claustrophobia and if it wasn't for Tyler she would've had to stop right there and turn around.

If Jenn had been on her own she'd have called. There was no doubt about that in Jessica's mind. It had been two days since her sister had gone silent. A lot could happen in forty-eight hours.

Her eyes adjusted to the darkness enough to see outlines by the time the trees thinned. She counted three sheds and her sister could be in any one of them. Then there was the main building, a relatively small two-story structure with a handmade sign on the porch that read The Bayou in big white letters on what appeared to be a large piece of driftwood. That was about the only thing she could see clearly because the trees around the house formed a canopy in the swamp making it impossible for light from the moon to shine through.

Two vehicles were parked in back, an old Toyota pickup truck and a Volkswagen van that looked like a relic from the sixties. Thankfully, there were no dogs on the premises or Jessica and Tyler's presence would already be known.

Tyler squatted down behind the Volkswagen and motioned for Jessica to come over. He flashed the light. The license plate on the VW read, Big Beau.

Jessica tried to wrap her mind around what this could mean. Her sister had mentioned The Bayou and then Elijah had referred to Big Beau. This had to be the place.

This could be a trap, a little voice said. Maybe she was right where Elijah wanted her.

Did that mean that Jenn was here somewhere?

Was this some kind of headquarters or meeting place for the group who was after the Infinity Sapphire?

A hand covered Jessica's mouth. Before she could scream she was dragged backward. She spun around out of her assailant's grasp, landed facedown and fumbled for the SIG Sauer she'd dropped in the struggle.

"Shhh. Don't scream. I'm here to help you and your sister. Don't say a word," the unfamiliar deep male voice said.

Tyler was there in the next beat, his gun at the man's temple. "Where do you think you're going with her?"

"Stay calm and we'll all get out of here alive," the man said.

From her vantage point, Tyler seemed the one in charge so it was bold of this guy to give orders. Her hand skimmed the surface of the ground until landing on her gun. She picked it up, sat up and pointed it directly at the male figure.

"I'm Big Beau. And if you want to know where your sister is, you'll keep quiet. We need to get out of here right now. If they know I'm talking to you I'll end up floating in that swamp. If the gators don't haul me off, the mosquitoes will."

"I have a car nearby," Tyler whispered.

She wasn't sure how Tyler knew to trust the guy. She had her own doubts, but desperation had her ready to do almost anything to find Jenn.

"Let's go before somebody wakes," Big Beau said. The guy was huge. Tyler was somewhere around six foot four so he was significantly taller, but Big Beau had the belly of a grizzly bear.

"Not so fast." Tyler patted the guy down to check for a weapon as Jessica scrambled to her feet.

"You won't find anything on me. I left my AR15 inside and there's more where that came from. But if you're smart, you'll move it along. If we wake anyone up or they know I'm helping you, I'm dead. And so is Jenn."

Chapter Twelve

At the SUV, Tyler kept his gun leveled at Big Beau. Getting a closer look at him Jessica saw what a big, burly man he was. A patchwork of scruff covered parts of his jaw and neck. He wore a flannel shirt with the sleeves cut off. His eyes were pale blue, his hair dirty blond. Jeans rode low on his hips, tucked underneath a pot belly.

"I know what you're thinking and I ain't like them others," he said, holding his right hand toward Tyler as if it could stop a bullet.

"Prove it," Tyler shot back, keeping his gun aimed at the big guy. "Tell us where she is."

"She ain't far. Unless they've moved her."

"Who has her?" Jessica asked defensively.

"It's complicated but I remember you from the first time your sister brought you here," he said.

"How? That was so long ago. I don't remember you at all," she said honestly.

Big Beau held back a laugh. "Your sister came out here and talked about you all the time since then. I hoped you'd figure out she was in trouble and come see me."

"If that's true, then why doesn't anyone else know me?" She seriously doubted Jenn spoke about her to anyone.

He rolled his big shoulders in a shrug. "Reckon she had

her reasons. She never talked about you where anyone else could hear and always asked me to keep it a secret."

"Because she was ashamed of me," Jessica said quietly. Then she glanced up apologetically. She hadn't intended to say that out loud.

"Ashamed?" He shook his head. "Proud's more like it. She went on and on about how smart you are and what a success you've made out of your family's business to help your parents."

"I had no idea she felt that way." True, she had expanded the cleaning business from houses to office buildings so her mother wouldn't have to do the heavy lifting anymore. And she'd hired two dozen workers, jobs she was happy to provide to people in order to boost the local economy.

Big Beau looked like he was examining Jessica and it made her uncomfortable. "I'm sorry for staring, but you two look so much alike. I'm surprised at how different you think or that you don't know how proud she is of you. She talks about you like you walk on water."

"Me and my sister have always been close but I didn't know." Jessica wiped an errant tear as it rolled down her cheek. She'd always loved her sister and had known on some level that Jenn loved her as much, but hearing that her sister was proud of her overwhelmed her with emotion.

"Jenn used to say all she had to work with was her looks," Big Beau continued. "And that she had to play her cards right or she'd end up with nothing. But you...she thought you hung the moon."

Jessica couldn't stop the sob that tore from her throat. Tyler moved to her side and put his arm around her protectively.

"I'm fine." She ignored the confused look on Tyler's face as she sidestepped out of reach. "Really. It's just very sweet to hear and my sister's in trouble. I let my emotions get the best of me but I'm good now."

Tyler eyed her up and down, clearly not convinced, but not ready to push the envelope either.

"Why didn't you do anything to help her?" she asked Big Beau, needing to redirect the conversation to something more productive.

"It ain't right how they're setting her up to look like she stole that necklace. They plan to kill her as soon as they get hold of it and make it look like suicide. As far as helping her, that's what I'm trying to do right now."

"She's innocent?" Jessica knew she shouldn't sound so surprised. She wanted to believe in her sister, but after learning about the affair, it was hard. "Who's behind this?"

She was so close that he could reach out and grab her if he wanted, but she didn't care.

"Ashton Brasseux. But now that Randall Beauchamp's involved it's a mess," Beau said, and turned toward Tyler. "She's my friend and I wouldn't do anything to hurt her. My family don't feel the same way. Everyone's afraid of Mr. Beauchamp so they do whatever he asks. They don't have no trouble with her personally but he said to find her, so they did."

"What's Beauchamp's involvement in this?" Tyler asked.

Big Beau shrugged. "All I know is he has a buyer for that stolen necklace and now that it's gone missing he'll do anything to get it back."

"Is she hurt?" Jessica asked Big Beau. "Did he do anything to her?"

"I can tell you where I believe he's keeping her, but that's as far as I can go. I have no idea what shape she's in. My guess is not good. If he knows anyone from my family helped you out he'll have us all fed to the gators." Big Beau shivered.

"But she's alive?" Jessica could barely ask the question.

"She was last I heard," he said honestly. "No way was she involved in this. Ashton used her."

That made a lot of sense.

"You can trust us. No one will know the information came from you," Tyler promised.

Big Beau half smiled and nodded. "My life depends on it."

"Why are you helping us?" Jessica asked.

"Your sister's a good kid." Big Beau's face broke into a smile talking about Jenn. She had that effect on people, and especially men. She was charming and beautiful, but there was something else about her that drew people to her. "She don't mean nobody harm. It's a shame what's happened to her and it's even worse that my family's to blame. I'll give you the address where we took her."

Big Beau relayed the coordinates of a place he said was in town.

"Elijah told us about you. He was trying to set a trap for us, wasn't he?" Jessica asked.

"He doesn't know Jenn and I are close, so I figure he thought he was sending you to your demise. Nobody's going to find out you were here from me," Big Beau said. "Unless the gators start talking, I reckon no one will ever know."

He winked.

"Thank you." Jessica hugged Big Beau. Not because he would cover their tracks but because he cared about Jenn and had opened Jessica's eyes to a whole new side to her sister. Jenn had always come across as so confident, letting everything roll off her. Inside, she was far more fragile than Jessica realized and she wanted to protect her sister.

He seemed taken back by the gesture and stiffened. "Go

on, now. Find Jenn and get her out of the state until this whole mess settles down."

"Do you know James Milton?" she asked.

"He that no-good lawyer she messed with last year?" Big Beau asked.

"He tried to kill me when he thought I was Jenn," she supplied.

"I reckon lots of folks want to get their hands on that missing necklace," Big Beau said, his anger evident on his face. "That's a stupid move, though. Everyone knows Beauchamp wants it."

"I thought he might be working for him."

"Doubt it. He could be trying to get in his good graces, though," Big Beau said. "Or pay off a debt."

"He's a gambler," she said, remembering the news they'd received from the sheriff.

"Well then, he might be trying to get himself out of trouble," Big Beau said.

"My sister sent me with him as a distraction. She wanted him out of town. You know anything about that?" she asked.

"Sure don't."

"What else do you know about my sister?"

"Not much. She liked to mix with men who wore shiny shoes and fine suits. Most of them hang in the same crowd and do a little too much sharing. She didn't like to be reminded that she was really just one of us," Big Beau said. "A man with shiny shoes usually has a slick tongue in my experience."

Jenn must've liked having some reminders of her past because she'd made friends with Big Beau. Jessica was less trustful of men in general and rich men in particular. She'd seen the way prominent men manipulated others. That was half the reason she stuck around to run the

business she'd grown with her mother. Greed was power-
ful and she'd seen the damage firsthand.

"I best get back," Big Beau said. "Be careful who you
trust. Folks around here have a way of knowing each other.
Families, connections, they sometimes make no sense but
go way back."

"We will," Jessica reassured him, as if she needed to
be reminded there was no one she trusted besides Tyler
and Big Beau.

Tyler set the coordinates in his phone as Jessica started
toward the side of the SUV. She turned around to thank Big
Beau once again but he wasn't there. He'd already disappeared into the bush. The thought of making that journey
again sent a shiver down Jessica's spine.

TYLER HAD BEEN expecting another place near the swamps
and was shocked when he pulled into an upscale family
suburb with rows of white colonials. If Jenn was here, she
was being held in plain sight.

"You sure this is the right area?" Red asked, echoing
his sentiments.

"These are the coordinates." Tyler motioned to his
phone, which had been giving the directions aloud.

Tyler's ringtone sounded. He pulled to the side of the
road, turned off his lights and kept the engine idling. He
glanced at the screen. "It's my brother, Austin." He answered the call. "Yo, what's up, Ivy League?" His second
oldest brother had gone to college in the northeast, earning the nickname.

"Russ called me because you didn't show up this morning," Austin said. His voice sounded as though he'd only
been awake a few minutes. "Everything okay?"

Damn. Tyler had meant to touch base at the ranch and

ask someone to cover his area for the next few days. "Yeah, fine. Had a last-minute trip. Personal business."

"Lyndsey?"

An awkward tension filled the cab of the SUV. "No. That's long finished."

"You sure about that?" Austin pressed.

Now was not the time to discuss her.

"Positive. That the only reason you called?" Tyler didn't mean to sound defensive.

"Can a man check on his favorite brother?" Austin scoffed, his sense of humor intact. "This is what happens when people wake me up before the sun comes out, by the way."

Tyler chuckled. Austin was no early riser. "Yeah. I'm good, though. No need to worry about me."

"Then I won't stress about the stranger who's been asking around in town for Tyler O'Brien," Austin said.

"You catch a name?" Tyler asked as Jessica shot him a concerned look.

"All I know is Tommy called and said you were helping out a woman who was in trouble. Next thing I know a stranger is looking for you and you're not showing up to work, which I don't have to say is unlike you," Austin said, more than a hint of curiosity in his tone.

"Janis didn't tell you that I'm out of town?" Tyler asked, thankful he'd remembered to talk to her. He wanted to tell his brother what was going on but needed to speak to Jessica about it first.

"It must've slipped her mind," Austin said.

"In her defense, I called after I left and never said I'd be gone long."

"Give Tommy a call when you can. He didn't sound himself," Austin said.

"I plan to touch base with him after breakfast." It

wasn't a lie, even though Jessica shot him a cross look. She couldn't object to him bringing in Tommy after they found Jenn. Jessica's concern so far had been that whoever had her sister would kill her if the cops were chasing them. No one would get rid of her until they had that jewel.

"You hear about the Infinity Sapphire going missing?" Austin asked.

A pleading look came from the passenger seat. Jessica's hands folded into prayer position.

"I read something about it the other day." Playing dumb would only make Austin suspicious. He knew that Tyler read the newspaper every day, just as he did. They'd also had the Brasseuxs at the ranch, so Tyler would notice a story about the prominent family.

"I wondered about the Brasseuxs after the gala," Austin said.

"You did?" Tyler was shocked. He hadn't heard anything and his brother had been quiet up until now.

"I overheard him telling his wife that her spending was out of control," Austin said. "And then her necklace worth millions goes missing a couple months later."

"You think he was involved in an insurance scam?" Tyler wasn't sure if he should tell his brother that the Brasseuxs might be in trouble, but he was certain about that call to Tommy later. Maybe his friend had dug up more information.

"Who knows? The only thing I'm sure of is crossing them off the list for next year's gala." Austin chuckled and then paused when he didn't hear Tyler do the same.

Right. His comment was meant to be funny.

"You sure everything's okay?" Austin asked.

"Yeah. Why wouldn't it be?" Tyler tried to laugh it off. It was too much, too late but Austin didn't press.

"Get in touch with Tommy later. You have any idea when you'll be back at the ranch?" Austin asked.

"Couple of days should be enough to tie up a few loose ends here," Tyler said.

"I'll let everyone know." Austin paused. "Take care of yourself, brother. And call when you're ready to talk about it."

"I will." Tyler didn't like holding back from his family and the secrets were racking up. He ended the call and looked to Jessica. "Might be better to park here and walk to the end of the block."

The neighborhood had decent-sized yards and plenty of trees.

"Okay," Jessica said. She made a move for the door handle but stopped. "I'm sorry that you're lying to your family for me. I can tell how much it bothers you."

"It's—"

"Don't say that it's okay." Her hand came up in protest. "Because it's not fine for you to be dishonest with the people you love."

"I'd argue, but you're right. Austin understands and I didn't fool him for a second." He looked her in the eye. "And I need to make that call to Tommy later this morning. Right after we find your sister. I've thought this through and there's no reason not to tell him what's going on."

He really looked at her, expecting an argument.

"You're right. I want you to contact him as soon as we get my sister to safety," she said.

"He has no jurisdiction here, so whatever we're about to get ourselves into we're on our own anyway."

She nodded and brushed her hand against his arm. "Thank you for taking this risk for my family. If you want out, though, I'd totally understand."

"We've come too far for me to walk away now." He

was rewarded with a small smile—it was sweet and sexy at the same time.

There was very little security at the house. Tyler didn't want to tell Jessica his real fear, that none was necessary because Jenn wasn't perceived as a threat. She would be immobilized and he had no idea what physical condition she'd be in when they found her. He was prepared to carry her over his shoulder for the mile and a half walk to his SUV if that's what it took.

The sun would be up soon, so they had to move fast.

Tyler wished there was a way to prepare Jessica, to soften the blow of seeing her sister in such a vulnerable state as they closed the distance between the tree line and the house.

They could go in through the raised basement. Tyler pulled his gun and motioned for Jessica to do the same. He walked policeman-style, gun and flashlight drawn, down a half dozen stairs.

The door was locked but he'd had enough experience with barn doors to figure out how to pick it.

Inside, the place was dark and dingy, and the floor slanted downward, resulting in water pooling in one corner of the space. Tyler immediately looked for alternate exits in case the cellar door was no longer an option. An old wall that divided the space was half-torn down. The stairs leading to the main floor were old and wooden. There would be people up there. They couldn't go out that way.

Tyler scanned the room for any signs of life. A woman sat crumpled over in a corner of the room. Her head was slumped to one side, her neck at an odd angle and for a split second Tyler feared the worst.

Jessica let out a little gasp before seeming to catch herself and going silent as she hurried over. She dropped down next to the woman and cradled her face. "Jenn."

Chapter Thirteen

Tyler took a knee on the other side of Jenn and checked for a pulse. Relief washed over him when he got one. "She's alive."

Jenn's eyes fluttered open and she immediately drew back. A cut ran down the side of her left cheek and her right eye was swollen and bruised.

"Don't be scared. It's me. I'm taking you home," Jessica said soothingly.

It took a minute for Jenn's eyes to focus, but when they did she scrambled toward Jessica, hugging her sister around the neck. She was aware and that was a good thing.

Tyler glanced around the room. He was a little surprised they'd left her alone in the basement. The lock on the cellar door had been easy enough to pick. This was an upper class suburban neighborhood and they must not figure that anyone would tie this place to criminal activity. It was the kind of place where he half expected to find a grandma upstairs, having risen early and gathered vegetables to begin preparing the roux that would cook all day until used in a dish such as crawfish étouffée for supper.

"I'm going to pick you up and take you out of here," Tyler said.

Jenn pulled back, fearful, and shook her head. Her lips were dry, cracked and he wondered how long it had been since she'd had water. Getting her hydrated would be his first priority as soon as he got her out of there.

"It's okay, sweetie. This is my friend and he's here to help," Jessica said, her voice rising in panic. "What's wrong?"

Jenn shifted her position to reveal her ankles. Her feet had been tucked underneath her bottom so they'd missed the thick ropes around her ankles. Tyler followed the bindings to a three-inch PVC pipe climbing up the wall that disappeared into a hole in the ceiling. He pulled out his cell.

"What are you doing?" Jessica asked, placing her hand on his arm.

"Calling the police."

Jenn shook her head again and Tyler stopped, his finger hovering over the nine.

"I have no choice. I can't take a chance and I sure as hell can't leave you like this. We make any noise down here and I guarantee the room will fill with more men with guns than you can shake a stick at. What else do you think we should do?" he asked.

"I loved him," Jenn managed to say, her voice raspy and she sounded so tired. "Get the necklace. Keep it safe."

"Or we get you out of here, find the necklace together, and then go to police," Tyler said, using a tone that said he was done talking.

"No police. Not yet," Jenn insisted. "Not while it looks like I did this. Who would believe that I'm innocent?"

She had a good point. Currently, evidence pointed directly at her involvement.

"The truth will come out," Jessica soothed her sister. She was putting up a brave front but it was clear to Tyler that she was fighting to keep her emotions in check. "All anyone would have to do is look at you to know you're innocent."

"I go to the police and I'm dead," Jenn said, and it looked like it took an incredible amount of effort to speak.

Her statement was true and he couldn't deny it. She was afraid for good reason. Tyler tucked his phone into his pocket.

"Then we find a way to get you out of here and figure this out," Jessica said emphatically, obviously not wanting to upset her sister with the information about Elijah and Milton. "But I am not leaving you here. Do you understand me? I won't do it."

Tyler slid his arm around Jessica's waist, trying to soothe her.

She smiled up at him and then scooted closer to her sister and out of his reach.

"Where's Ashton?" Jenn whispered. It was barely loud enough for Tyler to hear.

"I don't know," Jessica said.

Tyler searched the space for something he could use to cut the rope. Seeing Jenn like this, defenseless and in a basement, he understood why they didn't think they'd need security and this was just what he'd feared. They were hiding her in plain sight and were confident...too confident?

Even so, the move was pretty brilliant if anyone asked Tyler, and he'd have to keep that in mind moving forward. These guys were clever career criminals and neither Jenn nor Jessica would be safe until those men were locked behind bars.

There was nothing around to use to free Jenn. The sun would be up soon. That meant someone would most likely be down to check on her.

Old houses were notorious for having pipes that ran nowhere. Was it possible that the PVC pipe she was attached to would be the same? He stood and ran his fingers as high as he could reach on the PVC pipe. The ceiling wasn't more than seven feet high so he could reach fairly far into the ceiling. He curled his index finger around the end of the pipe. Jackpot.

Tyler twisted the pipe but it wouldn't budge. There was probably twenty years of grime holding it together. He clamped his back teeth together and gave another twist, netting a little movement this time. Digging deep, he squeezed the pipe and turned. This time, it gave. He pulled apart the pipes by threading one through the ceiling. They could worry about the ropes later. His first priority was getting her out of there. He scooped her off the floor and raced toward the cellar door.

Jessica went first, pushing through the door and into the beginnings of sunlight.

Two men in an SUV with dark windows burst from the vehicle. Tyler cursed and he heard Jessica do the same. They must've been reporting to work because they hadn't been there fifteen minutes ago.

"Run and keep running. No matter what happens," he said, figuring they still had a chance if Jessica could get away. She would have to call the police then. Of course, with criminals this smart, he and Jenn would be hidden in a new location.

Tyler had no intention of going down without a fight.

"Stop," one of the men shouted.

Tyler didn't look back. He ran on burning legs. At this distance, the men would have to be spot-on shots to hit him, although he liked his odds less since he was a good-sized target. Once he got to the trees, *if* he got to the trees, it would be even more difficult for them to get off an accurate shot. They could circle back to their SUV once they got away from the men. Try running there now and the men would catch them before they could get Jenn inside.

He could get to the trees, but then what? If he could set

Jenn down, turn around and pull out his gun in time then maybe he could hold them off.

Carrying roughly a hundred and twenty pounds of woman put him at a distinct disadvantage. He chanced a glance behind. The men were closing in fast.

The trees were too far and he realized that there was no way he was going to make it in time. Either of the men could stop and fire at this point and have a good chance at hitting him. His best guess as to why they hadn't fired already was that they wanted Jenn alive because they assumed she knew where the necklace was hidden.

All his and Jessica's efforts to save Jenn wouldn't matter the second these guys caught up with them. He couldn't outrun them and he could hear their footsteps closing in.

The next second, Jessica spun around with her gun leveled. "Duck."

Tyler dropped to the ground, holding on to Jenn, whose arms were wrapped so tightly around his neck she was almost cutting off his ability to breathe.

A bullet split the air, Jenn screamed and Tyler half feared she'd been shot by mistake. He looked behind him to see the men had scattered in the opposite direction, running for cover. His chest shouldn't fill with pride for Jessica's quick thinking but it did. And he was darn grateful she wasn't a lousy shot or he might've ended up with a bullet in his skull.

He popped to his feet and blazed past her. "Let's go."

Only when they were deep in the woods and there was no sign of pursuit did he feel it was safe to stop and catch his breath. "Way to think on your feet back there."

Jessica smiled and it quickly faded as she put her arm around her sister. "I can't take her home. That's the first place they'll look. I have to figure out a way to warn our parents without telling them what's going on. And we need to stay out of sight until we sort this out."

Tyler waited for his breathing to slow before talking. "I can make sure your family is safe. I'll send someone to pick them up and take them away for an extended vacation. And I have the perfect place to hide while we figure this out. There are blind spots on my ranch and I know just where they are. We can pitch a tent on my land and stay under the radar."

"She's too weak and she needs medical care," Jessica said. "And these guys won't let up."

"I have other plans for her and those men with guns are exactly the reason we need to find a place to hunker down for a few days and give her time to recoup. She needs medical care and I know where she can get it and still be safe." He examined the cut on Jenn's face. "All the wounds are superficial so they'll heal quickly as long as there's no infection. In the meantime, I'd put money on the fact that necklace has to be somewhere in Texas and I'm betting it's near Bluff."

"Of course, that's why Milton believed me and took me there," Jessica said. "I guess he figured he'd get me to tell him where it was and then he'd take it back himself. And then he could collect a reward from Mr. Beauchamp or use it to get in his good graces."

"Gambling" was all Jenn managed to say. She needed water, food and a day's worth of rest before she could say much more. Nearly three days of who knew what conditions she'd been in other than the basement. The only good news was that she seemed otherwise healthy and should bounce back given a little time to recoup.

"What did you say?" Jessica asked, leaning closer.

"She said gambling. I'm guessing Milton's trouble had to do with a betting addiction," Tyler said.

Jenn nodded.

"But you didn't think he'd turn on you," Tyler clarified.

"No." A look of horror crossed Jenn's weary features as she looked at her sister. "I would never have—"

"I know. Don't try to talk right now. It's okay," Jessica soothed. "I know you would never put me in danger on purpose."

"We need to stay on the move," Tyler said as he moved toward Jenn. "And get her into the SUV."

He scooped her up and she wrapped her arms around his neck again. He'd rather go straight to Tommy than to the ranch. There was no doubt that Tyler could trust his longtime family friend. Jessica and Jenn seemed to have other ideas. He needed to help them see the light.

So far the only thing the three of them agreed on was getting Jenn out of the state and keeping her off the radar while she gained her strength. But Tyler had every intention of calling his friend. Jessica had green-lighted the connection before and nothing in their present circumstance changed his mind.

THE FLIGHT HOME was smooth as the morning sun settled in the sky. Jessica was grateful to have her sister back. During the flight she'd racked her brain to put the pieces together. Milton had obviously been in some kind of gambling trouble and when Jessica couldn't deliver the necklace, he'd tried to kill her, believing her to be Jenn.

Jessica had an endless list of questions…would Elijah realize Big Beau had allegiance to Jenn now that she'd escaped? Elijah had figured Jessica out. But who stole the necklace in the first place?

Everyone seemed to believe that Jenn knew where this multi-million-dollar necklace was, but she was too weak to talk. Answers would have to wait until she was hydrated and feeling better.

"Checked the weather in Bluff before we took off," Tyler said, interrupting her hamster-wheel of questions. "It should be in the low sixties for the next few days. Perfect camping weather."

Images of the last time she was on his land flashed through her thoughts. Of turning to find Milton standing there, rock in hand, ready to bash her head in. That image was burned into her brain.

After settling the airplane in the hanger, Tyler helped Jenn into the backseat of his SUV. She was moving a little better now that he'd removed the ropes from her ankles. He'd given her ibuprofen and water from his emergency kit and Jenn had slept during the flight home.

Jessica was grateful for Tyler. She couldn't imagine doing any of this alone—and yet hadn't she been alone her entire life? Sure, she'd had her sister and her parents, all people who leaned on her, but who did she have to depend on?

Without the Texas cowboy she had no idea where she would've ended up. Dead, she thought. She would've died if she'd been left underneath that ATV. A wild animal would've gotten to her or she would've wandered around on the property, lost, until she succumbed to dehydration or, if she'd survived long enough, starvation. The important thing was that she and Jenn were together and her sister would be okay.

Tyler took a call, walking around to the back of his SUV out of earshot. A pang of jealousy tore through her, which was silly. She had no designs on the cowboy, even though the few kisses they'd shared in the past twenty-four hours had left a piece of her thinking otherwise. Dating hadn't been a priority of late and especially since Brent.

It was more than his infidelity that pierced her chest. It was the fact that she'd so easily given her trust to him, and how willingly he'd stomped all over it. Was she that bad a judge of character?

It would seem so, because she'd misjudged her sister, as well. It had taken a stranger, Big Beau, to tell Jessica what she really meant to Jenn.

How strange was that?

"That was my brother Dallas. Someone in a suit is still asking around for me in town," Tyler said, rounding the SUV to where she was sitting in the passenger seat with the door open.

"Why would they want you?" Then it must've dawned on her. "They must've figured out that you were helping me."

"When your sister wakes up, we need to talk to her."

"Do you think she'll be safe with us?" she asked. "I'm worried about her. She's been mumbling something and I think she's out of it."

"I was planning to call Dr. McConnell to have Jenn examined. We could check her into the hospital under a fake name. I can send security to keep an eye on her 24/7 while we continue to investigate. I'm certain the doc will accommodate us without asking a lot of questions."

Jessica chewed on that thought for a minute. She liked the idea of having her sister in a facility where she could be properly cared for. Looking at her in this condition was a cause for serious stress. Would Jenn fight them on it? Could she? As it was, she could barely lift her head and her ramblings were becoming more frequent and less distinguishable.

"She'll get well faster in a place she can be looked after properly," he said with a convincing look.

"Okay. Let's do that. If we can get her to agree," she said.

"Her eyes have barely opened since Baton Rouge. I doubt she has any fight left inside her." Tyler had a point. He walked away, presumably to give her time to think about it.

Jessica looked in the backseat. Her sister was resting comfortably but she needed medical care in order to get better. What if infection set in or she was bleeding internally? She already favored her right side, moving carefully as if one of her ribs was broken. She needed X-rays and an IV.

But that would mean leaving her in the hospital.

The thought of not staying with Jenn hit Jessica like a two-by-four to the chest. But what choice did she have? It wasn't like Jenn was waking up. She could have a concussion or worse. Even though Jessica couldn't imagine walking away from her sister, she wouldn't deny her medical service or put her in danger because of her selfishness.

Fighting tears, she walked over to where Tyler stood forty feet away. No way was she going to let the handsome cowboy see her cry again. This was the right thing to do for her sister. "Signing my sister into the hospital under an assumed name is the best way to go. Can you arrange it?"

Tyler took her hand in his and tugged her toward him. She leaned into his strong chest and he wrapped his arms around her. And in that moment, crazy as it might sound, she felt safe.

"You're making the right call. She'll be well cared for in the hospital and it's the last place Milton or anyone else will look since you've already been there."

She nodded. "Plain sight."

"That's right," Tyler said. "I'll call Dr. McConnell and set everything up."

Jessica wiped a rogue tear. "It's hard to see her like this. She's normally so strong and willful."

"We'll get her the care she needs and you'll be back to your twin antics in a few days," he said, an obvious attempt to make her smile.

It worked.

Chapter Fourteen

Tyler pulled off the highway and then around the back of the Quick Gas Auto Mart on the outskirts of town where an ambulance waited. Dr. McConnell had insisted this would be the best and safest way to transport Jenn to the hospital, and he figured she was right on both counts.

Jenn could begin receiving fluids immediately and, given that she was severely dehydrated, that should make a big difference in her general health. Glancing at Jessica as he parked had him wondering if she would be able to walk away from her sister. Agony darkened her features and she was chewing on her thumbnail.

"They're going to take good care of Jenn and the doc said she'd call the minute your sister wakes up and is ready to talk," he said to reassure her, hoping she wouldn't change her mind at the last minute.

"You're right," she conceded. "It's just hard to leave her again."

Tyler waved the EMTs over. Andy and Shanks greeted Tyler as they went right to work helping Jenn out of the SUV and positioning her on the gurney.

Jessica was at her sister's side as Jenn's eyes fluttered open again.

"You're going to the hospital," Jessica said.

Jenn barely nodded.

"Everything's going to be okay and I'll see you very soon," Jessica reassured, rubbing her sister's arm.

Jenn opened her mouth to speak but looked as though she lost the energy. She took in a ragged breath and mouthed, *Love you.*

"Love you," Jessica parroted.

"We'll take good care of her, man, I promise," Shanks said to Tyler, looking from Jessica to Jenn. Tyler could almost see the question mark in his mind at the resemblance between the two.

Tyler patted Shanks on the back. "I know you will. And we'd appreciate it if you kept my involvement between us for now. In fact, if you could keep quiet about this whole thing."

"Doc mentioned something about this being tied to a criminal case and her being a witness, but that's all she could say." Andy's eyes got wide and sparkly with excitement. He lowered his tone when he said, "Is she going into the witness protection program or something?"

"I'd like to tell you more but I'm sworn to silence," Tyler said, trying to sound disappointed. He didn't want to quell Andy's excitement, and figured his response would serve as a good reminder of how top secret this had to be.

"Right-o." Andy nodded and wheeled the gurney to the back of the ambulance with a satisfied smile.

As soon as Jenn was out of sight, tears started rolling down Jessica's face. Tyler glanced around, feeling exposed in their current location. He hugged her before ushering her into the SUV.

"Why do I feel like I'm never going to see her again?" Jessica said, wiping the tears from her face as she apologized. "I'm sorry. I'm not usually a crier."

"Never say you're sorry for showing your emotions,"

he said. Tyler had been an expert at stuffing his below the surface for too many years.

"I've always been the strong one, you know. It's why my sister always comes to me and this makes me feel weak." She motioned toward a rogue tear sliding down her cheek.

"Crying doesn't make you any less strong. Tears are just saltwater. The ocean is filled with it and that doesn't take away from its magnitude. Real strength means pushing through your boundaries when you're afraid and never giving up. Trust me when I say you have that in spades."

She smiled through red-rimmed eyes. "Thank you."

Tyler started the engine and navigated onto the highway, heading home. His heart fisted in his chest. He was in trouble. And this time, going home had a new meaning. Rather than rack his brain trying to crack that nut, he fisted the steering wheel and focused on something that made sense…the road in front of him.

"You're quiet all of a sudden," Jessica said.

"I just have a lot on my mind." It was partially true. Tyler couldn't stop thinking about Jessica and wasn't it his trick to shut down emotionally when he got close to someone or something he wanted? But then he hadn't wanted anything like he wanted her in his life and it confused the hell out of him.

Another thing he didn't want to think about right then.

Tyler decided to take her to the easternmost tip of the property, furthest from his house, where people would least expect him to be. His SUV was made for off-roading and he'd need it to reach the location. The drive took another two hours. Jessica leaned her seat back and rested for the ride. He almost woke her half a dozen times to tell her that he was confused and wanted to sort out what was going on in his mind, but he stopped himself. She needed the rest and he liked having her there.

"This location will be out of the way for most of the ranch business and should keep us flying under the radar," he said when she finally sat up.

Pitching a tent didn't take long. He'd decided on camping next to Hollow's Lake, figuring they'd need a water source if they were going to be out there for a few days. This land wasn't near where they kept the cattle and therefore no one would be riding fences. There were no hunts scheduled on this side of the property in the month of November, so unless something had changed they'd be good. He had cursory supplies, including toiletries, in his SUV at all times in case he wanted to spend the night out on the range and sleep under the stars, which had happened often since hearing the news about his parents.

He built a campfire and offered Jessica a protein bar before making coffee.

"I'm impressed," she said, taking a sip.

"What you're tasting is the result of years of trial and error." He laughed.

"It's even more than that," she said, and he knew exactly what she was talking about. "What is it about a beautiful landscape that makes everything taste so much better?"

"Fresh air does something to food and drink."

She nodded. "Thank you for taking care of my sister."

"No problem," he said, but he could see that it was a huge deal to her.

JESSICA DIDN'T WANT to like the handsome cowboy any more than she already did. As soon as they figured out who was behind this crime and could prove it to the law she'd go back to Shreveport and running the family business so she could resume taking care of her parents. The thought made her sad. Not the part about taking care of her parents, but returning to Shreveport. The place no longer felt like home and the job had never before felt so lonely.

Could she convince Jenn to come home?

Jenn? Come home?

Jessica almost laughed out loud. Her sister hadn't been able to wait to get out of Shreveport. If Baton Rouge was no longer an option, and Jessica was pretty sure it wasn't, then maybe Jenn could get a fresh start in Houston or San Antonio.

Thinking about her sister brought on too much sadness, so she pushed those unproductive thoughts aside for now and tried to clear her head with another sip of coffee. They needed to figure out why Jenn was being set up.

"Have you heard from Zander?" she asked.

"He was released from the hospital last night and is doing fine." He sat staring with his back to the sun.

Had a wall come up between them? When Jessica really thought about it, Tyler clammed up every time they got close. What was that all about? He had feelings for her, or at the very least an attraction, and yet he shut down every time they tried to act on it. She made a mental note to ask him about it. Maybe it had something to do with his past.

"Did you really play pro baseball?" she asked, remembering a conversation with Zander.

"Yep."

"And what happened?"

"Nothing." He rubbed his right shoulder, a move she'd seen him make several times when they'd done something physical.

"Everything okay?" She motioned toward the spot where his hand was rubbing.

He stopped midrub. "Peachy."

She pushed to her feet, unsure what she'd done to make him stop talking to her. All of a sudden they were at one-word answers and he looked uncomfortable. "I'm going for a walk."

"You want company?"

"No." What had happened? One minute he was comforting her and now they were barely speaking. What was up with that?

Jessica pushed those thoughts aside as she walked toward the lake. Every step away from Tyler was a giant leap toward being completely stressed. How had she become so dependent on a stranger in just a few short days?

Anger and frustration formed a tight ball in her chest, making breathing hurt. She had no right to feel this way about him and she needed to walk it off. Heck, she didn't want to feel this way about any man. And yet she couldn't deny that was exactly what was happening.

So the handsome cowboy had done a few nice things for her. Let's face it, his actions were nothing short of heroic. But that didn't mean she had to put up with his rollercoaster emotions—one minute on and the next keeping her at a safe distance.

At least this was better than her relationship with Brent. He'd been practiced and cool the whole time. He knew exactly the right words to say to throw her off the trail if she was suspicious…and it had all been one big act so she wouldn't catch him cheating.

Jessica paced from a mesquite tree to the lake's edge a few times before she looked up and realized that Tyler was standing right there watching her. She let out a little yelp before she could quash it. "What are you doing sneaking up on me like that?"

"I'm sorry." His wry grin belied the sincerity in those words.

"Great. The man *can* put two words together," she quipped and then regretted saying what she was thinking. She should probably bow at the man's feet for how much he was helping her family, so why did she want to claw his eyes out right now instead?

There he stood, silent, for a long moment with his arms crossed as he leaned against a tree.

Jessica would be damned if she spoke first. Two could play at that game, so she planted her fisted hands on her hips and stared right back.

"You want to scream or something? Go ahead. No one will hear you out here," he said, as if he dared her to.

His stance was casual. Hers was aggressive. *Well, get used to it, buddy.* She had no plans to back down from a challenge.

"I would if it would help," she shot back. "Can't see how that'll make it easier to be around you, though."

"*I'm* the problem?" He almost sounded sincere but damned if that grin wasn't plastered into place on his face. It was sexy, she had to give him that, but a little sexy—okay a lot sexy!—wasn't about to make her cave. Besides, she was getting whiplash from his mood swings. One minute his hands were all over her, making her want things she hadn't felt before. And then the next he couldn't put enough distance or a bigger wall between them.

"Glad you see this from my point of view," she said, knowing full well his was a question not a statement. Well, he'd put it out there.

The smile faded from his lips and his hand flew behind his back at a sound behind her. "Get down."

She dropped to all fours at the exact time his gun came around and leveled at a spot where her head had been seconds before. A bullet cracked the air as fire flared from the tip of his barrel.

"Stay down," Tyler said, already on the move.

Jessica pulled her gun and crouched behind the tree

where Tyler had been a few moments before, hoping to get a look at what he'd seen. She scanned the area next to the lake, the direction he'd fired, and couldn't see anyone. And now that it was getting dark, she'd lost sight of Tyler in the trees.

If anyone came near her, she'd have no qualms about shooting.

A few shots were fired at least forty feet away. She whirled toward the sound, trying to keep her hands from shaking as she gripped the gun and kept alert.

Rustling noises came from the same direction. Rather than move into the dangerous area, she maintained position. She wanted to call out to Tyler but did not want to compromise his position or hers. A thought crossed her mind. She was crouched in the spot from which he'd fired a few minutes ago. Her position was already compromised. She needed to move.

Staying low, she crawled toward the water.

It was eerie how everything had gone quiet.

Jessica sat near the water's edge, looking at her reflection in the moonlight. Still no sign of movement around her.

She completely stilled, quiet, for several minutes that dripped by like hours.

A hand touched her shoulder at the same time as he spoke. "It's okay."

She nearly jumped out of her skin. Using the momentum, she spun around on him. "It most certainly is not. I could've shot you."

That wry grin parted his lips. "You're not fast enough."

She let that slide, ignoring the sour taste in her mouth that came with knowing he was right.

Chapter Fifteen

"What happened? Who were you shooting at?" Jessica asked, trying to calm her fried nerves.

"I saw movement in the bush and something charged toward me. Turned out to be a wild hog," he said.

Tyler O'Brien was no doubt capable of handling any situation he came across, but Jessica couldn't ignore the fact that the cowboy lit up more of her senses than was good for either one of them.

Another noise sounded behind her. Jessica jumped and scrambled into his arms.

"Don't tell me you're afraid of a hog?" he asked, leaning back to get a better look at her.

"You're not?" she asked.

"They're mean but, trust me, I can be worse. I'm not going to let anything happen to you," he said and his voice was gravelly. "But *this* isn't a good idea."

"What?" she asked, but she was being coy. "Is *this*?" She reached up on her tiptoes and pressed a light kiss to his lips. Sure, she was frustrated with him and she figured half the reason their frustrations had built to this degree was all the sexual tension crackling around them every time he got near her. It was crazy and impulsive but all she could think about was the feel of his arms around her and how right everything felt when she was this close to him.

His heart thundered against her chest, its rhythm matching hers.

He closed his eyes and took a deep breath. "I can't stop whatever's going on between us and it scares the hell out of me."

"You don't have to be in control all of the time," she countered. "Maybe it's time we both let go."

With that, he closed his arms around her and pressed her body flush with his.

"I'm glad you feel that way, because this thing between us seems to have a mind of its own," he said. "I'm tired of fighting it."

A trill of need blasted through Jessica. "Those are the best words I've heard all day."

He dipped his head and claimed her mouth. She parted her lips and his tongue slid inside, tasting her, needing her.

Tyler picked her up and carried her to the tent. He set her down long enough to pull the sleeping bag outside, under the stars.

She shrugged out of her shirt, dropping it onto the ground, and he groaned when he saw her blue lace bra.

All it took was one step for him to be there, his hands on her breasts as her nipples beaded beneath the silk undergarment. He paused long enough to look into her eyes and she was certain he was searching for reassurance.

No words were needed as she tugged at the hem of his shirt. His joined hers on the ground a moment later and then his lips were on her neck, slowly moving down. He stopped at the heartbeat at the base of her neck, feathering little kisses there, and then slicked his tongue down the line between her breasts.

Her breath came out in little gasps as he explored her sensitized skin. She planted her hands firmly on either side of his shoulders to stop him.

"What? What's wrong?" he asked, and his voice was low.

"We're wearing too many clothes," she said, already grabbing for his zipper.

He shimmied out of his jeans and she did the same. Her bra came off a few seconds later and joined the other clothes on the ground.

Tyler stopped, his eyes dark and hungry, and looked at her. "You're beautiful."

"So are you," she said, tracing a line down the muscles in his chest. He was like touching silk over steel, raw power in physical form.

His hands roamed her breasts and she liked the rough feel of his fingers on her skin.

Her breath caught as he slipped her matching blue silk-and-lace panties down the sides of her hips with achingly slow movements.

She tugged his boxers off next and took a second to admire his glorious body in the moonlight. He was muscle and hotness with just the right amount of gruffness to be irresistibly sexy…damn. There was so much more to Tyler O'Brien than a hot body, although he had that in spades. He was warm, intelligent and caring…a potent combination. And she was hooked.

When this was all over and he walked away, the pain was going to be beyond anything she'd ever known…but she had tonight. And a little part of her mind told her she'd held back too long. She needed to take what she wanted… and she wanted the hot cowboy. Hurt would eventually heal and she would have this memory for the rest of her life.

Jessica made a move toward Tyler but he stopped her.

"I'm not done looking at you," he warned, naked and glorious.

She should be embarrassed but there was something about his presence that made her feel completely at ease.

She glanced down at the makeshift bed on the ground, smiled, and then took off running in the other direction, straight to the water.

The cool lake practically sizzled against her burning skin.

Tyler was behind her in the next moment, spinning her to face him. She wrapped her legs around his waist and eased him inside her.

"You're going to destroy me," he said, his muscles taut as he thrust deeper inside her.

"In the best possible way," she said. "Now shut up and kiss me."

He did kiss her, his tongue thrusting inside her mouth as he filled her with his erection. One hand splayed against her bottom, the other pressed and tugged at one nipple then the other until she shattered into a thousand tiny pieces around him.

And then he detonated inside her as they, bare-naked skin to bare-naked skin, held each other in the moonlight.

TYLER WOKE BEFORE light peeked over the horizon, feeling a little too refreshed. There was a chill in the air that didn't penetrate his warm body—warm because of the woman in his arms. And a big part of him wanted to stay right there and hold her for as long as he could.

Good news about Jenn's condition would be a welcome relief for Jessica and he wanted to deliver it first thing. He needed to move to a spot on the north corner of the lake where he could check his cell phone.

Slowly, so he wouldn't wake her, he untangled their arms and legs with a satisfied smile. Last night had been right up there with…no, had been *the* best sex of his life.

When they sorted out Red's situation they needed to have a conversation about seeing each other on a regular basis, explore where this could go. He picked a few supplies out of his pack and moved to the water. After brushing his teeth, he replaced the supplies and hiked to the other side of the lake.

His first phone call would be to Dr. McConnell. It was early but she'd be up making rounds. He walked along the lake, checking various spots for bars until he got at least three. Immediately his cell phone started buzzing and dinging. Fifteen missed calls and a half dozen text messages. Not good.

The first was from the doc. She was direct, as usual, saying that hospital security had been breached and her patient had gone missing.

Tyler immediately phoned.

"It happened an hour ago," she said, not bothering wasting time on perfunctory greetings. "I had to call the sheriff."

That second statement was a given. Jessica might be upset at first but she'd see that the doc had no choice.

"What did Tommy say?" he asked.

"He figured it was connected to the murder at the motel. I didn't link you to my patient. That's between you and Tommy," she said.

"What was her condition?" Jessica needed to know what they were dealing with. "Tell me in layman's terms."

"She'd had two bags of saline, so she was rehydrating. Overall, I've seen worse but I don't like her being gone before I had a chance to evaluate all her injuries." The doctor hesitated for a second. "How's her sister?"

"What gave her away?" Tyler asked.

"She doesn't have the same bruising on her arms, for one," Dr. McConnell said. "That was the first tell."

He should've known. "I apologize for not being up front.

This situation is sticky and some information wasn't mine to share."

"You have your reasons," she said quickly. "I've known you a long time and I trust they're good ones."

He thanked her and asked if he could see the security footage.

"I'll have someone drop a copy of the feed off at the ranch," she said. "It would be best if you stayed away from here for now."

"Understood."

"On that note, the images are grainy. We don't have a need for high-tech security here so the equipment's old," she said.

"How many people are we talking here?" he asked, hoping to get a better frame around who they might be dealing with.

"Just one," she said, and there was an ominous quality to her tone.

"Did you recognize him, by chance?" he asked.

"I'd swear it was the man visiting her sister the other day."

James Milton.

"I better get ahold of Tommy and see what he's found so far." And he needed to come clean to his close friend. The best way to help Red and her sister was to lay all the cards on the table. On second thought, he'd shoot a text asking Tommy to meet at the cabin. It would be easier to explain everything with Red there.

"I'm here if you need anything," Dr. McConnell said.

"We'll be out of cell range for a bit this morning. You hear anything or if anyone connected to this shows up at the hospital, I'd appreciate a heads-up."

"Already have you on speed dial." She paused. "At the risk of sounding motherly, be careful."

"You know I will," he said before ending the call.

Tyler made a beeline toward the tent. Jenn had gone missing and Milton had her. Tyler had miscalculated the man and her disappearance was on his head.

Jessica needed to know.

Chapter Sixteen

Tyler didn't like the idea of waking Red before she'd had a chance to get a proper night's rest, but this news couldn't wait. They needed to regroup and come up with a plan to find her sister, now. "I have news."

She blinked her eyes open.

"We need to talk," he said, kissing her on the forehead.

Red sat up, yawned and rubbed her eyes. "What's up?"

Bad news got worse with age so he didn't wait for the right words to come. "A man breached hospital security an hour ago and managed to get away with your sister."

The look of shock and horror playing out on her face fisted his chest. He'd let her down in the worst possible way.

"Who? How?" she asked, wide-eyed.

"I can't say for certain. Dr. McConnell is sending security films to the house. If we pack up now we should be there around the same time." Tyler was already gathering supplies. "She was doing better because she was getting hydrated, but doc said she didn't get a chance to get a full workup yet."

"And, let me guess, they have no idea who took her?" she asked again.

He looked her directly in the eyes. "Doc's pretty certain it was James Milton."

Panic crossed her features as she scrambled to her feet. "What do we need to do?"

"Pack up and go home."

Within ten minutes, the campfire had been tamped, the SUV packed and they were on the road. Tyler drove across the property, calling ahead to security to alert them he was coming. His next call was to his brother Austin.

"We have a situation and need to send out an alert to security," Tyler said as soon as his brother answered. "The woman I've been helping, Jessica, her sister is missing and they're both in danger. Everyone should stay vigilant and be on the lookout for Jessica's twin sister and a white male. If people want a visual, I'll be at my place in the next twenty minutes. I'm coming up from Hollow's Lake."

"I'll let everyone know. Dallas is in town this morning so I'll text him the situation. He'll want to meet up with us. The twins are in the barn so they'll be easy to round up. I'm not sure where Colin is, but he'll want to know what's going on and pitch in to help," Austin said.

Joshua, the youngest twin, had been traveling back and forth to his job in Colorado. He'd been having the most difficult time with the transition to rancher, given that he loved his job in law enforcement. Tyler was glad to have the extra help. He thanked his brother even though he knew Austin wouldn't see it as necessary. "I'll see you in a few."

"We're all here for you. Just let us know what you need and we'll make it happen," Austin said. "In the meantime, I'll watch your back as you enter from the south end of the property."

Tyler ended the call with the push of a button on his steering wheel. Red didn't immediately speak.

She finally leaned forward and said, "I didn't know there were twins in your family."

It was a distraction from the helplessness they both felt

being in the SUV driving home rather than being there to save her sister.

"The youngest boys, Ryder and Joshua," he said.

"Now I get why you seem to understand twins so well," she said with a hollow quality in her voice. She was talking, going through the motions, but her heart wasn't in the conversation.

He understood. Sometimes people needed to do something to keep busy or they'd go crazy. Given the current situation, Red had every right to be distant. And he had another bomb to drop on her. "Tommy's going to be at the cabin when we arrive."

Red shot a look at him.

"I didn't tell him anything. I said that I wouldn't go behind your back and I didn't. But he has to be involved now. He has resources that can help find your sister."

She started to put up more of a fight but seemed to lose steam as she blew out a defeated-sounding sigh.

"Whatever it takes to get my sister back alive," she said quietly. "I'll do anything to make sure she's safe."

JESSICA COULD BARELY BREATHE. Ever since she'd heard the news about her sister it felt as if the air had thinned and the walls were closing in on her. If Milton had gotten to her, and it had to be him, then Jenn was as good as dead. The man had a violent background and nothing to lose. There would be no incentive to keep Jenn alive if she didn't cooperate.

Based on her sister's condition, Jessica wasn't sure if her sister would be coherent enough to say where the necklace was even if she did know.

And what if she knew exactly where the necklace was? What if she'd figured it out? If she told Milton, he'd kill her and dump the body just as ruthlessly as he'd tried before.

"You said you were going to take care of my parents."

"They're on a ranch in Montana," Tyler said.

"My dad's always wanted to go fly-fishing," she said wistfully, trying to absorb all the information coming at her.

"That's how we convinced him to leave. Also, he thinks his daughters are joining him there for Thanksgiving."

"Does he know about all this? He and mother will be so worried," she said.

"Thinks you two arranged the trip with the caveat they had to leave immediately," Tyler said, and there was a sad quality to his tone.

"I'm more than happy to reimburse you for the expenses," she offered.

"It's not that. He sounds like a decent man and I hated lying to him," he said.

Their worlds had never felt so different. She and her sister were running from the law while Tyler's best friend was the sheriff. He was a good person who stepped in to help when most would run the other way. Would she do the same for a stranger? She liked to think she would, but then she'd never been asked to dodge bullets for anyone before.

But that was for her blood, her sister. No matter how crazy things got, Tyler stayed the course and offered his life to help. She thought about how much she'd been asking of him, forcing an honest man to lie to the people he loved, and a hard knot formed in her stomach.

"You can take me to the sheriff's office to file a report and leave me there. You've done enough for my family," she started, but his hand came off the steering wheel long enough to stop her.

"Don't push me away." His fingers closed around hers as he temporarily steered with one hand.

Was she?

"Every time we get close, you tell me to leave," he continued. "There's only one thing you need to know about a Texan—we don't quit when life gets tough."

Those words, his support, wrapped around her, bathing her in warmth. She couldn't deny his point. Every time they got close and she started opening up, she found a reason to shut down. He'd never left her side. "I don't know how to let go of the feeling that you're going to walk away at some point."

"I can't promise forever, but I do know that I've never felt like this about anyone before," he said.

"Me, too. That's exactly what I'm afraid of."

"Can you take a step back once we get Jenn back and life returns to normal and see where this leads?" he asked as he pulled into an area that finally looked familiar.

"I don't know," was all she could say. He deserved the truth.

"Do me a favor," he said.

"If I can."

"Don't make any decisions right now." He pulled into the garage, turned off the engine and held on to the key. He didn't make a move to get out of the SUV. "Not while everything's turned upside down."

For her own protection, she needed to tell him that was impossible. That she'd already made her choice…to go home and try to forget everything that had happened these past few days. And yet it would be impossible not to remember last night.

Before he could say anything to change her mind, Jessica opened the door and stepped out of the SUV.

They came from two different worlds, knew very little about each other, and trying to convince herself they could somehow magically make it all work would be foolish.

"The door's unlocked," he said, moving from the driver's side.

She walked in and forced her thoughts away from the feeling that this was home. It wasn't home. Home was with her parents in Shreveport.

He grabbed her elbow as she crossed into the kitchen, spun her around and pinned her against the wall.

"I get that you've lost a lot and that you're scared. But give us a chance." His steady gaze, those dark eyes—she could lose all sense of time. Even forget how messed up her life was right then.

The doorbell rang.

He didn't move and she didn't speak.

"I'll take that to mean you're at least thinking about what I said."

She looked away. No way could she look into those eyes any longer with what she was prepared to do.

An urgent knock sounded at the front door. No doubt it was the sheriff. She'd most likely be arrested for lying to an officer of the law. Would Tyler still want to have anything to do with her then? He wasn't thinking clearly.

He kissed her anyway, slow and sweet. She molded against him.

"Tyler, I saw you drive in," the sheriff said through the door.

Tyler pressed his forehead to hers and closed his eyes.

The next thing she knew, he'd gone into the other room and opened the door. The sheriff walked in first, followed by three men who looked related to Tyler, and a woman.

"I'm Stacy," she said, offering a hand.

Jessica took it and then the tears came.

Stacy pulled her into a hug. "It's going to be okay, you hear me? These men will find your sister and bring her back safe and sound. They're good men and they'll look out for you."

Those words were soothing, and a sense of calm radiated from Stacy.

"Thank you," Jessica said softly. She took a fortifying breath and straightened her shoulders.

Thankfully, the men had moved into the kitchen, gathering around the granite island and passing out mugs of coffee.

"These are my brothers, Austin, Ryder and Joshua," Tyler said.

"Dallas is on his way and Colin must be out of cell range," one of the men said. She recognized the voice as the one on the phone, so he had to be Austin.

"Nice to meet everyone." Each shook her hand and it was easy to guess who the twins were based on the fact that they looked so much alike.

They huddled around the coffeepot as Tyler moved to her side and took her hand.

No one made her feel the way Tyler did. And a big part of her didn't feel worthy of that kind of love. Wow. Was that why she took care of everyone around her? She didn't feel like she deserved real love?

Before she could talk herself out of holding Tyler's hand, he put his arm around her and she leaned into his strength. It was time to bite the bullet and own up to her fraudulence. "I haven't been completely honest with you, sheriff. My name is Jessica and I've been covering for my twin sister, Jennifer."

"I know," Tommy said, and she almost thought she didn't hear him correctly. She must've shot him one wild look because he put his hand up. "I didn't at first, but I started piecing things together and when I dug into your sister's background and found you everything snapped into place."

"I understand if you need to arrest me or something," she said. "But I'd appreciate it if you let me help find my sister first."

The sheriff made a face. "Arrest you? For what? Being a witness to a crime?"

Tyler squeezed her and she'd never felt more safe in someone's arms. But her sister was out there with a crazed man who had nothing to lose.

"Tell us what you know," Tyler said to the sheriff.

"We've been able to ascertain that James Milton owes Randall Beauchamp a large sum of money. His interest in the Infinity Sapphire is twofold—clear his debt and get enough money to start fresh somewhere else. He's been studying for a real estate license in Nevada, so my guess is that he's been planning his exit from Baton Rouge for a while."

"So, we know that he's involved and that Jenn was set up. Why does everyone think she knows where the necklace is?" Tyler asked.

"Because she does," Jessica said. "She might not even know it, but she does. It's the only thing that makes sense."

"What do you mean?" Tyler asked, clearly confused.

A picture was finally emerging. "Jenn said that Milton kept asking about the box. Maybe Ashton asked her hide something for him but she may not have known what it was."

"It would also mean that she trusted the person who gave it to her," Tyler said. "And we already know she was having an affair with Ashton."

One of the brothers set up a laptop on one side of the island and plugged in a thumb drive. "This is the footage from the hospital."

It was grainy, just as they'd been told, but it was so obvious that the person walking out was not James Milton. "That's Ashton Brasseux."

"How can it be? He and his wife, Emma-Kate were kidnapped," Tyler said, and then it dawned on him. "Or so he wanted everyone to think."

Jessica sipped from the mug she'd been handed earlier.

"Local police did some digging and found out that the Brasseuxs were having a little money trouble. Ashton and Emma-Kate were separating and she believed that he was seeing someone else," the sheriff said.

"My sister," Jessica said quietly. Jessica turned her full attention to the sheriff. "I know how this looks. All evidence points to Jenn taking the sapphire or at the very least being involved in stealing and hiding it. Other people seem to believe the same thing, bad people, but I know in my heart that my sister would never do that. She was in love with Ashton Brasseux and he set her up."

"I have to follow the evidence," the sheriff said. "But I promise to look at all the facts and keep an open mind."

She smiled, nodded. Under the circumstances, he was being generous. "Thank you."

"What's our next step?" Tyler asked. "We know that Jenn is in danger and we need to find her."

Tommy nodded.

"Do you know anything about the person who has been asking around for me?" Tyler asked.

"I tracked him down and he was an investigator for the Brasseux's insurance company," the sheriff said. "We just need to make sure he stays out of the way."

"Any chance that necklace is here on the property?" Tyler asked.

The doorbell rang.

Tyler excused himself and answered the door. "Janis, come in."

"I brought food," she said, carrying a full basket of muffins and pastries.

"Let me take that," he said, and she seemed to know better than to argue.

Janis followed Tyler into the kitchen. Her gaze moved around the island, stopping on Jessica.

"Good morning, Mrs. Templeton," Janis said. "I didn't know you were here."

Jessica shot Tyler a look. "I'm sorry, have we met?"

Janis stared, openmouthed. "You were here a couple of weeks ago with your husband."

"I'm afraid that I have no idea what you're talking about," Jessica said, but the light went on at the same time Austin turned the laptop around.

"Who'd she come with?" Austin asked.

"Her husband," Janis said, confusion knitting her eyebrows. "But I must be mistaken."

"Does Mr. Templeton look like this?" Austin asked, angling the screen toward Janis.

"Why, yes. It's a little blurry but that's him," she said emphatically.

"Which means that Jenn and Ashton came here, and Milton must've known she would come back to a place where they'd already been," Tyler said, and the sheriff nodded.

Tyler poured another cup of coffee. "Do you remember any details about their booking?"

"It's been a couple of weeks. Let me think," Janis said as he handed her a mug.

Hope blossomed for the first time since this whole ordeal started. If Jenn had been taken by Ashton, surely she'd be safe. If he loved her, he wouldn't do anything bad to her. Would he?

The man stole a family heirloom from his wife and gave it to his mistress to hide, promising her they'd be together forever. The short-lived burst of hope immediately died.

"If he gets the necklace, he'll hurt her," Jessica said. "We have to find them first."

"Is THERE ANYTHING specific you remember about the couple?" Tyler asked Janis.

"They stayed in their room most of the time. Didn't book a hunting trip, I remember that for sure because I thought it was odd this time of year," Janis said. "I remembered thinking that they must be honeymooners."

Reality hit Tyler harder than a ton of bricks. "She hid the necklace in the main house."

The sound of bar stools scraping across tile echoed as everyone stood at the same time.

"I can check the registry and tell you which room they stayed in," Janis offered, and they were already making a move toward the door.

"We'll tear the place apart if we have to," Austin said.

As soon as the group left, Jessica said, "They won't be on the property. We might find the necklace, but with security here he's not stupid enough to risk coming straight at us. He'll take her somewhere else until he comes up with a plan."

"First, let's get the necklace. That's the best thing we can do to ensure your sister's safety. He won't do anything to her if he thinks she's useful."

She followed Tyler to the garage where he fired up the SUV and backed out.

The drive to the main house took ten minutes. Denali was on the front porch waiting.

"Hey, buddy," Tyler said as the chocolate lab trotted over to greet him.

"I'll just check the registry," Janis said.

The main house was set back, but they could see the road from the porch. An older model, white four-door Mazda pulled up in front of the gate, someone was pushed out and the car sped off.

"It's her," Jessica shouted. "It's Jenn."

Chapter Seventeen

Tyler darted toward Jenn as the guards in the shack bolted outside. "She's clear. She's with us."

Most of the house emptied, with all the boys running close behind Jessica, and she had never felt so protected and secure in her life.

"Jenn," she said as she dropped down beside her sister, who was folded onto her side. She wore a jacket over her shirt, which was odd considering the weather had warmed up.

"Go," Jenn whispered, looking too weak to move. She made a grunting noise before repeating the word.

Sheriff Tommy knelt next to Jenn, his gaze sweeping over her. "Everyone back away."

"I'm not going anywhere," Jessica said, just as she noticed sweat beads on Jenn's forehead. She wiped them away. "It's okay. I'm here now and I won't let those men hurt you."

Jenn winced as she shook her head. "Go."

Her sister was weak and clearly not thinking straight. Jessica had no idea what those jerks had done to her sister but she hoped they rotted in jail for their crimes. She vaguely heard the sheriff in the background giving a description of the vehicle that had sped away.

"Everyone needs to step away," he said, unzipping Jenn's jacket to reveal a bomb strapped to her body.

Tears fell freely as Jessica held on to her sister's hand. "I'm not leaving you."

There was a piece of white paper sticking out of her jacket pocket. Jenn angled her head toward it.

"Sheriff—" Jessica started but was cut off.

"I see it. Everyone needs to get back," the sheriff demanded, leaving no room for doubt that he was serious.

The brothers did as instructed, except for Tyler. He didn't budge.

"I have protocol to follow, Tyler," the sheriff said.

"And I have my loyalties," Tyler retorted.

"If you're not going to make this easy, then scoot over so I can take a closer look," the sheriff said. He took out a pair of something that looked like tweezers and put on rubber gloves. He removed the folded piece of paper and peeled it open.

"It's easy. We get the necklace or she goes boom. You have one hour to leave it where you found her sister. No cops."

"He used the term *we*," the sheriff said. "We're dealing with a network."

"Which one of these guys has experience with explosives?" Tyler said.

"Chemical engineer," Jenn managed to say. "Ashton."

Everyone reacted to the news.

"She needs medical help." Jessica fought back tears as she whispered reassurances to Jenn.

The sheriff leaned back on his heels and evaluated the situation. "Ashton must be our guy. He's in charge."

Heads bobbed in agreement.

Tyler glanced up at his brothers and shooed them back into the house to search for the piece of jewelry.

"They must think we already have the necklace," Tyler said. "We'd have to hightail it to drive to Diablo's Rock in an hour. I can get there on Digby in forty-five minutes."

"Someone needs to show up whether we have the necklace or not," the sheriff said. "It'll be our best chance to nab them."

"They'll be watching for police," Jessica said. "We mess this up and they'll push the button."

"They can do that anyway once they get the necklace," Tyler warned, and he was right.

"This looks like pretty standard material." The sheriff rattled off names that didn't mean much to Jessica, then said, "They'd have to be using a wireless trigger mechanism."

"Cell phone," Jenn said through a coughing fit.

Both the sheriff and Tyler stiffened until she calmed again.

"So, if they need a wireless connection to detonate the bomb, then what happens if I take her out of cell range?" Tyler asked. "There are so many dead spots on the property, it would be easy to take her somewhere there's no signal. In fact, Diablo's Rock is a dead zone."

"We need to be careful moving her," the sheriff said.

"I'll get the SUV," Tyler said as Austin burst out the front door.

"Found it stuffed between the mattresses," he said, holding out the Infinity Sapphire. The brilliant stones caught the light just right, leaving sparkly streaks in the air.

"You're going to be okay," Jessica soothed, brushing Jenn's hair from her face. "You're here and we're not going to let anything happen to you."

"So stupid," Jenn managed to say. "Thought he loved me."

"I know, sweetie," Jessica said. "But he's not good

enough for you. And we're going to make sure he spends the rest of his life in jail."

Jenn nodded and a tear streaked her cheek.

"Move her carefully," the sheriff said as Tyler moved to the other side of Jenn.

"You might want to step behind the SUV," Tyler said to Jessica, but she was already shaking her head.

"I'm staying right here by my sister," Jessica said. She expected Tyler to put up an argument but he nodded and kept going, gently moving Jenn into the back of the SUV on top of layers of sleeping bags.

"I'll need you with me," Tyler said.

She moved to the passenger side as soon as Jenn was secure. "I have no plans to leave her."

"I was afraid you'd say that."

"We HAVE TO approach the same way you did with the ATVs," Tyler said to Jessica as he parked the SUV a few yards from the rock. Her body language screamed fear. No doubt she remembered the last time she'd been there a few days ago.

His brothers were near, they'd fanned out around the area, but there was no cell coverage out there. Good for Jenn but bad for overall communication.

"Stay here," he said, handing her the Sig Sauer she'd used before. "Don't let on that anyone's in the back of the SUV. Don't even glance back there, okay?"

"I'm good." She palmed the weapon and then double-checked the chamber.

"Remind me not to get on your bad side later." He kissed her. "I need to check the area. The boys aren't far and they know how to hide. The tricky part will be communicating with them if we get in trouble."

"We're going to be fine. We have to be."

She didn't say that their lives depended on it but they did.

Tyler moved to the rock and dug his boots in, moving to high ground to get a better look at the area. As he crested the rock he thought about how much his life had changed since the last time he was there. Everything had been turned upside down, he'd never been in more danger and never been more in love. The danger part he could handle.

He saw the glint of metal coming behind a bush on the east side just as the telltale flash of fire followed. The bullet pierced him. Shock registered as he missed his footing and tumbled the forty-foot drop from Diablo's peak.

JESSICA HEARD A gun fire. She bolted from the SUV in time to see Tyler tumbling down the face of the rock. Panic engulfed her and her pulse skyrocketed. Before she had a chance to rationalize her actions she was running toward him.

Please let him be okay.

Her stomach twisted as she got close enough to see him lying there, facedown, unmoving. All she could think about was getting to him and then she saw the blood through his plaid shirt.

There was no way to contact his brothers. Her own sister lay in the SUV, unconscious. All Jessica's hopes had been riding on the cowboy and now he was dying, leaving her, too. It was a selfish thought and she knew it. She tamped it down and spun around to the sound of footsteps running up behind her. There were three men, all with weapons pointed directly at her chest. She pointed her own gun at the ringleader, Ashton. "Stop or I'll shoot."

"Whoa," he said to the others, holding his hands out for them to stay behind.

They were out of cell phone range. Tyler's brothers had

to have heard the shot, hadn't they? And all of them were about to die.

Well, she planned on taking a couple of these jerks with her.

"Back off if you want the necklace," she said, taking a step away as the men slowed their approach.

"You don't have a play here, honey," Milton said, and her skin crawled at the sound of his voice.

She retreated a few more steps until her back hit a solid wall of rock. "Don't come any closer or I'll start shooting."

All three men stopped. The third fit the description of the man in the suit who'd been asking around for Tyler. It dawned on Jessica. The insurance adjuster must be in on it. Milton wasn't working for Beauchamp, he was in league with Ashton.

"How did they talk you into joining them?" she asked the third man.

"This guy?" A wide smile broke on Ashton's face. "Fraternity brothers forever."

He and Ashton were friends? He must've been offered a cut.

"My sister thought you loved her," she said as Ashton took another menacing step toward her. Anger burned through her chest. She hated the guy, but could she kill someone?

It was either kill or be killed.

Ashton ignored her comment and made a move to kick Tyler. "How'd this jerk get involved?"

Jessica closed her eyes and pulled the trigger. By the time she opened them a second later, chaos had broken out.

Ashton was on the ground, wrestling with Tyler, who had already shot Milton. She'd nicked the insurance guy who was diving on top of Tyler and Ashton.

Milton didn't seem to realize he'd been shot because he lunged toward her.

"Bitch," he said as he dived.

She whirled to the right and he smacked into the rock, shoulder first, but managed to knock the gun out of her hand. His thick hand clutched at her until he gained purchase on her shirt. He shoved her to the ground and she desperately felt around for the Sig.

Milton twisted until he was straddled over her. She glanced to the side in time to see that Tyler and Ashton were wrestling for a gun. Ashton's friend was rearing back to deck Tyler.

In a burst, the gun went off and Tyler managed to roll on top of Ashton.

There was so much blood.

Milton raised his hand high and she could see a rock in his palm.

And then she heard the footsteps.

"Put your weapons down," Sheriff Tommy's familiar voice said.

Milton ignored the request. She wiggled but he was too heavy to buck him off. And then another gunshot roared. Milton's eyes bulged after taking the second hit. He slumped to the side allowing Jessica to slide out from underneath him.

Austin wrangled Ashton's friend away, pulling him by the foot. But Tyler and Ashton were too tangled up. A shot was as likely to hit Tyler.

Jessica scooted away from Milton and gentle arms pulled her to her feet. She wasn't sure which one of the twins helped her, but she was grateful.

Tyler pushed Ashton off him and got in a solid punch.

Ashton's head bobbled and then he fell forward, unconscious.

The sheriff was by Tyler's side before she could open her mouth to speak. He zip-cuffed Ashton's hands behind his back.

Jessica ran to Tyler to see just how much blood he'd lost. His brothers were by his side as his eyes closed.

"He's going to be all right, isn't he?" Jessica asked, tears streaking from her eyes. She must've looked as torn on the outside as she was on the inside. Tyler was bleeding, unconscious. Jenn was alone in that SUV where anyone or anything could get to her.

"Austin is with your sister," the sheriff said, easing one of her fears as she heard the *whop, whop, whop* of the helicopter.

Chapter Eighteen

Tyler blinked his eyes open, quickly closing them again. His arm came up to shield them from the bright light shooting daggers through his retinas. His eyes burned as if they'd been branded.

"Hold on there, buddy," Austin said, and the sound of his voice moved toward Tyler until he felt his brother's presence at his side. "Let me get the nurse."

"I'm fine," Tyler blew him off, knowing full well it wasn't the nurse he needed. "Where is she?"

"About that," Austin started.

Tyler's hand came up to stop his brother from delivering bad news. Thinking about losing the woman he'd fallen for hit him like a physical punch. "Never mind. How long have I been out?"

"Just two days," Austin supplied. "And you've been in and out."

"Really?" Tyler needed to get well so he could find Red. There was so much he wanted to say to her. He squinted and a figure in the corner caught his eye.

"Hi, there," Jessica said, moving to his side. She was wringing her hands and that wasn't a good sign.

Austin winked. "I'll leave you two alone to talk."

All the words he'd intended to say died on Tyler's lips when he made eye contact. "How's your sister?"

"Dr. McConnell says Jenn will be fine," Red said, stopping just out of arm's reach. "She's down the hall, already sitting up and chatting. She confirmed that she'd been dating Ashton and he told her that she needed to take care of something to secure their future. He'd said he and his wife were in a loveless marriage and that he'd been planning to leave her for months. He gave her the box and Jenn naively didn't open it. He'd already arranged for Milton to steal it so there'd be a double payoff. His fraternity brother had planned to help him scam the insurance company and was going to get a cut for selling the Infinity Sapphire to Beauchamp's people."

"But Ashton was only using your sister. Setting her up to do the time for the theft," Tyler said, his hands aching to reach out to her, hold her.

"He planned to let her do the time or be killed by Beauchamp. Milton had secretly set up another buyer, and that's who showed at the motel room in Bluff," she said, shifting her weight from her left to right foot. "When Milton didn't produce the necklace, the guy figured he'd been duped. Their whole plan fell apart. Jenn was the only one who knew where the necklace was this whole time. And it turns out we were right that Elijah wanted the necklace to make money off his own sale."

"It can't be easy for Jenn knowing the person she fell in love with was using her," Tyler said.

"Those wounds will be harder to heal," Red admitted. "But just as fast as Jenn falls in love, she can fall out of it."

"And how about you?" he asked. "Do you fall in and out of love quickly?"

She stared at the floor instead of answering.

It was now or never, he thought. "It's finally over. But what happens next? You go back to your life and I do the same? I've never felt this way about anyone before, Jessica. I'm in love with you and I don't want this to be the end."

A little gasp escaped before she suppressed it. "I feel the same way. I've fallen hard for you, Tyler. But it would be crazy to throw away my life and you certainly can't throw away yours. Especially not when neither of us can be certain this isn't a circumstantial romance."

"Do you really believe that's true?" He did his best to mask the hurt in his voice.

"No, of course not. I want to believe this is real, but I need more than a few days to process what's going on between us and make sure it can become something permanent," she said, and there was no covering the confusion in hers.

"Come here," he said and she did.

She eased onto the side of the bed and he put his arms around her. "Let's just agree to keep seeing each other as much as we can until we figure it all out. I don't want to spend another day without you in my life but I'll wait for you."

He brushed a tear off her cheek. "No more crying. This is a good thing. *We're* a good thing."

She leaned into him gently. "Yes, we are. I was so scared when you were shot. I was so afraid of losing you."

"You don't have to," he whispered into her ear and then kissed her neck. "I'm right here."

JESSICA HAD WAITED six agonizing months for this day to come. She finished her breakfast and grabbed her car keys off the counter with giddy anticipation. Now that Jenn had returned to Shreveport and learned to run the family business, Jessica felt comfortable enough to let the employees know there'd be a change in the guard at Davidson Cleaning Services and Jenn would be taking over.

As she walked out the front door, she froze. "Tyler? What are you doing here? We aren't supposed to see each other until this weekend." And she'd been planning to drop the same bomb on him for weeks. She was ready. She knew that their love was real and could last.

"I couldn't wait to see you," he said with a smile.

She took the couple of steps from the porch quickly, ready

to share her good news. Before she could reach him, he dropped down on one knee and produced a small velvet box.

"You are the love of my life. When you're not with me I'm empty in a way I've never known before. I want you to spend the rest of your life with me and our children," he said.

Tears were already flowing down Jessica's cheeks, tears of pure joy.

"You want children?" she asked.

"At least four, but I figured I needed to talk to you about the number before I started making plans," he said. "Jessica, will you marry me?"

She nodded as she wrapped her arms around him. "I love you, Tyler O'Brien, and I can't wait to start our life together."

He kissed her, tenderly at first, but need built quickly.

"Will you come home with me and stay this time?" he asked. "The past six months have been killing me and I don't want to spend another day apart."

"Yes, I'll marry you. And, yes, I'll come home with you. I can't imagine a better place to bring up our kids," she said. "And you know what? I was just on my way to let the employees know that my sister is taking over."

"Good. Because when you come home with me this time, I'm not letting you go."

"You can hold on to me forever," she said. And she couldn't wait to spend the rest of her life with her Texas cowboy.

* * * * *

USA TODAY *bestselling author*
Barb Han's series,
CATTLEMEN CRIME CLUB,
continues soon.

Her frame trembled beneath his hands. "It was… terrifying… I'm going to hear that sound in my nightmares."

"What's it gonna take for you, Beth?"

"To leave Timberline? The truth. I'm going to leave Timberline when I discover the truth about my identity. Otherwise, what do I have?"

"You have me." He sealed his lips over hers and drew her close.

She melted against him for a moment, her mouth pliant against his. But then she broke away and stepped back.

"I just don't think you understand what this means to me, Duke. It's a lifetime of questions and doubts coming to a head right here. All my questions have led me here."

"You don't know, Beth. It's based on feelings and suppositions and red doors and frogs."

"And that's a start."

He closed his eyes and took a deep breath. He didn't want to take that all away from her—the hope—but he'd snatch it all away in a heartbeat to keep her safe.

SUDDEN SECOND CHANCE

BY
CAROL ERICSON

First Published in Great Britain 2016
By Mills & Boon, an imprint of HarperCollins*Publishers*
1 London Bridge Street, London, SE1 9GF

© 2016 Carol Ericson

ISBN: 978-0-263-91916-5

46-0916

Our policy is to use papers that are natural, renewable and recyclable products and made from wood grown in sustainable forests. The logging and manufacturing processes conform to the legal environmental regulations of the country of origin.

Printed and bound in Spain
by CPI, Barcelona

Carol Ericson is a bestselling, award-winning author of more than forty books. She has an eerie fascination for true-crime stories, a love of film noir and a weakness for reality TV, all of which fuel her imagination to create her own tales of murder, mayhem and mystery. To find out more about Carol and her current projects, please visit her website at www.carolericson.com, "where romance flirts with danger."

For Chuck,
one of the most avid readers I know.

Chapter One

Beth's heart skipped a beat as she ducked onto the path that led through a canopy of trees. The smell of damp earth and moldering mulch invaded her nostrils. She took a deep breath. The odor evoked the cycle of life—birth, death and rebirth. She'd smelled worse.

She gasped as a lacy, green leaf brushed her face. Then she knocked it away. If she freaked out and had a panic attack every time she delved into the forest, she'd have a hard time doing this story—and getting to the truth of her birth.

Straightening her shoulders, she tugged on her down vest and blew out a breath. She stepped over a fallen log, snapping a twig in two beneath her boot. The mist rising from the forest floor caressed her cheek and she raised her face to the moisture swirling around her.

The scent of pine cleared her sinuses and she dragged in a lungful of the fresh air. She'd definitely classify herself as a city girl, but this rustic, outdoor environment seemed to energize her.

Either that or the adrenaline was pumping so hard and fast through her veins, a massive anxiety attack waited right around the corner.

She continued on the path through the dense foliage, feeling stronger and stronger with each step. She could do this. The reward of possibly finding her true identity motivated her, blocking out the anxiety that the forest usually stirred up inside her.

She'd convinced Scott, the producer of *Cold Case Chronicles*, that she needed to come out ahead of her crew to do some initial interviews and footwork. She had her own video camera and could give Joel, her cameraman, a head start. Stoked by the show's ratings from the previous season, Scott had been ready to grant her anything. Of course, she had a lot of work to do on her own before she got her guys up here. She'd have to stall Scott.

The trees rustled around her and she paused, tilting her head to one side. Maybe she should've researched the presence of wild animals out here. Did bears roam the Pacific Northwest? Wolves? She was pretty sure there were no tigers stalking through the forests of Washington. Were there?

As she took another step, leaves crackled behind her, too close for comfort, and she froze again. The hair on the back of her neck stood up and quivered, all her old fears flooding her senses.

She craned her head over her shoulder and released a gusty breath of air. A man walking a bicycle stuttered to a stop, his eyes widening in his gaunt face.

"Ma'am?"

The relief she'd felt a moment ago that it hadn't been a tiger on her trail evaporated as she took in the man's appearance. He had the hard look of a man who'd been in the joint. She recognized it from previous stories she'd done on her TV show, *Cold Case Chronicles*.

"Oh, hello. My husband and I were just taking a walk. He went ahead."

He nodded once, a jerky, disjointed movement. "Come out to look at the kidnapping site, did ya?"

Heat washed into Beth's cheeks. She wanted to make it

clear to this man that she wasn't just some morbid looky-loo, but what did it really matter?

"We were in the area anyway, and it's so pretty out here." She waved a hand toward the path she'd been following. "Is it much farther?"

"Not much." He pushed his bike forward, wheeling around the same fallen log she'd stepped over earlier. "They were lookin' at me for a bit."

"Excuse me?" Beth tucked her hands into the pockets of her vest, her right hand tracing the outline of her pepper spray.

"For the kidnappings." He hunched his scrawny shoulders. "Like I'd snatch a couple of kids."

"Th…that must've been scary." She slipped her index finger onto the spray button in her pocket. "How'd the police get that idea?"

"Because—" he looked to his left and right "—because I'd been in a little trouble before."

Taking one step back, Beth coiled her muscles. She could take him—maybe—especially if she nailed him with the pepper spray first.

"And because I was there the first time."

"What?" She snapped her jaw closed to keep it from hanging open. Did he mean he'd been in Timberline at the time the Timberline Trio was kidnapped? He definitely looked old enough.

"You know." He wiped a hand across his mouth. "The first time when them three kids were snatched twenty years ago."

Twenty-five years ago, she corrected him in her head.

"You were living here during that time?"

"I wasn't the only one. Lots of people still around from that time." His tone got defensive. "It's just 'cause I had that other trouble. That's why they looked at me—and because of the dead dog, only he wasn't dead."

A chill snaked up Beth's spine. She definitely wanted to talk to this man later if he was telling the truth, but not now and not here in the middle of a dense forest with only the tigers to hear her screams.

"Well, I'd better catch up to my husband. A…are you going to the site, too?"

"No, ma'am. I'm just taking the shortcut to my house." He raised one hand.

Then he turned his bike to the right and her shoulders dropped as she released the trigger on her pepper spray.

"Ma'am?"

She stopped, and without turning around, she said, "Yes?"

"Be careful out there. The Quileute swear this forest is haunted."

"I will and I'm…we're not afraid of ghosts—my husband and I."

He emitted a noise, which sounded a lot like a snort, and then he wheeled his bike down another path, leaving the echo of crackling leaves.

Beth brushed her hair from her face and strode forward. He wouldn't be hard to locate later—an ex-con on a bicycle who'd been questioned about the kidnappings. Maybe he'd have some insight into the Timberline Trio.

She tromped farther into the woods but never lost sight of the trail as it had been well used recently. What was wrong with people who wanted to see where three kids and a woman had been held against their will?

If she didn't have a damned good excuse for being out here, she'd be exploring the town or sitting in front of the fireplace at her hotel enjoying a caramel latte with extra foam, reading—okay, she'd probably be reading a murder mystery or a true-crime book about a serial killer. The Pacific Northwest seemed to have those in spades.

A piece of soggy, yellow tape stirring in the breeze indicated that she'd reached the spot. Law enforcement had drilled orange caution cones into the ground around the mine opening and had boarded over the top. Nobody would be able to use this abandoned mine for any kind of nefarious purpose again.

She nudged one of the cones with the toe of her boot—it didn't budge. Wedging her hands on her hips, she surveyed the area. No recognition pinged in her chest. Her breathing remained calm, too, so nothing here was sending her into overdrive.

Not that she'd really expected it. Wyatt Carson had chosen this place to stash his victims because he'd discovered it or had searched for someplace to hide the children, not because he'd known it from twenty-five years before when he was just a child himself, when his own brother Stevie Carson had been snatched.

But one kidnap story might lead to another. Maybe the Timberline Trio had been held here before…before what? If she really were one of the Timberline Trio, those children obviously weren't dead. So, why had they been kidnapped? Why had *she* been kidnapped?

There was something about this place—Timberline—that struck a chord within her. As soon as she'd seen that stuffed frog in the window of the tourist shop during a TV news story about the Wyatt Carson kidnappings, she'd known she had to come here. She could be Heather Brice, and she had to find out.

Crouching down, she scooted closer to the entrance of the mine. When Carson had found it, the mine had a cover that he'd then blocked with a boulder. All that had been removed and cleared out.

She flattened herself onto her belly and army-crawled between the cones. Someone had already pried back and snapped off a piece of wood covering the entrance.

With her arms at her sides, she placed her forehead against one slat of wood and peered into the darkness below. She'd like to get down there just to have a look around. Maybe the local sheriff's department would allow it if she promised to get their mugs on TV.

A swishing noise coming up behind her had her digging the toes of her boots into the mushy earth. She'd just put herself into an extremely vulnerable position—an idiotic thing to do with that ex-con roaming the woods. A branch snapped. She slipped her hand inside her pocket and gripped the pepper spray, her finger in position.

A man's voice yelled out. "Hey!"

Then a strong vise clamped around her ankle. This was it. In one fluid motion, she dragged the pepper spray from her pocket, rolled to her back, aimed and fired.

The man released her ankle immediately and staggered back, one arm flung over his face.

Beth jumped to her feet, holding the spray in front of her with a shaky hand, ready to shoot again.

Her attacker cursed and spit.

Beth's eyebrows shot up. The ex-con had gotten bigger…and meaner.

Then he lowered his hands from his face and glared at her through dark eyes streaming with tears. Those eyes widened and he cursed again.

He cleared his throat and coughed. "Beth St. Regis. I should've known it was you."

Beth dropped her pepper spray and clasped her hand over her heart. She'd rather be facing a tiger right now than Duke Harper—the man she'd loved and betrayed.

Chapter Two

Duke's eyes stung and his nose burned, lighting his lungs on fire with every breath he took. Even through his tears, he couldn't mistake the woman standing in front of him, her shoulder-length, strawberry blond hair disheveled and her camera-ready features distorted by surprise and…fear.

She should be afraid—very afraid after the way she'd used him.

He kicked at the pepper spray nestled in the green carpet between them. "Is that the stuff I gave you?"

"I… I think so."

"Then I'll count myself lucky because that's expired. You should've replaced it last year, but if you had, I wouldn't be standing upright forming words." He pulled up the hem of his T-shirt to his face and wiped his tears and his nose.

Miss Perfect would hate that he'd just used his shirt as a handkerchief—and that was fine with him. He peered at her through blurry eyes and she still looked perfect—damn it.

She wrinkled her nose. "I'm sorry. I thought you were an ex-con attacking me."

She must be referring to Gary Binder, unless there were other ex-cons in Timberline who lived out this way. He'd already done his homework on the case but he had no intention of sharing his info with her. Oh, God, she had to be here for the same case he'd been assigned to investigate.

He narrowed his already-narrowed eyes. "You're doing a story for your stupid show on the Timberline Trio, aren't you?"

"That *stupid show*, as you call it, got a point-six rating last year, more than half of those viewers in the prime demographic." She tossed her hair over one shoulder as only Beth St. Regis could.

"Junk TV."

She clapped a hand over her mouth, her eyes wide. "Oh, my God. That's why you're here. You're investigating the Timberline Trio."

"What else would I be doing here?" He lifted one eyebrow and crossed his arms. "Do you think I followed you to Timberline?"

Red flags blazed in her cheeks. "Of course not. Why would I think that? What we had was…"

"Over."

"Yeah, over." She waved her hand in the general direction of his face. "Are you okay? I really did think you were that ex-con coming after me. Why did you grab my leg?"

"I thought you were falling in."

"Through that small space?"

"I couldn't see how big it was."

"I was fine. As soon as I heard you coming, I got ready for the attack. You told me once I needed to be more careful, more aware of my surroundings."

"Good to see you're taking my advice…about something." He ran a hand across his face once more and sniffled. "Where's the rest of your crew, or are you a one-woman show now? I guess Beth St. Regis doesn't need other people—unless she's using them."

Her nostrils flared but she ignored the barb. "I'm doing

some prep work. My cameraman and producer will be coming out later."

"And the circus will ensue."

"If the FBI is involved, there really must be something to investigate."

She brushed off her jeans that fit her a little too closely, so he kept his blurry eyes pinned to her face.

"Isn't that why this case is on your radar? You must've heard about the new information we got during the investigation of the copycat kidnappings." He cocked his head. "Come to think of it, I have a hard time believing the old Timberline Trio case is sexy enough for *Cold Case Chronicles*. Maybe *you* followed *me* out here."

Her sky blue eyes widened for a split second and then she giggled nervously, her hand hovering near her mouth. "I have no idea what happened to you after…that last case, Duke Harper. You dumped me, and it's not like I've been following your career or anything like a stalker."

A thrill of pleasure winged through his body at her lie. So she'd been tracking him. What did that say about him that the thought gave him satisfaction? It also meant she knew about the royal screwup that had resulted in the death of his partner, Tony.

"That's okay. I haven't watched one of your shows, either." The slight lift at the corner of her luscious lips told him she'd picked up on his lie, too.

"I suppose you're not interested in joining forces, are you? Pooling our resources? We're an unbeatable team. We proved that before."

He snorted. She didn't deserve an answer to that one. They'd been an unbeatable team in bed, too, but that hadn't stopped her from playing him.

"What were you doing crawling around on the ground?" He pointed to the cover over the mine.

"Prep work." She sealed her lips. "Where are you staying while you're here?"

"Timberline Hotel."

She raised her hand. "Me, too."

He pasted on his best poker face. "Makes no difference to me."

"Do you have a partner with you or are you working
alone?"

A partner? The FBI would have a hard time trying to
find someone to partner up with him after Tony. He shoved
his hands in his pockets and kicked at a gnarled root coming up from the earth.

"Oh, come on, Duke. Whether or not you're working
with a partner is not giving up any classified info."

He shrugged. He had no intention of giving this woman
one morsel of information. She should know that working a cold case was like being exiled to Siberia—for him,
anyway. This was punishment and he didn't want to discuss his failure with her.

"I guess you'll follow your leads and I'll follow mine."
He circled his finger in the air. "How long have you been
here?"

"Just a couple of days. I'm trying to get a feel for the
place. I even brought my own video cam."

A flock of birds shrieked and rose from a canopy of
trees and the hair on the back of Duke's neck stood up.
Hunching forward, he crept toward the tree line.

"What are you doing?" Beth's voice sounded like a
shout and he put his finger to his lips.

Voices carried in the outdoors and those birds had taken
off because something—or someone—had disturbed them.
The abandoned mine was in a clearing, but dense forest
and heavy underbrush hemmed it in on all sides.

The trail from the road had wound past an abandoned

construction site to the clearing, and it continued on the other side. The birds had come from the other side.

He reached the beginning of the trail and took a few steps onto the path, his head cocked to one side. Leaves rustled and twigs snapped, but that could be animals going about their business. His gaze tracked through the blur of green, but he didn't spot any movement or different colors.

City life had his senses on high alert, but a rural setting could pose just as much danger—of a different kind.

He exhaled slowly and returned to the clearing, where Beth waited for him, hands on her hips.

"What was all that about?"

He pointed to the sky. "Those birds took off like something startled them."

"I told you I saw a rough-looking guy out here on a bike. Maybe it was him."

"Doesn't explain why he was hanging around. I don't know that you should be traipsing around the forest by yourself." He snorted. "You're hardly an outdoor girl."

She kicked a foot out. "I have the boots."

He opened his mouth for a smart-ass reply but someone or something crashed through the bushes and they both jumped this time. Duke reached for the weapon tucked in the shoulder holster beneath his jacket and tensed his muscles.

He dropped his shoulders when three teenage boys came staggering into the clearing, laughing and pushing each other. The roughhousing came to an abrupt halt when they spotted Duke and Beth.

The tallest of the three boys stepped forward, holding a can of beer behind his back. "Is this, uh, official business or something?"

The other two edged back to the tree line, trying to hide their own beers.

"Nope. I was just leaving." Duke leveled his finger at the boy. "But you'd better not be operating a motor vehicle."

"Driving? No way, sir."

Beth flashed her megawatt smile at the trio of teens. "Do you boys live here? I'm from the TV show *Cold Case Chronicles*, and we're doing a show on the old Timberline Trio case."

"Oh, hey, yeah. My mom watches that show all the time."

One of the other boys, a pimple-faced kid with a shock of black hair, mimicked the tagline of the show in a deep voice. "*Cold Case Chronicles*…justice for all time."

"That's us." Beth nodded. "So, how about it? Any of you know anything about that case? Parents around at the time?"

The one who'd spoken up first said, "Nah, we just moved here a few years ago when my mom got a job with Evergreen Software."

The kid with the acne answered. "Same here."

The dark-haired boy with the mocha skin who'd been quiet up to now ran a hand through his short hair. "My family was here, but they don't talk about it. *We* don't talk about it."

"We?"

Duke rolled his eyes as Beth tilted her head, that one word implying a million questions if the boy wanted to pick one up. The teen had better run now if he wanted to avoid that steam train.

The tall, skinny boy answered for his friend. "Levon is Quileute. They believe in voodoo magic and boogeymen."

Levon punched his friend in the arm and the tall kid dropped his beer where it fizzed out in the dirt. "Hey, man."

All three boys picked up where they'd left off, crashing back into the woods, cursing at each other and laughing, startling a flock of birds with their raucousness.

"Well, that's interesting." Beth tapped the toe of her boot. "I wonder what that boy meant about the Quileute not talking about the crime. Did law enforcement ever question anyone from the tribe?"

"Not that I know of, but I'll leave that to your superior investigative talents." He jerked his thumb over his shoulder. "It's been real, but I gotta go."

"I guess I'll see you around, Duke. We are in the same hotel, same small town, same case."

"Don't remind me." He waved over his shoulder and hit the trail back to his rented SUV, putting as much space as possible between him and Beth St. Regis, his mind as jumbled as the carpet of mulch he was plowing through.

She looked the same, except for the clothes. Beth had always been a girlie-girl—high heels, dresses, manicured nails, perfect hair and makeup. The jeans, boots and down vest suited her. Hell, a burlap sack would suit Beth. She had the kind of delicate beauty that shifted his libido into overdrive.

He'd fantasized about those girls when he was a teen growing up on the wrong side of the tracks in Philly—the rich girls with the expensive clothes and cars, the kind of girl that wouldn't give him the time of day unless she wanted to tick off her parents by running with a bad boy.

He'd been drawn to Beth like a magnet for all the wrong reasons. You couldn't use a living, breathing person to fix whatever you'd missed in your childhood. But, man, it had felt good trying.

When he'd had Beth in bed, he couldn't get enough of her soft porcelain skin, the way her breast fit neatly into the palm of his hand and the feel of her fine, silky hair running down his body.

The thought of those nights with Beth's slim legs wrapped around his hips got him hard all over again, and he broke into a jog to work off the steam.

When he got to the car, he collapsed in the driver's seat and downed half a bottle of water. Just his luck to run into the woman of his dreams on this nightmare assignment.

He dug his cell phone from the pocket of his jacket and called his boss, Mickey Tedesco.

"I was just thinking about you, man. All settled in up there? I hear it's some beautiful country."

"Don't try to sell this, Mick. I checked into my hotel and took a walk in the woods to have a look at where the kidnap victims were held a few months ago, not that those kidnappings had anything to do with the Timberline kidnappings, except that the brother of one of the original victims turned out to be the kidnapper." He dragged in a breath. "Why am I doing this? Doesn't the FBI have more urgent cases that need my attention?"

"You know why, Duke." Mick coughed. "It's always a good idea to ease back into work after a…um, situation."

"I'm good to go, Mickey." His hand tensed on the steering wheel. "I don't need to be poking around a twenty-five-year-old kidnapping case based on some slim new evidence, which isn't even evidence."

"I don't know. It may not have started out too promising, but you might be getting more than you bargained for, Duke. You might have yourself a hot one."

A vision of Beth aiming her pepper spray—pepper spray he'd given her—at his face flashed across his mind. "I might be getting more than I bargained for, all right. That bogus *Cold Case Chronicles* show is out here nosing around."

Mick sucked in a breath. "Beth St. Regis is there, in Timberline?"

"Yeah." Mick knew a little about the drama that had gone on between him and Beth…but not all of it.

Mick whistled. "That makes total sense now."

"It does?" Duke clenched his jaw. "Are they promoting the segment already? She doesn't even have her crew out here."

"No. It makes sense that Beth's doing a show about the Timberline Trio because someone sent us an email about her yesterday."

Duke's pulse skipped a beat. "About Beth? What'd it say?"

"The email, untraceable of course, said 'Stop Beth St. Regis.'"

Chapter Three

Beth parked her rental car in the public parking lot on the main drag of Timberline and flicked the keys in the ignition. Why did Duke Harper have to be here mucking up her investigation?

She chewed her bottom lip. He'd been sent out on a cold case because of what had happened in Chicago. She'd read all about the botched kidnapping negotiation that had ended in the death of Duke's partner, a fellow FBI agent. But Duke had rescued the child.

Tears pricked the backs of her eyes. Duke had a thing about rescuing children…but he couldn't save them all.

She plucked the keys from the ignition and shoved open the car door. She couldn't get hung up on Duke again. This story had presented her with the opportunity to get to the bottom of her identity, and she didn't plan on letting tall, dark and handsome get in her way.

She locked the car with the key fob and dropped it in her purse. The chill in the autumn air had her hunching into her jacket as she walked toward the lit windows lining the main street.

If she recalled from the TV news story on the kidnappings, the tourist shop was located between an ice-cream place and a real-estate office. She started at the end of the block and passed a few restaurants just getting ready for the dinner crowd, a quiet bar and a coffee place emitting a heavenly aroma of the dark brew she'd sworn off to avoid the caffeine jitters. The Pacific Northwest was probably not the best place to swear off coffee.

A neon ice-cream cone blinking in a window across the street caught her attention. She waited for a car to pass and then headed toward the light as if it were a beacon.

The tourist shop, Timberline Treasures, with the same frog in the window, nestled beside the ice-cream place, and Beth yanked open the door, sending the little warning bell into a frenzy.

A couple studying a rack of Native American dream catchers glanced at her as she entered the store.

"Hello." A clerk popped up from behind the counter. "Looking for something in particular?"

"I am." Beth gripped the strap of her purse, slung across her body, as she scanned the shelves and displays inside the store. "I'm interested in that frog in the window."

"The Pacific Chorus frog." The woman smiled and nodded. "Timberline's mascot."

Beth's gaze tripped across a small display of the frogs in one corner. "There they are."

The clerk came out from behind the counter and smoothed one hand across a stuffed frog, his little miner's hat tilted at a jaunty angle. "They're quite popular and these are originals."

Beth joined her at the display and reached for a frog, her fingers trembling. "Originals?"

"These are handmade by a local resident." She tapped a bucket filled with more stuffed frogs. "These are mass-produced but we still carry the local version."

"Is there a noticeable difference between them?" Beth held the handmade frog to her cheek, the plush fur soft against her skin.

The clerk picked up a frog from the barrel. "The easi-est way to tell is the tag on the mass-produced version. It's from a toy company, made in China."

"The color is slightly different, too." Beth turned over the frog in her hand and ran a thumb across his green belly. She hooked a finger in the cloth tag attached to his leg and said the words before she even read the label. "Libby Love."

"That's the other way to tell." The clerk lifted her glasses attached to the chain around her neck. "Every handmade frog has that tag on it."

"What does it mean?" Beth fingered the white tag with the lettering in gold thread. "Libby Love?"

"It's the name of the artist, or at least her mother—Eliz-abeth Love. Libby's daughter, Vanessa, makes the frogs now."

Beth took a steadying breath. She'd already figured her childhood frog had come from Timberline, but now she had the proof. "When did her mother start making the frogs?"

"Libby started making those frogs over forty years ago when Timberline still had mining." The woman dropped her glasses when the browsing couple approached the counter. "Are you ready?"

While the clerk rang up the tourists' purchases, Beth studied both frogs. Now what? Even if she'd had a frog from Timberline, it hadn't necessarily come from this store. And if it had come from this store, any records from twenty-five years ago would be long gone.

The clerk returned with her head tilted to one side. "Can I help you with anything else? Answer any more questions?"

"So, these frogs—" Beth dangled one in front of her by his leg "—this is the only place to buy them?"

"The Libby Love frogs are available only in Timberline, although Vanessa sells them online now."

"How long has she been selling them online?" Beth held her breath. Surely, not twenty-five years ago.

The woman tapped her chin. "Maybe ten years now?"

"Is this the only store in Timberline that sells the Libby Love frogs?"

"Oh, no. All the tourist shops have them and even a few of the restaurants." The woman narrowed her eyes. "They all sell for the same price."

"Oh, I'll buy one from you." Beth studied the woman's pleasant face with its soft lines and had an urge to confess everything. "I... I had a toy like this frog when I was a child."

"Oh? Did your parents visit Timberline or get it from someone else?"

"I'm not sure." Her adoptive parents could've passed through Timberline and picked up the frog, but their taste in travel didn't include road trips through rural America.

"It's always nice to reconnect with your childhood. Can I ring that up for you now or would you like to continue looking around?" She glanced at her watch. "I do close in a half hour."

Sensing a sale, the clerk didn't want her to walk out of there without that frog tucked under her arm. She didn't have to worry. Beth had no intention of walking out of there without the frog.

"I'll look around for a bit." Who knew what else she'd discover in there? With her heart pounding, she wandered around the store. She felt close to something, on the verge of discovery.

Maybe in a week or two she'd be ready to track down the Brices and present herself to them as their long-lost daughter who had been kidnapped from Timberline twenty-five years ago. It would be a helluva story for the show, too.

She couldn't forget about the show—she never did. Being the host of that show had given her the recognition and attention she'd missed from her parents. How could she have put that into words for Duke two years ago without sounding pathetic?

Stopping in front of a carousel of key chains, she hooked her finger through one and plopped it down on the glass countertop. "I'll take this, too."

As the woman rang up the frog and the key chain, she peered at her through lowered lashes. "Are you here to do a story on the Timberline Trio?"

Beth dropped her credit card. "What?"

The woman retrieved the credit card and ran her finger along the raised lettering. "You are Beth St. Regis of the *Cold Case Chronicles*, aren't you? I recognized you right away. My sister and I love your show."

"Th…thank you." Wasn't that what Beth had always wanted? People recognizing her on the street, praising the show, praising her? Wasn't that why she'd betrayed Duke Harper?

"I…we…"

"Well, I figured it had to be the Timberline Trio case. We don't have any other cold cases around here. Our former sheriff, Cooper Sloane, made sure of that with the kidnappings we just had. Could've knocked me over with a feather when it turned out Wyatt Carson had kidnapped those kids. Why would he do that when his own brother was one of the Timberline Trio?"

"That was…interesting."

The woman put a finger to her lips. "I can keep a secret if you want, but I think most people are going to realize that's why you're here. Timberline is still a small town, despite Evergreen Software. Word will spread."

"It's no secret. I'll be interviewing Timberline residents and visiting all the original locations." Beth signed the credit-card slip. "I'm just doing some preliminary legwork right now and my crew will be joining me later."

Of course, the good people of Timberline would know the purpose of her visit. Word may have already spread, thanks to those boys in the woods. Soon everyone in town would know.

But nobody needed to know her ulterior motive for the story—including Duke Harper.

It would've been something she'd have shared with him two years ago, but now they had too many secrets between them. She'd noticed he hadn't offered up any explanations of why a hotshot FBI agent was wasting his time on a cold case, although she already knew the reason.

Beth hugged the bag to her chest. "Thanks...?"

"Linda. Linda Gundersen."

"You seemed knowledgeable about the stuffed frog. Were you living here when the three children were kidnapped?"

"No. My sister and I took over this shop when we both retired from teaching in Seattle. She'd dated a man from this area for a while, liked it, and suggested it as a place for us to retire." Crossing her arms, she hunched on the counter. "That was fourteen years ago when property was cheap. Turns out it was a good move because things started booming when Evergreen set up shop here."

Beth dug a card out of her purse and slid it across the glass toward Linda. "If you know anyone who'd like to talk to me about the case, have them give me a call."

"I will. My sister, Louise, would love to be on the show."

"Does she know anything about the case?"

"No, but she hired Wyatt Carson to do some plumbing on our house." Linda's voice had risen on a note of hope.

"I'll see if my investigation on the story takes me in that direction. Thanks again."

"Enjoy your frog."

Beth turned at the door and waved, stepping into the crisp night air. Darkness had descended while she'd been in the tourist shop, and her rumbling stomach reminded her that she'd skipped lunch.

Her hotel didn't have a restaurant on the premises and the yellow light spilling out of Sutter's across the street beckoned.

She had no problem eating alone—her job necessitated it half the time she was on the road, and her nonexistent social life dictated it when she was at home.

The plastic bag in her hands crinkled and she decided to make a detour to her car. If she had a bigger purse she'd stuff her frog in there, but her cross-strap bag had no room for her new furry friend and she didn't want to haul the frog into the restaurant. That part of this story she wanted to keep under wraps until she had more proof.

How many adults looking for answers had made the pilgrimage to Timberline, believing they were Stevie, Kayla or Heather? But she had a strong feeling she'd been here before.

She withdrew the frog from the bag and kissed him before stuffing him back in the bag and dropping it on the passenger seat. She'd kissed plenty of frogs in her day, but this one really was going to make all her dreams come true.

She locked up the car and strode back to the restaurant. It had just opened for dinner and a sea of empty tables greeted her—no excuse for the hostess to stick the single diner by the kitchen or the restrooms. She nabbed a prime spot next to the window, ordered a glass of wine and started checking the email on her phone.

Every time Beth looked up from her phone, more and more people filled the room, and she began to notice a few furtive glances coming her way. Linda had been right. News in a small town traveled fast.

If the locals showed an interest in the story, it would make for some good TV. She and her crew never went into these situations with the goal of actually solving the mystery, although a few times they'd gotten lucky. She'd gotten lucky when Duke had shown up during her story two years ago—lucky in more ways than one.

That *Cold Case Chronicles*' investigation had led to the arrest of a child killer who'd been living his life in plain sight of the grieving families. It had been one of her finest hours…and had cost her a budding relationship with Duke.

When the waitress brought her a steaming bowl of soup, Beth looked up just in time to see Duke walk into the restaurant.

She ducked her head behind the waitress and peered around her arm.

The waitress raised her eyebrows. "Everything okay?"

"Just thought I saw someone I knew."

"In Timberline, that's not hard to do even if you are from Hollywood."

"LA."

"You are that host from *Cold Case Chronicles*, aren't you?" The waitress had wedged a hand on her hip as if challenging Beth to disagree with her.

"I am, but I don't live in…" She shrugged. "Yeah, I'm from Hollywood."

"I wasn't here during the first set of kidnappings but—" the waitress looked both ways and cupped a hand around her mouth "—I could tell you a thing or two about Wyatt Carson. I used to date him."

"Really?" Everyone seemed to want to talk about Wyatt, but that case was one for the books. "Did he ever talk much about his brother and what might've happened to him?"

The waitress's eyes gleamed. "A little. I could tell you about it…on camera. I'm Chloe Rayman, by the way."

"We'll talk before we commit anything to video, Chloe." Beth held out her card between two fingers. "If it's something we can use, I'll have my cameraman film you when he gets here."

"Oh, I think it's something you can use." Chloe plucked the card from Beth's fingers and tucked it into the pocket of her apron.

Even if Chloe didn't have anything of importance to add to the story, the waitress would want her fifteen minutes of fame anyway. Beth's challenge on these stories had always been to separate the wannabes from the people with hard facts. Sometimes the two types meshed.

Beth lifted a spoonful of the seafood bisque and blew on the hot liquid.

"Digging in already, huh?"

She'd taken a sip of the soup and choked on it as she looked into the chocolate-brown eyes of Duke Harper. She dabbed a napkin against her mouth. "Dive right in. It's the only way to do it."

"It's the only way you know."

"I'd invite you to sit down—" she waved at the place across from her "—but I'm sure you have important FBI business."

The wooden chair scraped the floor as he pulled it out. "The only important business I have right now is dinner."

She gulped the next spoonful of soup and it burned her throat. What possible reason could Duke have for joining her for dinner? Maybe he wanted to grill *her* for information this time.

"The seafood bisque is good." She drew a circle around her bowl of soup with her spoon.

Chloe returned to the table, practically bursting at the seams. "Are you Beth's cameraman?"

"Would it get me a beer faster if I were?" Duke lifted one eyebrow at Chloe, who turned three different shades of red.

"Of course not. I mean, what kind of beer would you like?"

"Do you sell that local microbrew on tap here?"

"Yes."

"I'll have that and the pork chops with the mashed potatoes, and you might as well bring me some of that soup she's slurping up."

Beth dropped her spoon in the bowl. "Why did you join me if you're going to sit here and insult me?"

"That wasn't an insult. Are you getting overly sensitive out there in LA? You used to be a tough broad, Beth."

Rolling her shoulders, she exhaled out of her nose. Duke liked to needle her. It hadn't bothered her before—when they'd been in love. But now that he hated her? She couldn't take the slightest criticism from him.

"Pile it on, Duke. I can take it." She set her jaw.

"Relax, Beth. Your slurping made the soup sound good. That's all I meant."

Relax? Was that a jab at her anxiety? She squeezed her eyes closed for a second. If she didn't stop looking for innuendos in his conversation, this was gonna be a long dinner.

She scooped up a spoonful and held it out to him with a surprisingly steady hand. "Try it."

He opened his mouth and closed his lips around the spoon. "Mmm."

Heat engulfed her body and a pulse throbbed in her throat. My God, she couldn't be within five feet of the man without feeling that magnetic pull. And he knew it.

She slipped the spoon from his mouth and lined it up on one side of the bowl just as Chloe brought Duke's beer and another bisque.

"Are you done, Beth?"

"Yeah, thanks." She pushed her bowl toward the eager waitress.

When she disappeared into the kitchen, Duke took a swig of beer and asked, "What's up with the waitress? Is she your new best friend or what?"

"She dated Wyatt Carson and thinks that's going to get her camera time."

"You have that effect on people, don't you? They tend to fall all over themselves in your presence."

She stuck out her tongue at him and took a gulp of wine. She needed it to get through this meal.

"Interesting case, Wyatt Carson." Duke flicked his bottle with his finger.

"I know, right?" Beth hunched forward. "Why do you think he did it? Hard to imagine he'd want to put other families through that hell when he'd suffered the loss of his brother."

"One of two things." Duke held up two fingers. "Either he missed the attention and limelight of those days when his brother went missing or he really did just want to play the hero. He kidnapped those kids and then rescued them. Maybe he thought he could get past his survivor's guilt by saving other children when he couldn't save his brother."

"Twisted logic." Beth tapped her head.

"Do you want a slurp, er, sip?" He held his spoon poised over his soup. "I had one of yours."

"No, thanks. I have some fish coming."

"Yeah, yeah. I know the camera adds ten pounds. You still run?"

"There are some great running trails here. Did you bring your running shoes?"

"Of course. Running is the only thing that kept me sane…keeps me sane with the pressures of the job."

"Same here." So the loss of his partner must've weighed heavily on him. Did he suffer from that same survivor's guilt as Wyatt Carson?

"You doing okay with all that—" he circled his finger in the air "—panic stuff?"

"I'm managing." Did he care? He'd acted like he wanted to strangle her today in the woods. Of course, she'd just nailed him with some expired pepper spray.

"How are your eyes? They still look a little red."

"I'm managing."

Chloe brought their entrées at the same time and hovered for several seconds. "Can I get you anything else?"

"Not for me."

Beth shook her head. "No, thanks."

As Duke sliced off a piece of pork chop and swept it through his potatoes, he glanced around the room. "Does the entire town of Timberline know why you're here?"

"I don't know about the entire town, but everyone in this restaurant has a pretty good idea by now, thanks to Chloe."

"Do you think that's a good idea?" His lips twisted into a frown.

"How else am I going to investigate, to get information?" She squeezed some lemon on her fish and licked the tart juice from her fingers.

Duke shifted his gaze from her fingers to her face and

cleared his throat. "I guess that's how you operate. Stir up a bunch of trouble and heartache and move on."

Beth pursed her lips. "None of the original families is even here anymore. Wyatt Carson was the last of Stevie's family in Timberline. Kendall Rush, Kayla's sister, blew through town, got caught up in Wyatt's craziness and then hightailed it out of here. And Heather's family... They moved away from Timberline, to Connecticut, I think."

"You've done your homework."

"I always do, Duke."

"What I can't figure out—" he poked at his potatoes "—is why you were attracted to this cold case. It hardly has all the elements you usually look for."

"And what elements would those be?"

"You know—sex, drugs, grieving families, celebrity."

She chewed her fish slowly. Duke hated what she did for a living—had hated it then, hated it now. She didn't have to answer to Special Agent Duke Harper or anyone else.

She drained her wineglass. "I was following the copycat kidnapping story and got interested in the old story, like a lot of people. There seemed to be heightened interest in the Timberline Trio and talk of some new evidence, so I figure I'd capitalize on that. Right up my alley."

"Excuse me, Ms. St. Regis?"

Beth turned and met the faded blue eyes of a grandmotherly woman, linking arms with another woman of about the same age.

"Yes?"

"I'm Gail Fitzsimmons and this is my friend Nancy Heck. We wanted to let you know that we were both living here at the time of the Timberline Trio kidnappings and we'd be happy to talk to you."

"Thank you." Beth reached into her purse for her cards, ignoring Duke's sneer—or what looked pretty close to a sneer. "Here's my card. I'll be doing some preliminary interviews before my crew gets here."

Nancy snatched the card from Beth's fingers. "You mean we aren't going to be on TV?"

Duke coughed and Beth kicked him under the table. "I can't tell yet. We'll see how the interviews go."

When the two ladies shuffled away, their silver heads together, Duke chuckled. "This is going to be a circus."

"And what exactly are you doing to work this cold case?"

"I have all the original case files. I'm starting there." He held up his hands. "Don't even ask. You can do your interviews with Wyatt Carson's ex-girlfriend's ex–dog sitter's second cousin."

"Don't dismiss what I do. I helped the FBI solve the Masters case."

"You helped yourself, Beth."

Chloe approached their table. "Dessert?"

"Not for me." Beth tossed her napkin on the table.

Pulling his wallet out of his pocket, Duke said, "Just the check."

"You paying?" Beth reached for her purse. "I have an expense account."

"And you're using it to pay for your own dinner. I'm using my per diem to pay for mine. I don't want any commingling here."

She lowered her lashes and slid her credit card from her wallet. Was he talking about just their finances?

"Got it." She tapped her card on the table. "No commingling."

A loud voice came from the bar area of the restaurant, and chatter in the dining room hushed to a low level— enough for the bar patron's words to reach them.

"That TV show better not start nosing around. If anyone talks to that host, I'll give 'em the business end of my fist." The man at the bar turned to face the room, knocking over his bar stool in the process.

His buddy next to him put a hand on his shoulder, but the belligerent drunk shook him off.

"Where's she? I'll toss 'er out right now on her fanny. Tarring and feathering. That's what we should do. Who's with me?" He raised his fist in the air.

A few people snickered but most went back to their dinners. Duke didn't do either. He marched across the room toward the bar.

Beth groaned as she scribbled her signature on the credit-card receipt and took off after him. Duke had always been a hothead, and it looked like he hadn't changed.

"What did you say?" He widened his stance in front of the man. "Are you threatening the lady?"

"You with that show, too?" The man looked Duke up and down and hiccuped.

His friend picked up the stool and shoved his friend into it. "C'mon, Bill. Take it easy. Who knows? Being featured on TV might increase our property values."

The man, his dark hair flecked with gray, shook his head and stuck out his hand. "Sorry about that. My friend's a Realtor and has had a little too much to drink. I'm Jordan Young."

"Duke Harper." Duke gestured toward Beth. "This is Beth St. Regis, the host of *Cold Case Chronicles* and the woman your friend was threatening."

Jordan Young dismissed his drunken friend with a wave of his hand. "It's the booze talking. His sales numbers haven't been great lately, but it has nothing to do with the recent publicity we've been getting. Hell, Kendall Rush's aunt's place sold for top dollar. He's just ticked off that he didn't get that listing."

He took Beth's hand in his and gave it a gentle squeeze. "I'm a big fan of the show, Ms. St. Regis."

"Thanks." She nudged Duke in the back. "Are you a Realtor, too?"

"Me?" He chuckled. "Not really. I'm a developer, and I have a lot more to lose than Bill here if things go south, but that's not going to happen—Evergreen Software will make sure of that."

"You need to tell your friend to keep his mouth shut about Beth."

"Duke." She put her hand on his arm. His stint in Siberia hadn't done anything to temper his combativeness. "I'm sure he's not serious—at least about the tar-and-feathering part."

Young winked. "Good to see you have a sense of humor about it, Ms. St. Regis, but I can understand your...co-worker wanting to be protective."

Duke didn't correct him. If the residents of Timberline knew all about *Cold Case Chronicles* looking into the Timberline Trio, they didn't seem to be as knowledgeable about the FBI putting the case back on its radar. Maybe Duke wanted to keep it that way.

"You can call me Beth." Her eyes flicked over his gray-streaked hair and the lines on his face. "Were you here at the time of the initial kidnappings?"

"I was. Sad time for us." He withdrew a silver card case from his suit jacket and flipped it open. "If you're implying you want to interview me, I might be available, although I don't know how much I could contribute."

She took the card and ran her thumb across the gold-embossed letters. "You'd be the first one in town without some special insight."

"Can you blame them?" He spread his hands. "A chance to be on TV and talk to the beautiful host?"

"Thank you." The guy was smooth but almost avuncular. Duke could wipe the scowl from his face, but she didn't mind that another man's attentions to her irritated him.

"You should take care of your buddy here." Duke jerked his thumb at Bill, still resting his head on the bar.

"I'll get him home safely to his wife. Good night, now." Young turned back to the bar. "Serena, can you get Bill a strong cup of coffee? Make it black, sweetheart."

Duke put his hand on her back as he propelled her out of the restaurant—with almost every pair of eyes following them.

As Duke swung the door open for her, Chloe rushed up and patted her apron. "I'll be calling you, Beth. I don't care what Bill Raney says."

"Looking forward to it, Chloe."

When they stepped outside, Duke tilted his head. "Really? You're looking forward to talking to Chloe about Wyatt Carson?"

"You never know what might pop up in a conversation. Maybe Wyatt remembered something about his brother's kidnapping that he never told the cops."

"Why wouldn't he have told the cops?"

Beth zipped up her vest. "Because he turned out to be a nut job."

"Seems to be no scarcity of those in this town." He hunched into his suede coat, rubbing his hands together. "Where are you parked?"

"In the public lot down the block. This is Timberline. You don't have to walk me to my car."

"Just so happens I'm parked there, too." He nudged her with his elbow. "There have been two high-profile kidnapping cases in Timberline. I wouldn't take your safety for granted here. There might be more people here who feel like Bill."

"I'm hardly in danger of getting tarred and feathered... or kidnapped." She stuffed her hands into her pockets and lifted her shoulders to her ears. She may have already been kidnapped from Timberline once. What were the odds of it happening again?

Duke followed her through the parking lot to her car anyway, occasionally bumping her shoulder but never taking her hand. What did she expect? That they would pick up where they'd left off two years ago? Before he'd accused her of using him? Before she'd used him?

As she reached the rental, her boots crunched against the asphalt and she jerked her head up. "Damn. Somebody broke the window of my car."

"Safe Timberline, huh? Maybe Bill did his dirty work before he hit the restaurant." Duke hunched forward to look at the damage to the window on the driver's side. "You didn't have a laptop sitting on the passenger seat, did you?"

"No, but..." Her ears started ringing and she grabbed the handle of the car door and yanked it open.

Someone had taken the bag from the gift shop. Collapsing in the driver's seat, she slammed her hands against the steering wheel. "My frog. They took my frog."

Chapter Four

Duke's eyebrows shot up at the sob in Beth's voice. Someone had smashed the window of her rental car and she was worried about a frog?

"Beth?" He placed his hand against the nape of her neck and curled his fingers around the soft skin beneath her down vest. "What frog, Beth?"

She sniffled and dragged the back of her hand across her nose. "Some frog I bought in a gift store. I… It's particular to Timberline."

"I'm sure they have more." He released her and braced his hand against the roof of the car. Why was she overreacting about a frog? She must be driving herself hard again, maybe even succumbing to those panic attacks that had plagued her for years.

Because she didn't even know about the warning the FBI had received about her. He'd debated telling her but didn't want to worry her needlessly about an anonymous email. Who knew? The emailer may have sent the same message to Beth or her production company. Maybe that was why she was breaking down over a frog.

"You can replace the frog. Will your insurance fix the window on the rental car?"

"I'm sure I'm covered for that." She leaned into the passenger seat and peeked beneath the seat.

"It's gone?"

"Yep."

He kicked a piece of glass with the toe of his boot. "You're not sitting on glass, are you? The window broke inward, so there's gotta be some on the seat."

"There wasn't." She climbed out of the car and gripped the edge of the door as if to keep herself steady and upright. "He must've brushed it off."

"We're reporting this." Duke pulled his phone from his pocket, scrolled through his contacts and placed a call to the Timberline Sheriff's Department. "We have some vandalism, a broken car window, in the public lot on the corner of Main and River."

He gave them his name and a description of Beth's rental car before ending the call.

"Are they coming?" She cupped the keys to the car in one hand and bounced them in her palm.

"Of course. This isn't LA." He grabbed her hand and held it up, inspecting the dot of blood on the tip of her ring finger. "There *was* some glass in the car. Are you sure you're okay?"

Her wide eyes focused on the blood and she swayed— another overreaction. She seemed to be taking this break-in hard. Maybe she *did* know about the warning against her—and he didn't mean Bill's drunken threats.

Grasping her wrist lightly, he said, "Come with me to my car down the aisle. I have some tissues in there and some water."

By the time they reached his rental, she'd regained a measure of composure. "Idiots. Why would someone go through all the trouble of breaking a window on a rental car to get to a bag of stuff from a tourist shop?"

"Maybe if you hadn't left your bag on the passenger seat in plain view." He unlocked his car and reached into the backseat for a box of tissues, and then grabbed the half-filled bottle of water from his cup holder. "How many times have I told you not to leave things in your car?"

"Let's see." She held out her middle finger. "Must've been a hundred times at least."

"Very funny. It's your ring finger." At least she'd come out of her daze.

"Oops." She held out the correct finger and wiggled it.

He moistened a tissue with some water and held it against the bead of blood. "Apply some pressure to that. Did you get cut anywhere else?"

"Not that I can tell." She tipped her chin toward the cop car rolling into the parking lot. "The deputies are here."

As two deputies got out of the car, Duke whispered in Beth's ear. "That's what I like about Timberline. Two cops come out to investigate a broken window and a missing frog."

She stiffened beside him but a laugh gurgled in her throat.

She'd sure grown attached to that frog in a short span of time…unless there was something else in the bag she didn't want to tell him about. With Beth St. Regis, the possibilities were limitless.

The first deputy approached them, adjusting his equipment belt. "You call in the broken window?"

"And a theft. I had a bag in the car from Timberline Treasures."

The second deputy pointed at Beth. "You're Beth St. Regis from that show."

"Do you watch it?"

"No, just heard you were in town to dig up the old Timberline Trio case."

"I think Wyatt Carson already did that." She jerked her

thumb at Duke. "You do know the FBI is looking into the case again, too."

The officer nodded at Duke and stuck out his hand. "Deputy Stevens. I heard the FBI was sending in a cold-case agent. The sheriff already turned over our files, right?"

"Special Agent Duke Harper." He shook hands with the other man. "And I have the files."

The other officer stepped forward, offering his hand as well. "Deputy Unger. We'll do whatever we can to help you. My mother was good friends with Mrs. Brice at the time of the kidnapping. I was about five years older than Heather when she went missing. That family was never the same after that. Had to leave the area."

Beth was practically buzzing beside him. "Deputy Unger, could I interview you for the show?"

"Ma'am, no disrespect intended, but I'm here to help the FBI. I'm not interested in being a part of sensationalizing the crime. We've had enough of that lately."

"But…"

Duke poked her in the back. "You wanna have a look at the car now?"

"Sure. We'll take a report for the rental-car company and insurance purposes. Probably a kid or one of our local junkies."

Duke asked, "Do you have a drug problem in Timberline?"

"Crystal meth, just like a lot of rural areas." Unger flipped open his notebook and scribbled across the page.

When they finished taking the report, they shook hands with Duke again. "Anything we can do, Agent Harper."

"Well, they weren't very friendly." Beth curled one fist against her hip.

"I thought they were very friendly."

"Yeah, you get the cops and I get Carson's ex-girl-friend's dog walker's cousin."

"Second cousin's ex–dog sitter."

"Right." She tossed her purse onto the passenger seat of the car and hung on the door. "Thanks for seeing me through the report…and the words of advice."

He was close enough to her that the musky smell of her perfume wafted over him. "Do you want some more advice, Beth?"

She blinked. "If you're dishing it out."

"Find another case for your show. Get off this Timberline Trio gig. Since I'm in the Siberia of cold-case hell anyway, I can even toss a couple of good ones your way."

Her eyes narrowed. "Why would you do that? You must really want me off this case."

"It's not me." Raking a hand through his hair, he blew out a breath. "Someone else wants you off this case."

"What? Who? Bill?"

"We got an anonymous email and I don't think it was from Bill Raney."

"That's crazy. The FBI got an email about little, old me? How did anyone even know I was doing a show on the Timberline Trio?"

"How long have you been in Timberline?"

"Two days."

"We got the email two days ago."

She sucked in her bottom lip. "You think it's some-one here?"

"It has to be, unless the station has been doing promo for it."

"Not yet. We wouldn't release anything about a story we haven't even done yet. It might never come off."

"Then it has to be someone here in Timberline or someone related to someone in Timberline. You haven't exactly been shy about your purpose here."

"No point in that. But why contact the FBI?" She snapped her fingers. "It must be someone who knows the FBI is looking into the case, too. Maybe this anonymous emailer figures the FBI will have some pull with me."

Duke snorted. "Mr. Anonymous obviously doesn't know you."

"You know what's strange?"

"Huh?"

"Why didn't this person warn off the FBI? If it's someone who doesn't want me looking into the Timberline Trio, why would this same person be okay with the FBI dredging up the case?"

"I have no idea. Maybe he thinks *Cold Case Chronicles* has a better shot at solving the case than the FBI." He scanned her thoughtful face. "That was a joke."

"It's strange, Duke. I suppose you tried to trace the email."

"With no luck."

"Must be someone who's computer savvy, which isn't hard to find in this town with Evergreen Software in the picture."

He captured a lock of her silky hair and twisted it around his finger. "How about it, Beth? Why don't you back off? I'll find you another case, a better case for your show."

"You don't really think I'm in danger from an anonymous email, do you? I get a lot of anonymous emails, Duke. Some are unrepeatable."

"What about this?" He smacked his palm on the roof of the car. "Someone sends a threat and then someone breaks into your car. Do you think it's a coincidence?"

"Could just be a tweaker like Unger said. Besides, this could be good for you."

"How so?"

"If someone who was involved in the disappearance of the Timberline Trio twenty-five years ago wants me off the case and is willing to harass me about it, you might be able to pick him up and actually solve the case."

"You think I'd use you, put you at risk to solve a twenty-five-year-old case?" He clenched his jaw.

She swallowed, her Adam's apple bobbing in her slender throat. "I..."

"Just because you did it, don't expect the same treatment from me." He backed away from her car. "Drive carefully."

WITH TEARS FLOODING her eyes, which had nothing to do with the cold air coming through the broken window, Beth glanced at Duke's blurry headlights in her rearview mirror.

He hadn't forgiven her, despite his concern for her safety tonight.

Maybe that concern was all a big act. Maybe the anonymous email was a lie. Why would someone want to warn her away from the case but not warn the FBI?

Unless this someone knew her true identity. Did someone suspect her real purpose for highlighting the Timberline case?

She pulled into the parking lot of the Timberline Hotel with Duke right behind her. They even got out of their cars at the same time. He followed her inside, but made no attempt to talk to her.

She dreaded the awkward elevator ride, but he peeled off and headed for the stairwell. Once she stepped into the elevator, she sagged against the wall.

Was the warning to the FBI connected to the break-in? Had the thief grabbed the bag because she'd left it out, or had he wanted to send a message by taking the Libby Love frog? And what was that message?

She slid her card key in the door and leaned into it to shove it open.

She dropped her purse on the single chair in the room and sauntered to the window, arms crossed. Resting her head against the cool glass, she took in the parking lot beneath her.

Did Duke have a better view? If he'd taken the stairs, his room was probably located on the lower floors. The hotel had just five. Who was she kidding? Duke could run up five flights of stairs without breaking a sweat or gasping for breath. The man was a stud, but not the overly muscled kind. He had the long, lean body of a runner.

She banged her head against the window. No point in letting her thoughts stray in that direction. He'd been concerned about her tonight, but that could just be because he wanted her out of the picture.

Little did he know, she had more at stake here than good ratings.

She could tell him, confess everything…well, almost everything. He already knew that she'd been adopted and hadn't been able to locate her birth parents. If she explained to him her suspicions about being Heather Brice, maybe he could help her. Maybe he'd share the case files with her.

She pivoted away from the window. If she told him that now, he'd suspect her of spinning a tale to get her hands on the information he had. She wouldn't go down that road with him again.

Sighing, she swept the remote control from the credenza and aimed it at the TV, turning it on.

With the local TV news blaring in the background, she got ready for bed. Snug in a new pair of flannel pa-

jamas she'd bought for the trip, she perched on the edge
of the bed to watch the news. She hadn't made the local
news—not yet.

She switched the channel to a sitcom rerun and flipped
back the covers on her bed. Her heart slammed against her
chest and she jerked back as she stared at the head of the
Libby Love frog positioned on the white sheet, his miner's
hat at a jaunty angle.

Chapter Five

Beth slammed the frog head on the reception counter, squishing the hat. "Where did it come from?"

The hotel clerk's eyes popped from their sockets. "Ma'am, I'm sorry. I have no idea how it got in your bed. Perhaps it had been washed with the sheets and the maid thought it belonged to you."

"This—" she shook the head at him until some white stuffing fell onto the countertop "—does not look like it's been through an industrial washing machine. It looks brand-new, except for the fact that it's been ripped from its body."

"Ma'am, I don't know. I can talk to the maids in the morning."

"What's going on?"

Beth gulped and swiveled her head to the side. What was Duke doing down here? Might as well get it over with.

"I found this—" she thrust the frog head toward him "—in my bed when I got back to my room."

He held out his hand and she dropped the head into his palm.

"What the hell? Is this the frog you bought earlier that was stolen from your car?"

"Stolen?" The clerk turned another shade of red. "I can assure you, we don't know anything about any theft."

Beth released a long breath. "I don't know if it's the exact same toy I bought, but it's the same kind. So if the thief who broke into my car didn't put it in my room, it's a helluva coincidence that someone else did."

The hotel clerk reached for the phone. "Should we call the sheriff's department?"

Duke tilted his head back and looked at the ceiling of the lobby. "Do you have security cameras?"

"Just in the parking lot, sir. We can check that footage to see if anyone drove into the lot without coming through the lobby."

"That's a good idea. It would've been within the past ninety minutes. Do you have a security guard on duty…" He glanced at the man's name tag. "…Gregory?"

"This is Timberline. No security guard." Gregory lifted his hands. "Sheriff's department?"

"Will they come out for a stuffed frog head?" Beth crossed her arms over her flannel pj's, recognizing the ridiculousness of that statement. At least she didn't feel as if she were choking as she had from the moment she'd seen that frog in her bed. Duke had that effect on her—a calming, steadying presence.

Too bad she had the opposite effect on him.

He gave her a crooked smile. "You heard Gregory. This is Timberline. They'll come out for a stuffed frog. It's not just the head. It's the fact that someone broke into your room and put it in your bed…and the smashed car window before that. You want to report and document all this."

Gregory picked up the phone. "I'll call it in. We may learn more tomorrow when the housekeeping staff comes in. I'll make sure we question all of them thoroughly. The night crew was here until about an hour ago, so they could've been here when the, uh, frog was put in your room."

"Thanks, Gregory." Beth tucked her messy hair behind her ears and flashed him one of her TV smiles. "I'm sorry I got in your face earlier. That frog rattled me."

"I understand, ma'am. If you and the...gentleman—" he nodded toward Duke "—want to help yourselves to something from the self-serve concession while you wait for the sheriffs, it's on the house."

"Don't mind if we do. Thanks, Gregory." She crooked her finger at Duke and then charged across the lobby to the small lit fridge and rows of snacks, her rubber flip-flops smacking the tile floor.

She yanked open the fridge door with Duke hovering over her shoulder. "You're still in your pajamas."

Leaning forward, she studied the labels on the little bottles of wine with the screw tops. "Excuse me. I didn't have time for full hair, makeup and wardrobe once I realized someone had been sneaking around my hotel room beheading frogs."

She wrapped her fingers around a chilled bottle of chardonnay and turned on him, almost landing in his arms. She thrust the bottle between them. "What were you doing wandering around the hotel?"

His dark eyes widened. "Are you accusing me of planting the frog? I was with you, remember?"

"Now who's being sensitive? The thought never crossed my mind, but you were headed toward the stairwell the last time I saw you."

"I stepped outside for some air. My room was stuffy and I couldn't sleep." He held up the frog head. "It's a good thing I did. You looked ready to gouge out poor Gregory's eyes."

"I was spooked." She ducked back into the fridge. "Do you want a beer or one of these fine wines?"

"I'll take a beer." He ran his hand down the length of

her arm. "Must've freaked you out seeing that frog in your bed."

She handed him a cold beer. "It did. The fact that it was just his head made it worse. Was that some kind of warning?"

"Is this story worth it?" He took the mini wine bottle from her and twisted off the lid. "For whatever reason, someone doesn't want you digging into this case, and this person is willing to put you through hell to get that point across."

"Would you quit if someone started warning you?"

He twisted off his own cap and took a swallow of beer. "It's different. If someone started warning the FBI off a cold case, it would give us reason to believe we were on the right track."

"Maybe I'm on the right track."

"You just got here. It seems to me that some person or persons don't want a story on Timberline. Having the FBI investigate is a different ball game. Maybe these warnings to you are designed to stop you from dragging the town of Timberline through the mud again. You know, reducing the real-estate prices, like Bill said."

She took a sip of wine. "You saw the people at the restaurant. Most were eager to help."

"There could be two factions in town—one group wants the attention and the other doesn't. The ones that don't want the limelight have started a campaign against you—a personal one." He clinked his bottle with hers. "Give it up, Beth. Move on to something else. I told you. I have the cold-case world at my fingertips now and can turn you on to a new, sexy case."

She took another pull straight from her wine bottle and gritted her teeth as she swallowed. "I'm not going to quit, Duke. I want to investigate this case."

"Evening, Ms. St. Regis." Deputy Unger swept his hat from his head. "Gregory told us you had some more trouble tonight."

"It's the stuffed frog stolen from her car." Duke held out the frog head. "Someone planted it in her hotel room."

Unger whistled. "Someone really wants you gone—I mean off this story."

"Can you check the tape from the security camera in the parking lot?" Beth put her wine bottle behind her back just in case Unger thought she was a hysterical drunk. "Gregory said the hotel had cameras out there. Maybe someone will appear on tape who's out of place."

"I spoke to him on the way in. Gregory's getting that ready for us right now. Let's go up to your room and check it out. See if there are any signs of a break-in."

Duke proffered the frog head on the palm of his hand. "The frog's been manhandled by a bunch of people, but maybe you can get some prints from it."

Unger pulled a plastic bag from the duffel over his shoulder and shook it out. "Drop it in. We'll have a look."

They all trooped up to her hotel room and Beth inserted the card with shaky fingers. She didn't know what to expect on the other side of the door.

Nothing.

Everything was the way she'd left it, covers pulled back on the bed and the TV blasting. She grabbed the remote and lowered the volume. "It was there, on the middle of the bed, beneath the covers."

Unger looked up from studying the door. "No signs of forced entry. You're on the fourth floor. Does the window open?"

"No."

He had a fingerprinting kit with him and dusted the door handle and the doorjamb. Once he finished asking a few more questions, he packed up his stuff. "I'll have a look at the footage now. If I find anything, I'll let you know."

Duke stopped him. "One more thing, Deputy Unger. A Realtor by the name of Bill Raney was making some threats against Beth in Sutter's tonight."

"We'll talk to him. That man's been on a downward slide lately. I can't imagine him out breaking car windows and sneaking into hotel rooms, but you never know what people will do when their backs are against the wall."

Beth sighed. Why did this have to be happening on the most important case of her life? Maybe if she just explained herself publicly. She honestly didn't care who had kidnapped her twenty-five years ago and she wasn't interested in putting Timberline in the spotlight again. She just wanted to confirm her identity. She wanted to go to the Brices with proof. She wanted to go back to a loving home.

She'd already made a mistake. She should've done her sleuthing on the sly. She should've come to Timberline as a tourist, taken up fishing or hiking or boating. She'd just figured she had the best cover. Nobody would have to know her ulterior motive. Nothing would have to get back to the Brices until she was sure.

"Ms. St. Regis?"

She looked up into Deputy Unger's face, creased with concern. "Are you okay? Gregory offered to move you to another room."

"I think that's a great idea." Duke tossed her suitcase onto the bed. "In fact, the room next to mine on the second floor is empty."

Beth's mouth gaped open. Duke must really be worried if he wanted her rooming right next to him. Today in the forest he'd acted like he'd wanted to strangle her.

"That might not be a bad idea—if you're insisting on

continuing with this story." Unger slung his bag over his shoulder and walked to the door.

"Deputy Unger, who exactly doesn't want the old case dredged up from the cold-case files?" Holding her breath, she watched his face. *He* didn't. He'd made that clear before.

He shrugged. "People like Bill. People with a lot to lose—think property values, reputations, businesses— those are the people who want to put this all behind us. The executives at Evergreen about had a fit when Wyatt Carson kidnapped those kids and struck fear into the hearts of their employees—the people they'd lured here with a promise of safety and clean living."

"I don't see how a crime that occurred twenty-five years ago can still tarnish the luster of a city." She grabbed her vest from the back of the chair and dropped it next to her bag on the bed.

"C'mon, Beth." Duke scratched his stubble. "You've been doing the show long enough to realize what can happen to a town when all the dirty laundry is hung out for everyone to see."

"Maybe I won't end up doing the story. Maybe I won't even call my crew out here—but it won't be because someone wants to scare me off. It'll be because I decide to call it quits."

"Whatever you say, Ms. St. Regis." Unger pulled open the door. "Just keep calling us, especially if these pranks start to escalate."

"Escalate?" Beth licked her lips. "It's just a story, just a town's rep."

"You'd be surprised how far people will go to protect what's theirs."

She and Duke ended up following Unger back to the

reception desk to switch her room to the second floor—next to Duke's.

Unger scanned the footage while they waited and shook his head. "Nothing out of the ordinary. Anyone coming in or out of that parking lot is accounted for as a guest of the hotel."

Gregory slipped her the new card key. "As I said, Ms. St. Regis, I'll question housekeeping tomorrow morning and we'll try to get to the bottom of how someone got into your room. It won't happen again."

"Damn right it won't."

Duke got that fierce look he must've learned on the mean streets of Philly and Beth shivered. It meant a lot to have a man like Duke on your side—if you weren't stupid enough to throw it all away.

Gregory even looked a little worried. "I'll keep you posted, Ms. St. Regis."

Duke took the suitcase handle from her and dragged her bag toward the elevator.

She shuffled after him, yawning. "I am so ready to call it a night."

Duke gave her a sideways glance and stabbed the button for the second floor. The elevator rumbled into action and Beth closed her eyes. The wine had made her sleepy, and she felt the lure of a comfy bed with no surprises in it, although she wouldn't mind one surprise—a prince instead of a frog.

The elevator lurched to a sharp halt and Beth's eyes flew open. "Whoa. This thing needs service."

The elevator had stopped moving but the doors remained shut.

"Oh, God, not another prank—as Unger called it." Her gaze darted to Duke's face, still fierce but set, his jaw hard.

"I'm the one who stopped the elevator."

"What?" She braced her hand against the wall of the car. "Are you crazy? What did you do that for?"

Duke crossed his arms and widened his stance as if she could pull off an escape from the car.

"You're going to tell me what you're really doing in Timberline, and you're going to tell me now or this elevator isn't going anywhere."

Chapter Six

Duke felt a twinge of guilt in his gut as Beth's pale face blanched even more. Was she claustrophobic, too? He knew she had those panic attacks, and if she started down that road he'd cave. He had a weakness for this woman.

"I… I don't know what you're talking about. I'm here to do a *Cold Case Chronicles* episode on the Timberline Trio—come hell or high water."

"Cut it, Beth. That's not your kind of story and we both know it." He leveled a finger at her. "You're up to something. You may have fooled me two years ago, but I'm tuned in to the Beth St. Regis line of baloney now."

Her eye twitched and her tongue darted from her mouth. "It's personal."

He rolled his shoulders. "Now we're getting somewhere. I knew there was more to this story. Start talking."

"If I do, will you help me?"

He tilted his head back and eyed the ceiling. "Just like you to turn the tables. I'm not agreeing to anything. I just want to know the truth—for a change. Don't you think you owe me the truth?"

Tears brightened her eyes, and the tip of her nose turned red.

He scooped in a deep breath. If she shed even one tear,

he'd be finished. But that was how she'd gotten around him last time—pushed all his buttons.

"C'mon, Beth. What are you doing here?"

Drawing in a shaky breath, she covered her eyes with one hand. "You're right. It's not just the Timberline Trio case that brings me here, but in a way it is."

"Is this going to be a guessing game?"

"No." She sniffled. "I do owe you the truth, but do we have to do this here, like I'm some suspect you're interrogating?"

He punched the button. "Sorry about that. I just wanted to get your attention. You're not...?"

"Claustrophobic?" Her lips trembled into a smile. "Sort of."

The doors opened onto the second floor and he ushered her out of the car in front of him and then wheeled her suitcase down the hall after her, his gaze taking in the way the soft flannel draped over her derriere. Beth was probably the only woman he knew who could make flannel pajamas look sexy.

She stopped in front of the room next to his and swiped the card key. As she fumbled with the door, he reached around her and pushed it open.

"You want me to check for frogs in the bed?"

"My tormentor doesn't know my new room number, but go ahead anyway."

In three strides he reached the king-size bed and whipped back the covers. "Frog-free."

She climbed onto the bed and crossed her legs beneath her. "You ready?"

Pulling the chair from the desk in the corner, he straddled it. "I'm always ready for the truth."

"You know I'm adopted."

"And you hit the jackpot with a set of rich parents." He held up his hands. "I know they weren't the best parents, but at least they gave you all the creature comforts your teenage mother couldn't give you."

"I didn't have a teenage mother."

"What?" He hunched over the back of the chair. "You told me your birth mother was an unwed teen who gave you up to a wealthy couple for a better life and then disappeared."

"I lied."

He flinched as if she'd thrown a knife at his heart. What didn't she lie about?

"Okay. Who was your mother and what does this all have to do with Timberline?"

"Duke, I don't know who my birth parents are. My adoptive parents, the Kings, never told me."

"Maybe they didn't want you running after some bio parents and getting disappointed."

She snorted. "I doubt that."

"They wouldn't give you any information? The adoption agency? A birth certificate?"

"I… I think my adoption was illegal. My birth certificate is fraudulent. The Kings are listed as my biological parents. The only reason I even knew I was adopted was because I overheard them talking once. When I confronted them about it, they admitted it but refused to give me any more information."

"That's strange, but what does it all have to do with Timber…?" Her implication smacked him on the back of the head. She couldn't be serious.

"That's right." She dragged a pillow into her lap and hugged it. "I think I'm one of the Timberline Trio—Heather Brice."

He pushed up from the chair and took a turn around the room. "How in the hell did you come to that conclusion?"

She launched into a crazy tale of stuffed frogs and repressed memories of forests and news stories of Timberline until his head was swimming.

"Wait." He sank onto the edge of the bed. "Based on a stuffed frog you had as a child that happens to be Timberline's mascot, you think you were kidnapped and then what? Sold on the black market?"

"Don't pretend that doesn't happen. We both know it does, and the Kings were just the type to be involved in something like that. The rules didn't apply to them. Their riches always gave them a sense of entitlement."

"From what you've told me about your adoptive parents, I agree. But, Beth…" He reached across the bed and tugged on the hem of her pajama bottoms. "Maybe you have that frog because your parents, the Kings, passed through this area and bought it for you."

"I thought of that, not that I could ever see them vacationing in Timberline, but what about the hypnosis?" She waved her arms in a big circle. "I went to a hypnotist in LA, and I saw this place—the lush forest, the greenery—and it scares the hell out of me."

"There are a lot of places in the world that look like Timberline."

"But combined with the frog?"

"Maybe something traumatic happened here when your parents were passing through. Hell, maybe there was a car accident or you wandered away and got lost—God knows, you'd be the kind of kid to do that, and I mean that in a good way."

"The Kings never mentioned anything like that."

"Why would they? You said they were distant, uncommunicative."

"I just feel it, Duke." She pounded her chest with one fist. "From the moment I saw the Wyatt Carson story and the Timberline scenery on TV, I felt it in my bones. There's something about this place. I have a connection to it."

"Have you tried to contact the Brices?"

"No. I don't want to get their hopes up or make them think this is some cruel joke. I want to do some legwork first."

"I thought you were convinced you were Heather Brice."

"There's being convinced and then there's proving it. I came here to prove it."

"It would be easy to know for sure with a DNA test."

"I can't put those poor people through that if I'm not sure."

"What do you think is going to happen here? You're going to have some revelation? Everything that happened to you at age two is suddenly going to come back to you in perfect recall?"

She stretched her legs out in front of her and tapped her feet together. "I'm not sure. I just know I have to be here, and I have to investigate."

"You can't go to the Brice house anymore. It's been torn down along with its neighbors to make room for a shopping center."

"I know that." She drew her knees up to her chest and clasped her arms around her legs. "Does this mean you're going to help me?"

He jerked back. How'd he get sucked in so quickly? He planted his feet on the carpet. Was she even telling the truth now? Maybe it was all a trick to get him to turn over what he knew about the Timberline Trio so she could film her stupid show and maybe even piggyback on his success like last time.

She saw it in his face—the doubt.

She touched her forehead to her knees and her strawberry blond hair created a veil over her face. Her voice came out muffled and unsteady. "I'm not playing you, Duke."

A sharp pain knifed the back of his head. He was done—for now.

"You've had a crazy day. Get to bed and we'll discuss it tomorrow." He pushed off the bed and made it to the door. He yanked it open and paused as she rolled off the bed as if to follow him.

He raised one eyebrow.

"I have to brush my teeth again. Thanks for suggesting this room. I know it's just a frog and a broken window, but I feel better being close to you."

"Good night, Beth."

As the door shut behind him, a whisper floated after him. "I always did feel better close to you."

THE FOLLOWING MORNING Beth opened her eyes and stretched, feeling fifty pounds lighter. There had been a moment at the end of the evening when it looked like Duke was ready to bolt, but overall he'd taken her confession well. And he'd believed her.

She hadn't revealed everything to him, but she wasn't ready for that…and neither was he. Maybe she'd feel another fifty pounds lighter once she did.

Sitting up in bed, she reached for her phone and checked her messages. Scott had asked when she needed her cameraman and the rest of the crew. Maybe she'd never need them. If she played it cool and didn't make a big fuss, her tormentor might stop harassing her and she could get down to the business of her real investigation.

The tap on her door made her yank the covers up to her chin.

"Beth, are you up yet? I talked to the cleaning crew, and I think I know how the intruder got into your hotel room."

"I'm awake. Just a minute." She scrambled out of bed, ran her tongue along her teeth and lunged for the door.

"Sleeping in?"

"I was exhausted." She swung the door wide. "Come on in. What did the maids have to say?"

He put a finger to his lips and closed the door. "Let's not broadcast this. They had a cart on your floor at about the time we figured someone broke into your room. They carry master room keys with them, and Gregory thinks someone walked by and snatched one, letting himself in your room."

"Doesn't say much for their security, does it?"

"What security? But the hotel is going to change its policy, and now each maid will have a single master key—no more leaving them on the carts. I'm not sure they were supposed to be doing that anyway."

"I hope I didn't get anyone in trouble." She ran her fingers through her hair, wishing she'd told Duke to wait until she'd showered and dressed. "Have you had breakfast yet?"

"No. I went for a run and then met with Gregory."

"Wish I'd been able to join you." She glanced at the alarm clock. "Can I buy you breakfast?"

"To continue our discussion from last night?"

"To eat breakfast."

"Pound on the wall when you're ready."

She released a pent-up breath when Duke left. Still testy, but he seemed as if he trusted her a little more after sleeping on her revelation. She'd have to make sure that trust continued to grow. She could use his help…and maybe his protection while unraveling her past.

She showered and dressed for the weather in a pair of jeans, a sweater and the boots she'd been wearing every day since she got here. Before leaving the room, she called the rental-car company to report the broken window.

Instead of banging on the wall, she knocked on Duke's door.

He answered with a file folder in his hand. As he held

it up, he said, "You may want to just eat breakfast, but I have to get to work. Yesterday was a wash."

"There's a restaurant a few miles from here that serves breakfast." She averted her eyes from the folder. If he wanted to share with her, he would.

"We'll take my car. Did you call the rental-car place?"

"I just did. They're swapping out the car for me. Seemed so surprised about the vandalism and theft."

"I guess it is unusual for this town unless you're determined to dwell on its ugly past."

"You know what I was thinking?" She ducked into the stairwell as Duke held the door for her. "I should've come here as a tourist and done my own detective work without the glare of publicity."

"Without bringing the spotlight with you, a lot of those people last night at the restaurant wouldn't have any interest in talking to you about the case. They might've recognized you anyway and had their suspicions. You just didn't realize not everyone would be thrilled with the show coming to town."

"It's not like it hasn't happened before—people unhappy with the show coming to their town." She shoved open the fire door to the lobby. "I'm going to put those pranks out of my mind and concentrate on my goal. Nothing is going to stop me."

She glanced at the front desk on her way out but another clerk had replaced Gregory. When they reached the parking lot, Beth spotted the ex-con she'd run into before, straddling his bike and examining her broken car window.

"That's the guy I saw in the forest." She elbowed Duke and called to the man. "I saw you in the forest."

The man looked up, a green baseball cap low on his forehead. "Is this your car?"

"It's a rental."

"That's a shame." He scratched his chin. "I heard why you were here—from them teenagers drinking in the woods."

"Do you want to get on camera now, too?"

"No, ma'am. Some things are just better off left alone." He got back on his bike and pedaled away.

"Do you know that man was questioned for the Carson kidnappings?"

Duke waved the file at her. "I do. His name is Gary Binder and he's a former junkie and an ex-con."

"Were you going to tell me about him?" She walked to the passenger side and he followed her. "I mentioned him to you yesterday."

As he opened the door, he shrugged. "Would you blame me for keeping my research to myself?"

Before she could answer, he turned and walked back to the driver's side.

By the time Duke got behind the wheel, she'd decided not to push her luck. If Duke wanted to help her in her quest, he'd do it. She wouldn't push him, wouldn't cajole. When she'd started this journey, she'd had no idea that Duke would be here. His presence did give her a sense of comfort, but she was determined to dig into this thing on her own and to discover the truth with or without Duke.

While he drove, she gave him directions to the little café that sat near a creek bed and served breakfast and lunch only. As they entered the restaurant, she pointed to the back. "They have a deck next to a running creek, but it looks like rain."

"I have a feeling it always looks like rain in Timberline, and I don't want my papers floating away."

A waitress shoved through the swinging doors to the

kitchen with a row of plates up each arm. "Sit anywhere. I'll be right with you."

They took a corner table and Duke turned his coffee cup upright. "You still drinking decaf tea?"

"You remembered?" For some reason, the fact that he remembered she'd been trying to give up caffeine gave her a warm glow. "I've been to this place already for breakfast and they have a good selection."

The waitress approached with a coffeepot. "Coffee?"

"Just one. Black." Duke inched his cup to the edge of the table.

"I'll have some hot tea, please."

Duke blew the steam rising from his cup. "How much do you know about Heather Brice?"

"She was the youngest kidnap victim at two, and she was snatched from her toddler bed while her babysitter slept on the couch in front of the TV."

"She was also the last of the Timberline Trio."

"The FBI at the time ruled out any connection between the missing children—no babysitters in common, no teachers, no day care, not even any friends, although Kayla Rush and Stevie Carson knew each other."

"You *have* done your homework." He took a sip of coffee as the waitress delivered her hot water and a selection of tea bags.

"One thing I don't know?"

"Yeah?"

"The new evidence. After the Carson kidnap case was resolved, law-enforcement officials mentioned that new evidence about the older case had come to light, but nobody ever mentioned what that evidence was." She tapped the folder on the table between them. "I'm assuming that's what you have here."

"If you're expecting a bombshell, this isn't it. No confessions. No long-lost bloody handprint. No DNA evidence."

"But enough to send an FBI agent out here to take a look at this cold case."

"An FBI agent who doesn't have anything better to do with his career right now."

"I heard about what happened, Duke. I'm sorry you lost your partner."

"But we saved the child. Tony, my partner, wouldn't have wanted it any other way, and I'm not making excuses for our decision. We both went into that warehouse with our eyes wide-open, both knowing the risks. We were willing to take those risks. Believe me, I would've taken that bullet instead of Tony if it meant saving the kid."

"The FBI didn't blame you."

"Not exactly, but look at me now." He spread his arms.

"I'm glad you're here." She dredged her tea bag in the hot water. "Is your boss expecting any results out here?"

"Mick always expects results. The Timberline Trio case has been a black eye for the FBI for twenty-five years."

"Maybe Mickey Tedesco thinks you're the man to repair that."

"Doubt it."

The waitress hovered at the table. "Are you ready to order?"

Duke flipped open the menu. "Haven't even looked."

"I'll go first." Beth poked at the menu. "I'll have the oatmeal with brown sugar, nuts, banana…and do you have any berries?"

"Fresh blueberries."

"That's fine."

Duke ordered some French toast and bacon.

When the waitress left, he wrapped his hands around

his coffee cup. "I don't get why you just don't contact the Brices, tell them your story and get a DNA test done."

"You know about the Brices, right?"

"That they're super wealthy? Yeah, I know that."

"Don't you think they'd be suspicious of people popping out of the woodwork claiming to be their long-lost daughter? It's probably happened to them before."

"You're already rich. You don't need their money."

"I'm hardly in the same league as the Brices. Do you know how much of their wealth my adoptive parents left to charities and foundations, cutting me out?"

"You mentioned that before, but my point is you're not some pauper trying to cash in on the Brices' wealth."

"I couldn't put them through anything like that based on a hunch."

"Now it's a hunch?" He tilted his head. "You were one hundred percent sure last night that you were Heather Brice."

She linked her fingers together. "It just all makes sense. I can't explain it to you. Even if Timberline had never experienced those kidnappings, I would've been drawn to this town. The fact that a little girl went missing twenty-five years ago only adds to my conviction."

"I don't know why I can't reveal the new evidence. It's not top secret." Duke dragged the folder toward him with one finger. "It has to do with drugs—the methamphetamine market, to be exact."

"Drugs?" Her hand jerked and a splash of hot tea sloshed into her saucer. "What would drugs have to do with a trio of kidnappings?"

"That's what I'm here to figure out. At the time of the kidnappings, law enforcement wasn't looking at other illegal activities in the area. The Timberline Sheriff's Department wasn't forthcoming about the drug trade to the FBI. Who knows why not? These petty jealousies between the local law and the FBI always crop up in cases like this—most of the time to the detriment of solving the case."

"So, the FBI discovered that there was a thriving drug trade in Timberline during the investigation of the recent kidnappings."

"Yep, and we got a lot of our information from Binder, the ex-con on the bike."

"It's not hard to imagine he was involved in drugs. Is that what he went away for?"

"He's been in and out of jail—petty stuff mostly, but what he lacked in quality, he made up for in quantity."

She traced a finger around the base of her water glass. "Are you thinking some sort of human trafficking for drugs?"

"It's a possibility."

Beth shivered. "That's horrible. Why those children?"

"Could've been crimes of opportunity. Those kids were unlucky enough to be in the wrong place at the wrong time. A lot of crime is like that."

"Still not much to go on."

"I told you—Siberia." He planted his elbows on the table. "Now tell me what you think you're going to accomplish. How are you going to figure out if you're Heather?"

She paused as the waitress delivered their food. "Anything else for you?"

Duke held up his cup. "Hit me again?"

"I'm a little embarrassed to admit this, but I thought I might just show up here and it would all come back to me." She swirled a spoonful of brown sugar through her oatmeal without looking up and meeting Duke's eyes, although she could feel his dark gaze drilling her.

"I'm sorry, Beth."

She raised her eyes and blinked. "You are?"

"I'm sorry your parents were so cold and distant. I always thought you had it better than I did with your money and private schools and fancy vacations, but you suffered a form of abuse just as surely as I did."

"I would never compare my life of luxury to what you went through with your father, Duke."

"At least my mom loved me, even though I couldn't save her or my sister from that man."

"Your father and mine were two sides of the same coin, weren't they?"

"And now you're driven to find your real family, but what if this journey doesn't end well?"

"You mean what if I'm not Heather Brice, loved and missed by her family?"

"Can you take the disappointment?"

"Of course." She dug into her oatmeal to hide her confusion. She'd been so convinced she was Heather, she hadn't allowed any doubt in her worldview—until now.

"When do you start your interviews? I can probably get Deputy Unger to talk to you. Maybe if his mom's still in town, she can talk to you about Heather's family."

Beth took a sip of tea to melt the lump in her throat. Only yesterday after she'd sprayed Duke in the face with pepper spray and he'd stalked off had she figured she'd get nothing more from him, and yet here he was, offering to save her again.

Despite his hard shell, he had a soft heart. That was why he thought he could save all the kids of the world.

"I thought…well, I figured you were done helping me with cold cases."

"I don't see this as a *Cold Case Chronicles'* investigation. I see this as a Beth St. Regis investigation."

"I figured you'd be done with that, too."

"Maybe I should be." He bit off the end of a piece of bacon.

"Duke, it was never just about the evidence." She hunched forward. "I don't know how you could've believed that after what we had."

"You used me, Beth—straight-up."

"I took the case files from your room when I spent the night with you, but I didn't spend the night with you to get the case files. How could you think that?"

"Easy. We had sex and then you snuck out in the early morning hours, taking my files with you."

She sighed. If he'd let her prove to him that she wanted him regardless of what he could do to help her, she could convince him in one night.

She dropped her spoon into her bowl as the truth punched her in the gut. She *did* still want Duke Harper, had never stopped wanting him. She just had one more truth to tell him and she didn't know if he'd ever get over that one.

He turned the file toward her. "Do you want to see this or is it just more fun skulking around in my room?"

"I'll take a look."

While Duke polished off the rest of his breakfast, Beth sifted through the pile of papers in the folder. Apparently, Timberline had suffered from a flourishing meth trade as the town's economy tanked. A lot of money exchanged hands and there had been a spike in crime. Could the drug dealers have branched into trafficking? It happened all over the world. Why would a small town in Washington be immune?

She closed the file. "That's some scary stuff."

"You can see it's not a stretch to imagine that druggie bunch might've been into some other serious crimes."

The waitress tucked the bill between the salt and pepper shaker and Beth grabbed it. "I'll use my expense account in exchange for the information. You see? Everything on the up-and-up."

"Sounds fair." Duke stood up and stretched. "I'm going to have a few meetings today with local law enforcement. Are you going to start making calls and setting up interviews with tomorrow's budding TV stars?"

"I suppose I have to start somewhere." She handed her credit card to the waitress. "Who knows? Maybe someone will recognize me as Heather Brice."

She signed the receipt and joined Duke outside. "I hope the rental company replaced my car already."

"I'll drop you off at the hotel." He placed a hand at the small of her back, propelling her toward the car. "Stay alert. Don't leave stuff in your car and make sure nobody's following you."

"Following me?" She hugged herself. "That's creepy. I hadn't thought of that."

"Just watch it. I'll even replace your pepper spray for you."

He started the car and wheeled out of the gravel parking lot of the restaurant.

They'd traveled just a half mile when traffic slowed down and the revolving lights of some emergency vehicles lit up the gray sky.

"Traffic accident?"

Duke craned his neck out the window. "I don't see any cars except the ones on the road."

Beth powered down her own window and stuck her

head out. "It's a bike at the side of the road—a twisted bike."

Then she saw it—a gurney with a sheet covering a body…and a green baseball cap on the ground.

Beth's stomach churned and her nails dug into the seat of the car. "Oh, my God. It's Gary Binder and I… I think he's dead."

Chapter Seven

"What?" Duke slammed on the brakes and the car lurched forward and back. "How can you tell?"

"That's his bike up ahead and there's a body on a gurney with a sheet covering the head."

"How do you know it's Binder? Maybe his bike's there because he stopped to help."

"It's the hat—the green baseball cap. It's on the ground next to the stretcher." Beth covered her mouth. "We were just talking to him. Literally, he could've been hit right after he left the parking lot of the hotel."

"We don't even know if he's been hit. I still don't see any cars stopped except for the emergency vehicles and all of us on the road." He swung the SUV onto the shoulder of the road.

"What are you doing?"

"I'm still an officer of the law, and I'm going to find out what happened."

His tires churned up gravel as he hugged the shoulder, rumbling past the cars stuck on the road.

A deputy stepped up to block his progress, so Duke threw the car into Park and grabbed the door handle. Turning to Beth, he said, "Stay here."

When he slammed his car door, he heard an echo from

the other side and saw Beth heading toward the crash scene. Did he expect anything different from her?

He caught her arm and whispered, "Let me do the talking."

"Folks, you need to get back in your car and keep moving."

Duke flashed his badge. "Special Agent Harper. I'm here on FBI business, Deputy, and I think the victim here is—was one of my witnesses."

As the deputy squinted at his badge, he said, "Gary Binder. Is that your man?"

Beth stiffened beside him.

Duke said, "That's him. What happened?"

"Hit and run."

Beth grabbed his arm and squeezed hard. "Any witnesses?"

"Not yet. Follow me." The deputy jerked his thumb toward the ambulance. "Damn shame since the guy was finally getting his life together."

Beth kept a grip on Duke as they walked toward the gurney, draped with a white sheet, the outlines of a body beneath it, a bloodstain near the head.

Duke didn't need to see Binder and Beth really didn't need to see him. "Who called the police?"

"Someone on a cell phone in a car. She noticed the bike first, and when she slowed down, she saw Binder's body just off the road."

"Any evidence? Tire tracks? Brake skid marks?"

"Nothing yet, but we're going to let the accident investigators do their thing." The deputy shook his head. "Timberline seems to be losing its civility ever since Evergreen Software went in—too many city folks bringing the hustle and bustle with 'em."

Duke swallowed hard. Was that what you called a hit

and run out here? A lack of civility? "Maybe someone will step forward or the driver will have an attack of conscience."

"Do you need anything else from me, Agent Harper? We can forward the accident report to you once it's complete."

"That would be helpful, thanks." He started heading back to the SUV with Beth attached to his arm. Halfway to the car, he turned. "Deputy? What was Binder doing out here on his bike?"

"Not sure. He'd been working as a handyman, doing odd jobs, but as far as I know, most of his work was in town. He always rode that damned bike. Someone had even given him a truck recently, but he stuck with the bike."

"To the very end."

Duke climbed into the car and glanced at Beth, whose wide eyes took up half her face. "Are you okay?"

"That's so…creepy. We were just talking to him." She knotted her fingers in her lap. "What was he doing at the Timberline Hotel?"

"Riding on his way to work or wherever he was going." He drummed his thumbs against the steering wheel. "Maybe he was doing work at the hotel and that's what brought him out this way."

"If he was at the hotel…"

"You're thinking he was the one who broke into your room and left the frog head?"

She nodded. "But why would he do that?"

"He'd do it if he was the one warning you."

"He doesn't have any real estate to worry about. Why would he want to scare me off this story?"

"Maybe he was involved in the Timberline Trio disappearance more than he let on in his interview." He cranked on the engine. "I'm throwing that out there, but I have a hard time believing Gary Binder would be sending anonymous emails to the FBI."

"Do you think his death—a hit and run—is just coincidental to all this other stuff?"

"Maybe, maybe not, but it doesn't have to be related to his involvement in the kidnappings or to the threats against you. Binder's the one who gave the FBI information about the drug trade at the time of the kidnappings."

Beth clasped her fidgeting hands so tightly her knuckles turned white. "You think someone was trying to shut him up?"

"Could be, even though it's a little late. He already spilled, unless…"

"Unless he had more to spill." Her knees began to bounce.

"Maybe that's why he was at the hotel. He knew you were staying there and wanted to talk to you. He didn't want to open up in front of me, so he pretended to be looking at the broken window. I'm going to have to review his previous interview carefully." He pulled into the line of traffic, crawling past the accident site. "But if he had more information, I don't know why he didn't give it up the first time."

"I don't know, Duke, but there seem to be some real forces of evil at work in Timberline."

As they passed the last emergency vehicle, Duke looked in his rearview mirror just as the ambulance doors closed on Gary Binder's body. A chill touched his spine.

Whatever evil held sway over Timberline, he'd do whatever it took to keep it far away from Beth…even as she ran toward it.

WHEN THEY GOT back to the hotel, the rental-car company had dropped off her replacement car. Duke walked around the car, examining it. He ran his hand along the roof. "Don't leave anything out on your seat this time."

"C'mon, Duke. We both know the vandal would've broken into my car with or without that bag on the seat. He was sending me a message."

"Thanks for the reminder. I'm going to get you a fresh container of pepper spray. At least you proved you know how to use it."

"Are you going to take off for your meetings?"

"After I ask the front desk about Binder. You coming?" Maybe he was stalling, but he didn't want to leave Beth alone. Funny how he'd done a complete one-eighty from yesterday—a few threats could do that.

"Sure, I'll come with you. My interviews can wait."

They walked into the lobby together, and Tammy, the receptionist at the check-in counter, looked up from her computer screen and waved. "Hello. Can I get you anything? I heard about your room, Ms. St. Regis, and we want to make your stay here hassle-free from here on out. The maid staff is being extra careful now."

"I appreciate that."

Duke rested his arms on the counter. "Tammy, do you know a local guy, Gary Binder?"

Her mouth formed an O. "I just heard. He's dead—hit-and-run accident. Who could do that? I never liked Gary much, but you don't leave a dog to die in the street without stopping. Am I right?"

News did travel quickly in Timberline. "Absolutely. I hope they catch the bastard and string him up."

Her eyes popped. "Wh…what did you want to know about Gary?"

"Did the hotel ever hire him to do any work around here?"

"Gary? No way. Management knew his reputation, even

though Kendall Rush had given him a chance when she was here."

Beth cleared her throat. "Isn't Kendall Rush the sister of one of the Timberline Trio?"

"Twin." The clerk pulled the corners of her mouth down with two fingers. "She was out here to sell her aunt's house and got caught up with all the craziness with Wyatt Carson. But while she was here, she hired Gary to do some work at the house. I guess he did okay, but management here would still never hire him."

"Do you know why he'd have any reason to be at this hotel? In the parking lot?" Duke tipped his head in that direction. "We saw him out there, probably just before he got hit."

"Really?" Tammy's eyes got even bigger. "I don't know why he'd be here, just passing by, I guess." She licked her lips. "Do you think the sheriff's department is going to want to look at our security tapes of the parking lot?"

"Probably. In fact—" Duke slid his badge across the counter "—I wouldn't mind having a look myself."

"Okay. I know you're FBI and all, but can I call my manager first?"

"Sure." He glanced at Beth. "You can take off if you want, set up those interviews."

"I think I'd rather watch this video." She leaned in close, putting her lips next to his ear, and said in a low voice, "Why do you think Kendall Rush hired him?"

"Don't know. Maybe she felt sorry for him."

Tammy got off the phone. "My manager says it's okay."

She invited them behind the counter and into a small room. She hunched over a set of computer monitors and clicked through several files, launching a video. "This is from earlier today. How long ago did you see him?"

"Over two hours ago."

She cued up the tape, and after several minutes, Gary Binder with his green ball cap came into the frame, walking his bike.

Beth jabbed her finger at the display. "Is he talking to someone out of the picture?"

Binder kept looking over his shoulder, but Duke couldn't see his mouth moving.

"I'm not sure. Maybe he's just watching for cars as he comes into the parking lot, but he seems to have a purpose for coming into the lot."

"Yeah, he's looking at my rental."

After checking behind him once more, Binder wheeled up to Beth's rental car and poked his head inside the broken window. A minute later Duke and Beth appeared in the frame.

They watched a bit longer, but Binder never returned to the parking lot after they took off.

Tammy scrunched up her face. "Looks like he just wanted a closer look at your car."

"Why did he keep glancing over his shoulder? There's not that much traffic on the road." Beth stepped back from the monitors and folded her arms. "Because if there had been, someone would've seen the car that hit him."

"Maybe someone did." Duke backed out of the claustrophobic room. "Thanks, Tammy. I'll tell the sheriff's department about seeing Binder in the parking lot here, and they'll probably want to review that tape, too."

Her fingers flew across the keyboard as she closed down the recordings. "I just wish there was something on there. I suppose they told Gary's mom already. She's a tough, old lady, but Gary was her only kid."

"Sounds like the guy couldn't catch a break." He turned to Beth. "Are you taking off now? I'll be at the sheriff's station if you need me."

"And I'll be setting up shop somewhere to do some interviews."

"You could do them here in your hotel room, or maybe the hotel lobby."

"If I've learned anything from the show, it's that people feel more comfortable talking in their homes."

"Just don't go to Bill Raney's home to interview him." He pushed open the hotel door and they stepped outside.

"I'm not going to be interviewing people who don't want to talk to me."

"How do you know if they're being honest?" He aimed the key fob at his car and the horn blipped. "They could pretend and then change their story when they get you alone."

"I'm only going to talk to the ones I gave cards to last night—Chloe the waitress and a few senior citizens. You don't think I have anything to fear from them, do you?"

"Be careful, Beth. If the same person who's warning you is the same person who hit Binder, he's just added murder to his résumé."

She rubbed her arms. "If someone did kill Gary, it's because he knew something. I know nothing."

"Not yet and maybe you should keep it that way."

"I'll be careful, Duke." She got behind the wheel of her new rental and pressed her palm against the glass.

He waved back. He had no choice but to leave her.

When he drove past the accident scene, the ambulance had already left with its sad cargo and one cop car remained, directing traffic.

Was Binder's death really connected to his willingness to speak up about the Timberline drug trade twenty-five years ago? Deputy Unger had mentioned tweakers being responsible for the vandalism of Beth's car. Did that mean the drug culture was alive and well in Timberline today?

He hoped all Beth got today was half-baked stories of Wyatt Carson. She didn't need to be involved in this case any more than she already was.

He'd almost been relieved to hear about her ulterior motive for being in Timberline. Maybe once she found out she wasn't Heather Brice, she'd give up on this story.

And if she *was* Heather Brice? What could be the danger in that? She'd leave Timberline, reconnect with her long-lost family who now resided in Connecticut and live happily ever after...or not.

Duke's cop radar gave him an uneasy feeling about that scenario. What if the Brice family rejected her, too? She talked a tough game, but she had a vulnerable side she tried hard to mask.

He could speed up the entire process by requesting DNA from the Brices as part of this investigation. They wouldn't even have to know about Beth and her suspicions. Once Beth knew the truth—one way or the other—she could stop sleuthing around Timberline.

He pulled up to the sheriff's station and entered the building with a few file folders tucked under his arm. He hadn't met the new sheriff yet, who was probably just getting up to speed.

Deputy Unger greeted him at the desk.

"I'm here to see Sheriff Musgrove."

"The sheriff's expecting you. Go on back, first office on the right."

Duke thanked him and made his way to the sheriff's office. He tapped on the open door and a big man rose from the desk dominating the office.

"Agent Harper? I'm Sheriff Musgrove."

Duke leaned over the desk and shook the sheriff's hand. "Nice to meet you, Sheriff. What do you think of the hit-and-run accident that killed Gary Binder?"

"That's what I like about you fibbies." He smacked his hand against his desk. "Get right to the point. I think Gary Binder was a junkie who was probably riding his bike recklessly on the road, maybe even riding under the influence, if you know what I mean."

Duke studied the man's red face with a sinking feeling in the pit of his stomach. Clearly he had a sheriff on his hands who didn't have the ability to think out of the box. Too bad Sheriff Sloane wasn't still in the position. He'd heard nothing but high praise of Sloane from Agent Maxfield, who'd worked the Wyatt Carson case.

Duke took a deep breath. "You don't find it coincidental that Binder had just given us some information about the Timberline drug trade during the initial kidnappings?"

"The world is filled with coincidences, Harper. I don't find a junkie getting hit by a car all that coincidental."

Duke shoved his hands into his pockets and hunched his shoulders. "By all accounts, Binder was in recovery, hadn't touched drugs in over a year."

"Once a junkie, always a junkie." Musgrove sliced his big hands through the air. "Is that the course you're going to follow on this case, Harper? Are you going to dig up Timberline's sordid past?"

"No town, big or small, is exempt from drugs, Sheriff." Duke narrowed his eyes. "Are you one of the contingents that would rather not have the spotlight on Timberline?"

"Is it a contingent? I'll be damned. I know the town has worked hard to come back from its failures, and we're on the cusp of something great. I plan to work with the mayor and the town fathers to get it there."

Duke's gaze tracked over the sheriff's head to the awards and commendations on the wall, illustrating a career bouncing from agency to agency. He knew law-enforcement types like this guy, scrambling to secure the highest pension with the least amount of work, kissing ass along the way.

He'd have to report back to Mick that Sheriff Musgrove would be more of a hindrance than a help for this cold case.

His eyes dropped to the sheriff's face. "You weren't here during the Carson copycat kidnappings, were you?"

"No, I was over in Spokane. I read about it, though. Crazy SOB. I was hired in after Sheriff Sloane left for Phoenix—took off with that sister of one of the Timber-line Trio. Talk about getting wrapped up in the job." He shook his head.

Musgrove would never be one to get too wrapped up in the work. Put in the hours and go home. Duke never understood guys like that.

For him, the work was a calling, a duty. It had been like that for his partner, Tony DeLuca, too. Guys on the other side never got it.

"I understand Sheriff Sloane's daughter was the final kidnap victim."

"Yeah, yeah. Tough break. I guess he couldn't handle it." Musgrove puffed out his chest as if he could handle anything. "Deputy Unger was here for the copycat kidnappings and sat in on the interview with Binder. He's out front if you want to talk to him. Otherwise, you have free rein here, Agent Harper. Our files are your files, and we'll get you that accident report on Binder if you're interested."

"I am. Thanks, Sheriff Musgrove."

They shook hands again and Musgrove sank heavily behind his desk and returned to his computer. Duke didn't have a clue what the man was looking at, but he could guarantee it wasn't work related.

Duke sauntered up front and stopped at Unger's desk. "Can I ask you a few questions about Gary Binder and the whole Wyatt Carson case?"

"Sure." Unger glanced over his shoulder. "Maybe we can do this over coffee."

Duke got the hint.

"Sheriff Musgrove, Agent Harper and I are going out for coffee to discuss the Binder interview."

The sheriff called from his office. "Did you get those reports done yet?"

"Been on your desk for two hours, sir." Unger rolled his eyes at Duke.

The sound of shuffling papers came from the office. "Got 'em. Keep me posted, Deputy."

"I'll do that, sir."

When they stepped out of the station, Unger tilted his head from side to side, as if cracking his neck.

"The guy's a pain, huh?"

"I'm not gonna bad-mouth my superior, but he's no Coop Sloane."

"I heard good things about Sloane from Agent Maxfield."

"That just proves how good he was, since he and Maxfield didn't always see eye to eye."

"That happens a lot between the FBI and local law enforcement. It's a testament to both of them that they were able to work together and nail Carson."

They'd walked half a block and Unger pointed ahead. "Buy you a coffee?"

"Sure."

A couple of people on laptops huddled at tables and an older gentleman looked up from his paperback when they walked in.

Duke and Unger ordered their coffee and sat across from each other at a table by the window.

Duke stretched out his legs and popped the lid off his cup. "What do you think about Binder's death?"

"I think it's damned strange." Unger took a sip from his cup. "I overheard Musgrove and he's just wrong about Binder. Whatever the guy was into in his past life, he was clean and sober in this one."

"Do you think someone targeted him for his revelations about the Timberline drug trade twenty-five years ago?"

"Seems pointless, doesn't it? We already interviewed him and he told us everything he knew. No point in killing him now."

"Unless he didn't tell you everything. Maybe there was more to come and someone wanted to make sure he kept his mouth shut."

"The thought did cross my mind." Unger tugged on his earlobe. "It's funny that it happened after you showed up and after that TV host came to town."

Duke's pulse jumped. "What do you know about reaction to *Cold Case Chronicles* delving into the Timberline Trio case?"

"It's divided. You have one faction who wants their fifteen minutes of fame and another that's worried about the town's rep and doesn't want this case being rehashed every five years. Most folks want to move on. The families aren't even here anymore."

"Do you think Beth St. Regis is in any danger?"

"Honestly, if she wants my advice, it's not worth it. I don't think the current residents of Timberline are going to be able to give her any juicy new info about the case. She should find herself another one. I've watched that show before, and she can do a lot better than this."

"Yeah, I've been telling her to move on to something else, but the woman is stubborn."

Especially since she thought Timberline was the key to her past. Duke was still considering ordering DNA from the Brices just to settle this thing for Beth one way or the other.

In fact, that idea was sounding better and better.

Because as much as he wanted Beth right here in Timberline by his side, he had a cold dread that something bad was on the horizon.

Chapter Eight

Beth positioned her video camera on the tripod and smiled at Gail and Nancy. "Could you just start by saying your names?"

Gail jabbed a finger toward the camera. "Does this mean we're going to be on TV?"

Beth gritted her teeth behind her smile. "We shoot a lot of footage, Gail. If we can use it for the story, we'll put it on the show."

She patted her gray perm and smiled. "I'm Gail Fitzsimmons."

Leaning into Gail's space, Nancy said, "And I'm Nancy Heck."

"You don't need to lean over, Nancy. The camera is capturing both of you." Beth cleared her throat. "Did you both know the victims' families?"

Gail answered first. "My daughter used to babysit the twins sometimes."

Beth's heart banged against her rib cage. "Did she babysit Heather Brice, too?"

"Heather was too young. My daughter was seventeen at the time and wasn't interested in sitting toddlers or babies. Kayla and Kendall were older—five-year-olds—potty trained, talking."

"She wasn't babysitting them the night Kayla was kidnapped, though."

"Thank God, no. The parents had left the girls with their aunt. I don't know why. Cass was always a little scatterbrained. Don't you think so, Nancy?"

"Oh, yes, scatterbrained." Nancy seemed transfixed by the camera.

"Is Wendy Simons's family still here?" Beth scribbled on the pad of paper in front of her.

"The girl who was babysitting Heather Brice?" Gail cocked her head at Nancy. "I don't think so. Any of the Simons family around, Nancy?"

"They had a lot of children in that family. That's why Wendy would babysit the little ones. She was the second oldest in her family and helped her mother with her younger siblings."

"I know that, but are any of them still around? That's what Beth's asking."

Nancy reddened to the roots of her silver hair. "I... I don't know about that. I don't think so."

"What was the speculation at the time of the kidnappings?" Beth directed her question to Gail because she was clearly the ringleader and had probably just frightened Nancy into permanent silence.

"With the first one, Kayla, the police actually thought it was the father for a while." Gail affected a stage whisper. "The parents were having troubles."

"But once Stevie Carson was kidnapped, they realized it was something more...more sinister." Nancy placed both hands over her heart.

Gail rolled her eyes at the camera. "I don't know about you, but a father kidnapping or killing his own child is pretty sinister."

"Gail Fitzsimmons, I didn't say it wasn't. Why do you have to twist my words?"

"I understood what she meant, Gail." Beth waved her hands. "Were there any troubles in Stevie's family…or Heather's?"

Nancy had regained her composure and some confidence. "There were always problems in Stevie's family. Maybe that's why Wyatt turned out like he did. But Heather's family? Perfect."

Beth's gaze darted to Gail, waiting for her to disagree with her friend.

But she nodded with a smile on her face. "The Brices were a perfect family, weren't they? The parents adored each other and their children. It was lovely to see and so sad…after."

Beth's nose stung. A perfect family who adored their kids—just the kind of family she'd always dreamed of.

"Yoo-hoo, Beth?"

She snapped out of her daydream. "Yes, go on."

"Do you have any more questions? Because we have a lot more where that came from."

The ladies hadn't told her much she didn't already know, but she could sit and listen to stories about the perfect Brice family all day.

She continued with Gail and Nancy for another forty-five minutes. She'd gotten some colorful quotations from them she might be able to use in the story, but their answers hadn't done much to clear up the mystery—or to solidify her belief that she was Heather Brice.

Beth ended the interview and Nancy sent her away with a tin of cookies and an implied promise of more if their faces wound up on TV. She sent Duke a quick text to let him know where she was, since he'd seemed so concerned when she'd left.

She didn't mind one bit.

Munching on a snickerdoodle, Beth drove to her next appointment at Chloe Rayman's apartment in a new development near the Evergreen Software headquarters. She brought the cookies with her to Chloe's door.

Chloe opened at her knock in full makeup, the ruffle at her low neckline fluttering. "Hello. I'm ready for my close-up, as they say."

"Well, then, let's get set up." She stuck out the tin. "Cookie? They're from Nancy Heck."

"Nancy's famous for her snickerdoodles, but I'll pass. I just brushed my teeth."

Probably flossed and whitened while she was at it.

Beth set up the camera on the tripod and sat in a chair across from Chloe on the sofa. "State your name, please."

"Chloe Rayman. Six eighty-two Treeline Boulevard, number five, Timberline, Washington." She clapped a hand over her lipsticked mouth. "Maybe I shouldn't put all of my personal information out there on TV."

"We'll…ah…edit that out." Beth crossed her legs and took a deep breath. This was gonna be a long interview.

For the next half hour Beth allowed Chloe to chatter on about Wyatt Carson. She had very little insight into the man or what made him tick, and he hadn't talked to her about his brother at all. The interview was worthless to the show and worthless to Beth's personal quest.

As she was trying to think of a way to cut things short, a knock on the door had Chloe gasping and jumping from the sofa.

"That's my boyfriend, Jason. He's really jealous, so I don't want him to know I've been talking about Wyatt."

"Of course." Beth turned off the camera. "I think I got everything I needed."

Chloe ran to get the door as Beth collapsed the tripod

and shoved her notebook into her bag. She glanced over her shoulder as a compact man swept Chloe into a big hug. She met his gaze across the room and he released his girlfriend.

"Sorry. I didn't know you had company."

Chloe waved her hand toward Beth. "This is Beth St. Regis with that *Cold Case Chronicles* show. When she found out I used to know Wyatt Carson, she practically begged to interview me. Beth, this is my boyfriend, Jason Foster."

Jason tucked his shoulder-length dark hair behind one ear. "Hey, Beth."

"Nice to meet you, Jason. I was just leaving." She held out the tin. "Cookie?"

"Thanks." He took the tin from her and popped the lid. "You interviewed Nancy Heck."

"Her snickerdoodles have quite a reputation."

He took a bite of a cookie and brushed some crumbs from his chin. "You have a lot of people up in arms over this story."

"Are you one of them?"

He shrugged. "Doesn't bother me, but the elders are buzzing."

"Elders?" She hitched her bag over one shoulder.

"Jason's Quileute and they're kind of hinky about the Timberline Trio case."

"I met a teenage boy in the woods who told me the same thing. What is it about the case?"

"You got me." He pointed to the tin he'd placed on Chloe's coffee table. "Can I have another cookie?"

"Sure. I suppose anyone who did know wouldn't be willing to talk to me about it."

"Probably not, at least not the old folks."

"And the young folks, like you, probably don't know why it's a taboo topic."

"I sure as hell don't, but my cousin might have a clue." He brushed his hands together. "She's a shaman for the tribe, so certain customs and beliefs have been handed down to her more than the rest of us."

"Does she live in Timberline?"

"Yeah, and she happens to be in town. She travels a lot for her shows."

"Shows?"

Chloe curled her arm around Jason's waist. "Scarlett's an artist, has art shows all over the world."

"That's impressive." Beth's skin had begun to tingle with excitement. A shaman? Someone who knew about the case? Maybe she could help Beth with her own personal agenda.

"Do you think your cousin…?"

"Scarlett. Scarlett Easton."

"Do you think Scarlett would be willing to talk to me?"

"Probably. Her studio's out past the north side of town. You can tell her I sent you."

"Would you mind giving me her number?"

Jason pulled a wallet from his back pocket. "I think I have one of her cards. She only has a cell phone and reception isn't great out there, but you can give it a try."

He fanned out several cards between his fingers and plucked one from the bunch. "Here it is."

Beth scanned the black card with a reprint of a watercolor nature scene splashed on the front. "If this is her work, it's beautiful."

"Yeah, that's one of her more normal works. She does landscapes and then some freaky modern art—that's the stuff that gets her the shows and some big money. You couldn't pay me to hang some of that stuff in my living room."

"Don't tell Scarlett that." Chloe poked Jason's heavily tattooed arm.

Beth held up the card. "Thanks, Jason. In case I can't reach her by phone, can you give me directions to her place?"

"Chloe, do you have paper and a pen?"

"Will the back of an envelope work?" She took two steps toward her small kitchen and grabbed an envelope and pen from the counter, which she handed to Jason.

He squatted down next to the coffee table and sketched out a map. "Scarlett got all the artistic talent in our family, but if you head this way off the main road, you'll see an access road next to a mailbox that's all painted. Follow that and you'll run into Scarlett's place."

Looking at the map, Beth wrinkled her nose. "Do I need four-wheel drive to get there?"

"Nah, it's remote but the access road to the cabin is gravel."

Beth tucked the makeshift map in her back pocket. "Do you guys want the cookies or maybe I should bring them to Scarlett?"

"We'll take 'em." Jason grabbed the tin and hugged it to his chest. "Scarlett's a vegan or vegetarian or something and doesn't touch the stuff."

"I think you're exaggerating to get cookies." Chloe rolled her eyes at Beth.

"You can keep them anyway." Beth hitched the tripod beneath her arm. "Thanks for your time, Chloe."

Jason got the door for her. "Can I help you carry anything to your car?"

"I got it, thanks."

Beth loaded up the car and, seated in the driver's seat, pulled out her phone. She tapped in Scarlett's number and it went straight to voice mail.

"Scarlett, my name is Beth St. Regis. I'm the host of *Cold Case Chronicles*, and I'm in town to do a story about the Timberline Trio. Your cousin Jason Foster told me you might be able to give me some insight into the Quileute view of the crime. Would love to talk to you."

Beth left her number and checked her texts. Nothing from Duke. He must still be busy with the sheriff's department.

She'd give Scarlett an hour or so to get back to her and then maybe she'd head out to her place in case Scarlett never got her message.

She decided to try Sutter's again for lunch and brought her laptop into the restaurant with her.

The place buzzed with a lunch crowd from Evergreen Software, by the looks of their khakis, pocket protectors and firm grips on their electronic devices.

Beth flagged down the hostess. "Can I get a table for one?"

"Your best bet is a seat at the bar. We serve a full lunch menu at the bar."

"Perfect." Beth hoisted her laptop case over her shoulder and wended her way through the tables to the bar. Heck, she fit right in with her laptop.

She hopped up on a stool and opened her case. As she pulled out her laptop, the bartender placed a menu to the side of it.

"Are you ordering lunch?"

"Yes, and I'll have a cup of hot tea."

"Coming right up." The bartender ducked beneath the counter and clinked a mug on the mahogany bar. "You know Bill Raney wasn't serious about those threats, right?"

Beth focused on the woman's face and realized she'd been tending bar last night when Duke had confronted the loudmouthed Raney.

"Did I think he really wanted to tar and feather me? No. What's your name?"

"Serena Hopewell. And, no, I wasn't here twenty-five years ago." She poured a stream of hot water into Beth's cup.

"Why are you coming to Bill's defense, Serena?"

She shrugged. "He's been having a tough time lately. He's been drinking at this bar way too much. The cops questioned him about a few things this morning, and he doesn't need any more trouble."

"I didn't accuse Bill of anything, but I had a couple of…incidents and his name came up with the deputies." She dunked her tea bag in the water. "They were probably just following up. I don't think he's suspect number one."

"It was enough to get him in trouble with his wife, but that doesn't take much these days." Serena tapped the menu. "Do you need a few minutes?"

"Yeah." As Beth flipped open the menu, someone nudged her shoulder.

"I thought you were going out to Scarlett's place." Chloe's high-pitched voice carried halfway around the restaurant as several people craned their necks to take in the bar.

Beth gave her a tight smile. "Thought I'd have some lunch first, and I did leave her a message."

"Good luck with that. Scarlett likes to keep to herself when she's in town."

Jason came up behind his girlfriend. "Our table's ready. Oh, hey, Beth. Any luck with my cuz yet?"

"Left her a message, will probably pay her a visit this afternoon."

"That's probably the best way to get her attention." He took Chloe's hand. "C'mon, babe. We got a table in Austin's section."

When Beth looked up from her menu, she met Serena's eyes.

The bartender lifted one eyebrow. "You've been busy."

"It's my job. I'm here to work." She closed the menu and held it out. "I'd like the soup-and-sandwich combo—veggie chili and grilled chicken."

"You got it."

Beth flipped up her laptop and checked email. She answered an inquiry about a previous story, replied to an anxious message from Scott and opened a document to take some notes about the two interviews today.

When her lunch arrived, she checked her phone again. Nothing from Scarlett and nothing from Duke.

She took a bite of her sandwich, her teeth crunching through the grilled sourdough. Ever since Jason had told her about his cousin's extrasensory abilities, Beth's mind had been toying with a plan.

She'd seen a hypnotist a few times to try to uncover buried memories about her past. That was where she'd seen visions of the forest, which had evoked such cold terror. But she'd gotten no further with the hypnotist. Someone like Scarlett Easton might be able to help her uncover even more. She had to try…if Scarlett was willing.

She finished her lunch, and as she was slipping her laptop back into its case, a man took the bar stool next to hers.

"Give me that River IPA, Serena."

Beth slid a gaze to her left and Jordan Young caught her eye.

"Hello there, Ms. St. Regis. How's your story going?"

"It's going."

Serena put the beer in front of Young. "Little early in the day for alcohol, isn't it?"

"Rough morning, sweetheart." He raised the glass to Serena and took a sip. "I feel like I need to make up for my friend Bill's boorish behavior, Ms. St. Regis. I'd be happy to talk to you about the Timberline Trio case sometime. I was here—" he patted the top of his head "—with a little more hair."

"I'd be interested in what you have to say, and you can call me Beth."

"Pretty name. And you can call me Jordan."

"Thanks, Jordan."

She slipped off the stool just as Serena hunched toward Jordan. "What do you think about the hit and run that killed Gary?"

Beth didn't get a chance to hear what Jordan thought about Gary as she headed for the door, anxious to meet with Scarlett now that she'd decided on a plan.

When she got to her rental car, she checked all the doors and windows—nothing today. She loaded her laptop in the trunk and pulled Jason's map from her pocket.

When she sat behind the wheel, she flattened the envelope on her thigh and memorized the first few directions.

She made the turn from the main road and passed several houses and access roads until she reached the one with the mailbox painted with chickens. Why chickens?

She turned her rental onto the access road, her tires crunching the gravel and her car rocking back and forth. She drove into a tunnel of trees, feeling the chill as her world darkened.

Suddenly the road ended, but she did see the peak of a roof beyond the tree line. She would've needed a four-wheel-drive vehicle to get close to Scarlett's cabin, but the road had ended within walking distance and a path cut through the trees.

She got out of the car and slammed the door behind her. She glanced at the trunk, where she'd stashed her laptop. Duke had warned her about leaving her stuff in the car, but at least it was out of sight. Who would be out here in the middle of the woods, anyway?

Tugging on her down vest, she headed toward the cabin, her boots crunching through the underbrush.

She took one big step over a fallen log. As something whizzed past her ear, she heard a crack in the distance. She yelled, "Hey," as she fell to the forest floor on her hands and knees.

That was a gunshot—and she was the target.

Chapter Nine

Duke heard the report of a rifle from his open window. Beth could be out there.

He stepped on the gas pedal of his SUV and the car tore across the road, spewing gravel in its wake.

He almost plowed into the back of Beth's car. He lurched to a stop behind the rental and bolted from the car.

"Beth?"

"I'm here. Be careful. Some idiot is shooting a rifle."

"Are you okay?"

"I'm on the ground about twenty feet in front of my car."

Duke hunched forward in case the hunter—or whoever it was—decided to squeeze off any more shots.

He spotted Beth, still crouched on the ground, her eyes wide and her face pale.

"I yelled when I heard the shot and dropped to the ground. I recognized it right away, of course."

"Did you see anything? A hunter? I know it's hunting season right now."

"What the hell is going on?" A woman's voice floated out from the cabin.

Duke cupped a hand around his mouth. "Someone's taking shots out here."

She called back. "Everyone okay?"

"Yes." Beth started to rise. "Do you think it's safe?"

"Even those idiot hunters should know by now we're humans and not some defenseless beast."

Duke reached Beth's side and helped her to her feet.

She grabbed his arm for support. "What are you doing here?"

"Stopped by Sutter's and Jason told me you were planning to see his cousin this afternoon." With his arm around her, he led her to a small clearing where a woman with long, black hair stood in front of a rustic cabin, her hands wedged on her hips.

"And who the hell are you two?"

"Are you Scarlett Easton?" Beth brushed off the knees of her jeans and pushed her hair from her face.

"Who wants to know?" The woman stood even taller, as if challenging them to take one more step.

"I'm Beth St. Regis. Your cousin Jason gave me your number. I tried calling, and I left a voice mail but Jason said you don't always get reception out here."

The woman tossed back her head, and her mane of black hair flipped over one shoulder. "I'm Scarlett Easton, and I don't know why my cousin seems to think I need company, but since some moron almost shot you on my property, come on in."

They followed Scarlett to a wide, wooden porch, almost a deck, and Duke stomped his boots on the first step. "I'm Duke Harper. Does that happen a lot with hunters? Pot-shots in the forest?"

As Scarlett pushed open her front door, she tilted her head. "Happens a lot around here."

Duke exchanged a glance with Beth as they followed Scarlett into her place. Did that mean the shot wasn't meant for Beth?

Scarlett Easton didn't seem like good interview material for Beth, and it didn't seem as if she wanted anyone on her property. So why had Beth come here?

Beth pointed to a cell phone on a table that had been carved from a tree stump. "Are you going to call the sheriff's department?"

"Reception isn't good today." Scarlett dipped to pick up her phone. "If I didn't get your call, what makes you think I can get a call out to the cops?"

Duke tried his own phone and received a No Service message. "She's right."

"But if you could tell that idiot Sheriff Musgrove someone was shooting a rifle, too close to the road, I'd appreciate it."

Duke dragged a hand across his mouth, wiping away his smile. She had Musgrove pegged already and he hadn't been on the job even two months.

"Can I get you something? Water? Soda? Stiff shot of whiskey?" Scarlett jerked her chin toward Beth. "You look as white as a sheet."

"Maybe some water." Beth placed her hands on her cheeks. "That bullet flew right past my ear."

"Idiots." Scarlett shook her head and asked Duke, "Anything for you?"

"No, thanks."

Scarlett cranked on the faucet in the kitchen and filled a glass with water. "The stuff from the tap is actually better than the bottled stuff. Ice?"

"Just the water."

Scarlett handed the glass to Beth. "So what brought you to my doorstep? You friends with Jason?"

"I just met Jason today." Beth took a gulp of water, and her gaze darted to Duke's face. "I host a television show called *Cold Case Chronicles*."

"Never heard of it."

Duke scanned the decor of the cabin—a mix of hand-carved furniture, Native American crafts and original artwork—an explosion of colors and textures that overwhelmed the senses. A bookshelf took up one wall and hardback books and paperbacks jockeyed for space on the crammed shelves…but no TV.

Beth took a deep breath. "It's a reality TV show where we investigate cold cases."

"Let me guess." Scarlett raised her eyes to the beamed ceiling. "You're doing a story on the Timberline Trio."

Beth licked her lips. "Jason told me the Quileute are suspicious about the case. He told me you would have some insight into that."

"Jason thought I'd be willing to sit down with a reality TV show and discuss our Quileute heritage?" She snorted, the nostrils of her delicate nose flaring. "He must be smoking the good stuff these days."

Duke watched Beth, uncharacteristically hesitant. She should be halfway to convincing Scarlett an interview would be the best thing that ever happened to her. There had to be something more to this visit to Scarlett.

"I understand that." The glass of water Beth brought to her lips trembled. "That's not really why I'm here."

Duke's eyebrows shot up. "It's not?"

"It's not?" Scarlett echoed him.

"Can we sit down?" Beth hovered near a curved love seat.

"All right." Scarlett grabbed what looked like a hand-painted pillow and dropped into a chair, dragging the pillow into her lap. "Just let me warn you. I'm not doing anything related to some reality TV show, and I'm not exploiting my tribe's traditions and customs."

Normally, Duke would perch on the arm of a chair but didn't want to destroy anything in this room and end up paying thousands of dollars to replace it. He sat on the edge of the love seat, next to Beth.

"What I'm going to ask you has nothing to do with the show. It's about me."

"Let's hear it." Scarlett tapped the pointed toe of her cowboy boot.

Beth squared her shoulders. "I have a mysterious past. I was adopted, but my adoptive parents refused to tell me where I came from, and my birth certificate has their names as my biological parents."

"Go on." Scarlett drew her dark brows over her nose.

"Anyway, I tried hypnosis a few times to try to reveal any memories, but all I got was a cold terror associated with the vision of a forest."

Duke folded his arms over a niggling fear in his chest. Beth wanted Scarlett Easton to perform some ritual mumbo jumbo on her.

Scarlett held up one finger. "Hypnosis can really only work with the memories that are already there. I doubt you have any memories of being a baby."

"That's my problem. Even if I could dig up my earliest memories, they're not going to tell me who I am or where I came from."

"Right. So, what are you doing in Timberline? I'm known as an artist, not a Quileute shaman. You didn't come here for me."

Duke held his breath and tried to catch Beth's eye, but she'd started down a path and there was no turning back.

"I think I'm Heather Brice."

Scarlett whistled. "Are you kidding me?"

"A variety of sources led me to Timberline—that Pacific Chorus frog, the scenery and my response to it, and the missing children. I just feel it."

"Tell me all of it." Scarlett shoved off the chair. "But I

need to get comfortable first. Duke, do you want something to drink? A beer? A shot of whiskey?"

"Whiskey? Ah, no, but I'll take a beer. I have a feeling I'm gonna need it."

Scarlett went into the kitchen, her long hair waving down her back. She returned with a bottle of beer, which she handed to him, and her arm around a bottle of whiskey with her index finger and thumb pinching two shot glasses together. She put them on the tree table, filled each one about halfway with the amber liquid and then gave one to Beth.

"Tell me everything." Scarlett held up her shot glass and Beth touched it with hers.

They both downed the whiskey in one gulp.

Beth launched into her story—the same one she'd told him, except she hadn't mentioned the hypnotherapy.

Scarlett interrupted her here and there to ask a question or inject a comment. She was seriously considering helping Beth.

"You don't still have the original frog, do you?"

"No. I remember having that frog as a child and it's in my earliest pictures, but I don't know what my parents did with it. They probably threw it away."

"Do you have anything else from that time period?"

Beth nodded. "A locket."

Duke jerked his head to the side. That was news to him. She'd never told him about that, but then, their relationship hadn't progressed to the stage where they'd known everything about each other.

He'd broken it off when he discovered he couldn't trust her, but now he was beginning to see why Beth might've found it difficult to be completely open with anyone.

"You're sure the locket is from the time before your adoption?"

"I always had it. It's not the kind of thing you'd give to a toddler and it's not something the Kings, my adoptive parents, would've ever given to me."

"They didn't discuss the locket with you?"

"My mother just told me it was mine and that someone had given it to me when I was a baby."

"Do you have it with you?"

"It's in my hotel room. Is it important?"

"What is it you're asking me to do, Beth?"

"I want you to use your…sensitivity to help me confirm that I'm Heather Brice. Can you do that?"

"There are certain rituals I can perform. It might not be pleasant."

"For me? I can handle it."

"For me." Scarlett tipped another splash of whiskey into her glass and tossed it back. "You're not going to be seeing into your past. *I'm* going to be seeing into your past."

Duke felt Beth stiffen beside him. "I can't ask you to do that, not if it's going to bring any harm to you."

"I didn't say it would hurt me. It's just not the most comfortable feeling in the world."

Duke hunched forward, elbows on his knees. "What do you get out of it? Money?"

Scarlett whipped her head around, dark eyes blazing. "I don't do this for money. Do you think I'm back on the rez doing magic tricks for the white man?"

Duke held up his hands. "Just trying to figure out why you'd put yourself out for a stranger."

Scarlett collected her hair in a ponytail and wrapped it around her hand. "Let's just say I have my own reasons."

"Is it true what Jason said about the Quileute being skittish about this case? I heard it from a teenage boy in the woods, too."

"Yes."

"Can I ask why?"

"There's a Quileute legend about the Dask'iya, or basket lady, who steals children in the middle of the night without a trace—and eats them. After the kidnappings, most of the elders were convinced Dask'iya had come back and was responsible for the kidnappings."

"But none of the kidnapped children were Native American."

"Didn't matter. The thought of Dask'iya's return struck terror in the hearts of the old folks." Scarlett bit the tip of her finger.

"But?" Duke swirled his beer in the bottle. "You think there's more to it?"

"I'm not sure why that fear led to such secretiveness in our community at the time of the kidnappings."

"You think the fear had its basis in something more… earthly?"

"You could say that." Scarlett stretched her arms in front of her. "If we decide to do this, Beth, I'm going to need that locket. By the way, is there anything in the locket? No baby pictures?"

"Hair."

"As in—" Scarlett wrapped a lock of dark hair around her finger "—this?"

"On one side of the locket, there's a lock of blond hair, and on the other side, there's a lock of reddish hair." Beth shook her head so that her strawberry blond hair danced around her shoulders. "Like this."

"Yours and someone else's."

"I guess so. Are you sure you want to do this, Scarlett?"

"Like I said, I have my own reasons, but you can do something for me."

"Name it."

"You and Mr. FBI Agent here can report that gunshot when you go back to town."

One corner of Duke's mouth tilted up. "How'd you know I was FBI?"

"I heard you were coming. I'm not quite the complete recluse that my family thinks I am, and Cody Unger's a friend of mine—you know, Deputy Unger."

"Good man."

"Anyway, I figure the word of an FBI agent might carry more weight than the word of a flaky artist who complains about the hunters all the time."

Beth collected the shot glasses and bottle of whiskey and rose from the love seat. "We would've reported that shot anyway since it almost hit me. Is there anything else we can do?"

"I'll think about it. You think about it, too, Beth. Think about it long and hard… You might not like what you discover."

BY THE TIME they returned to town, reported the shot in the woods and drove into the parking lot of their hotel, a light rain had begun to fall.

Duke unfurled an umbrella he had in his backseat and held it over her head as they dashed for the hotel entrance.

Duke's father may have been an abusive alcoholic, but Duke had learned chivalry from somewhere. Must've been his military training. Beth had been attracted to Duke immediately when she'd met him two years ago. But he'd been a man who'd demanded complete openness and she'd found it increasingly hard to deliver.

Maybe she'd stolen those files from his room to sabotage their relationship and growing closeness. Would she make the same mistake today? Would she even have a chance to make the same mistake?

Duke hadn't changed. Had *she*?

A blaze in the lobby fireplace warmed the room and created a welcoming ambience.

Gregory waved from behind the counter. "We have our complimentary spiced cider tonight—spiked and un-spiked."

Beth headed for the cart next to the fireplace, calling over her shoulder, "If I grabbed a spiked cider after that shot of whiskey at Scarlett's, would you peg me as a lush?"

"Absolutely not as long as you don't judge me." Duke nodded at a couple sharing the sofa in front of the fire. "Mind if we join you?"

The man held up his cup. "The cider's good and not too strong."

Beth picked up two cups of cider from the tray and sank into the chair next to Duke's. "Here you go."

He took the cup from her and placed it on the table between them. "Good fishing today?"

The older man on the sofa glanced up. "How'd you know I was a fisherman?"

"You have the look."

"You mean the look of a fanatic?" The man's wife laughed.

"A dedicated sportsman. How about it? A good haul?"

"Decent."

"Do you hunt, also?"

Beth sat up straighter and watched Duke over the rim of her cup. As Scarlett suspected, Sheriff Musgrove had brushed off the shot in the woods. Deputy Unger indicated that it was protocol to post a notice to all hunters to stay in the areas designated for hunting.

"I've done some hunting, but not this trip." He half rose from the sofa and extended his hand to Duke. "Walt Carver, by the way, and this is my wife, Sue."

"I'm Duke Harper and this is Beth St. Regis."

Holding her breath, Beth waved, but neither Walt nor Sue showed a flicker of recognition. Must not be big reality TV fans.

"Why are you asking? Are you a hunter, Duke?"

"No, but my... Beth almost got hit by a stray bullet from a hunter."

Sue covered her mouth. "That's frightening. That's why I'm glad Walt gave it up."

"Some of these people don't follow the rules and accidents happen."

"How common are accidental shootings?" Duke blew on the surface of his cider before taking a sip.

"I don't have any statistics, but it happens." He patted his wife's knee. "I was always very careful, Sue. No need to worry."

Sue yawned. "For some reason, fishing all day makes me tired. I don't even know if I can muster enough energy to go out to dinner."

"We can order in." Walt took Sue's cup and placed them on the tray. "Nice to meet you folks. Will you be here long?"

"Not sure." Beth smiled. That depended on one beautiful shaman with an attitude.

They said good-night to the other couple and Duke moved to the sofa and stared into the fire, now a crackling orange-and-red blaze.

"What are you thinking?" She settled next to him.

"Wondering if that shot was an accident or intended for you."

"Scarlett seemed to think it had something to do with her." She held one hand to the fire, soaking up its warmth. "The sheriff indicated she called a lot to complain about the hunters and has even started a petition to push their hunting grounds farther north. She doesn't like the hunters and they don't like her."

Duke scratched his chin. "There have been other incidents at her place, but I don't like this, Beth."

"I don't like it, either, but I'm so close." She pinched her thumb and forefinger together. "With Scarlett's help I might finally discover who I am, where I came from."

"And like some fairy tale, you think your mother and father are going to be the good king and queen?"

"I'm prepared for anything, Duke."

"Are you?" He tapped his cup. "If someone could tell you tomorrow whether or not you're Heather Brice, would you leave Timberline?"

"If I *was* Heather, I'd contact the Brices immediately and arrange to see them in Connecticut—if they wanted to see me."

"If you're *not* Heather Brice?"

"I... I'd be back to the drawing board and I'd start following a different path." She leaned back against the sofa cushion and propped her feet on the table in front of her. Duke really wanted her to ditch the story, and this time it was for her benefit, not his.

"A different path away from Timberline and this case?"

"My producer, Scott, isn't all that excited about this case anyway. I could dump it and he wouldn't blink an eye. In fact, he'd be happy since he tried to talk me out of the case to begin with. If I dropped the show, it would make him look good in his father's eyes, since his dad owns the production company."

"Seems we all want you to drop the story, don't we?" He drained his cup of cider. "That was good. Do you want another or do you want to get something to eat?"

"I'm with Sue and Walt on this one. Maybe we can just order in. Pizza? Chinese?"

"Let's ask Gregory what he recommends."

Duke held out his hand and pulled her up from the sofa. She didn't want to let go, but he dropped her hand and put their empty cider cups on the tray.

"Gregory, my man. We're going to order in for dinner. Any recommendations?"

"There's a good pizza place down the road. They have pastas and salads, too." He pointed to the right of the reception desk. "There are a couple of menus there."

Beth reached for a red, white and green menu and held it up. "Vincenzo's?"

"That's it."

Duke joined her and hovered over her shoulder to look at the menu. "How come there's no restaurant on the premises?"

"I'm pretty sure Mr. Young made a deal with some of the town's restaurateurs to build the hotel only and not cut into their business."

"Jordan Young?" Beth ran her finger across the extra pizza ingredients.

"Yep. He developed the Timberline Hotel years ago. Bought the old one and renovated and expanded."

"He should update the security and get cameras in the hallways." Duke tapped the menu. "Pizza and salad?"

"That'll work." Beth shoved the menu into his hands. "You pick the pizza toppings and I'll grab a couple of twist-top bottles of wine."

"I have a better idea. I'll get the food and make a stop at a liquor store and pick up a decent bottle of cabernet."

"Sounds perfect. Do you want me to come with you?"

"I can handle it."

Beth tried to give him some cash, which he refused, and then went up to her room—the one right next to Duke's.

Not that she expected to get lucky tonight with that gorgeous man. She had a few things to tell him before they could reach that same level of intimacy they'd had before, which Beth had discovered hadn't been very deep.

Sleeping with a man didn't guarantee instant intimacy. She'd never had that level of intimacy with anyone before, but she'd come close with Duke. So close, the feeling had terrified her and she'd taken the surest route to torpedo the relationship.

She'd lied to Duke, betrayed him. He'd reacted as she'd expected him to—he dumped her. If she wanted him back, there could be no secrets between them.

Maybe tonight was the night—pizza, red wine and confidences.

When Beth returned to the room, she stepped into the shower and put on a pair of soft, worn jeans and the FBI Academy T-shirt Duke had given her two years ago. The shirt gave her confidence.

As soon as she turned on the TV, Duke knocked on the door. "Pizza man."

She peered through the peephole and opened the door. "I hope you got some paper plates and napkins."

"They're in the bag with the salad." He held up a bottle of wine. "Washington vineyard."

"This will be my third alcoholic beverage of the day. Really, this is unusual for me."

He placed the food on the credenza and turned to face her, his hands on his hips. "You don't have to excuse yourself just because my father was an alcoholic, Beth. Hell, you know I drink, too. I don't think a few drinks make you an alcoholic."

"I know that." She pulled the plates and napkins from the bag. "I just don't want you to get the wrong idea about me."

"I think I did have the wrong idea about you."

"I know." She popped open the plastic lid on the salad. "You thought you could trust me and I betrayed that trust."

"That's not it." He held up a corkscrew. "Bought a cheap one at the liquor store."

"What's not it?" She folded her arms across her stomach. Had he discovered something else about her?

"I've had plenty of time to think about what happened between us, and seeing you again and hearing your story has only confirmed what I'd begun to think about that time, about our relationship."

"Maybe I need some wine to hear this." Duke had uncorked the bottle, and Beth poured some of it into a plastic cup Duke had snagged from the cider setup in the lobby.

"It's nothing bad. I just didn't understand at the time that you took those files on purpose to push me away because we'd gotten too close, too fast."

The wine went down her throat the wrong way and she choked. She covered her face with a napkin. "Have you now added psychology to your other talents?"

"Tell me it's not true." He tugged at the napkin.

"It wasn't conscious at the time. I just really, really wanted those files."

"You could've asked me."

"You would've said no."

"Probably." He tore off a piece of pizza and dropped it onto a paper plate. "All this analysis is making me hungry."

She peeked at him over the rim of her plastic cup. "Is that your way of telling me you forgive me for that incredibly stupid act?"

"Hey, that incredibly stupid act did solve the case, didn't it?"

"Only because I didn't reveal that other piece of info to you that I got from my source."

"Are you trying to make yourself look bad?"

"I just want you to see me, warts and all...this time. I... If there is a this time."

Duke took a big bite of pizza instead of answering her and she let it drop.

He had a better handle on discussing this kind of stuff than most men she knew because he'd been through court-mandated therapy as a teen when his father had beaten his mother to death after he'd accidentally killed his younger sister.

Such tragedy and he'd risen from the ashes a strong man, a good man—and she could've had him if she'd been able to recover from her own tragedies.

They watched TV together, she from the edge of the bed and he from a chair he'd pulled up, and ate their salad and pizza. A meal had never tasted better, but she stopped at two cups of wine. She needed the relaxation but also needed a clear head for her confession.

Duke collected her plate and cup and stuffed them into the white plastic bag. "More wine?"

"No, thanks. Save it. I may need it after my session with Scarlett tomorrow."

"Tomorrow?" He checked his phone. "You set it up for tomorrow?"

"Expecting a text?"

"Work." He tossed the phone on the bed. "What time are you seeing Scarlett and when did you arrange this?"

"When you'd gone outside her place to look around. I'm bringing my locket and heading out there at dusk."

"At night? Really?"

"She works during the day and needs the natural light. She suggested it. At least it's not the witching hour."

"I don't think you'd better call Scarlett a witch. She'd go off on you for sure."

"I wasn't calling her a witch." She pointed to the pizza box. "Breakfast tomorrow morning?"

"Works for me."

Beth licked a crumb from the corner of her mouth. Now, if only they could settle the sleeping arrangements for tonight as easily as that. She could always make a suggestion, but she didn't want to push things.

Duke swiped his thumb across his phone again and placed it on the credenza. "I'll take the trash outside. You don't want to be smelling garlic all night."

He grabbed the white bag and left the room.

Beth blew out a breath. He didn't say "*we* don't want to be smelling garlic all night," so maybe he planned to go back to his own room.

She brushed some crumbs from the credenza into her palm just as Duke's phone vibrated. Was this the text he was expecting?

She spun the phone around to face her, touching the screen in the process. The phone was still unlocked from Duke's last usage.

The text message, from Mick Tedesco, sprang to life, and one word jumped out at Beth—*Brice*. Her eyes darted to the door and back to the phone.

She read the message aloud. "'The request to the Brices was sent and approved.'"

Pressing one hand to her heart, she stepped back. What request? Duke hadn't mentioned any request he'd made from the Brices. Did he plan to steal her thunder?

She heard the key at the door and retreated to the bathroom. How could she even ask him about it now without admitting she'd read his private text?

He stepped into the room. "That's better."

She poked her head out of the bathroom. "Would you

mind taking the leftover pizza to your room when you leave?"

His step faltered for a second but he recovered quickly. "Sure. You want me to leave the wine here?"

"You can leave the wine." She ducked back into the bathroom and called out, "Don't forget your phone."

"Got it."

A few minutes later he stood at the bathroom door, his boots back on and holding the pizza box in front of him with the cell phone on top.

Holding her breath, her gaze darted to the phone. Had he checked his very important message about the Brices yet?

"I'll see you tomorrow, Beth. And don't even think about going to Scarlett's without me."

"Of course not." She smiled as she unwound about a foot of dental floss. "We're partners in crime, right?"

A small vertical line formed between his eyebrows. "Right. Good night."

"Good night. Thanks for the pizza and wine."

When the door closed behind him, she threw the second bolt into place and marched to the credenza. She uncorked the wine and poured herself another generous glass.

Then she sat cross-legged on the bed and took a big gulp. It was a good thing she hadn't revealed her final secret to Duke…because the man was keeping one of his own.

Chapter Ten

Duke dropped the pizza box in his room and unlocked his phone to read Mick's message. Releasing a breath, he stretched out on the bed and texted him back. Rush order?

A few minutes later Mick confirmed and Duke ate another piece of pizza to celebrate. He'd hoped to celebrate another way tonight, but Beth had made it clear that she'd expected him to spend the night in his own room. Maybe she hadn't bought his forgiveness-and-understanding shtick, even though he'd been dead serious.

He didn't blame her for not trusting him. As recently as two days ago he'd been railing against her for her actions two years ago. That was before he'd discovered her real purpose for being in Timberline.

He finished the pizza and got up to brush his teeth. He leaned forward and studied his face in the mirror.

Maybe Beth had it right. This time they should take things slow and easy and not jump to any conclusions about each other.

He could do that.

Could she?

Duke spent the next day in meetings with the local FBI office and on the phone with the Drug Enforcement Agency. He'd touched base with Beth a few times and she'd been busy conducting more interviews and visiting relevant sites like the house of Kayla Rush's kidnapping.

He just wanted to make sure she didn't go out to Scarlett Easton's house by herself. He didn't trust those hunters—or anyone else in this town.

He ended his day in the sheriff's station, shooting the breeze with Unger. Musgrove had gone golfing with the mayor and Jordan Young.

"The local hunters don't much care for Scarlett Easton?"

"She complains about them a lot. She just doesn't like hunting."

"They've done things like that before? Shoot close to her property?"

"Sure, but they've never come close to hitting someone, like they did with Ms. St. Regis."

"Yeah." Duke chewed the edge of his fingernail.

"Do you think it was on purpose?"

"I'm not sure. Maybe someone was trying to scare her off, like with the broken window and the frog head, but that's extreme."

"If the guy was a good shot, he wouldn't see it as extreme since he never intended for the bullet to hit its mark."

"Still, that could be attempted murder."

"You and I know that, but someone willing to take that chance in the first place—" Unger shrugged "—that might not occur to him."

"I told Beth I'd ask you about your mom, if she'd be willing to talk to her about the Brices and what happened twenty-five years ago."

"I'd hate for my mom to wind up on TV."

"I understand. What if I could guarantee that her interview wouldn't leave Beth's possession?"

"Then why would Beth want to interview my mother if she didn't plan to use it for the segment?"

Toying with the edge of a folder, Duke said, "Information."

"Is that why Beth was talking to Scarlett Easton? Information? Because I can't imagine Scarlett wanting to get involved with a TV show. I don't think she even watches TV."

"Just a different perspective. These shows collect all kinds of footage and info they never use."

Unger lifted his shoulders. "I'll see what I can do."

"Thanks, man." Duke checked his phone. Did five o'clock qualify as dusk? "I'm outta here. Keep me posted on any new developments in the Gary Binder hit and run."

"Will do."

When Duke pulled into the parking lot of the Timberline Hotel, his shoulders relaxed when he spotted Beth's rental car. He'd had a nagging feeling all day that she'd take off without him.

He waved to Gregory at the front desk, avoided Walt and Sue in the lobby and jogged up the two flights of stairs to Beth's room. As he knocked on the door, he called, "Beth, it's Duke."

She opened the door. "I saw Scarlett in town. We're meeting at seven."

"Do you want to get something to eat on the way?"

"I had a bite to eat in town. I'll knock when I'm ready to go. About thirty minutes?"

"I'll be ready."

She shut the door in his face.

Had she read his mind and his body language last night? He'd wanted to bed her and, up until last night, he'd thought she'd wanted the same thing.

Maybe he wouldn't get a second chance with Beth, but he still planned to make sure nothing happened to her on this wild-goose chase.

He'd had a big lunch with the FBI boys and figured

he could skip dinner, anyway. He showered instead and changed out of his suit. He didn't know what to wear to a haunting, but he was pretty sure it wasn't a suit.

At around six forty-five, Beth tapped on his door.

He greeted her by jingling his car keys. "Let's take my SUV. It has four-wheel drive. Her place is remote, even by Timberline standards."

"Okay." She nervously toyed with a chain around her neck.

"Is that the locket?"

"This is it." She held it out from her neck with her thumb, where a gold heart dangled from the delicate chain.

As they hit the stairwell, Duke said, "I've worked with psychics a few times on cases. While they haven't solved anything for us, there's definitely something there."

"I hope Scarlett can tell me something. Even if it's some small connection to the Brices, it might be enough."

"Enough for what?" Duke pushed open the door to the lobby.

"Enough to warrant some communication with them, but like I said before, I don't want to give them any false hope."

"False hope is never good, especially in cases like this."

She tilted her head and shot him a quizzical look from beneath her lashes before she got into the car.

He started the car. "I'm guessing you didn't get to interview Jordan Young today."

"I didn't. How'd you know that?"

"I dropped by the sheriff's station to see Cody—Deputy Unger—and he told me Sheriff Musgrove was out playing golf with Young and the mayor." He snapped his fingers. "Mayor Burton. Have you met him yet?"

"Not yet. I spent my day videotaping different locations…and replacing my frog."

"You bought another?"

"I wanted to ask Linda, the shop owner, if anyone had come into the store after me or had asked about me later."

"Any luck?"

"Nothing suspicious, anyway. A few people chatted with her about the show, but these were people she knew. She was happy to sell me another frog, though."

"Are you going to keep this one under lock and key?" Duke made the turn off the main highway and the sky immediately darkened as the trees grew thicker.

"I'm going to guard him with my life."

He glanced sideways at her, expecting a smile, but Beth's jaw had a hard line that worried the hell out of him. How long had she been obsessed by this? He'd never seen this side to her two years ago.

As much time as they'd spent together, as many times as they'd made love, he'd never really known her.

The SUV bounced over the rough road and Beth clutched the locket against her throat.

"Are you having second thoughts? Because we can turn right around."

"No. Scarlett said it would be tougher on her than me."

"It's probably not going to be any picnic for you, either, especially if you discover something you weren't expecting."

"I have to do this."

"I know you do." He squeezed her thigh beneath the soft denim of her jeans. "And I'm gonna be right there with you."

She gave him a stiff nod.

He parked the car at the edge of the stand of trees circling Scarlett's house. He poked Beth in the arm. "Any more bullets start flying, hit the ground—and I'm only half kidding."

"Do you see me laughing?"

He kept an arm around Beth's shoulders as they approached the house, even though she'd stiffened beneath his touch. This meeting with Scarlett had put her on edge and he feared she'd drop over into the abyss.

As they reached the porch, Beth shrugged off Duke's arm. She didn't need a protector, especially one who kept important secrets from her. When was he going to tell her what he was doing with the Brices? Had he actually told them about her quest?

The heavy knocker that sported a bear's head gleamed under the porch light. Duke lifted it and tapped it against the plate several times.

Scarlett answered the door in a pair of black yoga pants and an oversize sweater that hung almost to her knees. "Did you bring the locket?"

"Right here." Beth held it out from her neck.

"Come in and have a seat by the fire." Her gaze raked Duke up and down. "Did that worthless sheriff tell you anything about the shot fired on my property yesterday?"

"He had a couple of deputies searching for a shell casing this morning, but that's about as efficient as searching for a needle in a haystack, and he sent a notice out to the hunters."

She tossed her long braid over one shoulder. "That figures. Do you want something to drink before we get started?"

"You girls aren't going to start tossing back whiskeys again, are you?" Duke raised one eyebrow and his mouth quirked into a smile as Scarlett gave a low chuckle.

Beth's gaze darted between Duke and Scarlett and something tightened in her chest. He liked her. What wasn't to like? The woman was gorgeous with her long, dark hair, mocha skin and sumptuous figure. Even the baggy sweater seemed to hug her curves.

The artist had an earth-mother figure, a body made for childbearing. Beth ran her hands down her own slim hips and a sob caught in her throat.

"I'm drinking a special tea tonight." Scarlett put her hand on Beth's arm. "Can I get you a cup? You look pale."

"That would be nice, thanks."

"You—" Scarlett leveled a finger at Duke "—don't look like a hot-tea kind of guy. Would you like a shot of that whiskey?"

"I don't touch the hard stuff, but I could use a beer."

Scarlett called over her shoulder as she sauntered into the kitchen. "You might need another when this is all over."

Beth sat in a chair near the huge natural-stone fireplace and curled out her fingers to the flame. "Is this okay here?"

"I'm going to sit in front of the fireplace on the floor." She must've already brewed the tea because she came out of the kitchen carrying two steaming cups. "Do you want sugar or milk?"

"No, thanks." She took the mug from Scarlett and sniffed the slightly bitter aroma of the pale brown tea.

Scarlett put her own cup on the broad base of the fireplace and returned to the kitchen for Duke's beer. Then she settled on a rug in front of the fire and took a sip of tea.

"A… Are there some times that are better for you to do this than others?"

"Like a full moon or something?" Scarlett shrugged. "No. You have the gift or you don't."

Beth sucked some tea onto her tongue and wrinkled her nose. Maybe she should've gone with the sugar.

Scarlett studied her over the rim of her mug. "Doesn't taste very good, does it? It's an acquired taste. I make it myself from roots and berries—an old recipe handed down through the generations."

With trembling fingers, Beth reached for the clasp on her locket. "I suppose you want this."

Three tries and she still couldn't unlatch the necklace.

"Let me." Duke crouched beside her and brushed her hair from the back of her neck. His warm fingers against her nape caused a thrill of excitement to race through her body despite the occasion. His touch always caused an immediate reaction in her body.

"Got it." He held out his hand where the chain pooled in his palm. He leaned forward and dumped the necklace into Scarlett's outstretched hand.

"May I?" She paused, her thumbnail against the crease of the locket.

Beth nodded and Scarlett popped open the gold heart. She flattened it open between two fingers. "This could be your hair—this strawberry blond. The blond could even be your hair at another age."

"That'll help, though, won't it? To have some hair as well as the locket?"

"It might." Scarlett crossed her legs beneath her and stretched her arms toward the fire, her dark eyes glittering in the firelight. "There are a few rules we need to cover."

"Rules?" Beth glanced at Duke.

"No matter what happens, do not bring me out of my trance."

"You're going into a trance?"

"What did you expect?" Scarlett's dark eyebrows jumped to her hairline. "Did you think I was going to search for your locket on the internet?"

"But a trance? Is it dangerous?" Beth bit her lip.

"Draining, but not dangerous—unless you yank me out of it." Scarlett tugged on her braid. "No matter what happens, no matter what I say or do, even if it looks like I'm having some kind of seizure."

"Seizure? Oh, my God. I can't let you do this, Scarlett."

"I've already decided I'm doing it. Like I said, I have my own reasons."

Duke sat on the floor next to Beth's chair and curved his hand around her calf. "Let her continue, Beth. Scarlett knows what she's doing."

"Listen to your man." Scarlett closed her eyes and cradled her mug. She took a long sip and placed it on the stone of the fireplace.

Her eyes opened to slits and she slipped her finger beneath the chain of the necklace and dangled it in front of the fire. The golden locket seemed infused with a flame as it swung from Scarlett's finger.

She curled her hand around the locket and held it in her fist. She exhaled slowly and her lids fell over her eyes.

Scarlett whispered something under her breath, but Beth didn't catch it. She raised her brows at Duke and he shook his head.

The whispers became a silent movement of the lips as Scarlett's knuckles turned white. Her head lolled back, her long braid almost touching the rug beneath her.

Scarlett's eyelids began flickering and her lips twitched.

Beth slid to the floor beside Duke, tucking her hand in the crook of his arm. She touched his ear with her lips. "I hope she's okay."

"I hope so, too."

Scarlett's chin dipped to her chest, her body still.

Beth whispered, "Did she fall asleep? Is this the trance she was talking about?"

Duke curled his arm around her waist and pulled her closer. "Shh. I don't know, Beth. I've never seen anything like this before."

Beth watched Scarlett's still form and it seemed as if the fire was swirling around her. Scarlett's long hair became the flames, dancing and curling around her face.

Beth put two fingers to her throbbing temple.

Duke whispered, "What's wrong?"

"I feel strange." She looked at the dregs floating in her cup. "Do you think that tea was some kind of drug?"

"What do you mean, like peyote or mushrooms?"

"I don't know." Beth ran her tongue along her dry teeth. "I feel funny."

"It is hot in here."

Scarlett gave a sharp cry and her head jerked back. Her lids flew open but her eyes had rolled back in her head.

"Duke!" Beth grabbed his hand. "Do something."

"You heard what she told us. We could actually do more harm than good if we interrupt her."

Scarlett brought one hand to her throat, clutching at it and gasping for breath.

Beth dug her nails into Duke's hand. She couldn't let this go on. What if something happened to Scarlett in this altered state?

Duke's arm tightened around her, as if he could read her thoughts. "Wait."

Scarlett gave another strangled cry and the hand not clutching the locket shot out. She grabbed Beth's upper arm, her grip like a vise. She pulled Beth toward her, toward the fire in the grate.

Duke held on to her, making her a rope in a tug-of-war.

"Let me go, Duke."

He released his hold on her and she allowed Scarlett to drag her beside her on the rug. Scarlett's hand slipped to Beth's and she laced her fingers with hers.

A flash jolted Beth's body. She could hear Duke's voice calling to her a million miles away as she traveled through darkness scattered with pinpoints of light. The heat from the fire had disappeared and a bone-chilling cold gripped her body. The blackness turned to a deep forest green, rushing and rustling past her.

Then it stopped. She jerked to a halt. The rushing sound became voices—loud, yelling, screaming, crying.

She smelled it before she saw it—metallic, pungent—blood. So much blood, waves of it, slick, wet. A baby crying.

Beth gagged, ripping her hand from Scarlett's.

Scarlett dropped the locket and pressed her palms against either side of her head. "The blood. The blood. So much blood."

Duke lunged forward and hooked his hands beneath Beth's arms, hoisting her up and against his chest. "Are you all right? What the hell was that?"

Beth's eyes felt so heavy she could barely raise them to Duke's face. "Blood."

"Sit." He pushed her into the chair and then hunched over Scarlett. "Are you okay, Scarlett? Should I get you anything?"

"Water, bring us some water." She stretched out on her back, flinging one arm across her eyes.

A few minutes later Duke pressed a glass to Beth's lips. "Drink."

She gulped the water so fast it dribbled down her chin and she didn't even care. After she downed the glass, she looked up, blinking, clearing her vision.

Scarlett's eyes met hers. "You saw it, too, didn't you?"

Beth nodded.

Dragging his hands through his dark hair, Duke paced to the window and back. "What the hell just happened? Did you drag Beth into your vision? Did you drug her?"

"Hold on there, cowboy." Scarlett held up her index finger. "That tea is not a drug. Yes, it does enhance my visions, but I had no idea it would have any effect on Beth. That's never happened before."

"What's never happened before? You giving someone that witch's brew or you dragging someone into your trance?"

Scarlett pressed her lips into a thin line and then she flicked her fingers at Duke. "How are you feeling, Beth?"

"I feel fine, amazing actually. It was like an out-of-body experience."

"Can you please get Beth more water instead of blustering around the room?"

Duke's mouth opened, shut, and then he growled. He took Beth's glass and stormed off to the kitchen.

"You'll be fine, Beth. I'm sorry I grabbed your hand like that. I am telling the truth. I've never done that before, didn't even know it was a possibility."

"Never mind all that. What did we see?"

"You tell me. What did *you* see?"

Beth's lashes fluttered. "I saw... I smelled blood. I heard people yelling and screaming. I heard a child or a baby crying."

"Amazing." Scarlett shook her head. "That's what I got, too. You shared my vision."

"What does it mean, Scarlett?" Beth took the glass from Duke and gave him a small smile. It didn't seem like he liked Scarlett all that much anymore.

"What do you think it means?" Scarlett settled her back against the base of the fireplace.

"If it's connected to the locket I had before my adoption, it has something to do with my past. Could it be the scene of my kidnapping?"

"Whoa, wait a minute." Duke held out one hand. "There

was no mention of blood at your kidnapping. There was no blood spilled at any of the kidnappings."

Beth tapped her water glass with one fingernail. "Could it just be a representation of the violence of my kidnapping, Scarlett?"

"I'm not sure about that. I guess so." She stood up and stretched. "Did you recognize the place?"

"The place?"

"The cabin. I'm pretty sure it was a cabin."

"Oh." Beth slumped back in the chair. "I didn't see a place, just the blood, the smells, the sounds."

"That's another problem. Heather Brice was kidnapped from her parents' house, which was not a cabin." Duke jerked his thumb at the necklace still glinting on the rug where Scarlett had dropped it. "How do you know this... vision has anything to do with you? It could be something connected to the previous owner of the locket. Right, Scarlett?"

"I suppose so, but I was compelled to take Beth's hand, to bring her in."

"The facts are you don't have a clue what you're doing here. You drink some herbal tea, you utter some mumbo jumbo, you have some visions and you leave your clients with more questions than answers."

"Clients?" Scarlett widened her stance and tossed her braid over her shoulder. "I'm an artist. The only clients I have are the ones who buy my art and sponsor my shows."

"Duke, Scarlett agreed to do this because I asked her. While frightened by what I saw and heard, I'm satisfied with what we did here tonight."

"Okay." Duke clasped the back of his neck and tipped his head from side to side. "I'm sorry, Scarlett. I just don't see how this helps Beth."

Beth bent down to sweep up her necklace. "What else

did you see, Scarlett? Anything more about the cabin? I didn't join your vision until later. You must've experienced more than I did."

"It was a cabin, a nice one, and it had a red door. I can't tell you anything else specific about it—I didn't see the location, any particular furnishings or the people in it."

Duke snorted and Beth shot him a warning glance.

"But I did see two birds."

"Flying around? That's helpful."

Beth jabbed Duke in the ribs for his sarcastic tone, but Scarlett didn't seem to notice.

"There were two birds...over the fireplace? I'm not sure. I just remember two birds—maybe on a painting, maybe they were those hideous stuffed taxidermy things."

"Anything else?"

"The people—there was a man, a woman and a child, wasn't there?"

"I certainly heard voices, but I'm not sure I could distinguish them, and I did hear a baby or a child crying."

"And the hair." Scarlett reached out and lifted a strand of Beth's hair. "The woman had strawberry blond hair."

Chapter Eleven

Beth took another turn around the hotel room. "What do you think it means? A woman with strawberry blond hair?"

"Who knows? Scarlett Easton is not exactly an expert at interpretation, is she?"

"She never claimed to be." Beth wedged her hands on her hips. "Why did you start attacking Scarlett when she was just trying to help me?"

"Help you? By dragging you into her dream state? I thought—" He raked a hand through his hair. "I was worried about you."

Beth gave him a sidelong glance. "I thought you had a thing for her."

"Scarlett's not my type—too artsy, too reclusive, too… weird." Folding his arms, he leaned against the window. "Would you care if I did have a thing for Scarlett?"

Before he'd started keeping secrets from her? Hell, yeah. Now?

She splayed her hands in front of her. "She's a beautiful woman. I could understand the attraction."

Rolling his shoulders, he pushed off the window. "What are you going to do with the information? What does it prove?"

Duke wasn't going to take the bait.

"It proves—" she dropped to the bed "—that I was in a

cabin here as a child, before the Kings adopted me. I plan to locate that cabin."

"And you're going to do that how? By running around Timberline and looking into all the cabins with red doors?"

"It's a start."

"Then what?"

She fell back on the bed and stared at the ceiling. "Why are you trying to discourage me? I thought you were all in. I thought you were going to help me with this."

"That was before someone hit and killed Gary Binder, before someone started taking shots at you in the forest."

"Gary's death doesn't have anything to do with me, and that shot could've been a hunter harassing Scarlett."

"You're doing it again, Beth." The mattress sank as Duke sat on the edge of the bed. "You're so single-mindedly focused on one goal you're not seeing the whole picture."

"I don't care about the whole picture." She puffed out a breath and a strand of hair floated above her face and settled against her lips. "I need to do this. Scarlett has given me the first real lead since I got here and I'm going to follow up on it."

He shifted on the bed and she held her breath. If he took her in his arms right now and kissed her, she'd kiss him back and to hell with the secrets between them—his and hers.

Standing above her, he shook his head. "Stubborn woman. I'll help you."

Bracing her elbows against the bed, she hoisted herself up. "I'll do it with or without you, but thanks."

"Get some sleep." He nudged her foot and stalked to the door, mumbling as if to himself. "What else am I going to do, let you wander around the woods on your own like Little Red Riding Hood?"

The door slammed behind him and Beth narrowed her eyes.

He could start by telling her the truth about what he was doing with the Brices.

BETH USED HER interviews the next day to discreetly ask about cabins in the area. She also scanned her videos to see if any of the cabins she'd captured had red doors—they didn't.

After her third interview of the morning, Beth slumped behind the wheel of her rental and gave Jordan Young's office another call. His assistant answered after the first ring.

"This is Beth St. Regis again. Just checking to see if Mr. Young has some time today for that interview."

"I'm sorry, Ms. St. Regis. Mr. Young is out of town today, but I know he's looking forward to talking to you."

"I know he's busy. Just tell him I called again and I'm available at his convenience."

"Will do."

Beth's stomach growled and she patted it. She'd skipped out on breakfast this morning because she hadn't wanted to share an awkward meal with Duke. The other night he must've thought they were growing closer, putting their bitter past behind them. He'd even apologized for cutting her off, had admitted misunderstanding her.

She could've had it all back with him if she hadn't seen that text from his boss, Mickey Tedesco. She could ask him about it point-blank, get it out in the open. Of course, then she'd have to admit she'd been sneaking around again and delving into his business.

Was that wrong if he really was keeping secrets from her? It was like the cheating spouse. If your spouse was stepping out on you, didn't that sort of excuse your checking his emails and text messages?

She exited her car and turned up her collar against the wind. A drop of rain spattered against the back of her hand and she hunched forward and made a beeline for the sandwich shop on the corner.

Ducking inside, she brushed droplets of moisture from her hair. The shop was more of a take-out place, but it did boast several wrought-iron tables to one side.

She ordered an Italian sub at the counter, picked out a bag of chips and waited for the self-serve soft-drink machine. The guy at the machine turned suddenly and almost spilled his drink on her.

"Sorry... Ms. St. Regis."

"Deputy Unger, how are you?" Her gaze dipped to his flannel shirt and jeans. "Off duty?"

"Yes." He held up a plastic bag, bulging with food. "Just picking up some lunch for my hunting trip."

"Oh, you hunt, too." She wrinkled her nose. She was with Scarlett on her distaste of the so-called sport.

"Most of us grow up hunting in these parts...and I always eat my game. I go for the turkey—" he pointed at the take-out counter "—probably a lot like your sandwich."

"I admit it. I'm a city girl. I don't understand the sport."

He sealed a plastic lid on his cup and grabbed a straw. "I talked to my mom about your show. She's actually okay with it."

Beth's heart did a somersault in her chest. "That would be great. Thanks so much for talking to her."

Unger pounded his straw against the counter. "I think she would've contacted you on her own. She heard you were in town doing the story."

"I'm sure a few words from her son didn't hurt." And a few words from Duke to Unger on her behalf.

Unger grabbed a napkin and asked the guy behind the counter for a pen. "Here's her number. Feel free to call her anytime. She's a retired schoolteacher and spends her days with knitting groups and book clubs and volunteering at the public library, but I think this is one of her free days if you have an opening."

"I do." She folded the napkin and tucked it in her purse. "I've been trying to set up something with Jordan Young, but he's never available."

"Yeah, Jordan. He's a big wheeler-dealer in town—has been for years. He seems to get the sweetest deals. We all joke that he must have a dossier on every public official."

"Sounds like he knows the town's secrets."

"He's been here for a long time, even though he's not a local. Came out of nowhere, married a local girl and set up shop pretty quickly—successful guy."

"Which is why he's hard to pin down." She patted her purse where she'd stashed his mother's phone number. "Thanks again."

"Save your thanks until after the interview. My mom just might talk your ear off." Taking a sip from his soda, he held up his hand and left the shop.

She filled her cup with ice and root beer and picked up her sandwich from the counter. She'd have to thank Duke for this interview.

As she sat down, Jason Foster walked through the door. He approached her table. "Hey, Beth. How'd it go with my cousin?"

"We, uh, talked."

"She's a trip, huh?"

Trip—yeah, that was exactly the word she'd use.

"I like her."

"Some do, some don't. Did she tell you anything?" He waved to the guy at the counter. "You got my pastrami?"

"She was helpful."

"Dang, that's not a word I'd use for my cuz." He pointed

at the counter. "I have to pick up my lunch and get back to work. Glad Scarlett could help."

He paid for his sandwich and left the store.

She didn't know how close Scarlett and Jason were, but she didn't feel comfortable talking about what went on at Scarlett's cabin. Hell, she didn't even know what had happened there.

She finished her lunch with no more interruptions and then pulled out the napkin with Mrs. Unger's telephone number.

Her anticipation was dashed when she heard the woman's voice mail. Beth left a message and got up to refill her soda.

Her phone started ringing and Beth sprinted back to the table and grabbed it. "Hello?"

"Is this Beth St. Regis from the *Cold Case Chronicles* show?"

"Yes. Mrs. Unger?"

"You can call me Dorothy."

"Dorothy, thanks for calling back." Beth pulled out her chair and sat down. "Your son said you'd be willing to talk to me about the Timberline Trio case, specifically about the Brices, since you knew them well."

"Such a sad time." Dorothy clicked her tongue. "I'd be happy to talk to you, Beth. Do you think I'll be on TV?"

Beth's lips twisted into a smile. "I'm not sure. It just depends. From what your son said, I thought you wouldn't be interested."

"Oh, that's Cody talking. Who wouldn't want to be on TV?"

"Can we meet at your house or wherever you're comfortable?"

"You can come by now if you like. I have a knitting circle at three o'clock, but I'm free until then."

"Perfect."

Dorothy gave Beth her address and she punched it into her phone's GPS.

A half an hour later, Beth reached Dorothy's house, which was located in one of the newer tracks and easy to find.

She pulled into the driveway behind an old but immaculate compact and retrieved her video camera and tripod from the trunk of her rental.

Before she walked up to the front door, she sent a quick text to Duke thanking him for convincing Unger to let her have access to his mother—even if Dorothy would've contacted her on her own.

Hitching the camera case over her shoulder, she walked up the two steps of the porch and rang the doorbell.

A small, neat woman who mirrored the small, neat compact in the driveway answered the door. "Hello, Beth."

"Dorothy. Thanks for talking with me."

"Of course. Come in. Coffee? Water?" She winked. "Something a little stronger?"

What was it with the Washington women and their whiskey? Must be the cold, damp weather.

"No, thank you. I just had lunch."

"Do you need to set up that camera?"

"I do." Beth gestured to the sofa where a magazine had been placed facedown on one of the cushions. "Sit where you're comfortable."

Dorothy sat on the sofa and folded her hands in her lap. "Is this a good place for lighting and all that?"

Beth extended her tripod on the other side of the coffee table in front of the sofa. "I'm no cameraperson. I have someone who does that for me. I'm just here doing some preliminary interviews. Just casual."

"Oh, thank goodness. Then I have nothing to be nervous about."

"Of course not." Beth's fingers trembled as she touched the video camera's display for the settings. She was the nervous one. This woman could've actually known her as a toddler.

Beth started the interview in the usual manner. Dorothy stated her name, address and the current date, and Beth questioned her about what she remembered twenty-five years ago.

It didn't differ much from the other accounts. The suspicions about Kayla Rush's father, and then the shock of Stevie Carson's disappearance, and the sheer terror when the toddler Heather Brice went missing.

"Three children snatched—" Dorothy snapped her fingers "—just like that. Those of us with young kids were terrified. I didn't let my boys out of my sight for one second for months after the kidnappings."

"And you were close with the Brices at the time?"

"We were friendly, socialized. Timberline wasn't as populated in those days. Evergreen Software brought in a lot of new people."

"Do you remember Heather?"

"A sweet little girl."

"She had blond hair, didn't she?" Beth had been twisting her own hair around one finger and dropped it. "I saw some fuzzy newspaper photos of her."

"It was blond, just like her mother's, although Patty had a little help from her hairdresser."

"Blond?" A knot formed in Beth's gut. "Mrs. Brice was a blonde?"

"She had been. Like I said, she lightened her hair. I think her real color was light brown."

Beth fingered the necklace around her neck. Light

brown, not strawberry blond? She dropped the locket against her chest. That didn't mean anything. The woman in Scarlett's vision could've been the kidnapper.

"Was there some evidence regarding hair?"

"No, no. I was just thinking about some pictures I saw that were related to the case."

Beth asked more questions about the family, as many as she could without arousing Dorothy's suspicions again.

She ended the interview with a warm feeling in her belly. By all accounts, the Brices were a close and loving family. They would welcome their long-lost daughter with open arms.

As Beth shut off the camera, she asked, "Did Mr. Brice already have his money when he lived here?"

"They were wealthy because Charlie had sold his first patent, but nothing compared to what they are now." Dorothy dragged the magazine into her lap and smoothed her hands over the glossy cover. "If little Heather had been kidnapped first, everyone would've expected a ransom note."

"Did you keep in touch with the family when they left town?"

"Exchanged a few Christmas cards, but I think Patty and Charlie wanted to put this chapter behind them."

"With all their money, did they ever do a private search for Heather?"

"I'm sure they did, but she never told me about it. They moved two years later." Dorothy pushed out of the sofa. "Would you like something now?"

"Water would be great."

Dorothy called from the kitchen. "I think I have a few pictures of Heather with my boys, if you're interested, but I'd have to find them."

Beth's heart thumped in her chest. She'd seen only the old newspaper pictures of Heather Brice. She'd felt no sense of recognition, but that didn't mean anything. Maybe clearer, color photos would reveal more.

"I'd love to see them if you can find them."

Dorothy returned with a glass of water. "I'll look later and give you a call if I have anything useful."

Beth took a few sips of water. "Do you know of any cabins around here that have red doors?"

"Not now, not anymore."

Beth's hand froze, the glass halfway to her lips. "Not anymore? There was one before?"

"There were several. It was a trend."

"How long ago was this, Dorothy?" Beth wiped her mouth with the back of her hand.

"Maybe thirty, thirty-five years ago. Designs follow trends, don't they? Remember the hideous avocado-green appliances? Now everything has to be stainless steel."

"How many cabins had these red doors?"

"Ten or fifteen?" She peered at Beth. "Why? Is this some new evidence, too?"

"I can't say right now. Were these cabins in the same area or scattered around?"

"I can't remember, Beth. They were here and there. Who knew at the time that any of this stuff would be important?"

"Are there any left? Any cabins with red doors?"

"There might be a few. You'd probably want to talk to a Realtor—not that lush Bill Raney, but you could try Rebecca Geist. She's a sharp gal. Just sold Cass Teagan's place."

"Maybe I will. I've seen a few of her open houses around."

"When are you going to make a decision about the story and the footage?"

"I'll submit everything to my producer and he'll make

the decision. Then the rest of my crew will come out and we'll put a story together."

"You won't solve it and neither will that handsome young FBI agent who's out here now." Dorothy put her finger to her lips and said in a hushed voice, "I'm beginning to believe it really was that Quileute basket lady who steals children away and eats them."

BETH COLLAPSED IN her car, a range of emotions assaulting her brain. Whose strawberry blond hair was in her locket? Her own? If so, who was the strawberry blonde Scarlett had seen in the vision? Maybe Scarlett had seen her as an adult.

Her mind shifted, another scattered piece of information in her brain taking shape, like a figure in a kaleidoscope.

Was there a way to find all those cabins that had red doors? If she tracked down each one, would she discover the cabin from her trance?

She threw her car into Reverse and backed out of Dorothy's driveway. She needed to touch base with Scarlett again. Had the shaman remembered more from her dream state?

She drove across town and hit the main highway. She took the turnoff, watching for the colorful mailbox that marked Scarlett's private access road.

Duke hadn't wanted her to come out here by herself, but he'd been busy all day and this couldn't wait. She pulled up when she saw the mailbox and tapped Duke's number on her cell phone.

"Where are you? I've been texting you for the past thirty minutes." His voice was gruff.

"I didn't get your texts. I'm on my way to see Scarlett."

"Damn it, Beth. You couldn't wait for me?"

"It's broad daylight."

"It was broad daylight last time. Stay put. I'm on my way."

"I'm at Scarlett's mailbox at the beginning of the access road. I'll just drive up to her place and wait for you. I don't even know if she's home."

"Stay in your car."

"Duke, I think you're overreacting."

"Let me overreact if it keeps you safe."

She ended the call and swung onto the access road leading to Scarlett's cabin. The rough road bounced and jostled her car, and she drove it as far as the road allowed.

She grabbed the handle, cracked the door open and stopped. She'd promised Duke she'd wait in the car until he got there—a ridiculous precaution, but one she'd honor.

Tipping her head back against the headrest, Beth drummed out a rhythm against the steering wheel and then checked the time on her cell phone. Scarlett must not be home if she hadn't heard Beth's car drive up the road.

She swung the car door open the rest of the way and dragged in a deep lungful of the pine-scented air. The mist caressing the copse of trees ringing Scarlett's cabin gave the area a mythical, mystical quality that suited its inhabitant.

A loud wail shattered the peace, sending a river of chills down her spine. She jumped out of the car and hung on the car door. "Hello? Scarlett?"

An animalistic shriek pierced the air and Beth bolted from the car and ran down the small path that wound its way through the trees to Scarlett's cabin. The front porch came into view and Beth charged ahead.

A vise grabbed her ankle with a snap and Beth tumbled forward onto her hands and knees as a sharp pain knifed up her leg. She hit the ground with a cry and rolled to her back to take pressure off her ankle.

Her eyes watering, she glanced at her injured leg and choked. A trap had her in its steely grip.

Chapter Twelve

Duke cursed when he saw Beth's car and the open door. Why didn't it surprise him that she hadn't stayed put like he'd asked? When had Beth St. Regis ever played it safe?

He slammed his car door and stalked to her rental. The open door gave him pause. He poked his head inside the car and swallowed. Why'd she leave her keys in the ignition and phone in the cup holder?

A low moan floated through the trees and he jerked his head up, the blood pounding in his ears. "Beth?"

"Duke? Duke, I'm here. Help me."

He crashed through the trees, and when he saw Beth on the ground, crumpled in pain, he rushed to her side. He dropped next to her, reaching for the cruel trap that had her boot in its teeth.

"Oh, my God. Did the spikes reach your flesh?"

Her chin wobbled. "I can't tell. It's almost numb with pain. I'm afraid to move or I would've crawled to my car to get my phone."

"Where's Scarlett?" He twisted his head over his shoulder.

"I don't know. I haven't seen anyone since I arrived." She ended with a hiss.

"Stretch out your leg. I'm gonna get this thing off of you."

Slowly she extended her leg, the trap clamped onto her ankle.

Duke placed both hands on either side of the trap's jaws and pulled them apart. The spring jumped and the trap snapped open.

The teeth of the trap had mangled Scarlett's boot, but he didn't see any blood. "I don't see any blood, but I'm going to leave it to the medical professionals to remove your boot."

"Thank God I was wearing them. My foot and ankle hurt like hell, but it's just a mass of pain. I can't tell what's injured."

"Let's get you to the hospital." He scooped her up and tromped back the way he'd come, keeping his eyes on the ground for any more surprises.

"Somebody placed that trap there on purpose, Duke, and lured me out of my car."

"How?" His arms tightened around her and he could feel the erratic fluttering of her heart against his chest.

"I heard wailing and a scream. It sounded like a wounded animal, but it could've been human." She tugged on his jacket. "We need to warn Scarlett. There may be more traps set around her cabin."

"I'm calling the sheriff's department." He settled her into the passenger seat and placed a kiss on top of her head, where his lips met beads of dew clinging to the strands of her hair.

"And Scarlett. That trap could've just as well been meant for her."

"Or you." When he got behind the wheel, he pulled his phone from his pocket. At Beth's urging, his first call went to Scarlett.

"Hello?"

"Scarlett, it's Duke Harper. I'm just leaving your place with Beth, who stepped into a trap outside your cabin."

Scarlett sucked in a sharp breath. "What kind of trap?"

"I'm not sure, but it could be a bear trap."

"A trap? You mean a real animal trap?"

"That's what it looks like to me."

"Is she okay?"

"I'm taking her to the hospital emergency room, but be careful. There might be more traps around your cabin."

"The police?"

"I'm calling the sheriff next. Where are you?"

"I'm at my granny's place on the reservation. How the hell did a bear trap get on my property?"

"I was hoping you could tell us."

"Duke, it could've been meant for me. It might not have anything to do with Beth."

"Yeah, except she's the one who was trapped."

He ended the call with Scarlett and tapped his phone for the sheriff's department. He told them about the wounded animal sound Beth had heard and gave them the location of the trap he'd removed from her ankle.

Tossing the phone onto the console, he said, "Scarlett thinks the trap could've been meant for her."

"It could've been meant for either one of us." Beth winced and rubbed her thigh.

"You doing okay? Hang in there." He sped back toward town, taking the bypass road to the new hospital near Evergreen Software.

He pulled up to the emergency room entrance and carried Beth inside. "She needs a wheelchair. She stepped onto a trap and injured her foot or ankle."

An orderly burst through the swinging doors, pushing a wheelchair.

Duke put her into the chair and followed the orderly back to the examination rooms.

The orderly lifted Beth onto an exam table and said, "A nurse will be right with you."

The paper on the exam table crinkled as Beth hoisted herself up onto her elbows. "Who would do that? You know that trap was deliberately set."

"Of course it was, but who was the prey? You or Scarlett?"

She crossed her arms over her chest like a shield. "It's Scarlett's place. No one could know for sure if I'd be back there, but Scarlett would be there, guaranteed."

"Just seems odd that both of these attacks at Scarlett's cabin happened when you were there. Is Scarlett even in an active battle with the hunters right now? I got the impression she hadn't been around much lately."

"Maybe—" Beth peered over his shoulder at the door "—maybe Scarlett was the target, but not for her anti-hunting stance."

"Then what? Her really creepy artwork?"

"The dream state ceremony last night."

Duke's pulse jumped. That would put Beth right back in the crosshairs since she'd participated, too. He rubbed his knuckles across his jaw. "Whoever placed that trap wants both you and Scarlett to stop looking into the Timberline Trio case. Maybe they didn't care who they snared."

"What I don't understand is why me? Why is this person just warning me and not you? The FBI is investigating the Timberline Trio case, too."

"Because targeting the FBI is a bigger deal than scaring off some reporter and an artist playing at being a shaman."

She smacked his arm. "Scarlett's not playing at being a shaman—she is one."

"For all the good it did."

"It did help. You know I spoke to Dorothy Unger today."

"I got your text. Did she take you by the shoulders and proclaim that you looked just like Heather Brice?"

"Shh." Beth glanced at the open exam room door again.

"She didn't, but she did tell me that quite a number of cabins in Timberline used to have red doors—seems it was a trend a while back."

"Those doors may no longer be red."

"I figured that, but she also gave me the name of a Realtor who might be able to help me figure out which cabins had the red doors. If I had that information, I could track down each one."

"Provided they're still standing. Not even the Brices' old home is still in existence."

"I know." She fell back against the table.

He hated to keep dashing her hopes, but she needed to get out of this town. The threats against her seemed to be getting more violent.

He smoothed a hand down her leg. Maybe he'd have some news for her shortly that would turn her away from this story and end this quest that seemed to be hazardous to her health.

The nurse bustled into the room. Touching the toe of Beth's mangled boot, she said, "Ruined a nice pair of boots, too. Let's get this off."

The nurse took a scalpel and sliced through the leather of the boot on Beth's calf. She peeled it off and clicked her tongue. "Your ankle is swollen for sure, but I don't see any blood. It doesn't look like the teeth of the trap made it to your flesh."

"I can't even imagine what that would've felt like." Beth shivered.

The nurse peeled off Beth's heavy sock and Beth grunted. "That looks bad."

"Swollen and the start of some massive bruising."

Duke leaned over and inspected Beth's injured ankle. "Is it broken?"

"The doctor will probably order some X-rays." The

nurse ran some antiseptic towelettes over Beth's ankle and foot. "How's the pain on a scale from one to ten, ten being childbirth?"

A red tide crested in Beth's cheeks. "I've never experienced childbirth, but I'd put this pain at a six now—definitely a nine when it first happened."

The nurse held out a small cup with two green gel caps in it. "I'm going to give you a few ibuprofens for the pain and the swelling. The doctor may prescribe some stronger painkillers for you."

A doctor poked her head into the room. "I'm Dr. Thallman. There's a sheriff's deputy here to see you, but we're going to take you over to get some X-rays right now."

"I'll talk to the deputy." Duke leaned over and cupped Beth's face with one hand. "I'm not going anywhere."

He watched as they wheeled Beth away and then went to the waiting room, where Deputy Stevens was talking to the woman at the front desk.

"Stevens, Beth's getting some X-rays." He shook the deputy's hand.

"We have a couple of officers scanning the area in front of Scarlett Easton's place. They already found another trap, closer to the cabin."

Duke pinched the bridge of his nose. "What a sick joke. Any way to trace those traps?"

"Probably not." He swept his hat from his head. "But if we find out who's playing games like this, not only will he never get a hunting license in the state of Washington again, but we'll send him to jail."

"Do you think it's related to Scarlett's war with the hunters?" Duke's jaw hardened. If only he could believe that himself.

"Maybe, but we're not going to rule out Beth's mission here in Timberline. There still are a lot of folks here who are uneasy about the Timberline Trio case getting rehashed again—and let's just say Bill Raney is a hunter."

"I thought you cleared him of the other...pranks."

"We're going to start looking at everyone more closely."

Scarlett Easton burst through the emergency room doors. "Where's Beth? Is she okay?"

"Getting X-rays." Duke pointed at Stevens. "Did you hear they found another trap on your property?"

"I did. Maybe one for me and one for her."

Stevens asked, "You don't have anything to do with Beth's Timberline investigation, do you?"

"Me?" Scarlett drove a finger into her chest. "Not a chance."

A nurse poked her head out of the swinging doors leading to the exam rooms. "Beth's doing fine. Dr. Thallman is looking at her X-rays if you want to come back now, Deputy Stevens."

Duke brought up the rear behind Stevens and Scarlett as the nurse led them to the examination room.

Beth looked up from examining the pink wrap on her foot and ankle. "Pretty, isn't it?"

Scarlett tripped into the room and put an arm around Beth. "I'm so sorry."

"It's not your fault, Scarlett."

"My cabin seems to be bad luck for you."

"It could've just as easily been you caught in that trap."

Stevens cleared his throat. "One of those traps—we found another one."

Beth's mouth dropped open. "Oh, my God. If that one hadn't gotten me, the other one could've done the job."

"And the other one was bigger, could've caused more damage."

"It's a good thing I bought those heavy boots for this trip."

Dr. Thallman squeezed into the crowded room. "It is a good thing. Those boots probably saved you from breaking any bones."

"My foot's not broken?"

"Badly bruised and the bone is bruised as well. Keep it wrapped, keep it elevated and I'm prescribing some painkillers if you need them." The doctor scribbled on a prescription pad and ripped it off.

"Is she okay to leave?" Duke took the prescription from the doctor.

"She is."

Stevens dragged a chair next to the examination table. "Before you leave, I'd like to ask you a few questions, Beth."

"We'll let you talk." Duke took Scarlett's arm. "I'll be in the waiting room, Beth."

When they reached the waiting room, Scarlett slouched on a vinyl chair. "I'm not staying in my cabin tonight. I'd been planning on leaving for Seattle tomorrow and then taking a flight to San Francisco for a friend's show. I can't help Beth anymore."

"You've done plenty."

She glanced at him sharply. "I just need to go back to the cabin to pack, and then I'll spend the night with my granny on the rez. Jason's driving me to Seattle."

"If something comes up, we can reach you on the cell phone number you gave Beth?"

"Yeah. Let me know when it's safe to return to my cabin."

Deputy Stevens caught the tail end of their conversation as he walked into the waiting room. "We have a couple of deputies canvassing your place, Scarlett. If we find anything else, we'll let you know."

"And if I remember anything else, I'll let you know, Quentin."

An orderly pushed Beth into the waiting room in a wheelchair.

Duke crouched beside her. "Can you walk on that ankle?"

She tipped her head at the orderly, holding a pair of crutches. "I'll have some crutches to get around at first, but once the swelling subsides a little more I should be fine."

The orderly handed the crutches to Duke and disappeared behind the swinging doors.

"We'll let you know if we discover anything else, too, Beth." Stevens clapped his hat onto his head. "Good night, all."

"Stevens? Scarlett's going back to her place to pack. Maybe it's a good idea if the deputies stay there until she leaves."

"I'll tell them."

When he left, Scarlett turned to Beth. "What did you want to see me about, anyway?"

"Oh, my God, I almost forgot." Beth pressed three fingers against her forehead. "The woman you saw with the strawberry blond hair in the vision—could she have been me as an adult, as I am now?"

"I don't know. Like Duke said, I'm not great at interpretation. I didn't get the impression that she was you. Why do you ask?"

"I spoke with someone who knew the Brices, and Patty Brice never had strawberry blond hair."

"I never said the woman was Patty Brice. I just don't know. I'm sorry, Beth. I can't help you anymore." Scarlett caught her bottom lip between her teeth. "What I haven't said yet to you or to Quentin Stevens is that the trap could've been a warning from my own people."

"The Quileute? Why?" Beth's eyes widened.

"They wouldn't want me talking about Dask'iya or the Timberline Trio case. I told you that before. The tribe doesn't discuss it."

"Would they really go that far to warn you?" Duke asked.

"It's a possibility. I just know I need to get away." She grabbed Beth's hand. "And you should, too."

"Thank you. I've been telling her that for a few days now."

"That's two to one, Beth. Find yourself another story. The Timberline kidnappings have been nothing but tragedy for everyone involved for as long as I can remember."

Beth squeezed Scarlett's hand. "Thanks for your concern, and thanks for all your help. I'm trying to reach a Realtor right now who can help me track down the red doors."

Scarlett rolled her eyes at Duke. "She's not going to listen, is she?"

"Don't worry. I plan to keep working on her. Are you okay if we leave now?"

"Yeah. You heard Quentin. The cops will probably still be wandering around my property when I get home."

Beth snapped her fingers. "My rental car is still at your place."

"You can't drive with that foot all wrapped up."

"Don't worry about it." Scarlett held up her hand. "I'll have Jason drive the car to your hotel and leave the keys at the front desk."

Duke dragged Beth's keys from his pocket and handed them to Scarlett. "Have a good trip."

They went to their separate cars, Beth awkwardly negotiating the crutches.

As he helped her into the SUV, he asked, "Did I hear you say you called the Realtor already?"

"Called her after my X-rays and left her a voice mail. If she's free for dinner, do you want to join us?"

"How could I possibly miss the discussion about cabins with red doors? Of course. And you're going to need some guidance before you get used to those crutches."

The drive back to the hotel was a quiet one. He was done trying to convince her to give up on this story. He knew one surefire way to do it, and if Mick would ever get back to him, it would be a done deal.

As he pulled into a parking spot, Beth's phone rang. She answered and he exited the car and leaned against the hood to wait.

When she got out, she held up her phone. "Dinner with Rebecca Geist at Sutter's tonight at seven. You in?"

"I'll be there." As she joined him, he took her by the shoulders before they entered the hotel. "I almost lost it when I saw you on the ground, that trap biting into your foot."

Her frame trembled beneath his hands. "It was…terrifying. The sound it made… Ugh. I'm going to hear that sound in my nightmares."

"What's it gonna take for you, Beth?"

"To leave Timberline? The truth. I'm going to leave Timberline when I discover the truth about my identity. Otherwise, what do I have?"

"You have me." He sealed his lips over hers and drew her close, burying one hand in her silky hair.

She melted against him for a moment, her mouth pliant against his. But then she broke away and stepped back.

"I just don't think you understand what this means to me, Duke. It's a lifetime of questions and doubts coming to a head in one corner of the world—right here. All my questions have led me here."

"You don't know, Beth. It's based on feelings and suppositions and red doors and frogs."

"And that's a start."

He closed his eyes and took a deep breath. He didn't want to take that all away from her—the hope, but he'd snatch it all away in a heartbeat to keep her safe.

"Okay. We have at least an hour before we have to leave for dinner. I'm going to take a shower. I'll stop by your room at around six forty-five."

She grabbed the front of his shirt. "Thanks for not pushing it, Duke."

Did she mean the topic of her identity or the kiss? Because he'd wanted to push both—especially the kiss.

AN HOUR LATER they drove into town and got a table for three at Sutter's. Beth had interviewed almost everyone she'd contacted, except for Jordan Young and a few others. As Beth had limped to their table, a few patrons glanced at her quickly, glanced away and then whispered among each other. Her reception in the dining room had cooled off compared to that first night.

Had the pranks and threats that had dogged her made the rounds and turned people off?

His gaze shifted to Beth studying the menu and his stomach sank. She didn't care how chilly the reception. She had a goal and to hell with anything and anyone who stood in her way—including him.

A flashy blonde entered the restaurant and made a beeline to their table. "Beth St. Regis? I'd recognize you anywhere."

Duke stood up and pulled out her chair as Beth made

the introductions. "Nice to meet you, Rebecca. This is Special Agent Duke Harper."

She shook his hand before taking a seat. "Now, aren't you the gentleman? These lumberjack types out here could learn a thing or two from a city boy like you."

Chloe was their waitress again and practically skipped to their table. "Jason told me someone had set some bear traps outside Scarlett's cabin and you stepped on one."

"Yeah, that happened." Beth lifted her wrapped foot in the air.

"That's crazy. Scarlett needs to stop ticking off those hunters."

"Did Scarlett get off to Seattle okay?"

Chloe nodded. "They're on their way. Jason texted me about an hour ago when they left. Can I get you guys some drinks?"

Rebecca ordered a glass of merlot while Beth got some hot tea. "I just took a couple of painkillers. If I mixed those with alcohol, I'd probably fall asleep at the table."

"I'll have that local brew on tap."

When Chloe walked away, Rebecca planted her elbows on the table and turned to Beth. "So, tell me everything. What secrets are you discovering about our little town?"

"Unfortunately the secrets seem to be piling up, and I don't have a clue."

"I heard what happened in here the other night between you and Bill Raney."

"His name keeps coming up, but since that initial threat from him, I haven't seen him at all." Beth glanced at the bar. "I don't think he's the only one who doesn't want me poking around."

Rebecca waved her manicured fingers. "Believe me, honey, the Timberline Trio case is the least of Bill's problems." She winked. "I'm his biggest problem right now."

Duke put his phone on vibrate and tucked it into the front pocket of his shirt. "You're taking away his business?"

"There was nothing to take away. I'm earning business and he's not—maybe if he'd lay off the booze."

"I heard from Dorothy Unger that you were the best, and that's why I called you."

Chloe stopped by with their drinks and they ordered their food while they had her attention.

"I helped Dot get out of her old house when her husband passed away and got her into a newer, smaller place." She folded her hands. "So, tell me how I can help you."

"Dorothy mentioned that there was a trend toward red doors for Timberline cabins a long time ago. Would you know which cabins had the red doors?"

Rebecca blinked her false lashes. "Red doors. Red doors. Not many of those cabins left."

"Are there some left?" Beth hunched forward, rattling her teacup.

"There are a couple, but I'm not sure if they're the original red-door cabins or if they're newly painted. I'm going to have to do a little research. I have a lot of archive photos of the cabins in Timberline. I'm sure I can find some of them."

"That would be great, Rebecca, and if you point me in the right direction, I can help you do the research."

Duke's phone buzzed in his pocket. He slipped it out and cupped it in his hand. When he saw that Mick had sent him a text, a muscle jumped in his jaw.

"Is that work?"

"Yeah. I'm just going to step outside for a minute, if you ladies will excuse me."

Rebecca patted Beth's arm. "True gentleman, that one."

Duke pushed back from the table and tried not to run

out of the restaurant. When he got to the sidewalk, he was panting like he'd just run a marathon.

He entered his code to unlock his phone and swiped his finger across the display. The blood rushed to his head when he read Mick's text and he braced one hand against the wall of the building to steady himself.

He placed a call to Mick. When Mick picked up, Duke said, "You're sure?"

"DNA doesn't lie, my brother, even on a rush job like this one. Is it going to help solve the case?"

"I think so."

"I have to get off the phone. It's late here and I'm helping my son with his math homework."

"Just wanted to verify. Thanks, buddy."

Duke strolled back into the restaurant. He didn't know how he was going to get through the rest of this meal.

When he got to the table, Rebecca was telling Beth all about her wedding plans.

She tapped her head. "Of course, it's all up here right now since my fiancé hasn't actually committed to a date yet."

"Nothing wrong with a long engagement, really get to know someone."

"What about you two?" Rebecca flicked her finger back and forth between him and Beth. "Any wedding plans?"

Beth's cup clattered into her saucer. "Oh, we're not… we're not together."

"Oops." Rebecca put two fingers to her lips. "I'm usually pretty good at things like that."

Duke grabbed Beth's hand. "We were together—once."

"You see? I knew it. I can always tell."

Beth tilted her head at him, a half smile on her lips.

Hadn't he made it clear he'd like to pick up where they'd left off? She'd been the one pushing him away. The night he'd told her he'd made a mistake two years ago had been the night she'd cooled down toward him. If a relationship came too easily for Beth, she'd probably dismiss it as unworthy of her efforts. She liked the struggle. It was what she knew.

Their dinner arrived and Rebecca did her part to keep the conversation going between bites of food. Thank God for talkative real-estate agents.

As they were finishing up, Bill Raney came into the restaurant with a few buddies, including Jordan Young, and bellied up to the bar.

Rebecca narrowed her eyes. "Honestly, Bill wouldn't have the guts to go sneaking through the forest laying bear traps for unsuspecting women. I wouldn't worry too much about him."

Duke asked, "I gather he's not your biggest fan. Has he ever bothered you?"

"You know, come to think of it…" Rebecca tapped her long nails together. "Someone sabotaged a couple of my open houses last month."

"Bill the Prankster strikes again?" Beth turned her head to take in the group at the bar.

Jordan Young waved her over.

She smiled and stuck out her bandaged foot. "At least Jordan won't think I'm too chicken to go up to Raney."

Young pushed away from the bar and drew up the fourth chair at the table. "Do you mind?"

Rebecca waved her finger at him. "As long as you give me a shot at your next listing, Jordan."

"I'm loyal to my friends, Rebecca, but I admire your success from afar." He tapped the table in front of Beth. "What happened to your foot?"

"I'm shocked you haven't heard yet."

"I've been fishing most of the day. What did I miss?"

"Someone set some bear traps in front of Scarlett Easton's place and I got stuck in one."

"Damn. Did you break it?"

"Just bruised it."

"Scarlett okay?"

"She's fine. Left town for a few weeks."

Jordan tsked. "That's no way to solve a disagreement over hunting. I'll talk to the mayor about cracking down."

"I'm sure Scarlett would appreciate that."

"How about you, Agent Harper? Any luck cracking the cold case?"

"We're investigating a few leads. They're not called 'cold cases' for nothing."

"And you're involved how, Rebecca?"

"I'll never tell. Maybe Beth just wants to buy some property after experiencing the beauty and serenity of the area."

Duke smothered his snort. Timberline had been anything but serene for Beth.

"Well, she's consulting the best." He rapped his knuckles on the table. "You folks enjoy your evening. And, Beth, I should be around for the next few days if you are."

"I'll be here. I'll try calling your office again to schedule something."

He took a card from his card case and called to Chloe. "Do you have a pen, sweetheart?"

She smacked a pen on the table and spun away.

Young scribbled something on one of his cards. "Here's my direct line, Beth. Give me a call when you're ready to interview me."

"Thanks, Jordan."

He sauntered back to his friends at the bar and a hard stare from Raney.

Maybe Bill Raney wasn't the hapless drunk everyone thought he was.

Chloe returned to the table with the check. "Sorry for the delay. I wasn't coming back with Mr. Young here. He can get handsy, if you know what I mean."

"Honey, at my age handsy isn't necessarily a bad thing." Rebecca laughed as she tried to grab the check from Chloe.

Beth was faster. "This is a tax-deductible dinner expense for me. You're going to help me find those red-door cabins, aren't you?"

"I'm going to do my damnedest. Now, if you don't mind, I'm going to scoot out of here and get back to the office to wrap up a few things."

When she left the restaurant after flitting to about five tables on her way out, Duke wiped the back of his hand across his forehead. "Whew. She's a dynamo."

"And efficient. I have complete faith in her to find those red doors."

Duke stroked her arm. "Let me get you back to the hotel and tuck you into bed. Maybe you can pop a few more of those painkillers and get a good night's sleep."

"You're being awfully...handsy tonight."

"I just want to take care of you, Beth." He laced his fingers with hers. "Do you believe me?"

"I believe you, and do you believe me when I say I just want the truth?"

"I can help you with that, too, Beth." He tugged on her hand. "Let's get out of here."

She leaned on him while she adjusted her crutches beneath her arms, and with a nod to Jordan, she navigated through the tables while Duke ran interference.

When they got back to the hotel, he followed her into her room. "I meant that about tucking you in. Do you want me to run you a bath?"

"I'd probably fall asleep in the tub and drown, but if you want to wait in here while I get ready for bed in case I topple over in the bathroom, that would be great."

"I'm your man in case of toppling." He stretched out on the bed and grabbed the remote control to the TV.

She gathered a few items and retreated to the bathroom.

While she ran the water and banged around in there, he ran a few lines through his head. He could put everything to rest tonight.

She emerged from the bathroom in her flannel pajamas and hopping without her crutches.

He jumped from the bed to help her. "Don't put any pressure on that foot yet."

She dropped some clothes in her suitcase. "I'm fine."

He pulled back the covers and helped her into bed. He wanted to crawl right in after her, but first things first.

She plumped up her pillows and eased back against them. "Aaah, this feels good."

"Do you need any more meds?"

"Not until after midnight. If the pain wakes me up, I'll take a few more."

He filled a glass with water from the tap and put her pill bottle on the nightstand. "For midnight."

"Thanks, Duke. You've been a big help."

"I'm going to be an even bigger help, Beth. I have something important to tell you."

Her face grew still. "What is it?"

He sat next to her on the bed and took both of her hands in his. "You're not Heather Brice."

Chapter Thirteen

She jerked away from Duke, banging her head on the head-board. His touch felt heavy, oppressive, and she snatched her hands away from his. "Why are you saying that? Why are you trying to discourage me?"

"It's more than that, Beth." He tried to take her hand again but she folded her arms and tucked her hands beneath her elbows. "I have proof."

Her tongue felt like sandpaper as she licked her lips. "How could you have proof? What did you do?"

"I requested a sample of the Brices' DNA through the FBI labs."

She clamped her hands over her ears as if that could stop the truth coming from Duke's lips. Bending at the waist, she touched her forehead to her knees. The pieces of her carefully constructed future began crashing down around her—the happy reunion, the loving family, her place in the world.

Duke's hand on her back felt like a lead weight, but she didn't have the energy to shrug him off. A black hole had sucked her into its vortex and she was spinning and spinning with no sense of time or place, no anchor.

"I'm sorry, Beth. I couldn't stand to see you twisting yourself into knots over this, putting yourself into needless danger." He swept aside the curtain of hair shielding her face. "I didn't cause the Brices any anguish. I didn't tell them about your suspicions. I let them know the FBI was working the cold case and needed their DNA. I ran it against yours from some strands of your hair and...no match."

A tear ran down her cheek and she let it drop off the edge of her chin. She managed a hoarse whisper from her tight throat. "Why did you do that? Why didn't you tell me?"

"The bigger question, Beth, is why didn't you ask me to do that? Your excuse for not going straight to the Brices was that you wanted to spare their feelings in case nothing came of your claim, but you always knew the FBI could request their DNA without arousing any suspicions. The fact that we'd taken this case out of mothballs made it easy."

She raised her head and another tear slipped down her face. "You know why."

"You were afraid of the answer. You were afraid of the truth." Duke caught her next tear on the pad of his thumb. "I get that. It's why I didn't tell you I was ordering the DNA."

"I knew." She rubbed her nose against the sheet covering her knees. "I saw a text from Mickey the other night about the Brices. I knew you were up to something. I just couldn't figure out why you wouldn't tell me what."

"Ah, that was it." He ran a hand down her leg and traced the edge of the heavy wrap around her ankle. "Maybe I should've told you, but then you would've been on pins and needles waiting for the results and if the results had been different..."

Falling back against the pillows, she said, "You're glad they're not different. You're relieved I'm not Heather Brice."

"I want you to be happy, Beth." He shoved a hand

through his thick hair and left it there, holding the side of his head. "I knew you'd been building up this perfect life with the Brices, envisioning them as the all-American family, a place for you to fit in at last. God, I want that for you, Beth, but you can have that with me. We can have it together. I'm looking for my perfect family, too."

A sob racked her body and she covered her face with her hands. "You can't have that with me. I can't help you create that perfect family because I'm broken. I'm damaged."

The mattress sank as Duke climbed next to her on the bed. He wrapped one arm around her shoulders and pulled her against his chest. "Don't say that. You're the most perfect woman I know—the girl of my adolescent fantasies come to life in living, strawberry blond color."

Taking a long, shuddering breath, she squirmed out of his hold. She grabbed handfuls of his shirt and pulled him close. "You don't know. I've already destroyed any family we could have together."

He touched his forehead to hers and smoothed the hair from her damp face. "I told you, Beth. I understand why you deceived me two years ago. I understand you."

"You don't know me."

"I didn't know you before. I saw you as the untouchable girl of my dreams, perfect in every way. Now I see the human woman that you are, with all your flaws and insecurities, and I still love you. I love you more."

She squeezed her eyes shut and ran her fingers across his rough beard. She'd been waiting so long to hear those words from him…and now she'd have to fling them back in his face.

"I don't deserve your love. I tricked you again. I deceived you." She pulled away from him so she could look into his dark eyes and see the love fade away. "I had a miscarriage. I lost your baby, Duke."

His eyes widened for a split second and grew darker as his pupils dilated. "When?"

"I found out I was pregnant when I got back to LA from Chicago—about three weeks after."

"What happened?"

"This is what happened." She slammed a fist against her gut. "Me. I happened. Unfit for a family."

"Stop it." His fingers pinched into her shoulders. "Tell me what happened to our baby, Beth."

"I don't know. I had the miscarriage just a few weeks after I discovered the pregnancy. It all came and went so fast, it felt like a dream."

She gritted her teeth and braced herself for Duke's anger, for his accusations. She welcomed them. Deserved them.

His hold on her shoulders melted into a caress and he dragged her back into his arms again, tucking her head against the curve of his neck. "I'm sorry you were alone when it happened. I should've been there for you."

"Don't you get it, Duke?" She sniffled. "I didn't even tell you about the pregnancy. I probably never would've told you about the baby."

"I don't believe that for a minute." He rubbed a circle on her back. "You would've told me. You never would've allowed our baby to grow up without knowing his or her father. Whatever your feelings for me were at the time, you would've recognized the value of giving our child a father. I know that about you…now."

"But it's over. I lost the baby."

"Did the doctor indicate that you'd have problems in the future? Was there a reason why you miscarried?"

His heart pounded beneath her cheek and she smoothed her hand over his chest. "No problems. He said it's something that happens in the first trimester sometimes."

"Then it wasn't your fault and you can get pregnant again." He kissed her temple. "You can have that family, Beth. You don't need the Brices. You don't need the Kings. All you need is me. And I sure as hell need you."

He wedged his thumb beneath her chin and tilted up her head. He traced the tracks of her tears with his fingertip until he'd dried them all, and then he kissed her lips. They throbbed beneath the gentle pressure of his mouth.

Between the kisses he planted along the line of her jaw, he whispered, "I. Want. You. More. Than. Anything."

"Duke, is this coming from pity?" She cupped his jaw in her hand, the stubble of his beard tickling her palm. "Because I'm okay now. I'm sorry I broke down. In fact, I—"

"Shh." He put a finger against her lips. Then he took her hand and guided it between his legs. "Does this feel like pity to you?"

She stroked his erection through the denim of his jeans. It felt like a visit to the candy store and a two-point rating share all rolled up into one big treat.

He growled and unbuttoned his fly. She took the obvious hint and peeled back his jeans while shoving her hand beneath the waistband of his black briefs.

The growl turned into a groan as she teased his flesh with her fingernails and kissed his mouth. He deepened the kiss and tugged at her pajama top, pulling it over her head.

He cupped one bare breast with his hand, dragging his thumb across her peaked nipple. She gasped against his lips and he shifted his mouth to the top of her breast. He kissed a circle around her nipple before sucking it into his mouth.

She arched her back, giving him more, her hips rocking forward, her hand stroking his hard-on.

She unbuttoned his shirt and rolled up his T-shirt, exposing his tight abs. She ran the flat of her hand along the ridges and then ducked her head and pressed a kiss in the middle, his skin warm against her lips.

Yanking on the edge of the shirt, she said, "That's the problem with cold weather—too many clothes."

"Sort of heightens the anticipation, don't you think?" He slipped off her pajama bottoms with one fluid motion.

"Says the man who has just a flimsy pair of pajamas to dispense with."

"There's still these." He ran a finger along the elastic of her bikini underwear clinging to her hips.

"What are you waiting for?"

He pulled down the panties and the silky material skimmed over her thighs. "This is a little more difficult. I'll try to be careful."

He inched the underwear over her knees and gently tugged them past her bandage. His gaze swept across her body, leaving tingles in its wake.

"Nothing but a pink bandage—incredibly sexy."

She wiggled her toes and rolled to her side. "You can get naked now."

He shed the rest of his clothing in record time and stretched out beside her again. He pressed his body against hers, along every line, and she let his warmth seep into her skin.

For a moment she let everything slip away—all the heartache and disappointment. She had her man by her side again and there were no secrets between them.

He followed her spine with one knuckle and caressed her derriere, fitting her against his body, his erection prodding between her thighs.

He traced over the rest of her body, as if drawing it from scratch. Could he recreate her? Make her whole?

His touch gave her goose bumps, made her believe anything was possible. He finished his exercise with a kiss on her mouth. Then he pressed her back against the pillows.

"I'm going to make you feel better than any painkiller in the entire pharmacy." He knelt between her legs and flattened his hands against the insides of her thighs. Lifting her injured leg, he rested it on his shoulder. "The doc said to keep it elevated, right?"

"That's one way to do it."

When his lips brushed her sensitive flesh, her eyes fluttered closed and her fingers burrowed into his hair. He circled with his tongue and then plunged it inside her.

She let out a long sigh, but then the tension began to build like a hot coil in her belly. Her fingernails dug into his scalp as he teased her higher and higher.

Her climax broke her apart into a million little pieces. All the anxiety and fear that had been building up since she'd started this quest shattered. She wouldn't let it take hold of her again.

Duke slid her leg from his shoulder. "Okay?"

"Mmm, more than okay and ready for you. Really ready for you this time, Duke. No more games."

"Nothing between us." He rose to his knees and she wrapped her fingers around his erection.

"Like one."

Bracing his hands on either side of her head, he drove inside her. A spasm of pleasure flashed across his face.

She clawed at the hard muscle of his buttocks, hooking her good leg around his hips, urging him deeper.

His rhythm was erratic, as if the tumult of his senses had overwhelmed him and he'd forgotten for a moment how a man loved a woman.

She touched his face. Their eyes met. He shivered and slowed his pace, plunging into her deeply and pulling out just enough to make it feel like coming home when he returned to her.

As his thrusts grew bolder and faster, she pressed her lips against his warm flesh, baring her teeth against his collarbone.

He moaned, a sound of such pure pleasure it made her toes curl. On the very next thrust, he exploded inside her. He sank to his forearms and took possession of her mouth. The motion of his kiss mimicked the waves of his orgasm and he didn't stop kissing her until he was spent inside her.

He hoisted himself off her body. "How's your foot?"

Her lips curled into a smile. "My foot had nothing to do with any of that."

"Is it feeling left out?" He slid to the bottom of the bed and kissed each of her toes sticking out of the bandage.

"Did you develop a foot fetish when we were apart?"

"I have a fetish for every part of your body. Don't you know that? I could worship your elbow and count myself lucky."

She crooked her index finger. "I have to admit I'm partial to one part of your body in particular."

"My brain, right?" He settled beside her again and scooped her into a hug, rubbing the gooseflesh from her arms.

"That's it." She kissed his chiseled jawline. "And that didn't feel like pity sex at all."

"As a man, that's the best way I know how to offer comfort. But pity? I don't pity you. So, you're not Heather Brice with the perfect family waiting for you at the end of the rainbow. I knew my family, knew where I came from—and it wasn't perfect. Maybe the Brices aren't perfect, either. You'll weather the storm."

"You're right. The news about the Brices' DNA was just a hiccup."

"I meant what I said, Beth." He massaged the back of her neck. "As long as I'm stuck in cold-case hell, I can turn you on to a few good stories."

"That would be great once I'm done here."

"Not that I won't miss you, but I can drive you to Seattle and you can get on the next plane to LA. I'll have to stay here, of course, but I'm sure Mick won't mind if I take a few weekends off and head to LA."

"I'm not leaving right away, Duke."

"You don't need to pretend with anyone. I'll make sure word gets out that your producer cut the story or you felt you didn't have enough to create a compelling enough episode of *Cold Case Chronicles*."

"I mean—" she pulled the sheet up to her chin, her heart thumping "—I'm not giving up here."

The massage stopped. "What does that mean? You don't have anything on the Timberline Trio. There's no story for you here."

She sat up, adjusting the pillow behind her back. "I don't care about the Timberline Trio case, especially now that I'm not involved in it at all."

His dark brows collided over his nose. "I don't understand. What is there for you in Timberline?"

"What was always here—my true identity. I may not be Heather Brice or Kayla Rush, but the secret to my origin is here in Timberline. And I'm going to stay here until I discover it."

Chapter Fourteen

A chill stole over Duke's flesh, still damp with the exertion of making love. He rolled away from Beth and planted his feet on the carpet. "You can't be serious."

"*You* can't be serious to believe I'd give up now that I'm so close."

"Close to what? For whatever reason, a person or persons unknown to you does not want you poking around Timberline, and as long as you continue to do so, your life is in danger."

"I don't give a damn what the people of Timberline want. I know my past lies here and I'm going to solve the mystery of my identity if it's the last thing I do."

"It just might be."

She flicked her fingers in the air. "There have been some warnings, but nothing life-threatening."

He smacked his forehead. "Someone shot at you."

"He missed. Do you really think an experienced hunter would miss his prey?"

"We don't know that the person shooting at you is an experienced hunter, and I'm sure hunters miss all the time." He fell back on the bed so that his head was in her lap. "Beth, it's not worth it. You don't know what you're looking for."

"I'm looking for a cabin with a red door and two birds

somewhere. If I can trace the property records for that cabin, maybe I can find out who had it twenty-five years ago and discover what happened there."

"I'm in awe of your..."

"Brilliance?" She combed her fingers through his hair.

"Stubbornness." He captured her fingers. "What if you do discover your true family? They may not be the loving family the Brices were. The Brices had their child stolen from them. Your family gave you away and didn't want to be traced. I'm not gonna stand by and watch you get devastated by the discovery."

"I... I'm not going to be devastated. It is what it is. I just want to know at this point. Wouldn't you?"

"I would." He pressed a kiss against the center of her palm. "I just don't want to see you hurt—physically or emotionally. You're back in my life now, Beth, and I don't want to lose you again."

"Stand by me. Stay with me. If you're going to be my family, then that's what it takes." She leaned forward and kissed his forehead. "I'm tired of secrets, Duke. I want a fresh start with you, a clean slate before we...do whatever it is we're going to do."

"If you're going to stay here in Timberline, I'll be with you. I'm not going to let you run off looking for red doors by yourself."

"I was hoping you'd say that because I don't think I can do this by myself. I'm better with you, Duke."

"I just hope you don't get hurt."

"If I do, I know you'll have my back."

"Count on it." He slid off the bed and swept her card key from the nightstand. "I'm going to my own room to brush my teeth, but I'll be back."

She snuggled against the pillow and closed her eyes. "I'll be waiting."

When Duke returned to his room he punched a pillow. He hadn't been happy when the Brices' DNA didn't match Beth's, but he'd been relieved. He'd figured she'd give up on Timberline and go back to LA, but she felt some connection to this place. He had to trust her instincts.

He brushed his teeth and splashed some water on his face. He pulled on a pair of running shorts and returned to Beth's room.

The TV flickered in the darkness and he crept over to her bed. She'd fallen asleep on her back with her foot propped up on pillows beneath the covers.

He dropped his shorts and slid between the sheets, next to her. She hadn't bothered putting her pajamas back on and he rolled to his side to press his body against her nakedness.

She murmured something through parted lips and he kissed the corner of her mouth. Beth had no intention of giving up her search, and whatever happened, he'd be there for the fallout.

THE NEXT MORNING after breakfast, he and Beth joined Rebecca in her office. She led them to a conference room and flipped open her laptop. She eyed Duke over the top of her computer. "This isn't part of the FBI investigation, is it?"

He held up his hands. "I'm off duty today. Would it make a difference?"

"I just don't want to get subpoenaed or have our records called into evidence."

"This is for the show only. You don't even have to be on camera if you don't want to be."

"Well, I wouldn't mind that as long as you get a shot of my sign out front. Unless—" she powered up her computer "—the story ends up driving potential buyers away from Timberline."

Beth shrugged off her down vest. "The case was twenty-five years ago. I don't see how that's going to affect Timberline's reputation. If anything, Wyatt Carson already did that by trying to play the hero."

As she typed on her keyboard, Rebecca gave an exaggerated shiver. "That was creepy, but I still managed to get a good price for Kendall Rush's house."

Duke cleared his throat. "What are you going to look up this morning?"

"I have access to all of Timberline's old housing records, along with some pictures. With any luck, I should be able to identify several of the homes with the red doors."

"Let's get started." Beth scooted her chair closer to the table and leaned over Rebecca's arm.

Rebecca's fingers flew over the keyboard. "Let's see. Twenty years ago, twenty-five, not much construction during that period. Thirty, thirty-five. Now we're getting somewhere."

Beth leaned forward, poking at the screen. "This is new construction for that time period?"

"Yes. I can click on the photos for this bunch."

A cabin filled the computer screen, but it didn't have a red door.

Beth slumped back in her chair. "That's not one."

"Let me click through these photos." Each time Rebecca tapped her keyboard, a new cabin popped up on the screen. None had red doors.

"There's another grouping. I'm going to close out this bunch." She launched another set of photos and Beth sucked in a breath when the first one appeared.

"This is it." Beth practically bounced in her chair. "These are the cabins."

Rebecca brought up the cabins one by one and each cabin sported a red front door.

Duke counted the red-door cabins aloud until she came to the end. "That's eight cabins with red doors. Do you recognize any of them, Rebecca?"

"I thought I recognized a couple." She minimized the window and brought up another application. "I'm going to copy and paste the cabin addresses in here to get their locations and to see if they still exist."

An hour later Rebecca printed out a list of five red-door cabins that were still standing. The other three had been demolished.

"You are the best." Beth plucked the pages from the printer. "If I ever know of anyone moving to this area, I will send them your way."

"Just give me a plug on your show." She squinted at her laptop. "I have to get ready for my open house. Have fun investigating, and if you annoy anyone by poking around, don't tell them I sent you."

When they got into Duke's SUV, Beth smoothed out the paper on her lap. "GPS?"

"Plug in all of them and we'll try to hit them in order of location."

Beth tapped in the address of each of the cabins on the list and they designed a route so they wouldn't be backtracking.

Duke turned the key in the ignition and glanced at Beth. "What's your plan? Are you going to invite yourself into someone's home, stand in the middle of the room and tell them you're waiting for a psychic experience?"

"I'm not sure yet. I'll figure it out when I get there."

"Okay, it's your rodeo. I'm just the technical adviser... and the bodyguard."

She squeezed his bicep. "I like the sound of that."

They drove out to the first two cabins, which resided on the same street. Civilization had encroached on the wilderness in this area as a wide, paved road cut through the forest, giving the houses on this street manicured back-yards bordering the forest edge.

Duke parked his car on the street in front of the first cabin and looked at Beth. "What now?"

"I... I'm going to get out and walk around. Maybe I'll knock on the front door and pretend I'm looking for some-one."

"Yeah, because you're not totally recognizable in this town by now."

"I could use that to my advantage." She unbuckled her seat belt and reached into his backseat. "I'll take my video camera. I was filming areas before."

"Let's do it."

He went around to the passenger side to get Beth's door. She looked up from the camera in her lap. "Might as well start filming now. In fact, this is a good way to get a record of each cabin."

He helped her out of the car. "Are you going to be able to hold the camera and navigate with your crutch?"

"I don't think so. Can you play cameraman for me?"

"Yeah, just don't tell Adam." He took the camera from her. "Where is your crew, anyway? Are they getting antsy?"

"They're working on something else right now. I al-ready indicated to Scott that this segment might not be a go and to hold off sending them."

"All right, then." He held the camera in front of him and framed the cabin in the viewfinder. "Cabin number one in the red-door cabin follies."

Beth poked him with her crutch and then appeared in his frame. "I'm going to knock on the door."

He followed her to the porch and then the door swung open and a boy cannoned down the front porch, leaving the door standing wide behind him. He tripped to a stop when he saw them.

"Hi there. Do you live here?"

"Mom!"

"Tanner, close the door." A petite woman appeared at the doorway. She put a hand to her chest. "Oh, you scared me."

"Sorry." Beth flashed her pearly whites. "I'm doing a little filming in the area. Do you mind?"

"Oh, I know who you are."

"Mom, can I go to Joe's house now?"

"Go ahead." She crossed her arms and propped up the doorjamb with her shoulder. "This area doesn't have much to do with the Timberline Trio, and I didn't even live here then."

"I know that, but a few of these cabins were standing twenty-five years ago. I'm just getting a sense of the area back then."

"You can film outside the house if you want, but I don't have time to talk to you and if the dog starts barking you're going to have to leave."

"I understand. Thank you."

But the woman had slammed the door on Beth's thanks.

Duke shifted the camera to the side. "Ouch. She's not too interested in appearing on TV, is she?"

"No, but I'm not getting anything from this house anyway."

"Like, recognition?"

"Like, any kind of vibe."

"You're not Scarlett." He snapped the viewfinder closed. "You felt those things with her because she let you into her vision."

"She told me I had a particular sensitivity. That's why

this landscape in Timberline, the forest, the greenery, sets me off. It always has."

He wasn't going to argue with her or convince her otherwise. He had a support role today and he planned to fulfill that role to the best of his ability. "On to cabin number two, then."

Cabin number two was similar to one—more like a house and inhabited with residents, none too eager to speak with Beth. Duke filmed the exterior for her, but this cabin didn't speak to her, either.

They had more luck with cabin number three. As they drove up to the front of it, Beth sat up. "This looks spooky, doesn't it?"

"It looks abandoned."

"I'm getting the chills already." Beth stretched her arms out in front of her.

Duke cut the engine and hoisted the strap of the camera over his shoulder.

He filmed the front of the cabin as Beth hobbled up to the porch without her crutches. "Hello?"

Duke tried the door, but the rotting wood held firm. He picked at a chip of paint with his fingernail. "I think this still has the original red paint on the door."

"Seems to be locked up tight." Beth stepped off the porch steps. "I'm going to look around the side."

"Hang on." He put the camera down. "The landscaping, if you can call it that, is overgrown with weeds. Grab my arm."

Taking his arm, she leaned against him. He navigated a path through the tangled shrubs and turned the corner of the cabin. The wild brush of the forest grew close to the exterior cabin wall.

Beth tugged on his hand. "The window's broken."

They crept up to the shattered window and Duke dug for

his phone. Poking his head inside the window, he turned on the phone's light and scanned the room.

"Do you see anything?"

"It's a big mess. Looks like animals, kids, transients or all three have been in here."

She yanked on the back of his shirt. "Let me have a look."

He backed away from the window and handed her the phone. "It's too high for you to see inside, especially without cutting yourself on the jagged glass."

He scanned the ground and spotted a stump of wood. "This'll work."

He dragged the wood under the window and helped Beth stand on it, holding her around the waist. "Do you see anything that grabs you?"

"No, but it's creepy. I'd like to find out more about it."

"I'm sure Rebecca can help with that."

Duke filmed more of the cabin before they got back in the car. "Three down, two to go."

Beth checked her phone. "They're in the same general area, farther out in the boonies."

"Let's go and you can review my awesomely professional video later."

He swung off the main highway, down one of the many roads that branched into the forest. Cabins and small houses dotted the road. "I wonder when housing for the Evergreen employees is going to creep out this way."

"I think there's something about the zoning that doesn't permit certain types of housing."

"I'm sure Jordan Young is working on an angle for that right now."

"And he'll probably give all the work to his worthless buddy, Bill." She tapped her phone. "Oops. I think the GPS lost its way."

"We don't have too many choices here until we plunge into the forest." He pointed to a marker up ahead on the side of the road. "There's an access road there." When they reached the marker, he made the turn.

Beth's knees bounced and she wedged her hands beneath her thighs. "Reminds me of Scarlett's area."

"Remote and rugged. These must be hunting and fishing cabins."

Beth scooted forward in her seat, her back stiff.

"Are you okay?"

Her lips parted and her chest rose and fell rapidly.

"Beth? What's wrong?"

She cupped her hands around her nose and mouth and huffed out a breath. "Feeling a little anxious. I'll be fine."

The trees crowded in on them, shutting out the light of the afternoon. Mist clung to the windshield and he flipped on the wipers. "We can stop right here, turn around."

Shaking her head, she hugged herself. "It's that feeling, Duke. The forest is closing in on me, suffocating me."

"I'm turning around."

"No!" She grabbed the steering wheel. "I can do this. I can get through it."

They came across a path leading from the access road. "My guess is the first cabin's back there."

"Then we'd better take a look."

He parked and helped her from the car. "How about one crutch?"

"I'll try it." She tucked it under one arm and he held her other arm.

The cabin arose from a clearing. A walkway paved with natural stone cut a path through a neat garden.

"It looks inhabited." He squeezed her hand. "Still getting the feeling?"

The door burst open and a man stepped out onto the porch with a shotgun.

Beth stumbled and Duke caught her.

"You lost?"

"Can you put the gun down?" Duke curled his arm around Beth's body and felt a tremble roll through her frame.

"Oh, this?" He lowered the shotgun. "Just came out here to clean it. Didn't know anyone was here. Got myself a turkey this morning."

Beth found her voice. "Do you own this cabin?"

"No, ma'am. My name's Doug Johnson, if you want to check it out. I rent the cabin once a year to do some hunting—turkey mostly. The wife likes it if I can bring one home for the Thanksgiving dinner." He tugged on his hat. "Are you looking for the owner?"

"Who is it?" Duke asked.

"I rent it from some management company—Raney Realty."

Beth pinched his side. "Bill Raney?"

"Might be, but I deal with a woman." He jerked his thumb over his shoulder. "I think I have a card, if you want me to get it."

Duke waved. "That's okay. We can look them up in town. There another cabin out this way?"

"About a mile up the road."

"Is that one for rent, too?"

"I think it is, but there's nobody there now. It's not as nice as this one."

"Raney Realty have that one?"

"I think so. I keep coming back to this place, so I'm not sure."

"Thanks. Sorry to disturb you." Beth dug her crutch into the ground. "Four down, one to go."

When they got back in the car, Duke touched her icy cheek. "Are you sure you're okay?"

"Do you find it coincidental that the cabin giving me the heebie-jeebies is managed by Bill Raney?"

"Yep." Beth had regained her focus and he didn't even bother asking if she wanted to check out the last cabin. She was like a dog with a bone at this point.

He drove almost a mile up the road until he spied another path with a mailbox at its entrance.

He pulled off the road as far as he could and met Beth at the passenger door. Her pale face and shallow breathing indicated another panic attack was on the horizon.

"Can I get you something, Beth? We don't have to do this now, or you can wait in the car and I'll take the camera."

"It's so strong, Duke. I wish I had Scarlett with me."

"I'm with you." He handed her the crutch. "Let's go face this thing head-on."

He adjusted his gait to hers, his head swiveling from side to side, his body tense.

Beth fell against him with a cry as she pointed to the mailbox. "Look, two birds. Just like Scarlett said—two birds. This is the place."

Chapter Fifteen

Beth swayed, but Duke kept her steady. The uneasy feelings had been building in her gut as soon as Duke had turned down the access road. Now, standing in front of the mailbox, they overwhelmed her.

Breaking away from Duke, she staggered toward the mailbox and grabbed it. She traced her finger along the edges of the two birds that had been carved at the top of the mailbox. "This is what Scarlett saw."

He placed a hand against her back. "Are you ready to have a look?"

"You're not going to try to talk me out of it again?"

"You've come this far. There's no turning back."

Dragging in a breath, she leaned on her crutch. "Let's go."

A path wended its way toward the cabin, which was a duplicate of the one down the road. The hunter had been right. His rental was in better shape, but this one hadn't been abandoned.

They approached the front door, which was no longer red, and Duke took the two steps in one long stride. He banged on the solid wood door. "Hello? Anyone here?"

"I suppose we won't find any broken windows in this cabin." Beth hobbled around to the side.

The brush had been cleared away from the structure,

creating a neat perimeter. Beth followed the outer wall of the cabin, the adrenaline pumping through her body. She pressed her forehead against one of the windows, but someone had tugged a pair of neat curtains across the glass.

She jumped as Duke put a hand on her shoulder. "Can't see inside this one, but this is it—the cabin of my nightmares. I'm sure of it, and the formerly red door and the two birds on the mailbox line up with Scarlett's vision."

"I doubt the owner of the cabin, especially if it's managed by Bill Raney, is going to allow us to just walk in and search around."

"Probably not. What if we rent the place?"

"Wouldn't that seem strange since you've been staying in the hotel all this time? And if Raney doesn't want you snooping around, I'm sure he could come up with a million reasons for the owner not to rent to you."

She traced a finger across the smooth glass. "I wonder who owns it. I really want to get inside."

"Can you get any reception out here? If you text Rebecca, she'll have the answer for you in a matter of minutes."

She pulled her phone from her pocket and tapped it. "No reception. That info is going to have to wait."

"But the rest doesn't have to wait." He brushed aside her hair and kissed the nape of her neck. "I'll be right back."

He headed to the back of the cabin and disappeared around the corner.

A wave of panic engulfed her again and she closed her eyes and pressed her hand against the rough wood of the cabin wall. "Duke?"

"Right here."

Her lids flew open to find him beside her. "What did you find?"

"Whaddya know? Someone left the back door open."

"You broke in?"

"Shh. We're not going to steal anything. We're just looking around to see if it's suitable for renting."

"I'm gonna end up getting you fired over this."

He took her hand. "If I'm going to get fired, we might as well get something out of it."

The forest edged up pretty closely to the back of the cabin, but the place did have a patio with a table, a couple of chairs and a barbecue pit.

Duke pulled the sleeve of his jacket over his hand and pushed open the back door. She didn't notice any broken glass or splintered wood, so he must've picked the lock. The less she knew, the better.

She stepped through the door into a small room off the kitchen with a compact washer and dryer in the corner. Her breath coming in short spurts, she edged into the kitchen as Duke closed the door.

She hesitated at the entrance to the living room where a large stone fireplace took up half the wall.

"Maybe they don't get many renters here because it's not completely furnished or ready." Duke hovered at her shoulder. "Do you want to have a look?"

Beth had to peel her tongue from the roof of her mouth to talk. "I... I'm scared. This room... There's something evil here. Do you feel it?"

Duke stepped around her into the dark living room and ran a hand along the mantel of the fireplace. "It's eerie, but I might be getting that vibe from you."

Beth took one shaky step after him. Curling her fingers around the gold locket at her throat, she closed her eyes. She could use some of Scarlett's magical tea about now.

She shuffled farther into the room, as if being drawn forward by some guiding force.

"Beth?"

Duke's voice seemed far away. Beth battled to get through the fear and revulsion to make her way toward a softer, more benevolent place at the end of this tunnel. The greenery of the Washington peninsula that had always caused her such anxiety rushed past her in a whirlwind. The blood-drenched terror that she'd faced in her shared vision with Scarlett swirled around her, but she kept her focus. There was something more, something sweet and precious, and she had to stay this course to get to it.

"Beth? Beth?"

The wood floor creaked beneath her and she fell to her knees. "I'm here. I'm back. I'll help you."

"Beth, my God."

Duke crouched beside her, his arm circling her waist. "Beth, are you okay? What's wrong with you?"

Twisting around to face him, she grabbed his jacket. "It's here, Duke. There's something here. Something led me here."

He stroked her hair. "I know, babe—the hypnosis, the visions, the red door and the birds have all led you here, but it's not enough. Even if we find out who owns the cabin, it might not be enough."

She pounded the floor through the Native American rug that covered it. "No, I mean it's here. There's something right here."

He dropped his gaze to the floor and ran his hand along the blanket, his brows creating a V between his eyes.

Just like that, he believed her.

"I don't see anything, Beth. It's just a rug." He flipped up one corner of the rug, exposing the original wood floor of the cabin, scarred and scratched. He pressed his hands against the slats of wood and one rocked beneath his hands.

"It's loose." His eyes flew to her face.

She breathed out the words. "It's here. I heard the wood creak beneath my feet. There's something here, Duke."

He reached into his pocket for his knife and flipped it open. He jimmied it between the loose slat and its neighbor. It lifted a half an inch.

"There's a cavity here."

Beth grabbed the knife, but Duke put his hand over hers. "Easy. We don't want anyone to know we've been here."

He took over and worked the blade back and forth until the wood came up from the floor. When he could get under the slat, he angled the knife and pumped it higher.

He eased up the slat and removed it. "Hand me your phone."

She knew what he wanted, and she turned her phone's light on before dropping it into his hand.

He aimed it into the space beneath the floor. "There's a box in there. Looks like a small fisherman's tackle box. It's too big to fit through this opening. I'm going to have to remove a couple more pieces of flooring."

While Beth held the phone, Duke worked on two more slats until the opening was wide enough to accommodate the box.

"You do the honors."

With trembling hands, Beth reached into the cavity and pulled out the tin box. She didn't know what she expected—her real birth certificate? Adoption papers? A letter from her bio parents?

When she flung open the lid, she gasped and fell back on her heels. Whatever she'd expected to find, it didn't include this.

Duke grabbed a handful of the photos in the box and held them to the light. "What the hell? Nudie pictures?"

Beth studied the pictures fanned out in Duke's hand and gasped.

As she opened her mouth, an explosion rocked the cabin.

Chapter Sixteen

Duke's ears were ringing with the sound of the explosion. He reached for Beth, whose mouth was hanging open in shock. "Are you okay?"

She managed a nod.

His nostrils flared as he sniffed the air. A window in the front had shattered, but the cabin was intact, and he couldn't smell fire.

"The cabin's fine. The explosion came from outside."

He gathered all the photos from the box and shoved them into the camera case. "We need to get out of here."

Beth reached for the wood slats and slid the first one into place. They put the floor back the way it was and Beth covered it with the rug.

Duke slung the camera case across his body and hoisted Beth to her feet.

With the crutch snug beneath her arm, Beth moved as fast as she could for the kitchen.

Once outside, Duke could see black smoke rising from the front of the cabin. He turned and shut the door, clicking the lock back into place with his knife.

"Let's get in the car and call 9-1-1 when we can. We were just driving by when we heard an explosion, right?"

She licked her lips. "Got it."

They got to the front of the cabin and started down the path to the road when Beth gasped. "It's a tire."

With a sinking feeling in the pit of his stomach, Duke pushed through the gate to the road, stepping over twisted metal.

He swore when he saw the shell of his rented SUV twisted, blackened and still on fire.

Beth tried her phone. "Still no reception. I suppose we're going to have to admit to being out here unless you can think of a way to move that burning hulk and all its pieces somewhere else."

"We were walking up to the cabin to do research for your show and heard the explosion."

"We're going to have a chance to try out that story real soon." She cocked her head. "Sirens."

"Doug must've called it in."

She hooked her fingers in his back pocket. "What do you think happened to your car, other than the obvious?"

"Since dynamiting a rental car seems too suspect, even for Sheriff Musgrove, my guess is that it was an expertly placed shot to the gas tank."

"Easily explained away by an errant bullet or teenage prank."

"Or another rogue hunter, but now that Scarlett Easton has left town, who's the target this time?"

"Someone knew we were here, Duke." She rested her forehead against his back. "Someone didn't want us to find those pictures."

"That's going a little far to protect a few naked photos, don't you think. As far as I could tell, they were all grown women."

"It's more than that."

A fire truck roared down the access road, followed by a squad car and an ambulance.

"Hold that thought, Beth. We have some explaining to do."

OVER TWO HOURS LATER, after being dropped off by a deputy, they collapsed in Beth's hotel room.

Duke downed half a bottle of water in one gulp. "That went smoother than I expected. We were the victims, so the deputies didn't seem to care what we were doing at the cabin."

"At least they think it was a threat directed at me this time and not related to Scarlett's feud with the hunters."

"Yeah, but their solution was to tell you to leave town."

"It wasn't too long ago that your solution was the same."

He ran a hand down her back. "Because I wanted to protect you, not because I didn't want to deal with solving a crime. Sheriff Musgrove is a piece of work."

"At least the explosion got him off the golf course."

"You realize it's going to take about two minutes before the entire town of Timberline knows we were at that cabin."

"Who cares?" She patted the camera case. "We found the stash of pictures."

"I'm not sure what good they're going to do us unless you want to start a girlie magazine."

"That's because you didn't look at the pictures." She opened the camera case. "I did."

His pulse ticked up. "Something incriminating."

"Not exactly, but something very, very interesting." She pulled a handful of the pictures from the case and dropped them on the credenza, fanning them out. "Look at this picture and tell me what you think."

"First time I've ever had a woman ask me to look at

provocative photos." He picked up the photo of a woman posing in the nude, tame by today's standards, and studied it. He dropped the picture as if it burned his fingers. "That looks like you."

"Exactly, and I can assure you I've never posed nude for anyone here in Timberline before."

He let that pass and picked up the picture again by the corner. He squinted at the pretty woman in the photo with the strawberry blond hair. Then he swallowed hard.

"Beth?"

She looked up from thumbing through the other photos. "Uh-huh?"

"Did you notice what this woman has around her neck?"

"No. An explosion interrupted my examination of the pictures."

He waved the photo in front of her face. "It looks like a necklace of some kind. I can't make out whether or not it's a locket, but I'm hazarding a guess it is."

Gasping, she snatched the photo from his hand. "You're right. A woman with strawberry blond hair wearing a necklace like mine."

Her bottom lip wobbled. "D-do you think this could be my mother?"

Duke plucked the photo from her hand and placed his thumb beneath the subject's chin, studying her face. He couldn't tell the color of her eyes, but the catlike shape matched Beth's, along with her wide cheekbones.

"You could be related, no doubt." Feeling like a voyeur, he turned the picture over. "What does it mean? Someone took risqué pictures of your mother and other women and then hid them under the floorboards of that cabin."

Beth lunged for her phone. "We need to find out who owns that cabin. All the deputy knew was that Raney Realty had the rental listing."

Beth tapped in Rebecca's number and left a message. "She's probably still busy with her open house."

Duke threw himself across the bed and rubbed his eyes. "I'm exhausted."

Beth stretched out beside him, propping up her head with her hand. "The strangest thing happened to me in that cabin. I felt like I was channeling Scarlett. Maybe some of her sensitivity rubbed off on me."

Duke's phone buzzed in his pocket and he pulled it out. "Mickey's calling. Hey, Mickey, this is my day off."

"How'd your meeting with the DEA go the other day? You never got back to me."

Duke's head rolled to the side and he watched Beth's eyelashes flutter closed. Had that meeting been before Beth's foot got caught in a bear trap or after someone had taken a shot at her?

"They're pulling all the files for me regarding drug activity in the area at the time of the kidnappings. Is someone getting anxious?"

"I'll tell you who's getting anxious—Stanley Gerber, that's who."

"Stan the man? The director of our division?"

"We had a situation, top secret. It all worked out, but Gerber wanted to know why you weren't on the case."

"And you told him I was in cold-case Siberia?"

"I did, and he wanted to know on whose orders."

"I guess Vasquez, his second in command, doesn't keep him up to date."

"I'm guessing he's having a few words with Vasquez right about now."

"Do you think he's going to pull me off the Timberline Trio case?"

Beth opened her eyes and nudged him with the heel of her hand.

"Maybe, but I'd like you to follow up with the drug connection first so we can show something for our efforts there."

"I'll see what I can do as soon as those files come through from the DEA." Duke sat up and swung his legs over the side of the bed. "What, no homework duty tonight?"

"It's Saturday. I've been coaching soccer all day."

"Father of the year, Mickey."

"I'm glad someone thinks so. Keep me posted on the drug angle and I'll put in a few hundred good words for you with Gerber."

When he ended the call Beth shot up next to him. "Are you getting yanked off this case?"

"Maybe, but not before I wrap up some loose ends."

She tapped her chest. "I'm your loose end. We need to discover what these pictures mean."

"Let's get some dinner while you wait for Rebecca's callback."

"I can't face going into town tonight. After hearing about that explosion, the townspeople just might come after me with pitchforks."

"There's that new development near Evergreen with a couple of chain restaurants."

"I could use a bland chain restaurant about now, but I need a shower after crawling around that cabin floor."

"Meet you back here in thirty minutes?"

"I think I can manage that."

He went back to his own room, his mind in turmoil. He and Beth had figured someone had to have been tracking them to know their whereabouts this afternoon—unless Rebecca had told someone.

If someone had put a tracking device on his rental car,

he'd never know now that the car had been destroyed. The rental company had already towed it away.

Why wouldn't someone want them to find some old pictures? Unless that cabin had something to do with the Timberline Trio case, these threats against Beth made no sense at all.

He'd been concerned when she'd decided to stay in town because he'd figured the people threatening her would assume she was still on the Timberline Trio case, but maybe the attacks had nothing to do with the Timberline Trio.

Maybe someone had objected to Beth's personal quest all along. But why? Why should one woman's journey to find her beginnings cause anyone to feel uneasy?

Showered and changed, Duke returned to Beth's room.

She opened the door, her face alight with excitement. "Rebecca called me back and she's going to look into that property as soon as she gets the chance. She's having dinner with her fiancé, but he's flying back to New York later and she's going to return to her office for some work."

"Then let's enjoy our dinner with some endless breadsticks and all-you-can-eat salad."

She paced in front of him. "I don't think I even need my crutches anymore."

They drove across town in Beth's rental to the newer area that owed its existence to Evergreen Software. When they walked into the restaurant, they barely warranted a glance from anyone.

These were the newer residents of Timberline and, except for that glitch with Wyatt Carson, they were far removed from the Timberline Trio tragedy.

Over dinner, Duke ran his new theory past Beth. "I was thinking in the shower."

"That's where I do all my best thinking." She bit off the end of a breadstick and grinned. That interlude in the cabin had transformed Beth from the scared creature of this afternoon. He'd expected her to be wrung dry from the experience and the discovery, but she'd been energized by it—vindicated.

"Beth, it occurred to me that the threats against you may not have anything to do with the Timberline Trio case. It could be that someone here doesn't want you to discover your identity. Maybe someone discovered your true purpose and has been doing everything he can to drive you away from that purpose."

She stabbed a tomato with her fork. "I thought of that, too. What if…? What if my birth parents don't want me?"

He dropped his fork and interlaced his fingers with hers. "Are you prepared for that?"

"I came out here to find the truth. I can handle it."

"Beth." He squeezed her fingers. "You came out here because you thought you were Heather Brice and you expected to be reunited with your long-lost, loving family. It's not going to be that way."

"I know." She gave him a misty smile. "But the fact that you stayed with me, helped me, didn't turn away from me when I told you about the miscarriage…well, that means more to me than ten loving families."

He brought her fingers to his lips and kissed the tips. "I'll ride this out with you until the end."

After dinner, they closed the place down over a shared dessert and coffee for him, decaf tea for her.

As they got in the car, Beth's phone rang.

"Hi, Rebecca. I'm with Duke. I'm putting you on speakerphone. Do you have anything for us?"

"I have the owner of that cabin for you. You know Serena Hopewell, the bartender at Sutter's?"

"Serena owns the cabin?"

"She's owned it for over twenty years."

"Does she live there?"

"Doesn't look like she ever lived there. It's been a rental, under Raney Realty, for quite some time."

Duke leaned toward Beth's phone. "Inherited property?"

"I don't think so."

"Who'd she buy it from?"

"Some management company—LRS Corp. Never heard of it. Hey!"

"What's wrong?"

"My lights just flickered."

Duke grabbed the phone from Beth. "Rebecca, are you in the office alone?"

"Of course I am. Who else would be nutty enough to be working on Saturday night?" She cursed. "The lights just went out in my office completely. Is it raining?"

Duke and Beth exchanged a glance and Beth asked, "Are your doors locked?"

"Of course. What's wrong with you two?"

"Rebecca." Duke kept his tone calm. "Your life is in danger."

As he uttered his last syllable, the line went dead.

"Rebecca? Rebecca?"

He tossed his phone to Beth as he tried Rebecca's number. "Call 9-1-1."

Rebecca's phone rang until it rolled over to voice mail.

Beth jerked her head toward Duke and covered the phone. "The operator is asking me what the emergency is. What should I say?"

He snapped his fingers and she handed the phone to him. "A woman I was speaking to on the phone thought she had an intruder and then her phone went dead. I can't reach her now."

"Name and address?"

"Rebecca Geist with Peninsula Realty." He gave the operator the address of Rebecca's office and his name, and then he ended the call. "A deputy's on the way, but so are we."

Beth had retrieved her phone from the console and had been trying Rebecca's number.

"Any luck?"

"Keeps going straight to voice mail." Beth hugged herself, bunching her hands against her arms. "I'm worried. Someone must've known she was doing all this research for us. We should've warned her against going back to her office alone."

"She was going back to do some work, not just for us. Anyone who knows Rebecca must know she burns the midnight oil at the office."

"Especially someone like Bill Raney."

As he hit the accelerator, Duke drummed his thumbs on the steering wheel. "She said some corporation had sold the property to Serena. Do you remember the name?"

"It was three letters. L something, but I'm not sure."

"Why harm Rebecca over information like that? She's not the only one who has access to those records. That's public information."

"I hope that's you thinking out loud because I have no idea."

"Unless it's just to further intimidate you, drive you away."

"Yeah, like that's going to happen."

"Beth—" he put a hand on her bouncing knee "—we can research that corporation and Bill Raney and Serena Hopewell from any place. Maybe you should spread it around that you're leaving, there's no story and you're tired of the pranks against you."

"And then actually leave?"

"Yes, leave. We can continue looking into all of it—the identities of those women, the history of that cabin."

"I'll think about it." She pointed out the window. "Look! It's a squad car in front of Rebecca's office."

"Good."

As he pulled in behind the police vehicle, an ambulance came up the road, sirens wailing.

"Duke." Beth grabbed his arm.

He threw the car into Park and shot out of the driver's side just as another squad car squealed to a stop.

His gut knotted as he charged up to the front of the building.

Deputy Stevens stepped in front of him. "Oh, it's you. You called it in, right?"

"What happened? Where's Rebecca Geist?"

Stevens gestured him inside and Beth grabbed the back of his jacket, limping behind him.

Holding up a hand, Stevens said, "Beth, you might not want to go in there."

"The hell I won't."

The revolving lights of the emergency vehicles lit up a hellish scene inside the offices of Peninsula Realty. Papers littered the floor, file cabinets lay on their sides, spilling their guts, computer equipment had been smashed and in the center of it all, Rebecca Geist broken and bloodied.

Chapter Seventeen

Beth cried out and staggered toward Rebecca. She dropped to the floor beside her. "She's still breathing. She's still alive."

"We know that, Beth. The EMTs are here—make way."

Duke touched her shoulder. "Let them do their work, Beth."

She covered her face with her arm as Duke helped her to her feet. "Oh, my God. It looks bad."

"She took a bad beating, but maybe we saved her life. There's nothing we can do for her now." Duke led Beth outside, where they spoke to the deputies.

They explained how Rebecca had been doing research for them on some cabins and how she'd complained of the office lights going out while she was on the phone with them.

Stevens asked, "Did she say anything else after that?"

"Her phone went dead and that's when we called 9-1-1."

"I was the one who responded first and I think I scared the guy off."

"Did he leave any footprints? A weapon? If he beat her with his fists, you're going to be looking for someone with some battered hands."

"I think he may have used a hole-punch."

"A hole-punch?"

"You know. One of those heavy, three-hole punchers? There was one next to the body. I'm sorry—next to Rebecca." Stevens wiped his brow beneath his hat despite the chill in the damp air. "She was conscious when I got here and her pulse was strong. I think she has a good chance of making it."

"Her fiancé." Beth folded her hands across her stomach. "She'd just had dinner with him and he was on his way to New York."

"Her coworkers will know how to reach him. From what I understand, he's loaded, flies a private jet into Timberline." Stevens waved the other deputy into the office. "What kind of research was she doing for you? Was it for the show?"

"There's not going to be any show on the Timberline Trio for *Cold Case Chronicles*." Duke curled his arm around her hip and pinched her. "Rebecca didn't come up with anything new, and Beth's decided there's not enough for a whole episode on the case."

"I'm sure quite a few people will be relieved to hear that. It's a little different when you have the FBI working on something behind the scenes and not splashing it all over TV."

"I may be wrapping up here soon, too."

"Well, maybe those kids were snatched by that Quileute creature."

"Not even the Quileute believe that, Sheriff." Beth's lips formed a thin line.

They said good-night to the sheriff and Duke caught Stevens's arm. "You'll let us know how it goes with Rebecca, right?"

Stevens shot a sidelong glance at Musgrove shouting

orders and nodded. "I'll let you know as soon as I hear anything."

Beth collapsed in the passenger seat. "I hope she's going to make it."

"I hope so, too. She had a lot of head wounds and those bleed profusely. It might look worse than it is."

She pushed her hair from her face and pinned her shoulders against the seat back. "Before I do leave, Duke, I'm going to talk to Serena about her cabin."

"Are you going to ask her who sold it to her? Because I can't remember what Rebecca told us."

"That's one question."

"You might want to ask her how she could afford to buy a cabin like that on a waitress's salary—be more discreet than that, but you know what I mean. Don't you think that's weird?"

"That and the fact that she doesn't even live in it and Doug told us it's not rented out much."

"Be careful, Beth. Let people know you're done with the story, that you're leaving town."

"I will. I don't want to get anyone else involved. I've put Scarlett in danger and now Rebecca."

"And maybe Gary Binder."

"Do you think he knew something about that cabin? Do you think he was at the hotel to talk to me?"

"Maybe, or it could be his drug connection." He tapped his phone. "I got an automated email from the DEA tonight indicating the files I requested are ready for viewing, so I'm going to work on that tomorrow. And you're going to work on getting a flight out of Seattle. I can drive you to Sea-Tac anytime."

That night they made love again and she held on to

Duke for dear life. If she had to give up her search in Timberline, he might be the only family she ever had.

THE NEXT MORNING DUKE, already dressed in running clothes, woke her up with a kiss. "Wish you could come with me."

She held up her foot. "As soon as this heals, I'll be right there with you."

"Do you want to have brunch at that River Café when I get back?"

"Okay, and then I'm going to find Serena and that'll be it for me."

"Which means you'll be on your laptop this morning looking into flights from Seattle to LA and on the phone with Scott to tell him the story's off."

"Yes, sir." She saluted. "Scott's going to be so happy this fell through. He warned his father it was a bad story."

"So, you get to keep your life and pump up Scott's ego in the process. It's a win-win."

Two hours later they parted ways after brunch. Duke's rental-car agency had replaced his SUV. Luckily for them, they had used different rental companies or one company would be left wondering just what the hell was going on in Timberline.

That was exactly what she wanted to know.

She drove into town, wishing she hadn't eaten so much at brunch. When she sat down at the bar at Sutter's she didn't want Serena to think she was there just for her.

A call to Chloe had already confirmed that Serena was working today. When didn't she work the bar at Sutter's? Maybe that was how she could afford the upkeep on that cabin.

All eyes seem riveted to her when she walked into the

restaurant. If someone wanted her out of Timberline, it could be any one of these people.

She hobbled to the bar on one crutch and hopped up on a stool.

Serena placed a cocktail napkin in front of her. "What can I get you?"

"I'm just going to have lunch again, if that's okay."

"Fine with me." Serena dropped a menu on the bar and got a beer for another customer.

Beth made a show of studying the menu and then closed it and folded her hands on top of it.

Serena returned. "Ready?"

"I'll have a ginger ale and a bowl of lentil soup."

Serena shot the ginger ale into a glass from a nozzle. "Not too popular around here anymore, are you?"

"No, and I can't do a show when the residents have turned against me. I'm calling it quits on this story."

"You can't blame people for getting cold feet. A lot of weird stuff has gone down since you've been here."

"Yeah, like someone shooting the gas tank of Agent Harper's rental car and blowing it up."

"Shows how desperate some of these people are. You don't mess with the FBI."

"That explosion—" Beth toyed with her straw "—happened outside of your cabin."

Serena's eyes narrowed.

"I mean, you own that cabin, right?"

"I do. Excuse me." Serena moved to the other end of the bar to take an order. She didn't return to Beth until she brought the soup.

"One lentil soup."

"Did you inherit that cabin?"

"Who, me? My folks never had any money, didn't even come from this area."

"So, you bought it?"

"I bought it after the Timberline kidnappings. Prices dropped off then. The lumber company had already pulled up roots. I got a good deal from an anxious seller."

"That person must've regretted it once Evergreen Software moved in here and prices went up again."

"Actually, it wasn't a person, just some big corporation that owned other properties. I got lucky."

"Is the corporation still around? What was the name of it?"

"Why do you care?"

Damn, she'd come across as too nosy. She took out her phone and feigned interest in her text messages. "I don't, really. Just curious—occupational hazard."

"I don't remember the name of the company. I'd have to look it up in my paperwork, wherever that stuff is now. Oh, hello, Jordan. Can I get you something?"

Smiling at Beth, he pointed to her soup. "I'll have some of that and a cup of coffee, if you've got some fresh."

"Coming right up."

Jordan swiveled on his stool to face her. "I heard you're not going to do the story."

"Word travels fast." She placed her phone on the bar.

"Small town." He lifted a shoulder. "Too bad."

"Are you one of those who was pro-story? I would've thought you'd be against it because of the business interests you have here."

"Thanks, sweetheart." He dumped some cream into the coffee Serena had brought him. "I'm a forward-thinking person. I think any publicity is good publicity. That whole mess with Carson kidnapping those kids and playing the hero didn't hurt business or our reputation. Some people are too sensitive."

"Like your friend Bill Raney."

"Bill has a lot to be sensitive about. He's a failure. People like me and that little firecracker, Rebecca Geist...we have nothing to fear."

"Did you hear what happened to Rebecca last night?"

"Damned shame, but then, you tend to attract unwanted attention when you're successful. Like you." He sipped his coffee and met her gaze over the rim. "Do you really want to give up?"

"I don't consider it giving up. There's just not enough here to produce a compelling story."

He winked. "You haven't talked to me yet."

"That's not from a lack of effort. You're a busy man, Mr. Young."

"Jordan, and I've got some time right now. Maybe what I have to show you will make you reconsider your decision."

Her heart thumped. Jordan had been around for a while. He just might know more of Timberline's secrets than anyone else since he also seemed to be tight with the town's movers and shakers.

"That depends on what you've got for me."

"You know that cabin you wanted to see out on Raven Road? The one where the agent's car exploded?" He hunched forward and cupped a hand around his mouth. "I can get you inside."

Beth's gaze darted to Serena counting money at the register. "It belongs to Serena."

"Yes and no. Let's just say it's more complicated than that."

"How can you get into the cabin?" She couldn't exactly admit to Jordan that she'd already been inside. She didn't want to get Duke into any trouble, especially if it turned out that Jordan knew the real owner.

"Let's just say I'm like this—" he crossed his fingers "—with the management company."

"H…he doesn't have to be there, does he?"

"He doesn't even have to know. It'll be our secret." He put his finger over his lips and glanced at Serena.

"Okay. What time?"

"How about right now? I don't have any meetings until later this afternoon." He rubbed his hands together when Serena put his soup in front of him. "Thanks."

When she walked away, he dropped his spoon. "I'll tell you what. You're staying at one of my hotels, the Timberline, right?"

"Yeah, the one that needs cameras."

"I have a little business to attend to there. Why don't you head back to the hotel, let me finish my lunch, and I'll meet you there and we can go over to the Ravens together."

"The Ravens?"

"That's what the cabin's called. Most of the owners of these cabins, especially the ones outside of town, named their places."

"I didn't even know that road was called Raven Road." Beth's hands grew clammy just thinking about the Ravens and she grabbed a napkin and crumpled it in her fist. Her breath started coming in shallow gusts, and she slid from the stool. "Can you excuse me for a minute?"

She made a beeline for the ladies' room and hunched over the sink, breathing in and out. Just talking about the cabin was causing her to freak out. How would she handle another visit there? But Jordan was offering her another opportunity to take a look at the place and she couldn't refuse.

She splashed water on her face and gave herself a pep talk in the mirror. Pasting a smile on her face, she returned to the bar.

"Sorry about that. So, the Ravens is on Raven Road."

Jordan studied her face for a second. "It's a local name, not on the maps. Ravens are important to Quileute legends, so I guess that's where it came from. Does that sound like a plan? You can wait for me in the parking lot of the hotel. I won't be long, and then you can decide if you really want to give up on this story."

"Okay. I'd love to see inside that cabin...for my own reasons."

"Excellent." He took a spoonful of soup into his mouth.

"Anything else?" Serena picked up Beth's bowl and dropped the check.

"No, thanks." Beth left some cash on the bar, swept her phone into her palm and nodded to Jordan.

Beth took her time getting back to the hotel, since Jordan had to finish his lunch anyway. She stopped by the market and picked up some water and a bottle of wine. If this was going to be her last night in Timberline with Duke, she might as well make it special.

She pulled her phone out of her pocket to leave him a text message. She tapped her screen, but her phone wouldn't wake up. She powered it down and tried again. The battery must've died.

Jordan had said he had meetings in the afternoon, so they'd be done at the Ravens before Duke finished working on the DEA files anyway.

When she pulled into the hotel's parking lot, Jordan was just walking out of the hotel.

She grabbed her crutch and scrambled from the car. "That was fast."

"It was just soup. What took you so long?"

She held up the plastic bag with one hand. "Stopped for a few things."

"Perishable?"

"No."

"Why don't you leave them in your car?" He looked at his watch. "My meeting was earlier than I thought, and I'm going to have to make this fast."

"Oh, okay." Leaning back into the car, Beth placed the bag on the passenger seat.

She used her crutch to navigate to his black sedan and the open passenger door.

"How's that foot of yours?"

"It's getting better. In a few days I think I can put more pressure on it and get around without using a crutch."

He helped her into the car and slammed the door.

On the way to the cabin he asked about her theories of the kidnappings.

She stared out the window at the passing scenery before answering. She really hadn't given the Timberline Trio much thought, especially once she'd found out she wasn't one of them.

"I'm not sure, maybe child trafficking, as awful as that sounds. Maybe those kids were just in the wrong place at the wrong time."

"It was a strange and scary time, especially for those with children."

"You didn't have children to worry about?"

"My wife and I were never fortunate in that regard."

"And then you lost your wife… I'm sorry. People do talk in a small town."

"Lorna drowned."

"I'm so sorry."

She'd changed the mood in the car by mentioning his wife. He seemed thoughtful as he gazed over the steering wheel.

He never remarried, so Lorna must've been the love of his life.

When he made the turn onto Raven Road, her fingers curled into the leather on either side of the seat and her pulse rate quickened. She'd thought getting into the cabin and finding the picture of the woman with the locket had dispelled her fears, but the anxiety still hovered at the edges of her mind.

Jordan dragged a hand across his face. "Did you call Agent Harper? I know he was interested in the cabin, too."

"My phone's battery died. He's working, anyway."

"On a Sunday?"

"He works when he gets the call."

"I have to admit I'm a little relieved."

She tilted her head. "Why is that?"

"He's an officer of the law and, technically, I'm entering the cabin without the owner's knowledge."

She smirked. If Jordan only knew Duke had been breaking and entering just yesterday. "I don't think he'd report you. So, do you think the Ravens is connected to the Timberline Trio kidnappings?"

"Could be. Back in the day, it was used for some illicit activities."

"Really?" Like prostitution? Her stomach felt sick at the thought of the pretty strawberry blonde involved in anything sordid.

"I don't know that much about it, but the Ravens had a reputation around that time. I thought that's why you were out here yesterday."

"I think Duke, Agent Harper, may have gotten some hint about something like that, but we barely got to the front door when the car exploded."

"Makes you wonder if some of those old characters are still hanging around, like what happened to Binder. Coincidental that he died in a hit-and-run accident right after telling the FBI a little about Timberline's drug culture."

A chill swept across Beth's body and she hunched her shoulders. She dug her phone out of her pocket and tried waking it up again.

"Still dead?"

"Yeah." She dropped it back in her pocket.

"Reception is bad out this way, anyway."

He swung around the yellow tape tied to a tree where Duke's car had been parked and rolled up the pathway to the cabin.

"Stay right there, Beth. I'll help you out."

He appeared at the passenger door and jingled a set of keys as he gave her his arm for support. "We can get inside the right way this time."

"This time?"

"Well, you didn't get in at all yesterday, did you?"

"N...no."

Her uneasiness still nibbled at the edges of her brain, but it differed from the sheer terror she felt yesterday.

He held her arm as they walked up the two steps to the front door. He used the key to unlock two locks on the door and pushed it open.

The front door opened right onto the sitting room where she and Duke had removed the floorboards and found the pictures.

"After you."

She hesitated, and Jordan put a hand on the small of her back. "We're not going to get caught."

As soon as Beth entered the room, beads of sweat broke out on her forehead. Her dry mouth made it hard to swallow. The room closed around her and she hung on to her crutch as the room began to spin.

"You feel it, don't you, Beth? She led you here, didn't she? Your mother led you to the place where she was murdered."

Chapter Eighteen

Duke pushed back from the desk in the conference room at the sheriff's station and stretched. If the Bureau pulled him off this case, at least he could leave with a good report regarding the drug trade in Timberline and who was behind it. A biker gang called the Lords of Chaos controlled the drug trade on the peninsula. They also ran women and weapons. A thorough investigation of that gang might lead to additional information about the kidnappings.

He checked his phone. Nothing from Beth. He texted her, but the message didn't show as Delivered. He tried calling and his call went straight to voice mail.

Maybe she was getting something from Serena.

Unger tapped on the open door. "Thought you'd want to know. Rebecca Geist is out of surgery. It looks like she's going to pull through, but they're keeping her in an induced coma until the swelling on her brain goes down."

"Thank God. Did her fiancé make it out here?"

"He's on a flight back right now. Do you need anything in here?"

"No. I skipped lunch, so I might take a break in a few minutes and pick up something."

"I can recommend the sandwich place two doors down."

"Thanks." When Unger left, Duke rubbed his eyes and went back to the Lords of Chaos and their dirty deeds.

As he scanned a bulleted list, a name jumped out at him—LRS Corporation. That was the name Rebecca had mentioned before she'd been attacked. He ran his finger beneath the text on the screen. The Lords of Chaos had rented several properties from LRS and used some of them for their illegal activities, including cooking meth.

Duke switched to a search engine and entered *LRS Corporation, Timberline, Washington*. He skimmed through the relevant hits.

LRS stood for and was owned by Lawrence Richard Strathmore, who'd passed away about twenty years ago. He'd been around during the time of the kidnappings.

He clicked through a couple of biographies. The man and the corporation had owned a lot of property in Timberline at one time. His wife had passed before he did and they had one daughter.

Duke whistled through his teeth. Strathmore's daughter, Lorna, had married Jordan Young.

Duke jumped up from his chair and stuck his head out the door. "Unger?"

"Yeah?"

"Need to ask you a few questions."

Unger walked around the corner with a sandwich in his hand. "Sorry, man. I would've gotten you something when I went over there earlier if I'd known you were gonna be holed up in here all morning."

"That's okay." Duke waved him to the chair as he perched on the edge of the conference table. "Jordan Young is a widower, right?"

"Yeah, his wife died about ten years ago—drowned."

"His wife was Lorna? Lorna Strathmore?"

"Not sure about her maiden name, but Lorna's right."

"Wasn't she loaded?"

"I heard something like that. Young got his money the old-fashioned way—he married it."

"You ever heard of LRS Corporation?"

"I've seen the name on a few things. Why?"

"That was the name of Young's father-in-law's company—owned a lot of property in Timberline."

"Now Young owns a lot of property in Timberline. Why are you asking?"

"Just a curious connection between him and something Beth was looking into." Duke rubbed his chin. "You know much about him?"

"Between me and you?" Duke poked his head out the door and then closed it. "He likes the ladies, and I think he shares that with my boss."

"Is the sheriff married? I don't see a problem for Young since he's widowed."

"I guess I'm being too discreet for the big-city boy, huh? What I mean is Young is into hookers, and I think Sheriff Musgrove is, too, which is a problem for both of them, as far as I can tell."

"Wow, you need to get rid of that guy. He's going to bring the department a world of hurt otherwise."

"Tell me about it." He swung open the door. "Anyway, that's about all I know about Young, about all I want to know about him."

"Thanks, Unger."

Duke tapped his thumbs on the edge of his keyboard. Jordan Young sold that cabin to Serena Hopewell. Why? Was he the one who'd stashed those pictures under the floorboards? Were those women hookers? Was the one who had Beth's locket a hooker?

He needed to reach Beth, tell her everything. He tried

her phone again, and again it went to voice mail. This time he left her a detailed message about Jordan Young.

Had she even seen Serena today? Maybe Serena had already given Beth the same info about Young.

He shut down the computer and stacked his files. Then he locked the conference room door behind him.

"Unger, I'm going to Sutter's for some lunch."

"All right, but the sandwiches down the street are just as good."

"I need something else at Sutter's."

The Evergreen lunch hour must've ended because Duke walked into a mostly empty restaurant. He noted Serena working behind the bar and wove his way through the dining room tables to get there.

"You just missed your girlfriend, the TV reporter."

"Did she talk to you about the cabin?" Duke hunched forward on the bar.

Serena's eyes widened. "Why are you two so interested in my cabin? It's just a cabin like any other on the outskirts of town, and it has no relation to the Timberline Trio case."

"That you know of."

"Do you want something to drink or are you just here to harass me?"

"Who sold you that cabin, Serena?"

"Oh, for God's sake. I don't remember—some corporation."

"Why are you lying? The LRS Corporation sold you that cabin—LRS, as in Lawrence Richard Strathmore, as in Jordan Young's father-in-law. Only, Young had control of the corporation when he sold the cabin to you. Why'd he sell it to you? Why'd he give you such a sweet deal?"

Serena backed up to the register, her arms across her chest. "What do you want from me?"

"Let's start with the truth. What was Young using that cabin for and why'd he want to get rid of it?"

He lunged over the bar and grabbed her arm. "And what's this tattoo on your wrist? Does that *LC* stand for the Lords of Chaos?"

She jerked away from him. "You want answers? Talk to Jordan Young."

"Is there a problem?" A restaurant employee wearing a shirt and tie approached them with his phone out. "Do I need to call the police?"

Duke released Serena and pulled out his badge. "I just have a few questions for Ms. Hopewell."

"It's all right, Randy." Serena flicked her fingers.

When the manager walked away, Duke asked, "Where can I find Young?"

"I'm not sure." Serena rubbed the tattoo on her wrist. "But he was in here the same time your friend was here when she was asking me questions about the cabin, sat right next to her. Maybe even did something to her phone."

Duke's blood ran cold. "What?"

"She went to the ladies', left her phone on the bar, and it looked like Jordan picked it up."

"Did they leave together?" Duke's heart was thundering in his chest.

"No, but…"

"But what?" Duke's hands fisted on the bar. "I'm sure the FBI can find something on you, Serena, from your years running with the Lords of Chaos."

Her jaw hardened. "But she left and then he left not long after they were having a hushed conversation—like he didn't want me to hear what they were saying."

"And did you hear anything they were saying?"

"I heard him mention the Ravens."

"The Ravens? What's that?"

"That's the name of my cabin—you know, the one you broke into before someone blew up your car."

BETH DROPPED TO the nearest chair, her crutch falling to the ground. "My mother was murdered? Here?"

"I'm afraid so, Beth." Jordan pulled a gun from his pocket and aimed it at her.

"The picture." Beth put a hand to her temple where her pulse throbbed. "The woman with the strawberry blond hair... Was that her?"

"I knew you'd found those pictures. I knew you and Agent Harper were out here, and I thought I could stop you by shooting out the gas tank on his car, but I was too late." He smoothed the pad of his thumb over his eyebrow. "I knew she'd led you to those pictures. How else could you have found them?"

Beth folded her hands in her lap, trying to hold it all together even though she felt amazingly relaxed—maybe because she'd reached the moment of truth.

"You don't seem surprised or skeptical that a dead woman could've led someone to a bunch of pictures."

He sat on the arm of the chair across from her. "That's because your mother was Quileute and so are you."

Scarlett reaching out to her and bringing her along in her dream quest made sense now, but with that hair color, her mother probably wasn't full-blooded Quileute.

Beth trapped her hands between her knees. Jordan Young most likely murdered her mother for reasons she didn't know yet, but she wasn't ready to go there with him. He still might let her go.

"Why did you take me here? Why are you telling me all this?"

"You want to know your identity, don't you?" He spread his hands. "That's why you concocted the story that you were here for the Timberline Trio, although you thought you were Heather Brice for a while, didn't you? I would've been content if you had continued along that path. Why didn't you?"

"Duke—Agent Harper—requested DNA from the Brices and ran a cross-check with mine." She plucked her useless phone from her pocket. "I've called him, you know. I told him I was on my way here."

"That would be hard to do with a phone without a battery." He dipped into his front pocket and held up a battery pinched between his thumb and forefinger.

Beth's stomach rolled. "Are you going to tell me about my mother? Her name? Why she was murdered?"

"Your mother." He stroked his chin. "Angie was lovely, delicate, so much more refined than Lorna, even though my wife was the one with the money."

"Your wife died. You said she drowned." Beth clenched her bottom lip between her teeth to keep it from trembling. Had he killed his wife, too?

"That was later." He ran a hand through his salt-and-pepper hair. "When Angie got pregnant, I realized it was my wife's fault we couldn't have a baby."

The knots in Beth's gut tightened, almost cutting off her breath.

Jordan Young was her father.

His blue eyes, the precise shade of her own, lit up. "That's right, Beth. I'm your father."

She gripped the arms of the chair and vaulted out of it, but her legs wouldn't support her and she stumbled backward, falling onto the chair's cushion.

"Why? Why did you kill her? Because she got pregnant and had your child?"

His brows collided over his nose. "If she had gone away quietly, like she did at first, it wouldn't have been a problem. But she decided to come back. I was married to a very wealthy woman and had a father-in-law who thought the world of me. How do you think he would've felt after discovering I'd gotten some Indian pregnant?"

Beth flinched. "But I must've been two years old. She'd kept the secret that long."

"You weren't two at the time. Your adoptive parents changed your age and birth certificate to mask your true identity. You were a baby, barely one year old. Angie left when you were first born, but then she returned. She shouldn't have come back, Beth."

"You murdered my mother to keep her quiet? To get rid of a messy problem?"

"It was more of an accident, to tell you the truth. She knew I was never going to leave Lorna, and she knew I wanted her to keep quiet." He clucked his tongue. "Your mother wasn't as sweet and innocent as she appeared. You have the pictures to prove that. She tried to extort money out of me."

"Maybe she just wanted child support for me."

"Whatever you want to call it. She also found the pictures of the other women—silly bitch to think she was the only one."

Beth's nose stung. How could she be related to this monster? Duke had been right. It would've been better to stay in the dark.

"Did you shoot at me? Set the bear traps? Beat Rebecca?"

"Bill was more than happy to help with Rebecca. I was just trying to scare you away, but you wouldn't go away—just like your mother. As soon as I heard Beth St. Regis of *Cold Case Chronicles* was in town, I knew there was a problem."

"Y...you knew who I was all this time?"

"Of course. When I offered you up to the market, I insisted on having some say in where you went."

"So, I have you to thank for my cold, unfeeling parents."

He shrugged. "What do you expect from a couple who would take a child off the black market? But I was your father, Beth. I followed your career with great pride—until you came here."

A movement beyond Jordan's shoulder caught her eye. Something had flickered at the window of the back door.

"What led you here?" Jordan glanced at the fireplace. "Did she speak to you from beyond? I knew she had the gift, not as strong as Scarlett Easton's, but I always feared it."

Was that Duke at the back door? She coughed. "It started with the Pacific Chorus frog. It was a toy I'd had from my earliest years. I finally tracked it down to Timberline because of the Wyatt Carson story on TV. And it was the visions and nightmares I'd always had of a lush forest filled with terror."

A glimmer of light flashed from the laundry room for a second and Beth held her breath as Jordan cocked his head.

She rushed on. "Why would I feel such fear? Was I here in the cabin at one point?"

"You were here when I murdered her."

Beth bent over at the waist, bitter bile rising in her throat. "You killed her in front of her child?"

"It wasn't planned. It was an accident. She just wouldn't shut up about what I owed her and how she was going to get it out of me." He waved the gun in her face and for the first time she really believed he'd kill her.

"I'm not like my mother. I don't want anything out of you. I was going to leave Timberline anyway. I'll never come back here."

"We're alike, you and I." He wagged a finger at her. "I

could see that when I watched your show. A hard charger. I admire that, Beth."

"I am like you. I understand why you did what you did. You were only protecting your position."

"I murdered Lorna, too, you know."

Beth covered her ears. "I don't want to know what you did. I don't care."

"I saved you that day, Beth. As I stabbed your mother and rivers of blood soaked your body, I saved you."

Beth choked and covered her mouth.

"But I don't think I can save you this time. If you'd just stopped digging. If you hadn't gone to Scarlett. If you hadn't asked Rebecca for help. If you hadn't been part Quileute and your mother's daughter."

"Where is she? What did you do with my mother's body after you stabbed her to death?"

Jordan rose from the arm of the chair and placed his hand against the wall above the mantel. "I left her here."

Beth cried out and staggered to her feet. "You bastard!"

The gun dangled at his side and she lunged for it.

Jordan raised his arm, but she was close to him and bumped his forearm.

"Drop it, Young." Duke burst into the living room, his weapon trained on Jordan.

Jordan grabbed her around the waist, gripping the gun in the other hand.

A shot rang out and Beth screamed over the ringing in her ears.

Jordan slumped against her, his blood pumping out of the wound in his chest, covering her body.

She'd returned to where she began.

Epilogue

Safe in the crook of Duke's arm, Beth watched the demolition crew enter the Ravens, followed by a hazmat team from the FBI and Deputy Unger.

"You don't need to be here, Beth."

"I do. My mother led me back here and I owe it to her to witness her release."

He rubbed her back. "He didn't admit to anything involving Gary Binder, did he?"

"No, everything else was him and Bill Raney."

"The sheriff's department has already arrested Raney for assault and attempted murder. They're going to try to determine how much he knew about Young's activities."

"Serena, too?"

"She's left town."

"I guess there's your answer."

"Maybe, or she's protecting herself against questions about the biker gang, the Lords of Chaos, she used to run with."

"Rebecca's doing better. I visited her this morning. Her fiancé is going to take her to Hawaii on a sort of a convalescence-slash-vacation in a week."

"You talked to Scarlett?"

"She's still in San Francisco and is heading for New York after." Beth rested her head against Duke's shoulder. "She wasn't too surprised when she found out about my mother's heritage."

"She didn't know Angie?"

"Her grandmother had known my grandmother, but they didn't live on the reservation and Angie was a free spirit. When she came back to the rez twenty-five years ago, pregnant, she'd talked about a rich fiancé who was going to take her around the world."

"And she never left Timberline." Duke shook his head. "Did Jordan talk much about the black market he used to...place you?"

"No. Do you think it's related to the disappearance of the Timberline Trio?"

"I do, and I think they're both related to the Lords of Chaos. I was at least able to give the Bureau a thorough report of the gang's activities in this area."

"Where to next for you?"

"Wherever you are." He kissed the side of her head.

"I'm sure the FBI is going to have a thing or two to say about that."

"After I tag along with you to LA, I think I'm headed back to Chicago, but not before we make some serious plans."

"I like the sound of that." She fluffed his hair back from his face.

"Are you going to do a segment on finding your mother? It definitely qualifies as a cold case, and the ratings would be sky-high."

She tightened her hold on his arm as the door of the cabin swung wide. "I don't care about the ratings, Duke. Some things are not for the public's consumption."

The hazmat crew navigated the porch steps, wheeling a gurney with a black bag on top of it.

Beth sucked in a breath and Duke pushed off the stone planter and helped Beth to her feet.

As the gurney made its way down the path, a surge of people, Quileute in their native ceremonial dress, gathered on either side of the procession.

A low chant rose and puffs of incense scented the air around them.

One of the elders approached Beth and bowed her head. "You have family now, Beth St. Regis, a whole nation behind you."

With tears in her eyes, Beth nodded and touched the old woman's silver hair.

When law enforcement, the emergency vehicles and the procession of Quileute had cleared out, Duke took her in his arms. "I'm sorry, Beth, for all of it."

"I'm glad I found out. Now I can get to know my mother for the person she was. All the doubts and fears are gone."

He stroked her hair. "It's time to rewrite the past for both of us now. I want to create what we both missed out on—a family. If that's just us or ten kids or one, it doesn't matter. Are you ready for that, Beth?"

She curled her arms around his waist and pressed her cheek against the steady beat of his heart. "I'm ready for all of it, and as long as you're by my side, I know I'm home. Duke Harper, you're the man of my dreams."

* * * * *

Carol Ericson's series
TARGET: TIMBERLINE
continues next month with
ARMY RANGER REDEMPTION.